DOUBLE
WEDDING

ALSO BY WILLIAM KATZ

Surprise Party
Open House
Facemaker

DOUBLE
WEDDING

William Katz

McGraw-Hill Publishing Company

New York   St. Louis   San Francisco
Toronto   Hamburg   Mexico

Book design by Eve Kirch

Quality Printing and Binding by:
Berryville Graphics
P.O. Box 272
Berryville, VA 22611 U.S.A.

advice

"The wife is the first to know and the last to believe," Woody Evans told Sarah as they sipped champagne. They were at a stock Washington party, with sixty guests rumoring away, and the divorce lawyer's comment was prompted by some hot gossip about a senator and his wife.

"How do you know?" Sarah asked.

"They tell me. They knew what their husbands were doing. Some even knew the name of the other woman. But, you know, it's human nature. They just couldn't believe what was going on, so they pretended it wasn't. Don't let that happen to you."

"Oh, it won't," Sarah laughed, placing her glass on a small, round table and taking a shrimp from a passing waiter's tray. "I have a terrific marriage. I can't be the first to know because there's nothing *to* know."

"Really?" Evans replied with a cynical smile born of forty years in the practice of smashing marriages. "You know what I call women who say that?"

"What?"

"Clients."

PART ONE

PART ONE

chapter
one

Washington, D.C.

Bret was surprised that he felt any guilt. After all, he'd known for months that he was going to end his marriage to Sarah. And he'd known for weeks how he would end it. His plan, which he'd drawn up with his usual attention to detail, was almost complete. But now, seated behind the wheel of his Lincoln in an early morning traffic jam, with Sarah beside him, he felt this sudden sting of guilt. It nagged at him. He was embarrassed, frankly. Why should a man feel guilty over something that was necessary to advance his career? The assistant secretary of the United States Navy should have steel enough to resist. A *calculating* man—how he loved that word—should be immune to childish sentiment.

But this was their twentieth wedding anniversary. Sarah had been talking about it for weeks, and she had slipped a card for him under his pillow the night before. That was probably it, he thought. That's why he felt that little tug at his conscience. But it hardly mattered. A tiny conscience doesn't put up much of a fight, and in his case it surrendered unconditionally.

They began to inch forward on 16th Street. The White House, bathed in the misty orange of a hot June morning, was ahead. It was 7:14 A.M. It would be one of the longest days in Sarah Lewis's life.

"I made reservations for tonight at Jimmy Lee's," she was saying.

"Great," Bret replied. He struggled to look interested, turning quickly to smile at Sarah, but his mind was racing. Maybe a flashlight would do it, he thought. Or the outer shell of a portable radio. Either one could hold explosives.

"I arranged for our usual table," Sarah went on. "With a setting for four. Jimmy is hauling out the same silverware they used twenty years ago."

"Wonderful." Get the grease, he remembered. Damn, that should have been done by now. Get the order number from the service manual in the trunk. Go to a Lincoln dealer, but one far from home. Pay by cash, and wear dark glasses.

"And I ordered that seafood special in advance. Not too spicy. Just the way we had it last time."

"Terrific." Fake the break-in. Make it look like an amateur job, and don't make a big deal out of it with the police. Maybe the break-in shouldn't be reported immediately . . .

"Bret, you're not listening," Sarah chided, poking him in the ribs.

"No. I mean yes, I am. Of course I'm listening." With the car totally stalled now behind a limousine from the Nigerian Embassy, he took his hands off the wheel and turned to her. "You know what I was just thinking about? How I used to travel up on that rattly bus from Columbia every weekend to visit you, trying to get a couple of hours of sleep along the way, and how you picked me up at the station. I asked you to marry me at the end of a bus ride, in the middle of a snowstorm after the bus was two hours late. Remember?"

"Sure, I remember."

"Has it really been twenty years?"

She smiled now, a full, bright smile. "Yeah."

"You know," he said, "I made a decision this morning."

"Oh?"

"I could go for another fifty."

"Fifty?" Sarah asked. "Well, fifty years from now I can see myself in a rocking chair, living with my memories."

Funny, Bret thought. Where *he* saw her, there wouldn't be any memories.

If Woody Evans, the divorce lawyer who'd given Sarah that cocktail-party advice, had been listening from the back seat, he'd have admitted that he was probably wrong on this one. Sarah Lewis didn't seem to suspect a thing. The man next to her was, at that very instant, planning the end of her life. She was planning a night out.

In fact, it was a commonplace in Washington that this was a very solid couple. Bret was a rising star in the Defense Department, one of the few people at his level to be *noticed*. How many assistant secretaries, Sarah liked to ask him, already had a scrapbook for their news clippings? Bret had two. Even this morning, stuffed between them in the console of the Lincoln, was the *New York Times*, already turned to page A16, where Bret was quoted on the latest hostage crisis in Lebanon. Washington *knew* him. His Christmas card rating was improving all the time—from a few cards from government officials when he first came to Washington, to enough now to fill the mantle and part of the top of the piano. He'd been told, although he could not confirm it directly, that he was in Dan Rather's Rolodex.

Sarah was a curator at the National Air and Space Museum, or, as some people still insisted, a *woman* interested in airplanes. Very interested. She had a commercial pilot's license and would have been a test pilot except for a slight heart murmur. She was Bret's age, but looked much younger. Her blond hair was short and straight, and her large, searching eyes were a sky blue. Bret always told her she looked like Grace Kelly. He kidded her for being every cool blonde from every Hitchcock movie. But when they were engaged, that's exactly the way he bragged about her to his friends.

They were opposites, an odd couple to some. She could have been happy teaching school in rural Nebraska, introducing youngsters to the world of flight, maybe recruiting a few astronauts. He was the sharp Washington go-getter—Mr. Charm when he had to be, Dr. Death when the need arose. Professionally, he lived in a world of Navy secrecy, which he liked. He enjoyed knowing things that others did not. It gave him a sense of power, made him feel more manly. He was sure that, just as he kept military operations inside him, he could keep his plans for Sarah a deep, deep secret. It wouldn't be a strain, for it wouldn't be long.

"Did you really mean that?" Sarah asked.

"Mean what?"

"Another fifty."

"Yeah, I did," he said, reaching out to touch her arm tenderly. It was a lie, like all his lies, especially the lie that he still loved her and was loyal to her. In fact, he was already thinking of the elegant woman who'd be sitting next to him once all the messiness was out of the way, the woman who'd ride to work with him each morning, the woman whose very presence would ease his way to the top. Maybe he'd buy a new car, he thought. That would start things off right. She deserved it, and it was important to impress her.

Sarah gazed at the White House up ahead. It was much too warm, she thought, even for Washington in mid-June. And with the choking traffic on 16th Street and the air conditioner blasting in her face, it wasn't the most romantic way to start an anniversary.

Then she spotted them, as she knew she would. The sidewalks were already filling with high school kids in cutoff jeans, loud shirts and hats with buttons pinned all over them. They were part of the annual ritual of senior-class trips to the capital. They were in Washington to breathe in their country's history, although they generally were more interested in the history they were making in the hotels at night. One wore a big Dukakis button, never forgetting, never forgiving. They horsed around, taking pictures of each other, trying to make out the tourist maps and reaching into backpacks for the required morning candy bar.

They reminded Sarah.

Laurie would have been just about that age now. She would have been going on trips, and Sarah would have been home worrying, just as the parents of these kids were probably worrying, demanding that the kids call nightly, wondering which one in the group had the drugs.

But Sarah forced the thought from her mind. Don't bring it up. Don't be morbid today. That was seventeen years ago.

"Do you remember when our class came to Washington senior year?" Sarah asked.

Bret hated questions like that. They made him feel nostalgic, and that could bring back the guilt. "Sure," he replied. "You wanted to drag us all to the Smithsonian."

Sarah laughed, and now a few slight age lines appeared at the corners of her eyes. "That's right. Did I bore you?"

"Yeah."

"Well, you weren't so interesting in those days yourself, Lewis, even if you were class president. God, could you be pompous. You went up those Capitol steps like you owned the place."

Bret just smiled. If she had any idea what he'd been doing on the Capitol steps in the last few weeks, she wouldn't have been joking about them. But she didn't know, he was sure. How could she?

The students' tour buses seemed everywhere—cylinders chugging, fumes hissing from their rear engines, obese drivers with bored expressions behind green aviator glasses waiting to pick up their cargo for a morning at the FBI or Arlington. They made the traffic even worse, and a Washington traffic jam is world-class. Unlike New York, where entrapped drivers simply forge ahead and hope their fenders survive, Washingtonians, reflecting the casual Southern tone of the city, are generally content to wait their turn, at whatever hour that might come.

"Come on!" Bret demanded, under his breath, to the driver ahead. He was one Washingtonian who wasn't so casual. "Another civil servant out for a morning drive."

"Come on, chill it," Sarah told him. "We've got plenty of time."

I've got plenty of time, Bret thought to himself.

Sarah actually was used to Bret's outbursts at traffic jams. She'd heard them for most of their married life. But she'd noticed that they'd become more pronounced in recent months, as if there were some extra burden on Bret's mind. The week before the anniversary he'd even gotten out of his car to lecture another driver on creeping up too close behind him. He'd never done that before. She turned and gazed over at him once more. *Was* anything wrong?

It wasn't the best route to take to work. In fact, it was the worst. But Bret always insisted on going this way. Approaching the White House was a daily high for the man the *Washington Post* once described as "utterly charming and chillingly ambitious." As the front columns now came into view, he tried to see himself in the future. Some day, he thought. Maybe some day he would live in that house. But not with Sarah.

"Isn't that Tim Curran?" she asked, motioning to a sixty-ish man in a blue, pin-striped suit walking out of the Hay-Adams Hotel, directly across from the White House, his head down to hide his face.

"Looks like him," Bret answered. "Yeah, that's him."

"What's he doing here at this hour? He's not one for breakfast, and he lives out in Langley."

"He's got a girlfriend at the Hay-Adams," Bret replied nonchalantly. "A redheaded lawyer."

"I see."

"Just your government at work, my love. The chairman of the
House Armed Services Committee is cheating on Betty. It's been going
on about three months."

"You know who she is?"

"Sure. She's with a law firm that specializes in defense contracts.
She's pushing a bill in Congress to give a tax break to a jet engine
maker."

"I get the picture," Sarah said.

"I'm sure you do. She goes down at night, the bill comes up in
the morning."

Sarah watched Curran evade the doorman and walk to the end
of the block to find a cab. He didn't want the doorman to get a close
look at him. Doormen remembered. And he couldn't be sure which
doorman was paid by which newspaper to take names.

Strange that they should see Tim Curran, Bret thought, as he
made the turn around Lafayette Park and past the White House. In
a way, Curran was responsible for his decision to get rid of Sarah.
Bret remembered the night it all came together, some five months
before. He was with the twelve-term congressman in the Rayburn
House Office Building on Independence Avenue around midnight.
They'd been discussing the Navy appropriation for the new fiscal
year—the Navy and Curran were disagreeing about the need for
another Aegis class cruiser—and were the only ones left in Curran's
office. Curran was a relaxed man of medium height, known for
political horse sense and an ability to master the details of every
major weapons system in the American arsenal. He was also known
as a man who had more skeletons in his closet than a medical
school, some of them young, female and willing, others older, male
and bearing envelopes of cash on behalf of companies looking for
favors. Curran had been touted for the Senate, even for vice president, but was smart enough to know that the skeletons would come
marching out in formation if he ever tried. So he'd made his pact
with destiny, checked out the pension that was due him, and decided to keep his safe House seat, going into history as the man
who brought more defense contracts to Ohio than anyone else.

They'd closed the book on appropriations that night when Curran, who had Nixon's five-o'clock shadow at three o'clock, swung around in his overstuffed leather chair and gave Bret Lewis the once-over. Leaning back, he took his time, plenty of time. Bret felt a cold unease come over him. Curran wanted something. Curran *always* wanted something, and Bret didn't like the predatory look in the chairman's bloodshot eyes.

"You're about forty, aren't you, Bret?" Curran asked.

"Forty-one," Bret replied, surprised at the question.

"You taught college before you came here, isn't that right?"

"Yes. I taught political science."

"Well, that's very nice. Greatest profession, teachin'. Inspirer of the nation's youth. You want to stay in government?"

"Sure. Why do you ask?"

Curran just kept staring at him. "You know, I've been watchin' you," he said. "I watch a lot of people in this town come and go, mostly go, mostly *should* go." He got up and walked over to a cabinet, reaching for an illegally imported Havana cigar. "Smoke?"

"No, thanks."

"Smart boy. Much healthier that way. But learn to accept a smoke occasionally." He winked at Bret, like a father giving intimate advice, then lit up with a gold desk lighter marked with the corporate seal of a major defense contractor that was under indictment. Bret instantly understood. This *was* a father giving advice. Be deferential, yet savvy, he told himself. No smart aleck, but no kid.

"You know, Bret," Curran went on, "you could go right up the ladder in this little village. You're young enough. Bright. Good-lookin'—or so the ladies tell me." Again, he looked Bret up and down, analyzing his six feet of well-toned muscle, his thick shock of dark brown hair, even the black designer frames of his glasses. "You could reach the top." He drew on his cigar, and smoothly blew out the aroma of Castro's forbidden island. "The tippy top. Are you readin' me, sailor?"

"That's very flattering, Mr. Chairman," Bret answered.

"What I'm sayin' is, you're packageable," Curran went on. "Unless you've screwed up somewhere down the line—you're not weird or anythin', are you?"

"No," Bret replied, with a smile. "Not that I know of."

"Now there—show a little anger when you answer that. Growl a little. Show you're a red-blooded American male. When they finally got Bush to do that, he got his tail elected."

"If anyone ever seriously asked me that question, you'd see a man growl," Bret replied. "There's nothing weird about me." And he glared at Curran. A good glare. A red-blooded glare. The kind that looked wonderful on a twenty-one-inch screen during a debate. Curran loved it.

"You maneuver well. You twist things when you have to. I know you fudged those shipbuildin' budgets last week, and you got 'em past my committee. I admire that. You've got enough snake in you to make it, even if you did teach school. And don't you dare think that what I'm sayin' is out of line. Hell, take Lincoln. We've got him sittin' up there in marble at the end of the Mall, with all the fancy words he talked, but let me tell you—the man was a snake. He had a guy in his law firm—Henry C. Whitney, you can look it up. You know what this gent said about Lincoln? He said Lincoln picked every friend for what he could do for him. You can do it, too.

"But you need a political base, Bret. Run for the Senate, maybe." Curran started walking over to a map of the United States mounted on a wall. He slapped the East Coast with his hand. "You come from New York."

"That's right."

"Crap house. No one should be from New York, but you can get around it. Franklin Roosevelt was from New York, and *he* was assistant Navy secretary too. You knew that?"

"Yes, I did. There's a picture of him right outside my office."

"Under Wilson he was. You build on that. The Roosevelt tradition. Servin' your country in the Pentagon. Y'know, it counters that liberal New York bushy-haired image. Someone told me you grew up there with your wife."

"We grew up on Long Island. Went all through high school together. We've never been apart since."

"Even when you were in the military? You *were* in the military, I hope, please God."

Bret smiled. "Sure. She joined too. We were Navy officers together in San Diego in the early seventies. Best years of our lives."

"I like the way you said that. The military years. The best years.

Nothin' New York in that. And it's a nice story. I've met your lady Certainly a looker. Beautiful blond hair. Flashin' eyes. A figure that could stop a . . ."

"I'm sure she'd thank you," Bret interrupted.

"You must give my best to Susan."

"Sarah."

"Oh, yeah. Sarah."

The mistake stung Bret. Curran wasn't the first Washington powerhouse to forget Sarah's name.

"Lovely lady," Curran went on. "But, uh, and this isn't a criticism of your bride . . ."

"But what?"

"But, you know, in this business wives are part of the game. She's goin' to have to help you, Bret. It's great that she works with airplanes. Doesn't she?"

"Yes. She's an aeronautical engineer. She's over at Air and Space as a curator."

"Very commendable," Curran said. "Plays great with the God 'n flag crowd. Y'know, you get a cute picture of her smilin' out the cockpit of an F-15. But to help you in politics she's got to be a little more . . . how shall I say it?"

"Calculating?"

"That says it."

"I know what you mean," Bret replied. And he knew exactly what to say next and how to say it. "Sarah," he went on, a look of mild contempt coming to his face, "is the kind of woman who chooses friends because she likes them."

"That bad, eh?"

"I'm afraid so."

Curran stared up at the ceiling. "Well, could she, uh, change? Be a little more . . . Lincolnesque?"

No doubt in Bret's mind where Curran was going. "I don't know," he answered. "It's not her style."

"Hmm. Not her style. That's really very sad. Well . . . is it a good marriage, Bret?"

"It's good."

"Nothin' for lawyer crud to worry about?"

Bret hesitated. The idea was forming. "Not really."

"Well, at least that part is okay. Divorce is bad stuff, Bret. Leaves a court record. Maybe a scandal." He looked directly into Bret's eyes. "Happy is the man whose bad marriage ends with his wife goin' off a bridge."

Bret's mind snapped back to the present as he passed the Treasury Building. He continued down Pennsylvania Avenue, then cut across the Mall, heading for the National Air and Space Museum. The Capitol Building was on the left. As always, his eyes swept the knots of people walking to work there. Mustn't miss a chance to wave to someone powerful, someone who could help, someone who'd remember a friend. That was Curran's way. That was the ball game in the capital city of the Free World. "Fred Saunders," he said, gesturing toward a tall, lanky man walking to the Senate with a slight limp, a thick manila envelope under his left arm. Saunders was on the Senate Finance Committee, a good buddy of bankers, a useful man to know, and Bret threw him a dignified wave. Saunders waved back, although Bret wasn't sure whether he actually recognized him or thought he was some constituent visiting Washington. An assistant Navy secretary, even one who was noticed, wasn't exactly hot stuff to a major senator. Sarah showed no great interest. If Saunders were homeless, Bret thought, she'd be interested.

Now a group of eight demonstrators, dressed in jeans and faded shirts, was forming on the Mall. Bracing against a sudden breeze, they unfurled a twelve-foot banner made of sewed-together yellow sheets, with writing in red paint: SAVE MANUEL RAMIREZ.

"Who's Manuel Ramirez?" Sarah asked.

"He's on death row in Virginia," Bret answered. "He killed a policeman who stopped his car for speeding." Virginia, of course, was just a few miles away, across the Potomac River.

Sarah stole a sideways look at him. As a rule, he didn't follow Virginia news. But Bret had learned all about Virginia law, especially as it applied to murder. There were simply things a man planning to get rid of his wife had to know.

"I'm still against the death penalty," Sarah said.

Isn't that wonderful, Bret thought. She really didn't understand what kind of monsters there were in the world.

Sometimes they even drove Lincolns.

chapter
two

Bret turned the car toward the museum, stopping at its front entrance on Jefferson Drive. Already, long before the doors opened, kids were pressing their noses and plastic camera lenses against the glass to get an early glimpse of the dreams inside. Bret had to admit that this was something he would miss—pulling up to that building each weekday morning, gazing in the giant front window and seeing the Wright Brothers' first plane, Lindbergh's *Spirit of St. Louis*, Chuck Yeager's Bell X-1 and John Glenn's *Friendship* 7 space capsule, all with one sweep of the eye. It was among the world's great pictures, and it still gave him a chill. This was power and glory—what it was all about, and what Sarah didn't quite comprehend. He'd take the new Mrs. Lewis there, he promised himself, after a proper period of mourning.

"Remember," Sarah said, "they'll be at our place at seven-thirty."

"I'll be home early," Bret said. "I told the Secretary it's our anniversary, and he's decent about these things. You know, it's a kinder, gentler Navy Department."

"Thank him for me."

"Sure."

They kissed. "See you tonight," she said.

"Be careful," he told her.

Picking up her brown leather briefcase, Sarah eased out of the car and started walking toward the entrance, maneuvering around some South Korean tourists who were photographing each other. When she turned back, as she always did, to wave a final good-bye, Bret was sure he caught an odd look on her face. He couldn't recall any expression of Sarah's that was quite like it. He found it impossible to understand, but it seemed a strange mixture of passion, questioning and worry, as if she really wasn't sure precisely where she stood with her husband of twenty years. It puzzled him. Did she know something? Did she suspect? No, that couldn't be. It was, he decided, a simple case of anniversary emotion. Women always worried on wedding anniversaries. They worried that their husbands would die.

He always had things figured.

Sarah entered the museum. "Hello, Frank," she said to the uniformed guard, a burly six footer who'd been a member of the Air Police in the Air Force.

"Hello, Mrs. Lewis," Frank replied. "Happy anniversary."

Sarah was startled. "Frank, how did you know?"

Frank winked, forcing his thick mustache to rise up the right side of his face. "I know. I ask Personnel about birthdays and stuff."

"That's very nice of you, Frank. I didn't know anybody really did that. Thank you."

Sarah walked on, and then stopped. She gazed over at one of the most popular displays in the museum—a piece of moon rock brought back by *Apollo 17* in 1972. She walked over and rubbed it. There was an instant of mild shame—an engineer, a scientist, indulging superstition like some schoolkid visiting for the day. But any woman who'd dreamed of being an astronaut, who'd joined the Navy, who worked in this museum, had to have a strong dose of the romantic inside her. So she rubbed the rock again. "I hope," she murmured to herself. "I just hope."

Bret pulled away, back into traffic, pausing for a moment to let a group of elderly tourists cross to the museum. He headed southeast, for the George Mason Memorial Bridge, which would take him to the Virginia side of the Potomac, and the Pentagon.

Then he began the ritual.

As the traffic crawled, he reached up and tilted the rearview mirror toward him so he could see his face. He checked to make sure that all four windows were tightly shut. He clenched his teeth, so no one in nearby cars or walking along the sidewalks could see his mouth move.

He focused his mind precisely, envisioning a specific scene in a motel parking lot. The scene had rolled over and over in his mind for months, appearing sometimes in dreams, sometimes during meetings with Navy officials, but most often when he was planning the actions that would rid him of Sarah. He saw himself in the scene, dazed, confused, hands flailing about in anger and frustration. He saw people running, and the police screeching up in patrol cars. He heard moaning, and crying, but mostly he heard the crackling of fire.

And then, with the scene etched in his mind, Bret Lewis, the cool and rational Bret Lewis, started to rant, a low, gut-crunching rant. "She's dead! Oh, my God, she's gone!"

He forced tears to his eyes.

He contorted his face as if in anguish.

"Jesus! It was meant for *me*! Goddammit, those bastards! Why didn't they get *me*!"

His chest heaved.

He grunted through teeth still tightly clenched.

"There's nothing left," he moaned. "Nothing. Dear God, there's nothing left!"

That was good, he thought. Very, very good.

chapter
three

The woman behind the counter recognized Al Durfee as soon as he came through the shop door. Durfee was forty-seven, short and stocky, with curly black hair and a side-to-side swaying action, like a discount-house John Wayne. Anyone could recognize him from front or rear. Besides, he was a well-known figure at Savannah PhotoLabs, a custom photofinishing service on one of the seedier streets in Northeast Washington that catered mostly to (A) professionals, (B) advanced amateurs, (C) weirdos who took pictures other labs wouldn't develop, and (D) people who needed pictures for strange purposes. Al Durfee was (D), people who needed pictures for strange purposes. He was a private detective, one whose history of three broken noses told the world that he specialized in matrimonials. And now he was coming to pick up the latest bulletins.

"How you doin', Al?" Evelyn Banks asked.

"Miserable. Up all night," Al replied. "Some of these people in this town, they got no shame. I don't know how a man cheats on his wife at three in the morning and still gets up at eight to make a speech in Congress."

"They do it for their country, Al," Evelyn smiled. She was a svelte brunette of thirty-three who went into photofinishing after her brief modeling career faded.

"I brought three rolls," Al said, removing three cassettes of thirty-

five-millimeter film from his suit pocket and clacking them down on
the counter.

"Standard process?" Evelyn asked, whipping out an order sheet.

"Yeah. No. Gimme eleven-by-fourteens of everything."

"That big?"

"I want my client to see her husband's face. And I'm picking up
an order."

"Yeah, okay, it's right here. These are good ones, Al. You've got
a good eye."

"Yeah, sometimes a black eye."

"I thought I knew the lady in these photos," Evelyn said. "But I
couldn't place her."

Al glared at her. "Evvie, I told you before. We are not to discuss
this. You just develop the pictures, okay? Don't look at them. Okay,
you can look at them. I mean, you got pride in your work, you got
to check the quality. But you're like a doctor here. You don't discuss
the patient with the outside."

"Okay, Al, okay." She handed Al a large brown envelope.

"Put it on my bill," he said. He quickly slipped out the eight-by-
ten glossies that Evelyn had given him, flipping through them with an
eye that, even when blackened, knew what to look for. He shook his
head sadly, but it was a bit put on. "These will bring unhappiness,"
he said.

Of course, they always did. Al Durfee made his living from the
bad news business.

chapter
four

"They were very sophisticated men," Sarah was saying, gazing at the first powered aircraft, flown by the Wright Brothers in 1903. The Wright flyer, looking like little more than a biplane glider with twin propellers, was suspended from cables in the Milestones of Flight gallery of the National Air and Space Museum. It was part of that great view that thrilled Bret each morning as he dropped Sarah off.

At Sarah's sides were two engineers from the Saab aircraft works of Sweden. She regularly took aeronautical engineers around the museum, showing off the displays and getting a sense of what was happening in their research labs and workshops. Now she stood with the Swedes on a balcony overlooking the gallery. Light streamed in through the building's tall, modern windows, giving an almost outdoors feel to the display space. "Most people," Sarah went on, "think of the Wright Brothers as two young boys from a bicycle shop in Dayton. Actually, they were in their thirties when they made their first flight in that contraption. They'd done years of research. There's a whole file of correspondence between them and the Smithsonian Institution in Washington. You really should read it."

"I'll make sure to do that," one of the engineers said, with Scandinavian courtesy. And, efficient as always, he even made a little note to read the file while he was in Washington. "Oh. Which one flew first?" he asked.

But Sarah seemed suddenly distracted, staring into space.

"Uh, I asked . . ."

"What?"

"I asked which one flew first?"

"Oh, I'm terribly sorry. I was thinking about . . . Wilbur Wright actually made the first flight. He won a coin toss with his brother. He flew in a business suit. The Wrights didn't really believe in wearing anything else."

A coin toss was her life right now, Sarah mused. Was she right? No, it would be awful to be right.

"And you're absolutely convinced," the engineer asked, "that this was the first powered flight?"

Sarah shot him a wry smile, aware that "first" always involved controversy. "The museum is convinced."

"Of course, there are other claims," the engineer said. "A man in Connecticut . . ."

"We're aware of the claims," Sarah replied, "and we investigate them. But we haven't found anything credible to challenge the Wrights."

"Didn't your museum take the flyer apart some years ago?" asked the other engineer, a man of fifty with a thick, blond beard.

"Yes," Sarah said. The question brought back memories. It had been a happy time—long before this strange feeling began. "I was involved in that. The fabric and wood parts were deteriorating. We disassembled it in a rear room here and restored it." She sighed. "It was like touching a religious object."

"I understand," the first engineer said, sensing that in Sarah he had found an engineer who was a romantic at heart.

"Before you leave," Sarah said, "we'll give you a book put out by the museum. The cover is made of the same material the Wrights used on the flyer's wings."

They walked a few feet to their left, Sarah scuffing her gray business suit against a railing and then brushing it off with her hand. Now they were face to face with the *Spirit of St. Louis*, the plane that took Lindbergh across the Atlantic in 1927. "*That* is a religious object," one of the engineers said, gazing at the single-engine plane, also suspended by cables. They were almost close enough to touch it, surely close enough to read the name on the nose, with the miniature paintings of flags of the nations under it. One of the engineers glanced at the tail, which had "Ryan NYP" printed in bold letters. "I know Ryan was the maker," he said. "What is NYP?"

"New York to Paris," Sarah replied. Everyone who saw the craft asked the same question. "Lindbergh picked the Ryan company to build the plane because everyone else wanted too much money. They built it for $10,580."

"I think you call that 'bargain basement' in the States," one of the men from Saab commented.

"That's right."

On the floor below the planes, hundreds of young faces were looking up, listening to tour guides explain the same things Sarah was explaining. Some gathered around the piece of moon rock that Sarah had rubbed earlier. The kids rubbed it, too, and Sarah wondered what their wishes were, what their fears were. They couldn't possibly have the fear that she had at the moment. A romantic she was, yes. But she was a frightened romantic.

Another bus pulled up and about sixty more kids, some of them singing high school fight songs, piled out and jammed through the museum doors. Immediately the singing stopped, and it wasn't simply common courtesy. There was the sense of adventure everywhere, of triumph in the heavens; but there was also the spectre of death and pain. Sarah always noticed that when high school students in particular looked up at the suspended planes, it was as if they were gazing at icons.

She was about to begin her comments about the chunky little orange-and-white Bell X-1 rocket, Chuck Yeager's *Glamorous Glennis*, when she spotted a man coming in the front entrance, squeezing his way through a clot of teenagers. He went up to Frank, the guard, and seemed to be asking a question. Sarah eased slightly to the right to get a better view and put on her glasses. Yes, that was him. She couldn't see his face clearly, but she recognized the walk, the style.

Her heart began to pound.

She knew this man.

She knew why he had come.

She saw Frank point to the area of the museum where her office was located.

"This Bell X-1," the bearded engineer asked, "it was carried under the wing of a B-29, am I correct?"

"Yes, yes, that's right," Sarah replied. "Or maybe it was a B-50. I'll have to look that up." She sounded distracted as she watched the man make his way toward her office.

Al Durfee. Private detective.

She had hired him.

She had hired him because she was far less innocent, far less accepting, than Bret ever thought. She had never let on, she had steeled herself to maintain composure in her husband's presence. But Sarah Lewis knew, and she *was* the first to know. She wasn't sure what—but she knew something was terribly wrong. And she wondered, as she watched this detective, this messenger, making his way through the crowd, whether she would believe, or whether, like so many women, she would teach herself to deny.

"Now it's time for me to turn you over to Dr. McGill," she said, matter-of-factly, to the Swedish engineers. "I think you'll have a very interesting dialogue."

"Yes, I'm sure," one of the engineers said. "He visited us at Saab two years ago."

Sarah quickly handed her guests over to Mark McGill, a young colleague who specialized in rockets and spaceflight. He had been standing by to conduct the rest of the tour, although he hadn't expected to be called in quite this early.

Then Sarah walked toward her office in the administrative section of the museum, as nonchalantly as possible, all the while realizing that this twentieth wedding anniversary could turn into a nightmare. Durfee had certainly picked a symbolic day to show up. Maybe it was in the hands of the gods and he was simply following instructions. She saw him now, waiting outside her office, carrying a battered briefcase and rolling back and forth on the balls of his feet. He was not the picture of elegance. But Sarah wasn't interested in class at the moment. Just information. Information that could change her life.

"Al?"

He saw her coming and straightened up. "Oh, hello Mrs. Lewis. Your office was locked. Otherwise I wouldn't loiter."

"You came without calling."

"Well, you use the phone, you never know who's listening. I was working for a European ambassador once, and. . . ."

"Al, do you have anything?"

Durfee's eyes shifted, a habit of twenty-three years in the business. "Y'know, maybe we better sit down in your office, Mrs. Lewis."

Sarah stood for a moment, staring at him. She was sure she could read his vagueness. "Maybe we better sit down" was not the preface to a love letter. She was determined not to break, not to dissolve, but she couldn't deny the turmoil building inside her. "I'd prefer not to meet in the office, if it's all the same to you, Al. It's a little too obvious. We'll go behind one of the exhibits."

"Anything you say, ma'am. It's on your meter."

Sarah was well aware of that. She kept her own, personal savings account and had drawn $1,200 from it to pay Durfee for his services. She knew the tab could be much higher if anything turned up and she needed him again. If she ran out of money, she'd have to borrow it from someone, for Bret was obsessive about studying every cancelled check and every withdrawal from their joint account. He kept a little calculator in each room of their apartment.

"Nice place you got here," Durfee said, looking around at the planes and rockets that hung from every ceiling and crowded every floor.

"You haven't been in the museum?" Sarah asked.

"No. Remember, when you hired me, we met in a restaurant?"

"Yes, that's right," she sighed, recalling her anxiety at actually speaking with a private detective. She had felt so sneaky, almost dirty.

They walked to the Pioneers of Flight gallery, Sarah's favorite. She had written a high school paper on the life of Amelia Earhart and had read every book she could find on the aviatrix by the time she entered college. Now, in this gallery, she could actually touch Earhart's single-engine Lockheed Vega.

They sat down behind a nearby photo exhibit. Durfee observed her carefully as she sat: how she kept her back straight, her head high; how she crossed her legs with a sharp, assertive movement. Image, Durfee knew. The first thing women in her position did was worry how they looked to the outside world, even to a private detective. The pride factor was at work. It could be positive, Durfee thought, but it could also lead to catastrophe.

Sarah took a deep breath. "So," she said, "I guess you've got a little tale to tell me."

"That's right, ma'am," Durfee replied. "Some people like reports in writing, but I'm not such a good writer, and then you don't ..."

"It's okay, Al. Just go on."

Durfee paused for a moment. This was the part that brought in the income, but it wasn't the part he particularly enjoyed. "Ma'am," he said, "I think your suspicions may be correct."

"Bret *is* having an affair?" It was less a question than a resigned statement.

"Possibly. I can't prove it, yet, but it looks that way." He caught the gradual moistening in Sarah's eyes, something no amount of pride could prevent. This wasn't a woman looking for a jackpot divorce settlement. This was someone facing the crumbling of her marriage.

"All right," she said. "Please answer the obvious question."

Durfee started to reach into his briefcase. "Does the name Alison Carver ring a bell?"

Sarah suddenly sat up straighter. "It's *her*?"

"None other."

"No," Sarah protested, ridiculing the thought. "Alison Carver is a congresswoman. She's on the Appropriations Committee. My husband's been dealing with her for years."

"Apparently so, ma'am."

"I didn't mean *that* way. No, it doesn't seem logical."

"Never is."

"Sure, she's single. Even attractive. But she's all business and she's from an ultra-conservative district in California. This is little Miss Careful. She's not the kind to get involved in something messy."

Durfee shrugged. He pulled the brown envelope out of his briefcase and from it slipped the eight-by-ten glossies. Then, in the gesture that symbolized the private eye for generations of movie goers and TV addicts, he spread the pictures in front of Sarah with the flourish of an ace poker player. "I think you'll recognize the lady," he said. "And I'm sure you know the gentleman ... intimately."

Sarah examined the photos, her eyes taking in each one, left to right. "Where were these shot?" she asked. There was a touch of anger in her voice, blaming the messenger for the message.

Durfee picked up one glossy. It showed Bret and a tall, slim woman wearing a Burberry trench coat and carrying a leather bag.

Some pillars were evident in the darkened background. "Well, this was taken outside the Capitol about 11 P.M. with a 300-millimeter telephoto lens. They walked out together."

"They could have been meeting on official business," Sarah said.

"Ma'am, you hired me because you said your husband was coming home late a little too often, and his excuses started to wear thin. Lemme ask you, did he ever once say he was meeting with this congresswoman?"

"No, he never mentioned her."

"If his meetings were legit, he wouldn't have hesitated to mention her, right?"

"I don't know."

"He deals with women. There's loads of women in the Pentagon. Does he mention some of them?"

"Yes."

"So why wouldn't he mention Alison Carver?"

Realizing there was no answer except a devastating one, Sarah returned once more to the photos. Her tone became defensive, skeptical. "And where were these others taken?"

"This one is in Virginia, not far from the District line. It was outside the, uh ..."

Sarah looked more closely at the photo. It showed Bret with the same woman, now in a wool topcoat. There was a long, low building in the background, with a neon sign. "A motel," Sarah whispered. "The Cheshire Motel."

Bitterness swept over Sarah's face. Her large eyes always flashed with intelligence, but now they simply showed hurt. "We stayed there the week we were married," she said. "Did he have to take her there?"

"I don't know," Durfee replied. "I didn't ask him."

"Maybe someday I will," Sarah said.

"Well, it's a strange thing, Mrs. Lewis. I tailed them, but they never went inside, if that does you any good. They just kinda parked, across the street actually, got out and looked the place over."

"Why?"

"I don't know, ma'am. Maybe she's a student of architecture."

Sarah shuffled through the other pictures. Then she stopped abruptly. Her face took on the look of sudden discovery. "Look," she said, eyeing Durfee head on, "this could be a mistake. I mean, there isn't any actual *proof* here."

Durfee knew that was coming. They *all* said it. No proof. A misunderstanding. Just a friend. Helping someone with a family problem. A temporary relationship that would be healthy in the long run. He had a whole list of rationales up on the wall of his office. And he also had an autographed picture of Woody Evans, who'd actually signed it, in purple ink, "The wife is the first to know and the last to believe." Sarah's reaction hardly surprised him. "No proof, that's true, Mrs. Lewis. I mean, they could just be pals . . . at around midnight every night."

"But people do that. Maybe he likes her company. Maybe there's a political problem she has, and he's helping her tackle it."

"Ma'am, anything's possible," Durfee told her. "But some things become obvious."

"Obvious to you, maybe," Sarah snapped, "but I'm not sure that . . ." Then she stopped, and let out an ironic, pained laugh. "Who am I kidding?" she asked, to no one in particular. "Who am I really kidding?" And then she lowered her head, her defiance giving way to a crushing reality. Her proud stance was taking a beating. Al Durfee, graduate of the tenth grade and life's school of hard knocks, knew what was entering her mind. He'd seen this before too. Wife loves her husband. Hears the bad news. Looks for a quick way out. Emotions take over.

"Don't even think about it," Durfee said. "You've got too much to live for."

Sarah looked up at him briefly, then lowered her eyes once more and did not respond immediately. She knew she'd never seriously consider suicide. She was too strong, too independent. It wasn't the kind of thing *she* would do. But she also knew she'd never again ridicule a woman who let the thought cross her mind in the face of shattering rejection. For her, this wasn't simply the loss of a man. This was a twenty-year marriage that was the envy of friends who hadn't been so lucky. "I've got decisions to make, don't I?" she asked.

"Afraid so," Durfee replied. "But I get the feeling you'd like to save this marriage."

"Very much."

"Okay. That's where you start. Sometimes a child keeps people together . . ."

"There are no children," Sarah said abruptly.

"And none planned, I guess," Durfee said, conscious of Sarah's age.

"We had a daughter once," Sarah told him. "Laurie. We certainly planned for that one. We did all the right medical things. We took all the classes. Everything was bought for her nursery. Bret even had an encyclopedia waiting for her at home. She was born with water on the brain and died the next day. I couldn't have any more."

"Oh, I'm sorry," Durfee said. He hesitated. "Uh, if you don't mind the question—have you ever thought of adopting?"

"No. I'm adopted, Al. I guess you didn't know that."

"No, ma'am, you never told me."

"Frankly, it wasn't a picnic—the only adoptee in a family of three kids. You know, they try to make you feel good by saying you're the chosen one, but it never works. You're always the guest at the table, the one the aunts and uncles point to and whisper about. I don't think I could adopt, not with those memories."

"Yeah. Yeah, I could see that. I got a cousin who's adopted. Yeah, I could see that."

"Look, that's another discussion. I've got to think this through."

"Sure. You want me to do anything else, I mean surveillance-wise?"

"No. Not right away. You've done what I needed." She finally tried to smile. "Thanks, Al."

"Any time, ma'am. I wish I brought better news."

Sarah sighed, the weight of the world on her shoulders. "In the back of my mind I know I'll still hope it isn't true. I guess I'm just another wife looking for a lie."

Durfee wondered what she was really looking for. Sure, she was decent and he liked her. But he'd liked a lot of women who then did things that got them a spot on the evening news.

chapter
five

"We're convinced they're here in northern Lebanon, in a little village just outside Tripoli. And we think we can pull them out."

"I like your spirit," Bret Lewis said.

"Thank you, sir."

Bret watched from a well-worn leather chair at the end of a long oak table in his office at the Pentagon. Lieutenant Commander Roger Eltron, a black officer with a muscular build and a clipped, aggressive style, was pointing to a spot on a five-foot-high map of the Middle East, outlining a plan to free two Americans from a band of terrorists. The hostages were medical workers who'd gone to Lebanon to render aid after an outbreak of influenza. They had been snatched, like so many others before them, despite their nonpolitical work. But this time some contacts in the country had been able to tip American authorities to their whereabouts. Under a secret agreement, the contacts would receive $25,000 if they were right, and if the United States was able to pull off a rescue.

Bret was uneasy about the reward scheme, for it reminded him of the attempt to swap arms for hostages during the Reagan Administration. True, this was a simple reward, but Bret had political nightmares about being assigned to deliver it. He could almost see the caption under the picture of himself: Navy official delivers check to group that shoots down airliners and massacres civilians. Americans just didn't like bribes and didn't care much for the people who paid them. And the reward money could *still* be used for arms. This was Bret's assignment, however, and he was skilled at keeping his misgivings from the men around him. In the Pentagon, it wasn't healthy to question policy.

"Do we have aerial photos of the village?" Bret asked.

"Yes, sir, we have KH-11 satellite stuff."

"Can you pinpoint the building where these people are being held?"

"Our intelligence is that it's one of three buildings, all of them two-story."

"Are they close together?"

"They're on the same block."

"Let's see if we can get the right address. We might make a special delivery."

There were four other people at the table; two Navy officers in summer khakis, and two civilian experts who had made careers in the growth industry of antiterrorism. Bret was almost amused by the civilians. As he looked at them, he thought of the kind of weathermen who went to bed at night praying for a blizzard or a hurricane. These boys seemed a bit too thrilled every time a hostage was taken. It was their time on the international stage, in the press, in magazines. And it was talk-show heaven.

As for the Navy men present, Bret was interested in only one: Captain Avery Masters, sitting at the far end, prematurely gray at forty-nine, a man who seemed to carry worry in his eyes. Bret had invited Masters to sit in, to give advice if need be. But he had another motive for inviting him. He had a job for Masters—something much more important, much more personal. It was ironic, Bret mused, that Masters had once given Sarah a ride home after a Pentagon reception for a retiring admiral. Now their lives would intersect once again. The circumstances would be entirely different, however.

For the moment Bret had to concentrate on the hostage crisis. He'd been put in charge of forming a new antiterrorist task force and, despite the honor, it worried him. Sure, it could boost his career. He was well aware of that. Even strategists behind desks could be marketed as heroes. But one mistake and he could be in the glare of an unwelcome spotlight. One blunder and his political dreams could be over. Americans insisted on instant success in any antiterrorist operation, but Bret knew the chance of successfully extracting those Americans was no greater than thirty percent, despite the hype of Commander Eltron, who seemed as schooled in the art of public relations as in the art of war. Bret had learned to discount military assurances when, as an intelligence analyst in the Pentagon, he watched the failure of the mission to rescue American hostages in Iran during the Carter Administration. It was Tim Curran himself who had once cautioned him, "Every military disaster begins with some officer guaranteein' success. And it ends with a politician gettin' the blame."

The fact was, Bret had already decided to recommend against a military attempt to rescue the hostages. But he had to go through all the motions—listening to briefings, showing concern, asking questions with his brow furrowed, talking to the relatives of the captives, making phone calls to congressmen and senators who'd been let in on the situation, even issuing the traditional public statement deploring "this scourge" of modern terrorism. He was protecting both himself and the leaders of the Administration. No one wanted to be nailed for not sifting the evidence, for not being ready. Avoiding blame was, after all, Washington's highest calling. "Not my fault, man" had replaced "Give me liberty or give me death."

"I assume you're considering an operation using the SEALs from the Sixth Fleet," Bret remarked, referring to the Navy's sea, air and land commandoes.

"That is correct, sir," Eltron replied, his Naval Academy ring flashing as a beam of light from the window hit it. "We have all the forces and logistics in place in the Med area, as the briefing book on your desk plainly shows."

"Yes, I've read it. Very good. Very thorough. How long do you estimate it would take to pull this off if we got the go?"

"We estimate we could have the SEALs onshore in about thirty hours, assuming weather conditions held."

"All right," Bret said. "Now, since they'd be Americans and wouldn't exactly be making family visits, I'm sure you think of this as a night operation."

"It would have to be."

"What is the operational condition of our night vision equipment?"

"The latest assessment is that approximately sixty-five percent is functioning."

"That's all?" Bret's tone was angry.

"Yes, sir. We have some maintenance problems. There's a shortage of technical personnel."

"Why?"

"Training priorities, sir."

"In whose command?"

"I'd have to find out where the problem originated, sir."

"Please do that. That's pretty critical equipment."

"Yes, sir."

Bret dutifully made some notes. The others at the table occasionally glanced at him, and it was obvious from the indifference, and at times the chill in their stares, that he was not about to be voted Mr. Popularity in a Pentagon poll. "Not one of us," was how Commander Eltron himself had once put it in a discreet conversation. In other words, Bret was a man whose cultural roots weren't in national defense. "A ticket puncher," someone else at the table had once said—a man building a résumé on the road up. It wasn't that they disliked him personally. Like Sarah, they'd always seen his charming side, and he was perfectly pleasant to everyone. But no one saw him leaving the Pentagon for a vice president's desk at General Dynamics or Lockheed, and returning a few years later as Undersecretary of Defense armed with corporate wisdom. No one saw him out golfing with retired generals and admirals. He wasn't family. People could tell. Family went hunting and got dreamy-eyed when savoring the latest missile or fighter. Family often talked Southern or tried to. Family found a "threat" lurking on every border and in every ocean, especially around budget time. Family liked polyester rather than wool. Family was a class apart. Even civilians in the family weren't civilians.

And it was true. Bret wasn't one of them. The dreamy look in his eyes was reserved for Capitol Hill, and his only exposure to "Southern" consisted of once getting lost near Charleston on a Navy inspection tour.

"Commander," he said finally, after asking all the obligatory questions, "I've got a heavy schedule. Why don't we wrap this up for now and meet again in three hours?"

Not missing a beat, Eltron climaxed his briefing with a ringing presentation of the Navy's capability to conduct a hostage-rescue operation. Then, pleased that he'd demonstrated maximum service loyalty, he took down the map, which was marked SECRET in large red letters, and the group started to depart, carrying their inevitable zipper folders containing the classified notes they'd taken. Bret rose from the table to see them out. He was wearing an elegant blue suit that was slightly beyond his means. With his black-framed glasses, one of the civilians thought he looked like Clark Kent before a visit to the phone booth.

"Uh, Captain Masters," Bret said, as Masters, the four gold stripes gleaming on each shoulder, was almost out the heavy, carved wood door.

"Yes, sir?"

"Would you stay a moment, please?"

"Of course, sir."

Avery Masters was a submarine officer who didn't have the advantage of a Naval Academy background. He had graduated from a small teacher's college in Texas and worked his way up through the ranks. He was attending the antiterrorism meeting as an expert in the role of landing men from submarines. There had been rumors around the Pentagon that Masters was in some kind of trouble, and the rumors had gotten back to Masters himself. He'd put on weight; he'd run up bills at a liquor store. The worry in his eyes had become more intense. Bret felt he was somewhat more rumpled than a Navy captain should be. But for Bret, this was all ideal.

"Shall I close the door?" Masters asked.

"Please."

Masters shut the door and stepped back into the office. He could tell that something serious was about to be discussed. Bret nervously took off his glasses, breathed on them with three short bursts and rubbed them with the bottom of his suit jacket.

Masters gazed around the office as Bret readjusted the glasses. Bret observed him carefully, without being obvious about it. "I don't recall your visiting here solo before, Captain," Bret said.

"Just once," Masters replied. "For a moment."

"You seem intrigued."

It was an understatement. Bret Lewis had one of the most spectacular offices in the Pentagon, an unashamed advertisement of his many interests. The room itself was fairly common, with light brown walls and a deep-pile blue carpet. Bret Lewis was based behind a pedestrian teak desk that bore the coffee stains, scratch marks and battle scars of four administrations. But it was the displays that made the difference, that had made this office the subject of a half-page feature in the *Washington Times* that created envy among those in the Pentagon who could only claim a ship model or a flag that had flown over an old battleship.

Bret walked over to Captain Masters, who was gazing into a glass-topped case. "Those are batons, Captain," he said.

"For military bands?" Masters asked.

"No," Bret replied, with slight contempt. "These are some of the old batons of major classical conductors. Each one is handcrafted, of course."

"I thought a baton was just a little stick," Masters said. "I thought they just bought them in stores."

"Most people think so. You can buy the garden variety in a music store. But a true connoisseur has his baton specially made. There are expert craftsmen for this kind of work, Captain. Each conductor requires a different grip and balance. That's why the handles on these batons have such individual shapes. Some maestros even require a special color. Now, take this white baton. The second from the left. It was selected by the conductor of La Scala in Italy so the singers onstage could see it. This one over here, with the handle like a child's top, was used by Leonard Bernstein."

"It's like a person liking a particular stock for a gun," Masters said. He saw Bret wince at that. Even in the Pentagon there was a time to check your weapons at the door, and Masters had forgotten. "Do you play an instrument?" he asked, trying to recover.

"No," Bret replied, somewhat abruptly. The answer bulged with frustration, a frustration that found an outlet in the display of batons. Like many men who sought power, Bret Lewis was trying to overcome a crushing disappointment. In this case it involved his desire, from childhood, to become a great pianist. He'd started lessons at six. He had a gift, his teacher had said. He had potential for the concert stage. He could have Europe and even Russia cheering. But suddenly, with no warning, his father cut off his lessons when Bret was eleven.

"You're too interested in that sissy business," his father had roared at him the day he fired the teacher. "It has no future. I won't have a bum for a son."

Masters could sense that his question about Bret's musical talent was not appreciated. He drifted toward another case, where model planes were kept. But then Bret gestured him to a visitor's chair. "Shall we sit down?" he said. Again there was the sense of seriousness, of something that Masters could not anticipate. Bret slipped behind his desk and into an orthopedic chair that he'd oiled himself so it uttered not a squeak.

"Is this about the mission?" Masters asked, sitting down.

"No," Bret replied. "I don't even know if there's going to be a mission. Right now I'd doubt it."

"I think we could pull it off," Masters countered. "I've studied the force dispositions in . . ."

"Captain Masters," Bret interrupted, "I'm sure you're aware of the Kearns inquiry."

Masters was stunned. It had come out of the blue. He started turning uneasily in his chair, and his did have a squeak that Lewis had left in because he knew it made visitors feel awkward and sometimes defensive. "Yes, I know about it," he replied.

"What do you know about it?"

"It's about torpedoes."

"Torpedoes, Captain? Only torpedoes?"

Masters's face became stiff with tension. "Defective torpedoes."

"Yes, that's right," Bret replied. He caught the strain in Masters's face. Everything was working. Masters was reacting exactly as he'd anticipated.

"Mr. Secretary, what are you getting at?" Masters asked, realizing that he wasn't about to have a nice day.

"You, uh, were involved in the purchase of these torpedoes, am I not right?"

"You have the report, sir. I'm sure it's there. There are stories around the building."

"In fact, you were very much involved. You accepted gifts from the contractor and two subcontractors. You went to hunting lodges, on them. Dinners, on them. Theatre tickets. Bottles. Many, many bottles—and I'm not talking about the kind you return for a five-cent deposit. In fact, the American Express card you never left home without was theirs." Bret paused for effect. "And we have some evidence that you also participated in the . . . let's say it delicately, Captain . . . the improvement of some of the test results on the prototype."

That was a matter of extreme sensitivity in the Department of Defense. Throughout the 1980s there had been rumors, and sometimes direct allegations, that tests of some new weapons had been faked to win a production contract and make the officers in charge of developing the weapons look good.

"The charges are false," Captain Masters said. "I may have gone slightly over the line in accepting some courtesies, sir. But that's all."

"That is your claim?"

"It is my claim."

"You realize it will be disputed."

"Yes, sir. But I'd want to retain counsel."

"Oh, I understand. These aren't formal charges, Captain. I hope they *never* turn into formal charges."

"Sir?" It seemed odd to Masters. This accusatory tone, and suddenly the seeming compassion. That is exactly the way Bret wanted it to strike the captain—as odd, confusing. Get Masters off balance. Make him want to cooperate.

"I'll make my point briefly," Bret went on. He glanced at a calendar, on which he'd penciled in his twentieth wedding anniversary. He caught himself almost smiling. "The report is preliminary. The evidence against you, while considerable, is, in my estimation, largely circumstantial."

"I'll say it is."

"But will a court-martial?"

Masters's face turned red. "What do you mean? A minute ago you said you hoped . . ."

"Take it easy, Captain. We haven't selected the plank for you to walk yet. But that wouldn't be too difficult, would it?"

Masters did not reply.

"I can accept the report, or reject it," Bret continued. "I can question its conclusions. I can recommend changes. I can ask for more information. In fact, Captain, I can do pretty much what I want to with it, including feed it to the shredder. Or, I can send it on to the legal people."

"That would be unjust, sir."

"I'll be the judge of that. Obviously, you're a man who'd like to be an admiral, a fleet commander some day. You've had a fine career. Distinguished service in Vietnam. Various commendations. Your father was an Army officer. Your brother is a federal judge. Disgrace wouldn't suit you, would it?"

Masters took a deep, pained breath, yet tried powerfully to maintain his military bearing. "It wouldn't," he replied tersely.

"It can be avoided. There are ways, Captain Masters."

Bret could virtually see Masters ready to bite at the bait. The man was in deep trouble. His fate lay entirely in other hands. The improper deeds were past. He couldn't change them. Only Bret stood in the way of his disgracing his family, his three children. He was a proud man, yet a practical man as well.

"All right, what would I have to do?" he asked.

"I need a favor," Bret replied. "A very sensitive favor. Shall I continue?"

"Yes, please."

"Captain, we both know that you have access to certain . . . materials . . . in your antiterrorist work. I have a short shopping list." At that point Bret reached into his vest pocket and took out a transparent plastic envelope. Inside was a piece of folded, lined yellow paper. He handed the envelope to Masters.

Masters slipped on a pair of glasses and examined the list, with no change whatever in his serious expression. "Explosive, Semtex type," he said. "Remote control device, as specified. Wiring. Fake labels and part numbers to make the device untraceable." He looked up. "I assume this is for an operation."

Bret glared at Masters. "Captain," he said, "you have no need to know."

"Sorry, sir."

"Now, can you get these materials?"

"Easily."

"How soon?"

"Almost immediately."

"Undetected?"

"Utterly invisible."

"You can deliver them here?"

"Yes."

"Will any of the explosives detectors or metal detectors in the Pentagon pick them up?"

"No, I know the routes around them."

"Does this present any other problems that I haven't ticked off?"

"No. None that I can see."

"I knew I could depend on you, Captain," Bret said, thoroughly pleased. "You're the kind of man I like to recommend for higher rank."

"Thank you, sir."

Bret finally smiled. "Obviously," he said, "this is not to be discussed. It is entirely between us. Any violation, and the Kearns report gets hot."

Again, Masters said nothing. He'd always sized Bret up as gimmicky, and he wondered what his shopping list was all about. Maybe some Pentagon officials were running an illegal operation, possibly at the request of the White House. That was logical, considering Iran-Contra and other strange activities of the seventies and eighties. But why was Bret Lewis handing out the shopping list himself? Why hadn't he passed it to a lower-ranking official, who would have given it to a military man?

Bret had perfect faith in Avery Masters. He knew the man. He knew his reputation. He was not one to probe too deeply, to wonder too much. He wanted to wear stars on his shoulders and avoid, at any cost, the damage of the Kearns report. Lewis knew, because it was in Masters's file, that Masters had once killed a man on a secret assignment in Greece. It turned out that the victim, who'd been fingered by American agents as a Soviet spy, had been totally innocent. When Masters found out about the mistake, it seemed to bother him not at all. He'd done his job. He'd gotten the credit. He was the kind of man Bret Lewis liked to do business with.

"Do you have any questions?" Bret asked.

"No, I think I know what you want," Masters replied.

"Good. I think we've completed our affairs, Captain Masters. Oh yes, one more thing. You'll notice that the list I gave you is typed. I used a typewriter in another office of the government to type it. You'll also notice that the list was sealed in a plastic envelope, so no fingerprints or fibers can be found on the paper itself. In other words, there's no way to link me to that list." He paused to let it sink in. "I just wanted you to be aware of my thoroughness."

"I'm well aware of it, sir. Thank you." Captain Masters got up and left with not another word.

Bret was pleased. He'd ended on a note of intimidation, exactly what a calculating man should do. The first phase of his plan to get rid of Sarah was under way. Of course, it would be successful, courtesy of the United States Navy.

chapter
six

Sarah was still numb from Al Durfee's snapshot show. Her head was filled with the picture of just one human being.

Alison Carver.

The name kept rolling over and over in her mind.

Alison Carver. With the squeaky-clean image and the wholesome Western values.

Alison Carver.

The fake.

Alison Carver.

And now, as Sarah sat in her office, closeted behind a locked door, she felt an almost uncontrollable urge to rush over to the House of Representatives and tell Carver to her face precisely what she knew, with her Congressional colleagues listening. But she thought better of it. She wasn't quite ready for that kind of scene. And once again, the god of wishful thinking dangled the thin shred of hope before her: Maybe Durfee was wrong.

On Sarah's desk was a packet of photos she had gotten from the museum's public relations office. She started to go through them. They had been taken at a number of official functions the museum held for Washington VIPs, including members of Congress. Carver had been a regular visitor, Sarah recalled. Maybe she'd be in these pictures. Maybe she'd be with Bret. Sarah knew instinctively that she was doing what every other woman in her situation did—going back to find proof, to study the signs she may have missed, to locate the smoking gun, and, most important, to size up her competition. It was normal. It was natural.

There, Alison Carver in one picture, smiling her head off with museum officials.

Another picture—Alison Carver, and, incredibly, Sarah beside her. Sarah didn't even remember it.

There were a few more with Carver, but none showing her with Bret. What did it matter? Maybe she was just being discreet. Maybe their relationship had not yet gotten going.

Eventually, Sarah put the pictures away. She knew she was delaying a fateful decision, one she dreaded. No, she would not pack up and leave Bret, not on the basis of one investigator's report. And no, she would not call Woody Evans for advice on divorce. She *did* want to save the marriage. The decision she was putting off was whether to confront Bret with Durfee's pictures, whether to have it out—whether to destroy this twentieth anniversary and ask him bluntly for the truth.

The decision was impossible. Don't confront him, and his apparent affair with Carver could go on to its logical, heartbreaking conclusion. Confront him, and he could react so strongly that the marriage could end instantly.

Sarah was practically frozen at her desk. Her logical mind functioned, but no answer emerged.

Alison Carver.

The name continued to burn itself into her mind. It was rapidly becoming an obsession.

Sarah had to decide. Quickly.

chapter
seven

The rider on horseback saw the two figures, almost a hundred yards away. A man and a woman. Serious talk. For a few moments the rider studied them. The man gestured sharply with his hands. He was convincing the woman of something. He was the salesman. Their bodies were hunched, leaning toward each other. This was secretive, insistently private. The woman's gestures were tight, as if she were very nervous. But she always looked directly at him. She had style. She'd learned how to cope. She was a woman who could confront things and handle them.

The rider's job had made him an expert at interpreting body movements. He'd seen them all before, and the sight wasn't unusual here. Couples came all the time, sometimes in crisis, sometimes in love, but always because there was something about this place that made them feel they had a kind of Divine approval.

So the rider turned away, directing his look forward. His eyes were not supposed to stray. His head was not supposed to turn. And he wasn't permitted to display any interest in the little dramas that the gesturing hands and shoulders always signaled. The rider was the definition of spit-and-polish. He wore the dress blue uniform of the Third Infantry, United States Army. The Old Guard. His haircut was the required "high and tight." He was astride one of six white horses tugging a caisson up a hill at Arlington National Cemetery. A retired general was being buried with full military honors. Three riders rode the white horses on the left of the team. The horses on the right were riderless. Ahead of the caisson marched a military band, followed by soldiers, then the colors, then another group of soldiers.

Tourists stood stiffly as the funeral procession passed along the narrow road, which cut through a forest of gravestones. The visitors were uncomfortable, some of them vaguely embarrassed. They were, in their jeans and creased denim skirts, dropping in uninvited at someone else's funeral, and had to admit to themselves that they were enjoying it. The pomp. The snap of the soldiers. The muffled drums with their excruciatingly precise cadence. The caisson that people associate with the deaths of presidents. The Old Guard always put on a magnificent show. Through the corner of his eye, the man on horseback saw some tourists aim their Instamatics in a common display of poor taste. One actually took a flash picture, startling one of the horses for a split second. And the rider saw the visitors whisper to each other as the coffin passed. Always the same question, at every Arlington funeral: "Hey, you think it's anyone famous?"

It was understandable. Arlington wasn't for real people. It was a movie set for legends.

The couple the rider spotted were oblivious to the final rites, seeing and hearing only each other. They had met many times before, but this was their first time at Arlington. Bret Lewis thought that he and Ramy Jordan would have more anonymity here than almost anywhere else. And he picked a telling location—a small bench near the grave of Dashiell Hammett, the crime novelist. It was, Bret thought, a wonderful place to plan a murder.

To a passerby, Ramy and Bret seemed absolutely right for each other. Anyone would have thought they were married. Ramy was also forty-one, and everything about her demeanor exuded style and importance. The hair—red, shoulder length, shaped by the best professional and held in place with a twenty-four-karat gold clip. The summer dress—very simple in subdued green, but clearly not off anyone's rack. The pearl necklace—Tiffany's, after a private showing by a company vice president. The sunglasses, which Ramy held in her hand—rimless, something of an elegant trademark with her. This wasn't a Washington housewife out for an afternoon fling. This was someone who rarely carried credit cards because they were rarely needed. Her credit was her name.

"It's not every day that I agree to kill my husband," Ramy was saying, lowering her dark green eyes. "God, I can't believe what I just said."

"It's not every day that I agree to kill my wife," Bret replied. "And I *can* believe what I just said." Now Ramy raised those green eyes and stared at Bret. She'd danced through affairs before, and each time she'd cut them off. All those men, or so-called men—the senators and lawyers and diplomats—were so inadequate, so full of themselves. But this one was forever. Bret Lewis could rescue her from Shel Jordan, who combined wealth, sleaze and dullness in one remarkable, smiling package. In her moments of sheer fantasy, Ramy saw herself glide off with Bret into some orange sunset, leaving behind no cares, no guilt, no scandal. And yet, in more realistic moments she knew it had to come to this. *All* affairs finally came to this, to two basic questions that have been asked since the first clauses of matrimonial law were chiseled in a lawyer's office in some ancient cave: How do you get rid of the other husband? How do you get rid of the other wife?

"I always hoped for a simple divorce," Ramy said.

"This is the same principle," Bret answered. "We're just skipping the legal work."

For a few moments they were silent, gazing at each other, their hearts pounding a counterpoint to the muffled drums of the funeral procession now only eighty yards away.

"You could live with yourself, Bret?"

"Easily. You know what Sarah is. She's a museum piece with no ambition. I've outgrown her." The words were tinged with a bitterness put on for effect. "In fact, I was thinking about that just last night. A lot of men complain that their wives aren't the women they married. I've got a different problem. My wife *is* the woman I married. She's had a no-growth policy for twenty years." He paused for a moment, dramatically. "And *you* could live with yourself, Ramy?"

Ramy sighed deeply. "Yes. Yes, if this is the way you want it. I believe in going to the wall with a man."

"You're superb," Bret said. "You'll never regret this."

How Woody Evans would have loved it. How he would have loved bumming around Georgetown parties and telling the tale of the assistant secretary and the Washington society girl: "The guy wanted to kill his wife. It was all part of his game plan to move up in politics, and he wanted the right wife to help him. He even blackmailed a Navy captain to get his little school supplies. As far as that went, it was very easy. But his wife knew something was going on. They always do. She hired a private eye to get the facts, and he brought back photos of 'the woman.' Terrific. The trouble was, 'the woman' was one of two. There was a midnight woman, and there was a noon woman. And each of them played a different part in this man's life."

And, once he finished with the parties, how Evans would have loved telling this all to a court. He would have stood at the bar, hands shoved into the rear pockets of his $1,000-dollar suit, pushing his jacket aside. He would have begun pacing slowly back and forth, in an unchanging, hypnotic rhythm. "Ladies and gentlemen of the jury," he would say. Then he would stop. He would face Bret Lewis, glare at him like a country preacher staring down the local hooker, and shake a lecturing finger at him. "This man," he'd thunder, "the assistant secretary of the most powerful Navy on God's great earth, is a gutter rat."

"I still wish there were some other way," Ramy said.

"I told you, there isn't," Bret insisted. "Divorces would be messy—especially in this town, with all the press. They'd go on forever. We'd both lose everything. Your sleazeball husband would hire the best lawyers in the world. You'd be dragged through hell. I won't let him treat you that way. I simply won't, and that's all there is to it." Bret amazed himself by his own power of persuasion. He'd convinced a woman who had never even gotten a parking ticket to help murder her husband. And he'd convinced her that murder meant a clean inheritance—100 percent of her husband's money, less legal fees and a token contribution to the deceased's favorite charity. Appearances, you know.

"And you're sure we won't be caught, Bret? You *said* that."

"How can we get caught? I plan things like this in my Pentagon work. This is very easy. And I have someone else getting the materials."

"Someone else knows?"

"He's safe. I've got him by the chops."

"What does that mean?"

"It means if he talks, I wreck his life. Believe me, the man wants to be happy."

They could make out each clomp of the horses' hooves now as the funeral procession approached. A tourist with a video camera ran past them, trying to position himself to catch the caisson.

"What if there's a slipup?" Ramy asked. "God, I'm talking like a hood."

"In this town, that makes you an honored citizen. There won't be any slipups. There's nothing traceable to us."

"We haven't discussed the method."

"Explosion."

"One?"

"Yes, of course."

"You mean . . . Shel and Sarah together . . ."

"Yes," Bret said. "It's so neat that way. We'll have to get them both in the same car, but that won't be hard. It'll be my car."

"Why yours?"

"Because when it blows up, everyone will think *I* was the target. It'll look like the work of a terrorist out to get an American official."

Now Ramy glanced over to the funeral cortege, which had stopped. All that could be heard was the shuffling of the horses and the movements of a few troops. Members of the Old Guard started removing the casket from the caisson. They pulled it once. Then a second time. Then a third. Always three pulls to remove the casket.

Then they held it even with the caisson for a few moments.

Ramy looked away. She and Bret were the only ones whose eyes weren't riveted on the ceremony. Her mind, which could negotiate the most difficult social minefields, was becoming a mass of confusion, of uncertainty. I'm a grown woman of forty-one, she told herself. An important woman. A woman who knows the top of the Washington A-list and calls them by nicknames. And I'm sitting in a cemetery planning to murder my husband and another man's wife. And I'm scared out of my wits. And yet I love it, because my life must change and this is the man I want to change it. And he knows about these things. He *knows.*

Bret looked at her intently. Her eyes showed both the confusion and the ecstasy. And he knew he had her. She would follow everything he said. He'd seen the look before. He'd seen it on the faces of soldiers embarking on an antiterrorist raid. Their eyes said the same thing: Why am I doing this? But I can't wait to go.

"When do we do it?" Ramy asked.

"In nine days."

She sighed, then shook her head slightly, as if surprised at herself.

"What's wrong?" he asked.

"When you said nine days, I mentally started going over my social calendar. Isn't that stupid?"

"No, I think it's normal," Bret answered. "Of course, if there's something really critical—I mean, if you and Shel plan to go to some important function—our little thing can be put off a few days."

Ramy couldn't believe he was that cold about it. Put off a murder for a dinner dance? "No," she said. "Let's get it over with."

"We'll have to grieve together, publicly," Bret said. "Ramy, we may have to practice that. I mean, we may actually have to practice in front of my video camera."

"Don't make me do that," Ramy said. "I hate the way I look on TV."

"All right. We'll practice some other way. Look, the press'll love us. Two close friends who lost their spouses together in an act of terror against the United States."

The general's casket was carried slowly to the gravesite now, where the widow waited. She was too young for widowhood, not looking much more than fifty. She wore black, and held back the tears.

"An act of terror against the United States," Bret repeated. It had a wonderful ring.

And as he said it, six white-gloved men of the Old Guard loosened the American flag from the casket and snapped it open.

Ramy's eyes now returned to the ceremony, focusing on the widow. "That's me in less than two weeks," she said. "And all those people who hated my husband will be there. They'll whisper about the will, and the size of the estate. Actual numbers will be thrown around, right at the grave. I know. I go to these things. I've made estimates myself."

In the distance they could hear faintly the words of an Army chaplain, and then the band played "Onward Christian Soldiers."

"It will all be over soon," Bret told Ramy. "You'll have no more pain."

The air was rent by three rifle volleys fired over the general's coffin. With each volley the widow shook, bearing up under the honor, and yet the strain, of a final military salute.

Then, taps.

Unseen by anyone, the leader of the casket team tugged gently on the flag, signaling the start of the final flag folding. The band struck up "America the Beautiful." The folded flag was given to an officer who walked smartly up to the widow with it. "This flag," he said, "is presented on behalf of a grateful nation, as a token of appreciation for the honorable and faithful service rendered by your loved one."

Ramy dabbed her eyes at the sight. "One thing," she said, as if extracting a concession from Bret.

"What's that?" Bret asked.

"I do want to continue my volunteer work."

chapter
eight

In the kingdom of sleaze, Phil and Francesca Black were the royal family. They were, together, the owners, publishers, editors, and sole staff members of *Flash*, a weekly tabloid that had never been confused with the *New York Times*. PREZ MEETS WITH VAMPIRE was the story that secured *Flash*'s place in the supermarket checkouts of a mighty nation. The White House did not dignify the story with a denial, but, then, *Flash* never published the pictures of the meeting that it promised its readers. BLOODSUCKER PHOTOS SWIPED BY CIA was the explanation, and Phil Black demanded a Congressional probe.

Phil Black had grown up in Brooklyn and had been expelled from high school. Francesca had been born and raised in Los Angeles and had been expelled from college. Both claimed to be Australian. They thought it gave them more class, more cachet with the international set. They rented cassettes of *Crocodile Dundee* and read books on Australian dialect to pick up the accent.

Flash was issued from a rented townhouse three blocks from Capitol Hill. Automatic telephoners operated all day, calling potential subscribers with a message that began, "Please don't hang up or you won't hear about the congressman who gets instructions from Jack the Ripper . . . in writing." The walls were covered with neatly framed "scoops" about the high councils of government: SENATOR COLLECTS HUMAN HEADS; GHOST OF JOHN WAYNE SEEN IN WHITE HOUSE; REAGAN'S SECRET PORNO TAPES.

But there was one thing about *Flash* that lifted it out of the category of laughingstock or ragbag. It had something called "Page 5." "Page 5" was well researched and documented, and it always exposed someone in public life. It had brought down Cabinet officers, ambassadors and a powerful senator. "Page 5" made *Flash* feared, and Phil Black loved it.

The Blacks were at their word processors, putting together a story on transvestite conservatives in Congress. Phil was in his fifties, and even in the office he wore a black, three-piece suit with black, silk shirt and black tie, the better to reflect his name. Francesca, whose real name was Frances, overfilled an oversized chair, and the droplets of alcohol that populated her breath destroyed all disease within sneezing range. She was twenty-six, but her face was forty.

The buzzer on their steel security door rang. Phil dragged his bloodshot eyes toward a black-and-white TV monitor that showed who was outside. While *Flash* didn't advertise its address, and there was nothing on the door to indicate that a yellow rag was published within, Phil always feared a firebombing aimed at his sizzling files. This time he knew the caller and flipped on the intercom. "Come in, Al," he said, trying to jump start his Australian accent. "I'll buzz the lock." He buzzed. The door lock clicked open.

Al Durfee entered, and the door closed automatically behind him. He walked slowly up the wood staircase and knocked on the door to the main office. Phil Black went over and opened.

"G'day, Al," Black said, ushering Durfee in. "You leg over?" He'd read in a book that this was Australian for "Did you walk?"

"I took a cab," Durfee replied, slightly out of breath from the trip up the stairs.

"Come from a job?"

"Yeah."

"You look rotten. You go down the gurgler?" In other words, fail.

Durfee shot Black a queer look. "Phil," he said, "I'm tired. I was up all night. Cut the Aussie crap. Me, I'm a private eye. I know you came from Brooklyn. You know I know."

"Got to practice the accent," Black said. "It's like Spanish class."

"Olé. Cut it out."

Black and Durfee understood each other. They'd often worked together. The Blacks hired Durfee to conduct spy missions and document checks. Durfee's work was always winding up on "Page 5," and his thoroughness was legendary. He'd once spent weeks reconstructing a single night at a restaurant some two years earlier to prove that a Cabinet officer had been there with a woman who turned out to be a Soviet spy. Durfee got the restaurant's credit card slips from that evening and tracked down every patron. If the story had run in a legitimate paper, it might have won a Pulitzer.

"To what do we owe this honor?" Phil asked. "I assume you're not here to show us art studies."

"Me? Art? That's an allergy."

"You got a beaut?"

"Why else would I come? Hello, Francesca."

Francesca, absorbed in her story, her face reflecting the green glow of her computer screen, simply waved a chunky arm and typed on.

"All right, let's skip all the nice questions about our health," Phil said. "Look, Al, it's a pressure day. These right-wing transvestites are hot. Let's get to it."

Without a word, Al slipped an envelope from his briefcase, pulled out the standard eight-by-ten glossies and flipped them onto a table in front of Phil Black.

Black studied them with an educated eye. Despite his British Empire affectations, something in that craggy face and exaggerated nose smacked of a pit bull in search of a kill. Durfee liked that look. He thought it read money. Did it read $5,000? He figured at least that. Maybe $7,500.

Black looked up from the photos. "So?"

Durfee had misread the look. Maybe $250. "What do you mean, so?" he asked.

"So, what's so special?" Black explained. "It's a guy and his doll having a stroll."

"You don't recognize her?"

"No."

"Alison Carver."

"Hooker?"

"Congresswoman."

"Who cares?"

"From California. Conservative. Affiliated with church groups. She's having an affair with Bret Lewis."

"Who?"

"The assistant secretary of the Navy."

Phil stared at him with sublime incredulity. "The *assistant*? The assistant *secretary*? Of the *boats*? Al, Al, Al, I'm surprised at you. Look, this isn't the *Washington Post*. Our readers don't know from the tiny assistants."

"They'll know Bret Lewis," Durfee said. "He's being groomed for better things . . . by Tim Curran."

"Ah," Phil said.

"Yes, ah. He could go far. Cabinet. Senate. Maybe higher. These photos aren't for now, Phil. They're an investment. Remember Gary Hart with that model on the boat?"

"Yeah, yeah." Traces of Australia were fading.

"I can sell these to you with the usual provisions—a bonus if you use them after he reaches higher office. Right now I'm being reasonable. You wait 'til later, I become a little crazy."

Phil smiled at the standard line. Al Durfee always played brave, but he always needed cash. These pictures meant dinner and dry cleaning.

"Where'd you get them?" Phil asked.

"The wife hired me."

"Shame, Al. You're using the pictures you got paid for." Phil laughed. They both laughed. Durfee had, on discreet occasions, sold Black some pictures paid for by clients. There were restrictions, though: Durfee's name would never appear on them, and the pictures were extras, never seen by the clients. If they were printed, and a client became suspicious of their origin, Durfee would say they were taken by *Flash* photographers, who had smoked out the story on their own.

"Tell me about the chick," Phil said. "You say she's a God botherer?"

"A what?"

"I slipped, Al. That's Aussie for religious."

"Yeah, she is," Durfee answered. "But a fake. She just puts on the act. There's buzz that she's running for governor. If she does, these pictures are news. Husband stealing ain't in Scripture."

"Lord, no," Phil Black said. "So we have here an up-and-coming young man and a going-down young woman. Well, these aren't must haves."

"Think of their value in the future," Al goaded. "America must invest."

"Well," Phil said, "I guess I agree with that. Look, I'll take a shot that one of these peanuts makes news. Five hundred down, with escalators."

"Five hundred? Phil, I'm not a missionary."

"Six, because it's you."

"Phil, Phil. You aren't buying pictures. You're buying my judgment. Like a brain surgeon. These are people to watch."

"All right, a thousand. I'll mortgage my Mercedes."

Actually, Phil Black was buying the pictures simply to keep Durfee happy. He didn't want to lose a top investigator to the competitive rags that were always rumored to be starting up in Washington.

"You won't regret this, Phil," Durfee said.

"I probably will. Tell me, Al, now that you've got the large bucks, be straight. What's the very biggest story you see here?"

Durfee took in a deep breath and let it out slowly. "Murder," he finally said.

"What? You think this Lewis'll kill his wife?"

"No."

"Then what?"

"She'll kill *him*."

"Come on. How you figure that?"

"I know her, Phil. She hired me. She's a high-steppin' lady— educated, big job at the airplane museum. But she's a volcano inside. I see this a lot. The lady with the sheepskin who always tries to keep her feelings bottled up. They're the ones who do it. They're the ones who pull the trigger. She'll do it."

"When?" Black asked, now starting to take notes.

"Soon."

"You'll try to stop her, Al?"

"Nothing I could say would help."

"God," Phil Black said, "I hope you're right." Then he looked down at the photos he'd just bought. "I think I got a bargain."

chapter
nine

Ramy Jordan drove her red Mercedes sport coupe back to her fifteen-room house in McLean, Virginia, not far from the Central Intelligence Agency. She could think only of her meeting earlier that day with Bret, a rendezvous accompanied by the muffled drums of a military funeral and highlighted by constant reminders of death and mourning. Now she was living with a death in the family, a death to be, and the thought was becoming oh so delightful. The plan to eliminate both her husband and Bret's wife was beginning to wear well. It felt right, and she was glad that Bret had selected a method that was sudden and uncomplicated. Why cause pain and suffering? A refined woman would never do that.

And yet, she still had a sense of disbelief. This was murder. *I'm* involved in a murder, she kept telling herself as she turned onto her street. No one like Ramy Jordan ever expected to be involved in a murder, but she knew it was the electric attraction of Bret Lewis that was keeping her anesthetized to the reality. She didn't feel "murder." All she felt was "Bret, mine, soon."

Now, as she pulled into the driveway of her colonial and surveyed the three-car garage, she sensed a burden being lifted from her shoulders. Shel would be gone within two weeks. No more hearing him pull into the driveway in his BMW, honking three times as if announcing the arrival of a king. No more entertaining half-drunk defense executives ready to pay Shel obscene fees to get a quick visit with a bored senator. Shel could never be the man Bret was. Bret Lewis was a statesman. Bret was going places that money couldn't buy.

Ramy had always needed someone to believe in.

As she eased her car into the garage, placing it next to the Cadillac—which Shel kept to show a respectable loyalty to American manufacturing—Ramy leaned back in the seat and, permitting herself a smile, started planning his funeral. She'd design the paper program for the chapel, just as Jacqueline Kennedy had. She'd have white carnations—Shel always said he wanted white carnations at his funeral, and after all, the grief-stricken widow had to show full respect for the deceased. There'd also have to be an organist playing "Nearer My God to Thee." It had been Shel's favorite hymn ever since he saw a TV movie about the sinking of the Titanic and heard it played by the ship's band in the final moments.

And the casket, no matter how little might be left of Shel, would have to be bronze, Ramy knew. Shel had said he'd wanted a casket that would withstand an atomic bomb—a matter, apparently, of some moment in a cemetery.

The plot, which Shel had already picked out, would be surrounded by flowers. Shel Jordan wanted to be buried in a garden, just like Franklin D. Roosevelt.

Ramy got out of the Mercedes and spoke these words: "A Jordan is home." Automatically, a voice-activated mechanism closed the garage door. Ramy shook her head, laughing.

She entered the house by punching a three-digit code on a security lock. The door led to the kitchen—the first symbol of Shel Jordan's success. It was fifteen by twenty, with all the facilities needed to cater a small wedding. Shel loved to show off the kitchen's computer, built into a wood cabinet, that allowed the Jordan compound to keep track of party planning and stocks on hand. As in all Jordan rooms, there was a telephone, a tape recorder and a locked copy of Shel Jordan's Rolodex, with the right Washington numbers. There were four yellow pads placed strategically around the kitchen, each with a Cross pen at its side. For Shel Jordan was constantly making notes, trusting nothing to memory. No note was ever thrown away.

The lighting, even in this kitchen, was indirect. And of course there was a meeting table. People with power had meetings in the kitchen.

Ramy flipped her Gucci bag onto a spotless black lacquered counter and headed to the refrigerator for a Diet Coke. Just then the phone rang, or, rather, buzzed, which Shel thought was far more impressive. Ramy picked up.

"Hello."

"Ramy?"

It was Bret. He was in his office, at his desk, the door closed.

"Well . . . hello," Ramy replied with a tingling warmth, as she sank into a leather meeting chair.

"He's not there, is he?" Bret asked.

"Of course not." She checked her watch. "Right now he's meeting with a close personal friend of Imelda Marcos."

"I just wanted to call you," Bret said, speaking quietly. "This was a very important day, wasn't it?"

"Yes, it was."

"Your problems will be over soon. He'll be out of your life, safely tucked away."

"I can't wait."

"Neither can I. He's been bad for you, Ramy. He's been bad for someone I care very much about."

"You'll never know how bad," Ramy said.

"I'm glad you agreed to everything I suggested."

"You were right. It's the only way. It solves everything."

"If I'd only known before how unhappy you've been with Shel . . ."

"Well, it's something I kept inside me for a long, long time. But when you . . . appeared . . . is that the right word?"

"It's as good as any."

"I just let it all come out. What you've done means so much to me. I really don't know what would have happened to me without you."

"You don't have to worry about that now. We'll solve our problems together. I spoke with the person I mentioned."

"Person?"

"You know . . ."

"Oh, sure." She guessed it was the person who was getting the explosives.

"He doesn't seem to think there'll be a problem."

"Good," Ramy said.

"I have complete trust in him. I don't think there's a better man for this kind of thing."

"That's great to know. So much depends on him."

"And look—actually this is why I was calling—if you want to talk about this, if you have any worries or thoughts—I want you to call me."

Just like Bret, Ramy thought. He was always so considerate, so much more sensitive than Shel had ever been. Shel would have had his secretary make the call. "I will," she said.

"And soon we'll be together."

At that moment the buzzer on Bret's desk rang. An assistant crackled onto the intercom announcing that the Secretary of Defense was on the phone. "Got to go," Bret told Ramy, and their conversation ended.

Ramy placed the bright red Scandinavian-design phone back in its cradle. She stared at it, almost caressing it with her eyes, as if Bret were somehow inside it. How lucky I am, she thought to herself. Some women go through life in misery, never knowing what a deep, satisfying relationship can be. I have Bret Lewis. And soon, thanks to this wonderful man, my joke of a marriage will be over.

She couldn't know, she couldn't possibly guess, that the secret little conversation she'd just had with her beloved Bret would be reported in newspapers around the world. She couldn't realize the role it would play in her own fate, in the fate of Bret Lewis, in the fate of everyone connected with the strange Lewis and Jordan marriages.

Fate. It would not deal Ramy Jordan quite the hand she was expecting.

Sarah Lewis made a critical decision, possibly the most critical of her life. It was inevitable. It was necessary.

Sitting in her office, her door shut as tightly as was her husband's during his sneak phone call to Ramy Jordan, she decided to confront Bret that night. She knew it wasn't a completely rational decision. It came more from the gut. But she *did* decide: Confront him. Purge the fever. Try to save the marriage.

Her feelings were wavering between hurt and rage. Woody Evans could have scripted her thought process for her. He'd read the scene in court depositions a thousand times before. On the other hand, it *had* been a good marriage, she reasoned, and she wanted it to continue. It was tempting to think of Alison Carver as an aberration, a short-term fling, maybe a normal variation after twenty years. But Bret was thoughtful. He'd probably stop that behavior if she had it out with him. Of course. He'd realize what he might lose, what twenty years of marriage really meant.

On the other hand, he might not stop. Unlike some women who believed only the fantasy, Sarah was determined to be ready for the worst. If it had to end, let it end cleanly. I will not beg, she promised herself. I will not run after him. If he wants out, I will ask him for nothing. I have my independence, my position at the museum. I was single for half my life. I can be single for the remainder.

She was assuming, of course, that she still had half her life ahead of her.

When Sarah first hired him, Al Durfee had scribbled a series of phone numbers on the back of his business card—elegant places where he could be reached. One was a bar, another was his mother's room at a rest home, the last the lab of an inventor who provided him with some of his surveillance gadgets. He wasn't at the first two numbers. A man with a gravel voice answered the third.

"Kean Observations. Bill Kean speaking."

"Is Al Durfee there?"

Sarah heard a phone being clunked down and someone calling. "Hey, Al, pick up. Don't hog it."

Durfee got on the line. "Durfee," he said, very formally.

"Al, this is Sarah Lewis."

"A pleasure, Mrs. L," Durfee replied, trying to impress his inventor friend. "You have some surveillance for me?" Recalling that he'd just sold some of her photos to Phil Black, he felt a twinge of guilt. But, like Bret Lewis, he was able to contain it.

"No, Al, that's not why I called," Sarah answered.

"Oh. Something happen? He didn't walk out already, did he?"

"No. As far as I can determine, he's still at the Pentagon and we're still married."

"Thank God. They walk out, the wives get angry at *me*. Shoot."

"Al," Sarah said, "I've been thinking about confronting my husband—tonight."

"Spoil the anniversary, eh?"

"It's an inside feeling," Sarah explained. "I just think it's something I must do."

"You gonna sit down in some classy restaurant," Durfee asked, "like in a movie?"

Sarah's mind was too focused on her problem to be offended by Durfee's flipness. "No," she said. "I'm going to do it at home. And that's why I called you. You showed me the photos, but you didn't leave them."

"Intentionally."

"Oh?"

"Pictures like that shouldn't be left around, ma'am. If someone discovers them—a husband, that is—it could cause indigestion."

"I'd like them."

"Why?"

"When I confront Bret, I want to lay them in front of him—just as you did with me."

Durfee was silent for a few moments while he framed, as best he could, his reply. "Mrs. L," he answered, somewhat somberly, "if I can say so, that may not be wise. Men are capable—well, I'll put that different—men get angrier than women. A psychiatrist'll tell you that. The best way, in my experience, is to sit down with the man and just say that you're hurt, that you never expected anything to damage the marriage—but that you found out about this other woman."

"Without the pictures? Without proof? He might deny it."

"They don't. When they're caught, they're almost relieved. Besides, they plan to tell the wife eventually anyway. It just forces the issue."

It took only a moment for Sarah to mull it over. She wasn't much for sitting down with her husband "like in a movie" and just discussing things. She wanted the evidence in front of her. Maybe it was the scientist in her, but she felt more secure with hard facts. "Al, I'd like the pictures," she said.

"Ma'am," Durfee replied, "would you mind if I asked a few questions?"

"No, I guess not."

"Does your husband have a gun?"

Sarah hesitated.

"Well, ma'am, does he?"

"He has a pistol."

"Does he have a temper?"

"Now look, I know what you're getting at," Sarah replied, sounding angry, but really just frustrated. "I don't know what's at the bottom of Bret's little fling, but he's never so much as raised his voice to me. And he would *never* hurt me physically. You have to *know* the man. He's not the type."

Durfee weighed Sarah's request for the photos before saying anything more. Sarah could almost hear his concern, his worry, in the erratic pattern of his breathing. "All right, Mrs. Lewis," he said finally, "you're an intelligent woman with good judgment, and you have a right to your property. I'll bring the pictures. But I urge you—I'm on my very knees—to sound your husband out first."

"I'm not afraid of him. I told you that."

"Just sound him out. Tell him you know what he's doing and wait for his reaction. Then present him with the goods. Lead into it. He'll ask you how you got the pictures."

"What should I say?"

"Say a friend took them. They hate it when they learn the wife hired a private eye. It's the male ego thing."

Sarah went along with this part of Durfee's advice. She knew she'd be mortified to admit to Bret that she'd hired a detective. In fact, she was more mortified by the prospect of the confrontation than she was afraid. She almost laughed when she realized that she feared *embarrassing* Bret.

But why should that be unusual? She had to love him, she knew, no matter what he'd done. She'd always love him.

*   *   *

He'd have to choke up with tears during his eulogy for Sarah,
Bret thought, as he flipped on the paper shredder in his office.
It was the decent thing to do.

chapter
ten

One by one, Bret fed a file of papers into the shredder. He envisioned the long, tantalizing strips being sealed in brown bags and then burned in the Pentagon's incinerator for classified waste. These papers surely deserved the highest level of classification, he thought. He handled them with greater care, greater thoroughness, than he had ever handled a state document. This is my future, he said to himself, as each sheet was sliced into confetti by the blades of the machine. With these sheets I begin Sarah's final chapter.

The first to go through the shredder was a sketch of a car parked in the lot of a low building. Lines leading from three locations in the building to the car had figures running along them: "42 steps," "98 steps," "116 steps." The sketch also showed locations of floodlights in the parking area. Sharp shadows from the floodlights could be useful, Bret thought to himself, especially if they fell between cars.

Sketch number two was a diagram showing lines of sight from the low building to the car, with the car alternately parked in four separate locations. On this Bret had written, "Park farthest spot from building—no light, no people."

The third sketch was a rough portrait of a remote-controlled bomb sealed in a small container, resting inside a woman's handbag. Bret had circled the location of the antenna, a strip of thin metal running down one side of the container. He'd also jotted down a question:

"Steel beams stop signal?" He'd have to check it out in equipment manuals.

The fourth sketch was of a remote-control transmitter taped inside the jacket pocket of a man's tuxedo. The sketch showed several locations for the operating lever. Bret had scrawled, "Top best for thumb leverage."

The fifth sketch showed the probable blast radius of a bomb set off in the parked car. "Avoid window," Bret had written.

It took Bret only thirty seconds to send all his artwork to shredder heaven. He knew he would have to draw each sketch over again at least twice before the murder was carried out. Still, that was preferable to hiding them. He was obsessed with security. Documents, no matter how well hidden, had a strange way of being discovered.

When he finished, he shut off the shredder and walked over to his Linn Sondek turntable. He regarded it, and his other audio equipment, with some pride. This was the installation of a *music* lover, not a hobbyist. His equipment used *tubes*. He was proud to say that. Tubes—as in the old days. For he knew what every music lover knew, that tubes reproduced music more accurately, more sweetly, than any transistor. A vulgarian would have the "solid state" equipment that he loathed; Bret Lewis had tubes. And he *only* played records. He would not even consider compact discs, even if they were the modern rage. His sensitive ear was offended by the stridency of the compact disc and soothed by the subtle reproduction of the best European records. Fighting these new gadgets was a constant battle against degradation.

Bret realized that some people derided him for his insistence that every shading of the music be correct. But he knew that those on his level would understand.

After cleaning it with Last Formula 3, he put on a record of Ormandy leading the Philadelphia Orchestra in Beethoven's *Eroica*. As the music began, he flipped open the display case and fingered a baton actually used by von Karajan in a visit to America. Bret started to conduct an imaginary concert, straining to imitate the style of the Austrian conductor—his hands in sweeping, graceful motions, his eyes closed, as if one with the music. Nothing made him feel more powerful, more in control, than this. In these moments he felt he had missed his vocation. Leading a great orchestra would have pacified his every drive, would have fulfilled his lust for glory. He would have been a very happy man. Alas, now it could never be.

But wiping out Sarah was no small consolation prize. It was the first step on another ambitious road. And the plan he'd devised filled him with a sense of supreme professional accomplishment. It was too bad, he thought, that something so perfect had to be kept secret.

Sarah came home early that day.

Now, meticulously, she placed Durfee's pictures side by side on the bed she'd shared with Bret for twenty years. There were twelve in all, each an eight-by-ten color glossy. They were grainy because Durfee had to use high-speed film at night, but the speckles of grain gave the photos of Bret and Alison Carver an artistic look that was almost appealing. They could have been clothing ads in a slick magazine, or used in travel brochures to show the joys of Washington after hours. But each one drove a shaft of pain into Sarah's heart.

She placed the photos around the rim of the plain white spread so Bret would see at least some the right way up, no matter where he stood. For a few moments her mind wandered back to the day she and Bret bought that spread—traveling in a driving rain to an auction of old American handicrafts in Virginia. They'd done that so often. The apartment was filled with antiques, from old wood furniture to an assortment of cuckoo clocks. Every piece brought back memories, memories now blurred by crisis.

After arranging the photos, Sarah went to the door, left the bedroom, then immediately reentered. She wanted to gauge for herself the impact the pictures would make. Her eyes were first drawn to one of Bret smiling affectionately at Alison on the Capitol steps. That was enough. When Bret saw that picture, Sarah predicted, he'd realize that his wife knew everything, that he had no place to hide, no alibi to save him.

Sarah then examined her strategy. Where should she be when Bret walked into the room? Right behind him, ready for his reaction? Or should she be in the kitchen, allowing him to see the pictures alone for a while? She decided to be right behind him. I want to be there, she said to herself. I want to see everything, in living color and glorious 3-D. I want to see the look on old cool and collected's face.

But what would she actually see?

Never before had she had to confront Bret with anything even approaching this. Never before had she challenged his fidelity. Never before had she spied on him. Would his response be soft and gentle, as always? Or would he be the Bret Lewis of government rumors? Tough. Biting. Someone who could sting with words . . . and actions?

She started to imagine it.

He'd walk toward the bedroom. She'd be behind him. He'd enter. He'd spot the pictures from the door, but wouldn't instantly realize what they contained. He'd think, "This is about our anniversary." He'd smile, thinking Sarah had pulled out some old pictures taken through their twenty years together.

He'd approach them.

He'd look down.

He'd see, and know.

But he'd stay calm. Bret was always calm. He'd look at the pictures, possibly walking slowly around the bed. Only when he'd examined each would he look up at his wife. Then he'd speak. Sarah guessed that he *wouldn't* ask, "Where did you get these?" He was too sophisticated for that. He knew surveillance work when he saw it. He would more likely ask, "How did you know?" In other words, what did he do wrong that alerted her in the first place?

She'd tell him. Late nights too frequently. Stories about emergency meetings. No national crisis. A wife suspects.

Then he'd admit it was true. No lame excuses for Bret Lewis. He might even congratulate her for her spunk, her gutsiness. He'd never look toward the dresser drawer, where the pistol was. He'd never threaten her, or harm her. He had too much class for that.

In fact, he'd probably give her a status report: "I'm still seeing her," or "I saw her for a while, but I've broken it off," or "I intend to marry her, so let's talk," or "I've been unreasonable and I'm going to stop." That's it. He'd say "unreasonable." He'd never say, "I've been stupid." He wasn't the type to play dumb. Nor would he apologize. He'd simply assume that she understood how the game was played, and he'd proceed from there.

And by night's end she'd know if she'd be with him for those next fifty years, or flying solo.

Sarah felt strangely relieved.

The most important night of her life lay before her.

She'd grow old with Bret Lewis. Or without him.

While Sarah made her plans, Bret felt an odd compulsion returning.

He felt he *had* to visit the murder site almost every day. Like a scout before battle, he had to know every inch of the turf, every chance for error, every trap that fate lay for him. What were the traffic patterns? How many cars were usually parked? How did the shadows fall as darkness came? And so he left the Pentagon at five-thirty, telling his secretary that it was his anniversary. She made some comment about how lucky he was to be so happily married. His reply was gracious.

He walked to the Pentagon parking lot, nodding greetings to a few senior officers. Like the morning, the dusk was steamy. There was still a haze, and Bret's shirt started clinging almost immediately.

He turned and looked up at Captain Masters's window. The light was still on. Poor Masters, he thought. He'd better be working on that shopping list. He'd better get everything that was on it.

Bret slipped into the Lincoln and left the lot. Within minutes he was on the Jefferson Davis Highway, and minutes later on the Lee Highway.

Then he drove to the small Cheshire Motel, in a corner of Arlington, Virginia.

The Cheshire had been more elegant at one time, to the extent that a motel can be elegant. Now it catered to quick visitors doing business with the companies and agencies in Washington. Bret never actually drove into the motel's parking lot. He feared having a minor accident that would leave a record of his presence. He normally cruised by; sometimes he stopped, got out and mailed a letter from a nearby box or picked up a copy of the *Washington Times* from a local dispensing machine. He never spoke to anyone, and if it was still light, he wore sunglasses.

Tonight he stayed in his car. He had a particular objective: studying

the line of sight from the motel office to a large catering room that
the establishment rented out. Could anyone in the office see what
was happening? Would they be able to make out faces?

He observed. He took notes. Then he started back to Washington.

He turned on the radio, tuning in the local CBS station. The first
few stories dealt with the state of the economy, with the newscaster
reeling off some statistics that had just been released by the Labor
Department. Then there was this report:

> The FBI announced today that it has arrested two
> Iranian students in Washington and charged them with
> planning to destroy a telephone relay station in
> northern Virginia. The two students denied the charge,
> although the FBI alleged that they had explosives in
> their northeast apartment.

Wonderful, Bret thought. There'd been periodic reports like that,
but this one could be very useful in the next two weeks.

There was a *threat*.

He didn't say so.

The FBI did.

At 7:03 Bret pulled into the garage underneath the white-brick
apartment building on Massachusetts Avenue, the street known as
Embassy Row. The building was considered luxurious, but not particularly rich. There was the customary twenty-four-hour doorman
service, and the doormen did wear white gloves and blue uniforms,
with military caps. But this was not the place where the elite of
Washington lived. It was just a very good apartment house for those
who dreamed, but had not yet accomplished the dream. All around
him in the garage Bret saw diplomatic license plates. He knew that
only one belonged to an ambassador, and he wasn't from a major
power. The rest belonged to the second and third levels at the local
embassies and chancellories. Bret hated it. Every return to the garage
was painful, a reminder of his relatively low rank. Assistant Navy
secretary might have looked great in the class news section of his
college alumni magazine, but in Washington it was the B-list.

Someday, he promised himself, I'll have a chauffeur who'll open the door.

Someday the DPL plates in my garage will belong to ambassadors from nuclear powers.

Someday I won't have to shred personal papers or run around to sleazy Virginia motels.

Someday I'll have a wife who counts.

He set the anti-theft alarm on the Lincoln and locked the door. The car *had* lost its radio twice while parked in the garage, and Bret suspected that the perpetrator was attached to one of those diplomatic plates. He had absolutely no evidence to back up his suspicions, but it was comforting to think that he was targeted by foreigners.

Now he carried more than his briefcase. He carried twenty perfect long-stemmed roses, one for each year of his marriage to Sarah.

He knew there'd never be a need for twenty-one.

Sarah was still in the bedroom, staring at the photos, when she heard the doorbell. A rippling chill shot up her spine and lingered at the base of her neck. Her heart started to pound. The moment had come. Now there could be no retreat. As she turned to answer the door, it hit her that she hadn't scripted anything to say. She'd just anticipated what *he'd* say. For an instant she wished she had some of those flashing lines out of romantic novels, zingers shot by wounded women at wandering men.

Slowly, she left the bedroom and walked toward the front door. She hesitated and looked back toward the bedroom. It was as if her whole life was in there. She turned again and continued on.

The apartment had two bedrooms and a large foyer. Sarah entered the foyer, losing her footing for a fraction of a second on the polished parquet floor. She caught herself, then went to the door and snapped the two heavy locks.

She opened the door.

He was smiling. His best celebration smile, just as she'd expected. "Happy anniversary, love," he said.

God, he seemed to mean it, she thought. There was not a touch of hesitation in his warm, resonant voice. "Happy anniversary," she replied softly.

With a grand gesture, he handed her the roses. "Bret, they're beautiful," she said.

Now he entered the apartment. There was a long kiss, longer than any since precisely one year before. But he immediately realized that something wasn't right. "What's wrong?" he asked.

"Nothing."

"You're trembling."

She feigned a laugh. "Bret, I'm not."

He wouldn't buy it. "Did you have an accident?"

She had to think quickly. "You really are *so* perceptive."

His face became grim. "Sarah, are you hurt? Was *anyone* hurt?"

She turned away. "It was nothing," she assured him, smiling now. "These roses are really gorgeous. I know you picked them out yourself. Look, it really was *nothing*. I was crossing the street. I had the light. Some guy in a Corvette didn't, and it didn't matter to him. But he missed me."

"You get his plate number?"

He *would* ask that, she thought. "No, I really wasn't interested. Come on, it's over. I'm safe. The trembling will go away, and this is a wonderful night. Let's only think about anniversaries."

Bret shook his head, as if to say how lucky she was to be alive. "Okay," he said, "as long as you're all right. You just never know these days. Maniacs. They're all maniacs. And driving a Corvette, no less. Probably some fast-buck Washington lawyer on his way to cheat the Defense Department. But I'm glad you told me about it. You should never hold anything back. I mean, that's what I'm here for."

He smiled benevolently, then followed Sarah to the kitchen, where she started arranging the roses in a tall, cut-glass vase. "I'll put these on the piano a little later," she said. She didn't want to leave him, even for an instant. She wanted to see *everything*, every expression, every nuance. He was only a hall away from Durfee's pictures. It would be only minutes, maybe seconds. His own whims would determine when the moment would be.

"It's roasting out there," he said. "I'll just look at the mail and take a quick shower."

"Okay. But remember, they'll be here soon."

"I know, but I can't go without the shower." He reached for the pile of mail on the kitchen counter. Picking it up, he sorted through it quickly, stopping at one business-sized envelope. "I forgot the car insurance was up this month," he said. "You know we're getting a twenty percent hike."

"Why? We're safe drivers."

"But lawyers in Corvettes aren't. I get the feeling we're paying for them. Try fighting it."

Sarah glanced toward the bedroom. How would he fight *that*? she wondered. She watched as he meticulously went through more mail. Each tick of the kitchen clock was an eternity.

"Look at this *Newsweek* cover," he said, flipping the magazine around. "Sam Bissell, United States senator from the great state of South Carolina, supreme patriot, and possible future president of the United States. Wait'll they find out he faked his medical records to stay out of Vietnam."

"How do you know that?"

"You'd be surprised what we know . . . and what we suppress." He loved lines like that.

More mail. Sarah shot another glance toward the bedroom. She saw Bret perform this ritual regularly. She knew mail absorbed him. It was like a series of gifts every day. He leaned against the yellow kitchen wall to sift through some ads, but then he suddenly stopped. "Hey," he said, "this isn't very important. Not on our twentieth. I'm sure the flower society can wait."

"I'm sure they can," Sarah said, finding her own wait maddening.

"Maybe we'll stay out all night," Bret said, moving toward her. Not a man who seemed to be having an affair, Sarah thought, as they kissed again. "I'll be finished in a flash," he said. He dropped the mail back on the counter, uncharacteristically letting it scatter in front of the toaster.

Then he started out of the kitchen.

He headed toward the master bedroom.

Sarah bit her lip. Was this wise? Was she right? *Was* this the way?

Thoughts, doubts, began swirling inside her head. Maybe Bret was totally innocent and Durfee had been exaggerating to make himself look more important. Maybe Bret's meetings with Alison Carver *had* involved national security.

But it was done.

The pictures were neatly laid out on the bed.

She followed him, just as she'd planned.

He was halfway there.

This could be the end of the marriage. Right then. That minute.

But then he stopped. He turned. "God, I'm thirsty," he said. "They should air-condition this town." He started back for the kitchen.

A reprieve. The moment would be put off.

Sarah followed Bret back to the refrigerator. He opened it with a firm sweep of the hand, rattling the bottles inside. He grabbed a plastic bottle of Diet Coke, then poured some into a glass and watched it fizz. "Something for you, sweet?" he asked.

"No, thanks."

Curious look on her face, he thought. It wasn't like the look he'd seen that morning outside the museum. Now Sarah seemed almost frightened. Maybe it was a delayed reaction to her meeting with the Corvette. Maybe that encounter had been a lot closer than she'd admitted. Spunky of her not to complain, he thought. Gutsy. No doubt about it. She'd been the only woman in her aeronautical engineering class at school. Always that terrific spark.

But he put a fast brake on his thoughts. Let's not get sentimental. Let's have no more guilt trips. That kind of thing was dangerous for a man planning to turn his apartment into a bachelor pad.

He gulped down the Coke. He couldn't wait to hit that shower.

Sarah knew he'd rip off his clothes and toss them on the bed.

He put down his glass.

The reprieve was over.

chapter
eleven

It hit Sarah like a flash.

It was irrational, thoroughly unlike her. Yet she knew instantly that it was probably wise. "Excuse me, I forgot something," she said, then turned and rushed back to the bedroom. As she entered, she felt Bret's footsteps behind her.

She darted to the bed, grabbing the first picture and sliding her hand along the spread, sweeping up the others as she went, wincing at the heat generated by her hand's friction with the spread. She was almost finished when Bret appeared in the doorway.

Her heart sank.

"What's that?" he asked.

She didn't reply.

"Pictures?"

"Yes."

"For me?"

She forced a smile, holding the pictures against her chest. "Of course for you. But for later."

Seemingly touched, he smiled back, not that the moment would cause him to grant any stay of execution. "I'm barred from seeing them now?"

"You sure are. I forgot that I'd left them out."

Bret shrugged. "Okay," he said, "I never argue with a woman who knows more about aircraft engines than I do. I'll see them later."

In reality, he wasn't that interested. He just assumed, as Sarah had guessed, that they were old family photos. He disappeared into the bathroom, thoroughly satisfied. I really have her fooled, he told himself. She's even getting into nostalgia. She suspects nothing.

Sarah sank onto the bed, exhausted, still clutching the photos. Okay, she admitted inwardly, she'd chickened out. The risks were too high, her information too uncertain. But what other woman in her position, she asked herself, would have acted with more assurance? There'd be other moments to confront him, moments when she was more confident of her actions.

She listened as the shower went on, then heard the pitch of the water change as Bret made his seemingly endless series of adjustments. He was precise about this too, having had six different shower heads in the apartment.

Forcing herself to act, Sarah stuffed Durfee's artwork into her personal, locked file, then hauled down an old album from the top of her closet. She hurriedly pulled out some pictures to show Bret, just to maintain her credibility.

"Did you confirm our reservation?" Bret called out, his voice muffled by the shower.

"Sure," Sarah answered, fidgeting with a picture, realizing her hands were still shaking.

"I can't wait to get to the old place. That'll bring back memories."

The old place, Jimmy Lee's, was a Chinese restaurant on Connecticut Avenue that was rumored to be a rendezvous point for Asian spies. It had been Sarah and Bret's favorite place before they were married, and they'd gone there on every anniversary. So there were memories, as Bret had said. And his comment confused Sarah even more. No, he really didn't sound like a man who was about to leave. Men like that don't talk about memories.

In the shower, Bret could think clearly. The temperature of his skin began to drop, cooled by the soothing spray he'd adjusted so perfectly. He'd installed a fog-proof mirror in the shower and now could practice his lines, just as he did while driving to work. He knew how crucial this night would be to his plan. "A toast," he said into the mirror, keeping his voice low so Sarah couldn't hear. He couldn't even hear himself over the sound of the shower, but felt the vibration of his words, and sensed each nuance. "A toast to all of us," he continued.

Then he smiled broadly. "I had this idea," he said. He wasn't satisfied with how he'd said that. "I had this terrific idea," he continued. And he practiced and practiced, all the while realizing that it *was* a terrific idea.

He glanced at his waterproof Heuer watch. It was seven eighteen. Company would arrive in twelve minutes, and this company was generally punctual.

In a way, as he looked into the mirror and went through a series of planned expressions, he wished that Tim Curran could be watching him. It was true, as Curran had advised, that happy is the man whose bad marriage ends with his wife going off a bridge. But, in the absence of such good fortune, some plan had to be devised. And it couldn't be ordinary. Curran would be disappointed in his protégé if he simply dumped his wife in a ditch or hired some hit man from the résumé files of world terrorism. But Curran would be impressed with *this.* Not only would Sarah be eliminated, but her husband would end up as a sympathetic figure, possibly even a hero . . . and a hero to women. If he'd heard the plan outlined, Curran would lean back in his chair, take a long draw on his cigar, contemplate the tobacco for a moment, and say, "talent." It was his highest compliment.

Sarah set out the old photos she'd selected in the living room, which was filled with nineteenth-century American furniture, also picked up at tag sales and auctions. She tried not to look hard at the photos, which chronicled her life with Bret. It was too painful— strangely similar, she thought, to looking at pictures of departed relatives. The memories Bret mentioned were real, and wonderful, but she knew they could now become the memories of another failed marriage.

As she worked, the phone rang. It was on a small, folding-top desk in a corner, a desk that had once belonged to Theodore Roosevelt's Secretary of the Treasury. Sarah walked over and picked up.

"Hello." She reached for a pencil. "Oh, I'm sorry, he's not available now. May I take a message?"

The caller's message was brief. Sarah wrote it down on an ordinary yellow pad. She refused to have those pink "while you were out" pads, which she thought were far too antiseptic for a home. "Thank you," she told the caller. "I'll see that he gets this."

A few moments later she heard the shower go off and the shower door roll open. Soon after that drawers in the bedroom slid out and snapped shut. Bret was a lightning-fast dresser. He'd once told Sarah that he doubted the potency of men who lingered too long in front of mirrors. Sarah could never have imagined what he now did in front of those mirrors—what expressions of grief and outrage he practiced, what defiant lines he rehearsed.

Bret finally entered the living room, wearing a tan summer suit and still maneuvering the knot on his chocolate brown tie. In his lapel was the insignia of a civilian commendation he had been awarded by the Secretary of Defense, for outstanding service in the fight against international terrorism. He always wore it, transferring it from suit to suit. Once, when he realized he'd sent it to the cleaners, he made the owner of the place open on Sunday so he could retrieve it. One never knows whom one will meet.

Bret spotted the pictures instantly. "Now do I get my chance?" he asked. He flashed another put-on smile, gazing at the pictures one by one, an intensity in his eyes. "Look at this," he said. "You really searched these out. What a terrific job."

"Thank you," Sarah said, observing every nuance in Bret's actions, looking for clues.

Bret looked at a few more pictures, but he knew what a calculating man would do in this situation. He left the pictures, crossed the room to Sarah and kissed her. "How are you feeling now?" he asked.

"Oh, just fine," Sarah replied, almost forgetting her accident story.

"He didn't sideswipe you, did he?"

"No, Bret, he really didn't. Please, you're mothering me."

"I like it," Bret grinned. "You deserve mothering."

Sarah didn't know what to make of it. Was it put on? Or was this real? He *could* have broken off with Carver. Men did that, didn't they? "Oh, before I forget," she said, "there was a call for you."

"Oh?"

"A Captain Masters."

Bret stiffened, and knew that it showed.

"What's wrong?" Sarah asked.

"Nothing. Masters is involved in sensitive things. What did he want?"

"He just had a message. He said he could get everything you ordered. He said you'd know what he meant."

"I see," Bret replied, relaxing. "Well, that's good news."

"Classified?" Sarah asked, teasingly.

"Oh, very." Bret relished the moment. Sarah had passed on the message that would lead to her own doom.

But he wanted to get off that subject, and so he returned to the pictures that lay around the room. "I haven't seen some of these in years," he said. "This one, in Manila. Remember that guide the Navy provided?"

"He couldn't answer any questions," Sarah recalled.

"Probably from Naval Intelligence. It figures. And look at this one. Right outside the sports stadium in Grenoble."

"That was a terrific month we spent at the university there," Sarah said. She eyed her husband up and down, wondering whether these pictures were really having any effect, or whether he was just going through the motions. "Of course," she said, "some of those pictures may be a little hard to look at. There's twenty years of wear and tear on both of us."

Bret didn't reply. After all, Sarah's wear-and-tear problems would soon be over. "How many husbands and wives have been photographed in Navy uniforms?" he asked.

"Very few, I'll bet," Sarah answered.

Sarah wished she and Bret could recapture the fun of those years. All wives in her situation, she knew, wished the same.

"You know," Bret said, "some of the officers in these pictures are captains now. Look at Lloyd ..."

Suddenly, the intercom from the building's front door buzzed. "I'll get it," Sarah said. She rushed into the kitchen and snapped the switch on the intercom box next to the telephone. "Yes? Oh, yes, we're expecting them. Please send them up." Then she returned to the living room. "They're here."

"Great. You know, they'll really get a kick out of these photos."

"I hope so. I took out the ones from London. I still think that was our best trip together."

"Yeah, it was." Now he was starting to find the pictures more interesting than he'd thought. Each one gave him still more ideas for that eulogy he'd eventually deliver for Sarah. An image of himself suddenly flashed before his eyes—he was standing in front of the chapel, his voice cracking, his face flushed with anger. He could almost hear himself recalling how Sarah was a woman of the world, how she liked to meet people, especially scientists, from other countries. It was so unfair, he'd say to the assembled mourners. And, he'd add, with firmness and passion, that he'd never believe what people were saying about her. He wanted to be sure to emphasize that point.

He examined a photo of Sarah smiling with two kids in Guatemala. That should be blown up and displayed at the funeral.

The doorbell rang. Sarah started for the door. "This'll be a great night," she said, as Bret joined her.

"Who is it?" Sarah asked, although she already knew.

"Do I have to give my federal I.D. number?" asked a male voice, muffled by the door's thickness.

Sarah snapped both locks. She opened.

There, before her, were two of the dearest people in her universe, as close as a brother and sister. "Come in," Sarah said.

Ramy Jordan stood there beaming.

Shel Jordan was just slightly behind her.

At first they didn't move. Sarah, baffled, pulled the door open wider. "You just gonna stand there, you two?"

Slowly, Shel Jordan reached into his jacket pocket and slipped out a paper. As he did, his wife glanced into Bret's eyes, eyes that had met hers with intense yearning just hours before at Arlington Cemetery. Then, just as quickly, she forced her glance away.

"I have a poem," Shel said. Poems were a little fetish of his. He cleared his throat, and read:

We plot, we plan, we calculate
To know just where we're heading,
But tonight, who cares?
It's twenty years,
Since our glorious double wedding!

DOUBLE WEDDING

chapter
twelve

Shel and Ramy Jordan strolled in, twenty years to the night since they and Bret and Sarah had been married in a double wedding at the Cheshire Motel in Arlington, Virginia.

Now, again, for a brief moment, Ramy's eyes locked with Bret's. This time they both turned away. Drop no hints. Create no suspicions.

"Congratulations ... to all of us," Shel Jordan said, kissing Sarah firmly and moistly on the cheek and shaking Bret's hand with the vigor of a practiced influence peddler, which he was.

There were congratulations and kisses all around. As Bret moved to kiss Ramy he whispered softly in her ear, "Don't look at me. We'll have years for that." He felt her whole body smile back.

They hugged. The men slapped each other's backs. There were tears in four sets of eyes, although the reasons varied considerably.

"Can you believe it?" Ramy asked Sarah, warmly grasping the hands of the woman she planned to help murder and then replace. "Can you absolutely believe twenty years with the same guys?"

"And I hope twenty years from tonight we're together again, just like this," Sarah said, smiling at Bret.

"We will be," Ramy replied. "I promise." It *would* be like this, she said to herself—she and Bret together, kissing and hugging.

"First we have to drink," Bret announced. "Wine, everyone?" Hearing no dissent, he went off to the kitchen.

Sarah couldn't get over the way Shel and Ramy fairly glistened.

They always put on the flash, but this was above and beyond—his and hers jeweled watches, a new multicarat ring on Ramy's finger, solid gold monogrammed cuff links in Shel's French-made shirt. Sarah knew a Dunhill suit when she saw one, and also recognized Shel's Gucci loafers.

But even the glitter couldn't hide certain realities. Shel was forty-six, the oldest of the four, and the waistband on this particular Dunhill had already been taken out several times to accommodate his "improved" stomach, as he preferred to call it. His face was round, his dark brown hair thinning where it wasn't graying. He wheezed regularly, especially in the Washington heat. He could pass for fifty-six on a bad day, although recent plastic surgery had removed some of the extra years.

In the movies Shel Jordan would have been the sugar daddy. In real life he was the sugar daddy.

"You both look elegant," Sarah said, typically gracious. She had a normal, even healthy resentment of the Jordans' wealth, but she never let it interfere with their friendship.

That friendship, though, was a source of wonder to their other friends. It was a strange picture—the Washington social climbers with their major real estate, status cars and lavish parties, and the middle-level government official and curator wife, with their respectable apartment and occasional dinners. How could they stand each other? What was the secret of this curious bond that went back more than two decades?

In fact, there wasn't any. Friendship, like love, often can't be explained.

"Hey, look at this stuff," Shel said, spotting the pictures in the living room. "It's a regular 'This Is You Life.' Hey, Ramy, you gotta see this."

Hey, Ramy, Ramy thought. That pretty much defined their marriage. Hey, Ramy. Shel Jordan was no Bret. He didn't have Bret's charm or class. He wasn't even close.

Shel picked up a picture of all four of them together, taken in front of the Lincoln Memorial. "About the time we met," he said. "Like yesterday. Jesus, I mean it. I even remember the watch I had on."

They'd met in Washington when Bret and Sarah were undergoing special naval training before shipping out to San Diego. Ramy had been a legal secretary looking for marriage and wealth, in one convenient package. Shel had been a staff assistant to a member of the Senate Finance Committee. No one on Capitol Hill had any doubt what "staff assistant" meant in his case. He dug up campaign funds, legal or otherwise, putting the arm on businessmen whose lives could be shaped by legislation before the committee; then he devised the legislation in accordance with their degree of generosity. Shel was never accused of being a public servant.

"Do you remember this?" Ramy asked, picking up a picture of the four of them in the Senate chamber, after hours.

"Yeah," Shel said. "It was just before I went into my own business. I love this shot. I always thought the Senate was home."

Sarah winced a bit, but didn't let it show. Like Ramy, she knew he wasn't the picture of elegance.

Either because they'd been naive, or because they just didn't see, Bret and Sarah hadn't been repelled by Shel's activities in those early days. They'd just all gotten along. Shel had been—and stayed—a fun-loving butterball with an easy laugh. He'd liked having Navy friends—they were respectable, and he got some insights into military procurement. And the Jordans had provided some relief from the Lewises' daily frustrations with the Navy bureaucracy.

The idea of a double wedding had come up spontaneously. It was a modest affair at the Cheshire Motel—Bret's and Sarah's budget was particularly microscopic—with only a few friends and close family attending. But the four had celebrated the anniversary together ever since.

"I hope Jimmy Lee won't disappoint us tonight," Shel was saying, slapping his chunky hands together.

"He won't," Sarah replied. "I made the reservation myself and told him it's our twentieth."

"Simple little place, but I still love it," Shel said. "Nothing wrong with simple." He made the comment, as he'd made many others over the years, to reassure Sarah that the difference in their economic levels didn't bother him. It was true that he earned more than $300,000 a year from lobbying, but he was like the millionaire who'd give it all to walk down the aisle at a college ceremony with a $40,000-a-year professor. He genuinely liked having friends like the Lewises.

It was true, of course, that some of Shel's work could potentially embarrass Bret. There was no secret that Shel had been questioned about his attempts to pressure the Pentagon into granting contracts to his clients. As a result, there was an unwritten understanding between Bret and Shel—no discussion of business, no use of Bret's name. Shel wasn't offended. There was little that could offend him.

And so they'd remained the closest, if oddest, of friends. Now, all Ramy could think of as she chatted with Sarah was how this intimate bond that began with a double wedding would end with a double funeral within days. And now she wondered—what kind of flowers were appropriate when death was sudden and violent? She made a mental note to check discreetly. Some things were important, God knows.

"The apartment looks so cozy," she told Sarah, as they continued to look at pictures.

"Hasn't changed a bit," Sarah replied, caught off-guard. Ramy rarely mentioned the apartment.

But tonight she looked things over more carefully. After a respectable period, she said to herself, she and Bret would marry, old friends who came together to heal their grief. The apartment would be a suitable city place. She'd redecorate, of course. This early American junk would go to charity.

"The London trip," Shel said, picking up another picture. "It was the best. What can I say? This Imperial War Museum. Everyone should go there." Then he picked up a picture that lay on a Knabe piano that Sarah had bought, more than used, from an opera company. "Hey, Ramy, come here."

Ramy hated these constant orders. But she did as he directed, as she always had. Bret had stressed to her that the first rule in a conspiracy is never to change your habits. Never make anyone suspicious. Besides, Shel had wild emotions—he could explode, or cry. Just keep him calm until he was disposed of.

"Remember this?" Shel asked, nudging her toward a picture of the four of them on a beach in 1976. "I invested in property near there."

"We lost a bundle," Ramy said.

"Ramy, it was a write-off."

Now Bret came in, bearing four glasses of wine on a silver tray. "There he is," Shel said, "smartest guy I know."

"You're right," Bret replied, only half joking. He gave everyone a glass. "A toast," he called out.

They all fell silent. Shel put down the picture he was examining.

"To all of us," Bret said. "Twenty magnificent years past, and an unlimited number in the future."

"Here, here," Shel replied. They all drank. "How many friends do you know," Shel then asked rhetorically, "who are still married to their first wives or husbands?"

"Not many," Ramy replied.

"No, the casualty rate is pretty high," Sarah agreed, glancing over at Bret.

"I think we're terrific," Shel continued. "I am absolutely certain we'll be here twenty years from today, like Ramy promised."

"Any other toasts?" Bret asked.

They all looked around at each other. "Well, I have one," Ramy said. And now she looked straight at Bret. "To all our endeavors. May they all work out to perfection."

Bret hardly responded, simply smiled at Sarah, raising his glass and sipping slowly. "And now I have a surprise," he announced abruptly. "And I mean a *surprise*. Not even Shel—who knows everything that goes on in Washington—knows about this."

Shel shrugged. "It must be true. I don't know what the guy is talking about."

"Bret, you didn't buy a present for us, did you?" Ramy asked.

"No, I didn't."

"Thank God. I'd be mortified. We didn't get you anything."

Good, Bret thought. She said that exactly right, just as they'd rehearsed it. "No," he said, "this is an idea, a proposal."

"Shoot," Shel asked.

"We were married twenty years ago tonight," Bret said. "You ever hear of these people who renew their vows?"

"Sure," Ramy replied. "They actually get remarried."

"Exactly. They go through the whole thing again. Sometimes they even get the same minister."

"Ramy, the Millers did that," Shel said.

"Why don't *we* do it?" Bret asked.

Sarah was stunned. "*Us?*"

"Why not?"

She couldn't get over it. "Why *not? Why?*"

"Because it's exciting," Bret answered. "We could have another double wedding. We were married right out there at the Cheshire. Okay, we wouldn't do it there today. But for old times' sake ...."

"It's a terrific idea," Ramy said. "I think it's so romantic. Don't you, Sarah?"

At first, Sarah said nothing. Sure it was romantic. But Bret was having an affair with a member of Congress. Men with affairs don't rush to renew their vows ... not rational men at any rate. "Sure," she finally managed. "It could be a great memory." But her words had no feeling, no punch. This was entirely out of character for Bret, even a Bret without an affair. Handsome, yes. Dynamic, absolutely. But an incurable romantic? Not even a bronze medal.

"Wait a second," Shel broke in. "I don't know." He had this odd, worried look about him. Sarah noticed that his right eye twitched a bit, a certain sign that he was under tension.

"Come on, Sheldon, don't be a party pooper," Ramy said.

"Hey, I'm no party pooper. I mean, I think it could be fun and all that."

"So?" Bret asked.

"So is this really for people like us?"

"What does that mean?" Ramy wanted to know.

"Well ... who does this? I get the feeling it's people who go to Tupperware parties."

Ramy rolled her eyes. "Mr. Congeniality," she mumbled, just loud enough for everyone to hear.

"Shel," Bret explained, "Sarah and I went to a renewal of vows just last year. He was an attorney. His wife was a copywriter. Terrific couple. Young. With it. Look, we'd be doing this together. We could invite a few close friends ...."

"Well ..."

"Okay," Bret said, "if you don't want to do it, we won't do it. Can't have a double wedding with a groom missing, can we?"

"I guess I'm a little stodgy," Shel admitted.

"A little," Ramy quipped, then caught a firm glance from Bret. No ridicule, he'd warned her.

"I guess," Bret went on, "I'll have to cancel the reservation I made for the party room at the Cheshire."

"For when?" Ramy asked, knowing the answer.

"Next weekend. Could have been great ..."

They all looked at Shel. Suddenly, he began to smile, his round face creasing up like shriveled fruit. "You conniving sonofa ..."

"Guilty," Bret conceded, now breaking out in laughter.

"Arright, let's do it," Shel agreed. "What the hell. How many chances do you get to marry the same beautiful woman?"

They were all laughing now. Murderers and intended victims. All laughing.

"You know," Ramy said, "you mentioned people who use the same minister ..."

"Hired," Bret announced.

"Really?" Shel exclaimed.

"Well, not exactly hired. I reached him through his church. He's retired now, living down in Manassas. I called him."

"Did he remember us?" Sarah asked.

"No, but it didn't matter. He said he'd be glad to renew the vows, if that's what we want."

"Of course that's what we want," Ramy said.

Sarah still found herself wondering if this was really happening. If the suggestion had come from Shel or Ramy, she could understand. But Bret? Maybe Alison Carver could be maid of honor. Still, she played along.

"We should have flowers," Ramy was saying.

"That's right," Sarah agreed. "Look, we've got our albums from our *real* wedding. We'll study the pictures and just duplicate."

"All taken care of," Bret said, with a broad, self-satisfied smile.

"What has this man committed?" Shel asked.

"Well, I just looked at those albums too," Bret answered. "And I tried to match the original. I haven't made my order final ..."

"I'm starting to like this," Shel admitted. "You know, it *is* exciting."

"One thing," Sarah said. "Do we have to use the same photographer? The man spent most of his time eating, and the rest taking pictures that were blurry and crooked or caught guests with mouths open."

"He moved to Alaska," Bret reported.

"Good." Now, as they all laughed, even Sarah felt the electricity in the air. It was to have been just an anniversary dinner out, but now it was a planning session for this new double wedding. Looking from one smiling face to another, she realized how she would have loved it, except for that huge shadow over her marriage. How lucky Ramy was, she thought, to have a loyal husband, and to be loyal to him in return.

Some people had a reason to celebrate.

chapter
thirteen

Jimmy Lee's was less than glittering. In fact, it was so plain that restaurant critics assumed the blandness had to be intentional. Maybe Jimmy thought that nothingness was chic. Or maybe he thought the spies who ate there wanted even their restaurant to be invisible.

The entrance was part of a nondescript storefront on upper Connecticut Avenue, with the menu taped in the window. There was no doorman, not even an awning outside. And, although the long front window had curtains, these were sheer enough to allow anyone strolling by to look in, through some stains, and see who was staring down the spare ribs at the first three tables. The red neon sign saying "Jimmy Lee" in Jimmy's own signature had a perpetual on-the-blink buzz that drove Bret up a wall every time he passed it.

On one side of Jimmy Lee's was a pet supply shop that furnished the area with the muffled sound of air filters gurgling in the twelve fish tanks on display. On the other side was a travel agency that specialized in tours to the Orient. Bret knew for a fact that the firm's owner was a deep cover agent for the CIA, arranging shipments of weapons, chemical explosives and poisons all over the world. He was known to stimulate his business by issuing false tickets ... so intelligence agents could get extra credit on their frequent flyer cards.

"Table for four for Secretary Lewis," Shel Jordan told the reservations clerk who sat near the main door, a chipped lectern in front of him bearing the reservations for the evening. Jimmy Lee was nearby and overheard. He strolled over with a huge smile on his face. "Secretary Lewis, how delightful to see you again," he said, shaking Shel's hand. Although Jimmy could remember an entire dinner order for six, including special cooking instructions, he wasn't sharp on faces.

"He's Lewis," Shel said.

"Secretary Lewis, how delightful to see you again," Jimmy Lee said to Bret, not missing a beat.

"Evening, Jimmy," Bret replied.

"Your table is waiting, Mr. Secretary," Jimmy said, with a mixed Oriental/British accent that reflected his half-Chinese, half-Scottish parentage.

He started to escort the party in personally, but suddenly a man who'd been waiting in line with his wife blocked him. "Excuse me!" the customer demanded, in a voice loud enough to attract half the restaurant. He was smallish and light, but with the kindness of a shark. "*We* had reservations, too, and you *distinctly* said we were next."

Jimmy calmly placed a hand on the man's arm. "I apologize," he said. "The gentleman has a special condition."

Jimmy was a genius at keeping people waiting and giving priority to the more important customers, even those whose faces he failed to recognize. At one time or another almost every regular guest had been assigned a medical misfortune to hurry him in. One ambassador even developed a mysterious limp each time he passed under the buzzing neon sign.

Now Jimmy escorted Bret and his party to a table in the nearly filled restaurant, and handed them four oversized menus, each with a long, gold tassel. "Enjoy," he said. "The seafood special you ordered in advance is particularly good tonight. I know you'll want all the usual extras."

"Thanks, Jimmy," Bret said. "The protein in that seafood is very good for my condition." He winked at Jimmy, who winked back, then turned his attention to an Army colonel at the door.

It wasn't a noisy place, thanks to the thick carpeting and the soundproofing on the ceiling. The decor emphasized reds in the cushions, the carpeting and even the waiters' jackets. There was a lot of smoke from the smoking section, blurring everything and creating at least the suggestion of a political back room. With some of the narrowest aisles in town, rushing waiters were constantly sideswiping customers, never expressing even the slightest remorse.

There was little to indicate that this was a Chinese restaurant, except for the two decorative lanterns inside the front door—the bulb in one was always out—and the Chinese lettering on the covers of the menus. The lighting was subdued, but, if the smoke wasn't too thick, you could still recognize an indicted public official across the large, single room.

"Just *love* this place," Shel was saying, flipping open his menu. "Does anyone remember the very first time we came?"

"Don't remind me," Ramy answered. "Pretend it was yesterday."

"Jimmy was just a kid. His father—he was the Chinese one of the parents—he had the place and we were all a bunch of bright eyes out on the make. You could get a whole meal for four for ten bucks. Don't any of you guys remember? I've still got the receipts, for tax purposes."

"You've got every scrap of paper anyone ever gave you," Ramy said.

"Keep records, Ramy. Always keep records." Shel threw on his tiny rectangular reading glasses and buried his head in the menu.

With everyone immersed in menus, Bret glanced over at Ramy. They stole a quick, secret smile. Soon, Ramy thought, they wouldn't have to listen to Shel's inane chatter. Soon it would be the two of them together ... and they would go to finer restaurants than Jimmy Lee's.

"Why don't we order soup first," Bret suggested.

"Fine with me," Shel said.

Now Bret turned his glance toward Sarah. Was this the last time they'd be at Jimmy Lee's?

Sarah gazed back at Bret, their eyes meeting, as if it were some romantic evening years before. It wasn't, though, and Sarah was keenly aware of it. She fought to hold back the tears as the reality hit her. She'd been in turmoil all day, but this was the worst moment.

It was, after all, in these surroundings that she and Bret had marked the years of their marriage.

In the future, she mused, she might come to Jimmy's alone, just for old time's sake. The thought surprised her.

"One won ton, two egg drop, one hot and sour," Shel was saying to the waiter.

Bret stared through the stained curtains and out the front window at some other people about to enter the place. Something began nagging the back of his mind. To set off the charge he'd have to know exactly the right moment, which meant watching. But the blast could shatter the window in the motel reception room and send glass back in his face. He'd have to work out the problem. He made a mental note.

"Daydreaming?" Sarah asked him.

"Oh, no. Just thinking about that window in our living room that has to be replaced."

"I'll call someone," Sarah replied. "Windows are dangerous."

"Yeah," Bret said.

Then Bret caught Sarah suddenly stiffen. "See a ghost?" he asked.

She forced herself to relax. "No, a little heartburn—I think from the wine before."

"Oh, you want a Tums or . . . ?"

"No, it went away."

But it didn't go away, and it wasn't heartburn, at least not the kind caused by wine. Sarah was looking toward the rear of the restaurant. A woman was leaving the ladies' room and making her way back to her table. She was in the shadows, walking closer. Sarah was sure . . . almost sure. The trademark black suit. The inviting walk.

No. This couldn't be.

She glanced at Bret, who was sitting with his back to the woman and returning to his menu. Could he have . . . ? Impossible.

Sarah kept staring at the woman advancing through the restaurant. She came out of the shadows.

There was no doubt.

Sarah felt herself fill with rage.

What the hell was Alison Carver doing there?

The congresswoman was only six feet away. Her eyes met Sarah's. She recognized Bret's wife, whom she'd seen at functions. But she didn't break her stride or show any surprise whatever. Sarah kept staring her down. Oh, to be a bitch right now, she thought. Her mind spun with all the lovely things she'd want to say.

Then Carver stopped—right at their table.

She turned to Bret, his face buried in the seafood section. "Mr. Secretary," she said.

"Mr. *Secretary*!" Sarah thought. Is that what she always called him? In her office? In her bedroom?

Bret looked up. "Why, Representative Carver, what a pleasant surprise."

"*Representative*?" Sarah thought. Okay, here come the games.

"Sarah, Ramy, Shel, you know Congresswoman Carver, of California. She's on Appropriations. We work together on the military budget."

They all nodded their hellos. Shel and Carver had never met. He considered her too far down for cultivating, at least in the political sense.

"Are you here alone?" Bret asked her.

"Yes, I am, actually," Carver replied, glancing over to include Sarah in the conversation. "I've got to go back to the Hill for some late work."

Sarah *knew* she'd come to see Bret. Of course. What other explanation was there? Coincidence? This was simply a way for them to be together, even with the wife present. Bret must have been proud of the way he arranged this stunt.

Now she looked Carver over carefully. Independent and proud though Sarah was, she couldn't help asking herself the ancient question: What has she got that I haven't? Well, a congresswoman outranked a curator in anyone's pecking order, but that couldn't have been the sole attraction. It was, rather, Carver's glamour, her cultivated TV voice, her drop-dead style. That had to be it. What else was there? A life with a woman who worked nights?

"Is this some celebration?" Carver asked.

"Twentieth anniversary for all of us," Shel replied.

"How wonderful," the sixth-ranking member of the California congressional delegation replied. "Well, I wish you all fifty more."

There, Sarah realized, she'd used the same number that Bret had used in the car that morning. This was all set up. Or, if it wasn't, then

Bret had told Carver he'd be at this restaurant. Maybe she was spying on him, checking, or just trying to see if he'd be rattled by her sudden presence.

"By the way," Carver said, looking directly into Sarah's eyes, "whenever I see your husband he mentions you and your work. It must be wonderful to have a man who respects you so much."

Wham. Sarah felt the stiletto go right through her. "Yes," she replied, "it's great having a husband who's so supportive . . . and so loyal."

"Right," Carver answered, and for an instant Sarah was sure the congresswoman became flustered. "Well, I'd better get back now," Carver said. "I've got my staff waiting for me." She turned again to Sarah. "How nice meeting you. We should get together sometime."

"I'd love to," Sarah replied. "I'm sure we have common interests."

The congresswoman was careful not to direct her attention to Bret. She simply walked off with a quick "Bye, now," to everyone, said a few words to Jimmy Lee and left the restaurant.

"Terrific lady," Ramy said. "I read about her in the paper all the time."

Thanks, Sarah thought. A real friend. But, of course, how could Ramy know?

"I heard she was marrying some Houston lawyer," Ramy continued. "She's on the committee for the drug program I work on. I heard it from one of our people. Maybe it's just a rumor."

"I think so," Bret said.

"You follow these things, Bret?" Sarah asked.

"Oh, not really. But we hear. I'm close to Appropriations."

"Who cares?" Shel asked. "Let's talk about *our* wedding. Look, if there's a big cost, I'll pick up the tab."

"Accepted," Bret agreed. "We should use the reception room, just like the first time."

"Lovely," Ramy said.

"Remember, the last time we left that place, our friends threw rice," Shel added.

"Maybe they could do it again," Ramy suggested. She winked at Bret. If rice were thrown, it could only be at the two of them—the only two to leave the reception alive.

Moments later a waiter approached their table carrying a large silver container. Inside—a bottle of champagne.

"We didn't order that," Shel said.

"No," the waiter responded. "This is from Congresswoman Carver. With her compliments. She wishes you a happy anniversary."

"How gracious," Sarah said. "How very gracious."

And so, over a Chinese dinner, in the same restaurant where they had made some of the plans for their first wedding more than twenty years before, they planned each aspect of their renewal of vows. Sarah was still utterly baffled by the whole thing, by the fact that Bret had suggested this strange, yet sentimental ceremony.

Now, as they spoke, she caught Bret glancing at her, then immediately glancing at Ramy. She thought nothing of it. They were all such old, close friends. She could think only of Alison Carver. What did Bret really have going with her? He had to have something going. He was the kind who always did.

What Bret had going, of course, was murder. All his plans were falling into place, and at their center was the double wedding. He continued to glance back and forth between Sarah and Ramy, two women who were playing critical roles in those plans. This was probably the last time he'd be able to look at both of them at the same time, at least before the new ceremony. There was Sarah—everyone's favorite friend. Accomplished, a role model for young nieces, a terrific wife by any standard. But he had tired of her lack of ambition, her indifference to the needs of an aggressive husband. She'd soon be replaced by someone who understood his destiny.

And there was Ramy. So perfect. So Washington. She could chat up an ambassador or a senator and each would think she dreamed only of him. When she entered a room, even the room noticed. This was a woman who enjoyed playing a role, and always knew what role to play. Now, again, she was playing a role—a role crucial to Bret Lewis's future.

When they finished their meal, the waiter reappeared. "Fortune cookie," he said. And he placed before them a dish with four fortune cookies, intermingled with slices of orange.

Naturally, Shel grabbed his first.

"What does it say?" Ramy asked.

He cracked the cookie open and pulled out the little white slip. "It says, 'Your intuition will win out in the end.'"

"Hey, not bad," Bret observed. "Sarah?"

Sarah opened hers. "Nothing ever is exactly as it appears." She shrugged. "I wonder what that means?"

"Probably some old Chinese proverb," Ramy answered.

"Now," Bret said, "mine says, 'What you don't know will always hurt you.'"

"Absolutely," Shel agreed. "You gotta have the facts." He turned to his wife. "Ramy?"

Ramy was already opening hers. She read it to herself, then smiled.

"What does it say?" Shel asked.

"It says, 'You will do something important for someone you love.'" She turned to Shel, but then shot a quick look toward Bret. "I certainly hope so," she said.

chapter
fourteen

"I love you too, and I can't wait to be with you . . . forever."

It was the next morning. Bret was speaking from his office, on his private line, and Ramy loved every word. She lay on her king-size four-poster bed, covered with a satin spread with a large SJ monogram, in a huge master bedroom in which almost everything was pink, at her request, including the telephone. She was still in her pink nightgown. She knew Bret would call at this hour, as he did almost every day.

"Wasn't it boring last night?" Ramy asked.

"I almost couldn't stay awake," Bret replied. "The only thing that kept me going was the thought that the problem would be taken care of soon. I'm getting the materials in just a few minutes. It looks good. It looks very good."

"Shel wants to try to fit into his original tuxedo for the ceremony next week," Ramy said. "He actually got it out after we came home."

"He might have use for a black suit fairly soon," Bret replied.

"When I saw you and him together last night, I couldn't believe which one I was married to," Ramy said. "To think I've made this mistake for twenty years."

"And now you're correcting it," Bret told her.

"I'd better go," she said. "Make sure to get me the goods."

"I will," Bret replied. "It's only days now, and it'll all be over."

"By the way," Ramy added, "you know what the idiot said last night after we got home?"

"No."

"He was so excited about this double wedding business that he kept saying, 'It'll be a blast.'"

Bret barely laughed. "Let's hope so," he said. "I wouldn't want my old friend to be proved wrong."

Their conversation ended.

He immediately dialed another number.

As Bret made his second phone call, Captain Masters approached his office, walking down the long, carpeted corridor outside. "Captain Masters to see Mr. Lewis," he announced to Bret's receptionist.

"He's on the phone, Captain. Would you have a seat?"

"Uh, this is urgent," Masters said. "Could you interrupt him?"

The receptionist knew never to argue with the word "urgent." She buzzed Bret.

"Yes?"

"Captain Masters, sir. Says it's urgent."

"Have him wait a moment," Bret answered. "This is pretty urgent, too. It's the police."

Masters, surprised, took a seat.

"I don't want to alarm my wife," Bret was saying on the phone. "But I'm pretty sure I'm correct. It's the business I'm in. When we got back to the apartment I saw signs that the lock had been tampered with. But, I tell you, nothing was missing. Nothing I *know* of."

He listened for the reply. "No, I just want to make a report. But, as I said, I didn't even mention it to her. She had a little accident yesterday . . ."

The officer on the line suggested that Bret change the lock. "I'm having it done," Bret replied. "I'll just tell my wife the lock broke. Frankly, I think it might have been a member of the building staff looking for a quick buck. But there was nothing there."

The officer made some other comments and asked some questions. "Yes, I have a gun," Bret replied. "I pray God I never have to use it."

He completed his verbal report, then put the phone back down and smiled. He was thoroughly pleased. Now there'd be a written record of the "break-in" at his apartment, the break-in that never happened. He'd damaged the lock himself.

"Send Captain Masters in," he ordered through his intercom.

The door opened and Masters appeared. He was in his dress white uniform with four gold stripes on his shoulder, ready to attend a formal reception at the Canadian Embassy later that morning. He was carrying a small black satchel made of ballistic cloth—a fabric that can be resealed easily, even if punctured by a knife or small projectile. "Morning, sir," Masters said.

"Morning, Captain," Bret replied. "I got your message last night. Thank you for being so efficient."

"We try."

"I assume you have the merchandise."

"I do. It's right here. Everything you need, in triplicate as you ordered."

"And you're sure there are no substitutions?" Bret asked. "Manufacturers and model numbers are exactly what I asked for?"

"Exactly. As I said yesterday, this stuff is pretty standard."

Pretty standard is exactly what Bret wanted. There was to be nothing exotic. Captain Masters put the satchel on his desk. "Thank you," Bret said. "I assure you this will be well used."

"I have no doubt, sir," Masters replied.

"As to the Kearns report," Bret went on, "I reviewed it again last night. Awfully circumstantial evidence against you, don't you think, Captain?"

"I've always felt that, sir."

"I'll file the report in some inactive box," Bret told him. He could see the relief on Masters's face.

But Masters got the full message loud and clear. He'd done what was required, and now he just had to keep his mouth shut. The inactive box could always be activated.

"I think we can relax a bit," Bret said. "You know, Captain, I'm sure you'd enjoy a little tour of my air fleet."

At first, Masters was baffled. Then he turned around to the display case filled with handmade model planes from the 1950s. It was a curiosity that had attracted the attention of everyone from the Secretary of Defense on down. Masters considered it somewhat of an honor to be given his own tour of the display.

Bret got up and walked over to the case. As usual, he was dressed in an immaculately cut suit, charcoal gray this time, with vest and a muted maroon tie. He'd spend anything on clothes, not because he personally cared, but because his father had taught him that the man who dresses like a million dollars is treated accordingly. Tim Curran had also encouraged him to maintain a well-to-do, comfortable image. People instinctively wanted their leaders to be better than they were, Curran had told him. A leader had to look the part. "Jimmy Carter carried his own bags," he recalled Curran saying at a Capitol Hill smoker. "Right back to Plains, Georgia." Bret remembered the lesson.

"Those were great days, when these models were being built by kids all over America," Bret declared, opening the glass case. "They don't make most of these solid models anymore. They make this plastic junk, the kind of thing you can put together in a couple of hours and give to your dad to stick behind his office desk. They have no character. Everything stamped out. You can't put a plastic model together with love, Captain."

"I quite agree, sir," Masters said, always sensing when a word of encouragement was called for.

"Now you take this B-29 from StromBecker. God, I remember that name. A StromBecker solid model was every kid's dream back then. Two and a half bucks for this bomber. Big money to a kid. But you see, you had to work on each part. Now, look at the trailing edge of the wing here. It's sharp. But it didn't come stamped that way. It came squared off. What you did was, they gave you a piece of sandpaper with the kit, and you glued that to a piece of hardwood, and you had a sanding stick. Then you sanded the rear edges of those wings until they were razors—and you matched one wing against the other. Sometimes it took hours, but you had pride."

"I built a few myself," Masters said. "I loved them, too."

"There's a metal weight in the nose to keep it down," Bret went on, intensely serious. It was as if he were revealing some national secret. "I remember holding it in my hand. It had heft. There was something to it. You put the weight in the nose and covered it with a wood cap; then you sanded that to make the nose nice and round. Then, when you were finished, you hand painted everything. Testor's paint. I remember the smell of those little paint bottles after you opened them. It was like perfume to me."

"Yes, sir."

"And after you gave it a primer and a couple of coats of silver, you put on the decals. And you had your Superfort, and you knew what went into it. Only the propellers were plastic."

"It's a beautiful piece, sir."

"A nation's toys tell a lot about its culture, Captain," Lewis said. "We worked in those days."

"I'll bet you wish you had a son to build planes with," Masters suggested.

"You don't need a son for planes," Bret replied, with no explanation and no invitation to ask for one.

Avery Masters, despite his moral ambiguity, had a far sharper mind than Bret had realized. What kind of man, he was thinking, would have model planes in one case and conductors' batons in the other? Was there a link between the two? There probably was, Masters reasoned. Both reflected this man's dance with power—the power over an orchestra, the symbolic power of model military planes. Masters could just see Bret Lewis staring at those planes and imagining himself in command. He could see Bret as a child holding model planes in his hands and "flying" them around a room, bombing targets, strafing the ground.

Masters recalled sitting on a court-martial board that was judging an officer who'd shot an enlisted man who'd defied him. That officer, too, had built hundreds of models as a boy. A psychiatrist's report commented that, for some boys, spending time building models is related to a drive for mastery, for control.

That was Bret Lewis.

And yet, Masters realized, the guy never even got a pilot's license. This was no hero, not even a leader—except in the Walter Mitty imaginings reflected in these displays. Bret Lewis, like many men

Masters knew in Washington, was simply obsessed with running things.

Not a man to cross, Masters was thinking. He'd have to stay loyal to him, act loyal to him.

"I built some flying models, too," Bret was saying, although by this time Masters was far more fascinated by the character of the man than by his toys. "You built the entire frame of the aircraft and glued light paper over it. I'm sure you've seen that. It was a wonderful experience, flying them by remote control. I don't think kids today have as much fun—everything is so prepackaged. Back then you sent a plane up, you controlled it, and you knew part of yourself was in that plane. *You* were up there. You pressed a button, things happened."

No doubt, Masters thought. No doubt at all. But even he, in his wildest imagination, could not anticipate the button that Bret Lewis would press next.

chapter
fifteen

Sarah was in her museum's Hall of Air Transportation, which housed a silver 1930s-vintage, twin-engine DC-3, the heaviest plane to be suspended in the museum from wires. On its sides was the logo FLY—EASTERN AIR LINES. Sarah had come across some documents dealing with the early development of the plane and was discussing them with a curator who specialized in propeller-driven airliners. Around them were members of a Boy Scout troop from Baltimore, in tan uniforms, who seemed a little bored by the calm lines of the civilian plane and were hurrying through, eyeing the combat planes nearby. They were noisy, their chatter and horseplay echoing through the cavernous halls, forcing Sarah to speak above their din for the other curator to hear.

Everyone knew how serious Sarah Lewis was about her work, how she often put in extra hours on weekends to be sure an exhibition was just right, or volunteer to give tours to visiting airmen and engineers to boost the image of the museum. Right now she tried mightily to be businesslike, to describe carefully the documents she'd found. But that's not where her mind was. Even her professionalism couldn't keep her head focused on yellowed documents from an obscure file. Her mind was on the pseudofestive evening before. It had been so utterly bizarre. Something out of a movie, though not the movie Durfee had in mind when he'd asked Sarah how she intended to approach her husband.

She'd brought Durfee's pictures with her, stuffed in her attaché case as she rode to work with Bret. She had planned to leave them at home, locked in her desk, but an irrational fear had grabbed her, a fear that there'd be a fire and that the pictures would be rescued and turned over to Bret. How could she explain? What could she say except to confront him at that moment? But she knew that her fear of a fire was practically a fantasy, maybe a psychological trick her head was playing on her to avoid the real subject. And there was never any doubt what the real subject was.

Alison Carver.

She'd actually *been* there last night. And she'd been alone.

No, it couldn't have been coincidence. Bret had to know she'd be there. It was intentional, but why? Did he need her that much that he had to see her, even on his twentieth anniversary? Was it just an inside joke? Was it related to this crazy idea for a new double wedding, a renewal of vows? But why the vows, the whole ridiculous ceremony, if Alison Carver was the permanent fixture on Bret's call pad? Sarah couldn't fathom it. At best, she felt her husband was a confused man who didn't know which way to go. But she felt her spirit drained. She'd literally chickened out of confronting Bret once. She couldn't do it again. Alison Carver's imposing herself on their anniversary made that impossible. Now it was not only a question of saving her marriage. Now it was saving her self-respect.

As she finished with the other curator, she glanced out one of the museum's huge windows that faced the Mall. A light drizzle was falling, making everything outside glisten. The tour buses bunched at the entrance looked almost clean. Most people ignored the drizzle, but a few held newspapers over their heads or ducked under trees. Suddenly, she saw a man get out of a white chauffeured Cadillac and snap open an umbrella. Even at this distance—more than 100 yards—she was almost sure who it was.

But why would Shel Jordan be coming to the museum?

She watched the man as he walked toward the entrance, holding the umbrella in one hand, a thin briefcase in the other. No doubt. Shel Jordan. Now he was walking faster, darting around people, clearly anxious and very nervous. Why?

He approached the entrance. He wasn't running, but almost trotting. The umbrella leaned to one side. He was getting wet. He didn't seem to care. His face came into clearer view. Pained. Anguished. This wasn't the butterball from last night.

Something was wrong. Seriously wrong. Sarah knew that she was the only one Shel knew at the museum. He was coming to see her. Unannounced. With that look on his face. Her heart began to pound. She felt her muscles tense.

Ramy. Maybe it was Ramy. Something's happened and Shel would logically want to tell her close friend first. Ramy had never been a good driver. Her vision was narrow. She'd had close calls. Maybe she'd had too many last night. Maybe she'd been exhausted.

But wait. Maybe not. Maybe it was Bret. Of course. Everyone who worked with Bret in the Navy Department knew that Shel Jordan was his best friend. Shel hung around there frequently, buttonholing officers and officials on behalf of defense contractors. If Bret had been hurt, or become ill, or worse, no one would want to call his wife. They'd call Shel. *He'd* tell her. And with that look on his face, the news was bad.

My God, Sarah thought, is this the way out that Providence was providing? No. She couldn't believe it. But Shel Jordan was rushing through the door, gripping that little briefcase, his now-dampened face oozing with powerful strain.

As she'd done when she'd spotted Al Durfee the day before, Sarah rushed back to her office. That was best. She didn't want to face Shel in the main gallery, with all those visitors and guards around. He was an emotional man. He looked on the verge of crying.

She swung behind her desk, now stacked with blueprints of a British jet fighter that the museum was trying to acquire. As expected, there was a sharp knock at the door. "Come in," she said.

The door swung open. Shel Jordan stood there. He seemed winded, and very tired. Sarah didn't want him to know she'd spied him. "Shel," she exclaimed, "what are you doing here?"

"Can I come in?" he asked. He never asked that, Sarah knew. He would just come in.

"Of course." Sarah's curiosity, and fear, were overflowing. "Sit down, Shel. Something's wrong. I can tell."

Jordan slumped into an ordinary antiseptic visitor's chair—aluminum, with plastic cushions. He tossed his umbrella to the floor.

"Shel, just be calm," Sarah advised, now concerned that the man might collapse or suffer a heart attack. "Can I get you some water?"

Jordan just waved his hand and shook his head no. "I don't need water," he said. "I need some good advice, and so do you."

"What? Shel, what are you saying?"

Shel Jordan raised his hand, as if asking for time. "Let me cool down," he said, trying to catch his breath. "I'm sorry to barge in. I should've called. But I had to come."

"Just tell me," Sarah said.

In a few moments, Shel was reasonably calm, although his bulbous stomach heaved beneath his usual black silk vest. "Something's happened," he said.

It was Bret. Sarah was sure. That's the way they tell people. "What's happened?" she asked.

Shel's eyes seemed glazed over, as if about to cry. "Sarah," he asked, "has Bret had any problems recently?"

"Problems?" It had to be medical.

"Any kind of problems," Shel said.

"No. Shel, has something happened to my husband?"

"In a way, yes."

"In a way?"

"Sarah, this is hard to ask, but I've got to. You'll understand. Has anything gone wrong with your marriage?"

Sarah's mouth almost dropped. That came out of the blue. She was ready for any kind of medical disaster, and in a corner of her mind the opening lines of a eulogy for Bret were ready. But what was this? Did Shel know? Did Alison Carver say something, or call him, or what? "That's hard to answer," she replied. "Why?"

"Can you take it?"

"I can take anything."

"Sarah, love, I found out something, and it isn't going to be pleasant to hear. But, we're such old friends, and I thought it was only fair . . . , I mean, if I could help . . ."

"Tell it straight, Shel."

"I'll tell it straight. Here it goes. Bret may be, well he is, having an affair."

"Yes," Sarah replied, with a deep sigh.

"Yes? What do you mean, yes?"

"I know."

Shel leaned back in his chair. He seemed utterly flabbergasted. "How?"

"I suspected something months ago. Bret started coming home at all hours. It wasn't his work. I can tell when he's under pressure from work. It's the oldest cliché in the book, Shel. A woman knows."

"Oh," Shel said, the word drawn out to a semimoan. "You knew all along."

"Well, I suspected all along. And I guess you found out the same thing. If you can keep a little secret ..."

"I'm born to keep secrets."

"I hate to admit this, but I hired a private eye. He followed Bret around. He took pictures. In fact ..." She looked toward her attaché case. She hated to show Shel those pictures. Was it that she hated snooping? Or was it that they were so humiliating? It was probably both, with an emphasis on the latter.

He read her eyes. "You have them?"

"Yeah."

Even Shel Jordan knew not to ask to see them. But he watched as Sarah reached for her case and slowly opened it. Although she did hate to show the photos, Shel could understand why she'd do so. Anyone could understand. The pictures may have been humiliating, but showing them would be cathartic, a purge of a secret. "She's an elegant woman, of course," Shel said.

"Oh, yes. I studied her last night."

"But I can't understand it. Bret's got *you*. Why he would do this ..."

Sarah didn't reply. She grasped the brown envelope with the photos and then reached inside, slipping them out. They were face down.

"You sure you want to show me?" Shel asked. "I mean, I know what the woman looks like."

"You're Bret's closest friend, *our* closest friend," Sarah said. "I know you only mean well. Look at them." With a dramatic snap, Sarah flipped them over.

Shel stared down. For a moment, he said nothing. Then he winced. He picked up the top picture, studied it.

"Interesting?" Sarah asked.

"That's not her."

"What?"

"This is Alison Carver."

"Yes."

"Sarah, that's not who Bret is having an affair with."

"*What?*"

"It's Ramy."

"It's *who?*"

She was dumbstruck. At that instant a military-school chorus that was entertaining outside in the museum struck up, "Off we go, into the wild blue yonder . . ." It was wonderfully inappropriate.

"Shel, you've got to be kidding."

"I wish I was."

"Oh come on, now. This is crazy. You're imagining things. Shel, he's having an affair with this congressperson. She was even in the restaurant last night, probably keeping tabs on him. Shel, these pictures!"

Slowly, Shel reached into his briefcase and pulled out a small box. "Sarah, this *tape!*"

"Tape? Oh, Jesus. What's on it?"

"Lovebirds."

"Where'd you get it?"

"You've been in my house a million times. You know I have all this telephone and FAX equipment. Well, I've got this device—look, I don't snoop on Ramy—but it can automatically record a call. I use it for business. Yesterday I accidentally left it on. When I came home I realized it, but I also saw some tape had been used. Naturally, I played it. It was luck."

Sarah gazed at the tape, then back at the color photos that decorated her desk. What the hell was going on? "Does he have . . . two?" she asked.

"God, I don't know," Shel replied. "All I know is what they said."

"I'm not believing this," Sarah said, her voice now quivering with the impact of hurt, hurt compounded. "I'm absolutely not believing this."

"Believe it," Shel said.

"You knew about this last night, when we were all together. How could you . . . ?"

"I didn't want to tip what I knew. We're both in this. I wanted you to hear the tape first before I did anything."

Sarah sighed deeply. "Well, I guess I appreciate that. Of course I do. You have a player with you?"

Shel reached into his case and took out an old minicassette recorder that he used for dictation. He snapped in the tape. "You're sure you want to hear this?" he asked.

"Yes," Sarah replied firmly. "It can't be any worse than these photos."

"Don't be so sure," Shel said. "A word is sometimes worth a thousand pictures." He pressed the button with the little green arrow next to it. The motor began to whir. There was a slight crackling sound as the tape began.

"Hello."
"Ramy?"
"Well . . . hello."
"He's not there, is he?"
"Of course not. Right now he's meeting with a close personal friend of Imelda Marcos."
"I just wanted to call you. This was a very important day, wasn't it?"
"Yes, it was."
"Your problems will be over soon. He'll be out of your life, safely tucked away."

Shel shook his head in despair as Bret spoke those words.

"I can't wait."
"Neither can I. He's been bad for you, Ramy. He's been bad for someone I care very much about."

"Oh my good God," Sarah said, and Shel saw tears well up in her eyes. How much of this was she supposed to take?

"You'll never know how bad."
"I'm glad you agreed to everything I suggested."
"You were right. It's the only way. It solves everything."

"They're probably talking about a divorce from both of us," Shel interjected.

The tape continued.

"If I'd only known before how unhappy you've been with Shel ..."

"Well, it's something I kept inside me for a long, long time. But when you ... appeared ... is that the right word?"

"It's as good as any."

"Appeared?" Sarah asked, her voice flaked with an anger she fought to control. "He's been around for two decades."

Ramy continued.

"I just let it all come out. What you've done means so much to me. I really don't know what would have happened to me without you."

"You don't have to worry about that now. We'll solve our problems together. I spoke with the person I mentioned."

"Person?"

"You know ..."

"Probably a lawyer," Shel said. "They're playing cute about not mentioning people's names."

Ramy went on.

"Oh, sure."

"He doesn't seem to think there'll be a problem."

"Good."

"I have complete trust in him. I don't think there's a better man for this kind of thing."

"That's great to know. So much depends on him."

"Might be Saul Kaplan or Woody Evans," Shel said.

And Sarah recalled Evans once more: "The wife is the first to know and the last to believe."

Bret went on.

"And look—actually this is why I was calling—if you want to talk about this, if you have any worries or thoughts—I want you to call me."

"I will."
"And soon we'll be together."

Then there was the sound of a buzzer, followed by an unintelligible voice through Bret's intercom.

"Got to go," Bret said.

Shel snapped off the machine.

Sarah stared at the recorder. "That conniving little ... *those* conniving little ..." She jutted her finger toward the machine. "Did I really hear that?"

"Yeah," Shel said quietly.

"I still don't believe it," Sarah retorted, trying desperately to contain the explosion that was building inside her. "Ramy's my oldest friend, my ..." She stopped. She gazed once again at the pictures. "It's impossible!"

It had been only twenty-four hours since Al Durfee had shown his pictures to Sarah. Her life had tumbled over then. Now it tumbled again. "He has two," she conceded quietly. The humiliation was painted all over her, but so was the fury. "Two women, and he comes home with roses."

"Well, at least it took two to replace you," Shel said, with a nervous laugh. "Well, I mean ..."

"It's okay," Sarah said, raising her hand to stop him from getting in deeper. "No one knows what to say at a time like this. It would make a good book, wouldn't it? 'Things to say to a woman who's losing her husband.' I could write that. I'm becoming an expert." Then she stopped. "Shel, I'm so sorry. I forgot that it's *your* Ramy."

Shel's eyes drifted downward. "It's all right," he said. "Maybe it was bound to happen. I'm kind of a boring guy, with a a few bucks maybe, but that's all."

"Don't say that about yourself."

"Oh, look, come on, it's true. Ramy looks for a little more excitement. Bret, I mean, she's always had good things to say about him. He's going places. Where am I going? The bank?"

His head hung down to his hundred-dollar shirt, his double chins tripling. It was true, Sarah thought. He wasn't any woman's idea of excitement. But he surely wasn't the worst man in the world. "Don't lose your self-respect," she said. "It's not us who's cheating."

"Does it matter?" he asked.

She smiled ironically. "We've all been so close. We've all been so *very* close. I can't accept this. The congresswoman, at least I could almost comprehend that. But Ramy . . ." Then her large brown eyes became animated. "Something's wrong here, wrong with both of them. People go through these crazy stages. I mean, this business with the new vows, the new double wedding. Bret must have told Ramy. They're both involved in this. Why? Why go through it?"

"When Bret brought it up," Shel explained, "I had that tape in my mind. I couldn't believe it either."

"Any ideas, Shel?"

"Nothing great. Maybe they're doing it to show their affection for us. Then, a few months down the line, they announce they're filing for divorce. They can say they always loved us . . . but. They can use the renewal of vows in the divorce hearing to prove it. Maybe they think it'll ease things legally."

"That sounds like Bret, not like Ramy," Sarah said.

"He could be running things."

"As usual. Look, I'll take an optimistic point of view. Maybe they're trying to put our marriages back together. Maybe they're trying to break off their little affair and renew the old flames, and they think the double wedding would help."

"That *is* an optimistic point of view, but I don't buy it," Shel said. "That tape didn't sound like two people returning to sanity."

"True," Sarah conceded.

"We can sit here all day and make theories," Shel argued. "I mean, how do we explain Alison Carver?"

"We don't."

Shel gestured in his chair, as if ready to leave. "Look," he said, anger evident on his lips, "I'm going home to have a little talk with my wife."

"No!"

"Why?"

"Because you're not ready. And neither am I. I was going to confront Bret with the pictures. Well, I didn't, and don't ask why not. Now I hear this tape. God knows," she said, her voice heavy with strain, "there might be some new surprises. Maybe Bret has a whole deck crew."

"If we don't say anything," Shel asked, "what do we do?"

Sarah thought it odd that Shel would ask such a question, or ask any question at all. He was bull-headed, and always the first to propose a solution. But here he seemed lost, as if his will had been broken, and again she was reminded of the blunt fact that no one is really prepared for these situations. "It depends on your feelings," she replied.

"My *feelings*? I'm hurt. I'm angry."

"I don't mean those feelings. Your feelings for Ramy."

"The bitch."

"Did you feel that way before the tape?"

"No."

"Did you love her?"

"Sure. Of all people, you know that."

"Do you still love her?"

Shel paused for a moment. Sarah could read the anguish in his eyes. "That's complicated."

"It's complicated for me, too," Sarah replied. "And I've got more competition. *Could* you love her . . . again?"

"Yes," Shel said, without hesitation. "If things got straightened out. Why?"

"Shel, this may sound nuts," Sarah explained, "but this isn't the Bret and Ramy that we know. If we helped, if we worked together, if we got some professional guidance—who knows, maybe we can save these marriages."

"You mean, you want the guy *back*?"

Sarah took in a deep breath and let it out slowly. Although she'd always prided herself on being rational, she knew she couldn't make an entirely rational decision. Instinct and feeling simply took over, as of course they had to. "Yes," she said, "I feel the same way now that I felt after I saw these photographic masterpieces. I'll fight for Bret. I've got to believe this running around isn't what he wants. In time, things can heal. I can't guarantee it. No one can. And if Bret persists in what he's doing now, then I'll drop him. I will not beg. I won't come on my knees. But I'll give this a try."

Shel looked at Sarah with a kind of grudging admiration. "I like the way you said that," he told her. "I guess that's the way I feel too. Why shut the door on twenty good years?"

"I'm glad we agree," Sarah said quietly.

"Should we go through with this ridiculous double wedding?" Shel asked.

"Why not? I can't see where it can hurt, whatever their motive. But before that, we've got to get some counseling. Maybe see a psychiatrist. *We're* the ones who need help now."

"I wonder," Shel mused, "what they'd say if they realized we knew."

"I have a feeling," Sarah replied, "that they'd be for us, that they'd want to end this sickness they're going through. They'd wish us well."

"You're an optimist, Sarah Lewis," Shel said.

"Find me something else to be in a situation like this," Sarah replied. "I once wrote a paper for a history of science class on the conflict between science and religion. I finally came to the conclusion that there was really no conflict. Each served its purpose. All that we know about Bret, and now Ramy—that's science. My feeling that we can save what we've both built over twenty years—that's religion."

At that moment, Bret Lewis, behind a locked office door, was examining the explosives and detonators that Captain Masters had brought.

D-day was eight days away.

Freedom, and a new life, lay ahead.

chapter
sixteen

Shel left, and for a few minutes Sarah sat at her desk, thoroughly ignoring the clutter in her office, just staring into space. She could hear the occasional shouts of little kids in the museum, and the blower that cooled her office, but otherwise all was silent. She felt shell-shocked, as if all her mental and emotional systems had been overloaded by the convulsions of the last twenty-four hours. She had suspected, but the confirmation of those suspicions, and now the bizarre addition of Ramy Jordan to her other-woman club, was as traumatic as if everything had come as a surprise. I was the cool one, she mused. The cool blonde, just right for a Hitchcock picture, the Grace Kelly of aeronautical engineering. Right now a good scream wouldn't hurt this cool blonde, she thought. One loud shriek that would sound like some of the jets on display no more than a hundred feet down the hall.

But she didn't scream. She kept it in, and knew she always would. Eternally the cool blonde, she muttered to herself. And yet, that is precisely what she wanted to be. She would not break under this assault.

There was a knock at the door, and Hal Tennis swung it open without even being invited, banging a doorknob against a wall. Tennis was a public relations aide for the museum, a skinny twenty-four-year-old who could drive even a Kiwanis fanatic mad with his steady diet of "golly" and "gee." Sarah was sure he ate Wheaties for breakfast and collected Captain Marvel comic books, and that each year he celebrated his fifteenth birthday.

"Hello, Hal. Thanks for barging in."

"Oh, sorry, Sarah. But I was just so excited. There's a woman in Texas who claims to be Amelia Earhart, and she seems to have some proof. Isn't that incredible?"

Sarah knew that there'd been any number of women who'd come forward since Earhart's disappearance, on her round-the-world flight, near Howland Island in the Pacific in 1937. She assumed this one would get the standard news coverage, appear on a few talk shows, maybe write a book and have it published by a publisher no one ever heard of, and fade away. "Interesting," Sarah said, gazing at her young associate the way one gazes at a man who'd just said he'd bought the Brooklyn Bridge.

"Just interesting?"

"I'm a scientist, Hal. It sounds like a lie."

"I'm a flack," Hal replied. "All lies welcome."

"Hal, Amelia would be in her nineties now. Just leave the proof of the lady's identity on my desk sometime, huh? Right now I've got calls."

Hal Tennis shrugged, surprised that Sarah Lewis wasn't jumping out of her chair, and closed the door behind him. Now Sarah actually smiled, reflecting on the absurdity of what Hal had told her. It was her week for absurdity. A fake Earhart. A fake husband. A fake best friend, Ramy Jordan. People are wonderful, she thought.

She worked for a time at her desk, and then minutes later the phone rang. She picked up. "Hello?"

"Hi, love. I'm glad I caught you in."

She almost couldn't believe the man had the nerve to call her "love." Either he was sick, he was going through some terrible period of uncertainty, or he was a very different man from the one she'd known for more than twenty years. And if he was, she couldn't believe he could fake it so well. "Hello, Bret," she said. There was a chill. She couldn't help it.

"Someone in your office?" he asked, believing the chill was just official correctness.

"Yes, you're right," she replied.

"Okay, I just wanted to tell you I'll be very late tonight."

"Oh?"

"Yeah, I've got to go over to CIA. These threats around Washington have us concerned. I don't know exactly what office we're meeting in."

"I thought the FBI handled domestic threats," Sarah said.

There was a pause. That was an odd comment from Sarah, Bret thought. She'd never challenged him before. She'd generally not shown much interest in the details of his work. "They do," he replied, "but you never know the foreign implications."

"Right. Well, I'll keep something warm for you."

"Would you do that? What about the doggie bag from last night?"

"I'll heat it up."

"Look, I'll make it as fast as I can," Bret said. "I don't like these late nights. You know that."

"Sure I do, Bret."

"I wish I could stay home with you. You know, I was thinking today—we should take that time off I talked about. Just go away somewhere, maybe California, or even Europe or South America."

"Japan?" Sarah asked.

"I'd love to go," Bret said. "I know plenty of Navy people in the Far East. We'd have a wonderful time. You know, I've been so busy recently I just get the feeling I've been ignoring *us*. We'll have a second honeymoon—right after our little lark next week."

"Terrific," Sarah said, practically choking on the word. "We'll talk when you get home."

"Bye, love."

"Bye, Bret."

They both hung up, Sarah still gazing at the phone in disbelief. Nothing figured. All right, he was having an affair. All right, he was probably having two ... that she knew about. But why these ornaments? A new double wedding, with one of his "affairees" standing a few feet away, renewing her vows to another man. Mention of a second honeymoon, as far away as Japan. Showing a level of affection that had not changed in twenty years. And continuing the lies that he was going to late meetings, when in fact he was almost certainly going to be with Alison Carver.

Almost certainly.

Sarah went for her address book. Time for another call to Al Durfee. Check Bret out one more time. Would it be Alison or Ramy tonight? Or was there a *third*?

"I'm going to tell her within two weeks," Bret said. "I'll just explain that things haven't worked, that twenty years is a long time, that the marriage is tired, that I want out. She's a mature woman. There may be some anger, even tears, but she'll accept it."

"I'm glad it's all coming to a head," Alison Carver answered. "I can't wait any longer."

"Well, there'll still be a *respectable* period of waiting, Ally."

"I understand that. You know I wouldn't just march in and steal you after you dump Sarah. We'd have to be two people finding each other, and ending our loneliness. It's the kind of story they put in *Parade* or *Redbook*. Great copy."

They spoke in Carver's office in the Rayburn House Office Building. It was a cozy office, with a warm oak desk and several cushiony visitors' chairs. The walls were filled with the usual battle ribbons—a plaque from a California right-to-life committee praising Carver for her fight against abortion (except in the case of rape or incest, or where the life of the mother is concerned, or in the case of Alison Carver's own abortion at age twenty-two); an honorary diploma from a high school in her district; another plaque from the Navy League of the United States praising her for her untiring devotion to a strong Navy, rather easy for a congresswoman from a coastal section; and, most important, a picture of Alison Carver with George Bush. There were assorted other awards, each one dutifully displayed in case the giver happened by. Carver particularly liked the one from an ice-cream dealers' association praising her for her bill to make chocolate ice cream the national snack. Carver was a superb politician. She'd have introduced a bill to make rattlesnakes the national pet if there were enough venom lovers in her district to swing an election. But most of them had already moved to Washington.

"The divorce won't take long," Bret assured Carver. "I'll hire Woody Evans and have him make some phone calls to the courts."

"It's too bad," Carver said, looking at an obligatory photograph on her desk of her mother and father. "Your wife seemed like a rather nice person last night."

"That describes it," Bret told her. "Nice. You can take only so much 'nice' in twenty years."

Carver smiled, the cynical smile of one who dropped a compliment one moment and swiped it away with a sabre the next. Bret kept looking her over, looking at the prize that any man would want. He could not get over how sleek she was. He knew she worked out every day in a nearby gym and was often seen by reporters jogging around the Mall on weekends. But it was the shoulder-length jet-black hair and that modulated, TV-trained voice that tied up the package and made it so saleable. She was forty. She passed for thirty. And she was *important*.

He knew her history thoroughly. Alison Carver had been Phi Beta Kappa at Berkeley and had begun her career as a reporter for the *Los Angeles Times*. Then a California congressman had offered her a job as his press aide in Washington. The political bug bit her, and she returned to California to serve two terms in the Legislature, before being elected to Congress.

She had always said that she'd never had time to marry, but inevitably there'd been rumors that she didn't care much for men. The rumors worried her. They were one of the prime motivators for seeking an affair with a man she'd eventually marry. Her district was conservative, heavily Catholic. She had to keep carrying it by large majorities in order to get a shot at her real objective—the United States Senate. Marrying Bret Lewis and being seen as a family woman could help her. In Washington, people were the usual tools of the trade.

At first, Carver had worried that Bret's divorce could create image problems. But both of them realized that the stigma of divorce had faded. In the 1950s, Carver liked to recall, Adlai Stevenson's divorce hounded him in two Presidential campaigns. But there was barely a whisper when the divorced Ronald Reagan ran, and won.

"After we marry you'll have to start building a political base," Alison said. "It's a good time. People are always curious about the newly married."

"Tim Curran wants to introduce me to some finance people in New York."

"Can't hurt," Alison replied, "but check them out first. Tim knows a lot of people you wouldn't want in the family scrapbook."

"Yeah, I figured that. But I've got to have money to build that base."

"If you do it Tim's way."

"Come again?"

"You're here. I'm here. I've been thinking about it. In a way, you can build a political base right in Washington."

"Not if I want to run for something," Bret said.

"George Bush only served briefly in Congress," Alison replied. "In fact, he lost for the Senate against Lloyd Bentsen, and lost against Reagan for the Republican nomination in 1980. He kept going with appointive jobs."

"Yeah, but one of those jobs was Republican National Chairman," Bret pointed out. "You pick up a lot of IOUs behind that desk, and I'm just not exactly known as a hot party man."

"True," Alison said. They were both standing, both pacing in their own way, doing a kind of brain dance around the room. They were two people obsessed with a virulent Washington disease, something that transcended any possible romantic involvement. "You've got to move into a more visible position," Carver asserted. "No, no, it can't be through appointments. You're right. There's just nothing in any appointive job that automatically makes people think of higher office. Even secretary of state is a dead end down here. I mean, they all go do specials on public television. Unless you can get someone to make you vice president . . ."

"The longest shot."

"No doubt. No, you've got to build something in a state."

"I had this idea," Bret said. "What if I didn't build a political base immediately? What if I went into business?"

"Business? What kind of business?"

"Ally, I get offers—feelers, really—from the defense industry. Look, we all know the way the system works. I know things they want to know. I know *people* they want to meet. I could literally walk in at the vice presidential level."

"Business," Alison Carver said. "Well, it's been done. But it usually leads to appointive jobs again. And unless you're a CEO, it doesn't wash down here. Vice presidents are a dime a dozen—forgive me for insulting my one true love."

"Maybe I can hit that CEO level. And I'll use it for elective office. Look, it's the right era. American business is respectable again."

"Bid-nus," Carver said.

"What?"

"Bret, my sweet, you've got to learn to speak English like the natives. We're Republicans. We're a Western and Southern party now. It's not business. It's bid-nus. You're going into bid-nus. And never say 'American.' It's 'Murkan.' You're a red-blooded Navy man and you're going into Murkan bid-nus. Say it."

"Murkan bid-nus."

"Perfect the first time."

"Jesus," Bret said, "I feel like Eliza Doolittle."

But Carver turned somber. "Some industry might work out," she said, "especially if there are people in it with a pipeline to the Administration. But where would you be? God, Bret, I hope we're not separated."

"So do I. I'd give up any ambitions to be with you, angel Ally."

"It's so wonderful to hear a man finally say that. Let's forget politics now. We'll have years for that. Let's talk about us."

"My favorite subject."

"You know, I was wondering—do you think Sarah suspects anything?"

"No," Bret replied, with utter certainty. "She's not a suspicious person. She's very simple in a way, not at all like her looks. You've got to understand these women engineering types. She goes to her museum, tinkers with the airplanes and comes home. She doesn't suspect an affair any more than she suspects a divorce."

"I wish there were something quicker than a divorce," Carver said. Then she realized the implications of what she was saying. "Strike that."

Bret stared at her incredulously. He wanted her to remember that look. "I'm glad you took that back," he said. "You know, I wish Sarah well. You and I'll have each other some day, but I don't want to hurt her any more than I have to."

"You're a kind man, Bret Lewis," Carver said, and she walked over and kissed him ... for about a minute.

Bret was beginning to feel a sense of personal power that he'd never felt before. He had his wife conned. He had Ramy Jordan on a string. And he was even able to deceive the sophisticated, savvy Alison Carver. He could never let her in on what he really intended to do. She had her limits, and he had a good idea what they were. Ramy was developing a romantic view of murder because she was so desperate to get rid of her husbandly burden, and because she'd always had a secret feeling for Bret Lewis that Lewis had sensed years before. Alison Carver was a little more realistic.

Outside the Rayburn Building—actually, standing in the shadows of the Longworth House Office Annex—was Al Durfee. He watched the lights at Rayburn go off, one by one. The light in Alison Carver's office remained on, and periodically he could see two figures. The telescopic viewfinder on his camera identified them as Alison Carver and Bret Lewis. This time, Durfee caught that kiss on film. This time he had the smoking gun. In a way, he felt badly. He liked Sarah. Everyone did. Now he had the proof of what she had feared, and he had to report it to her. Previously he'd given the marriage six months, a year tops. Now, based on the geometric aspects of the embrace he'd just witnessed, he reduced his estimate to three months, four on the outside.

Durfee lingered near the building after the now-documented kiss. He was a bit apprehensive over a disheveled man who meandered nearby, a white man about six feet tall with two days' growth of beard and movements suggesting either addiction or some kind of mental derangement that went beyond even the Capitol Hill norm. But as a streetlight hit the man's face, Durfee recognized him as a police undercover agent, someone he'd met several times while on assignments. Durfee guessed, and he was right, that the agent was waiting for a prearranged drug buy, to be followed by a bust. Considering the location, Durfee hoped the buyer was a political big one. It made conversation with the cops so much more interesting.

He was watching ten minutes later as Bret left the Rayburn Building ... alone. Durfee's job was essentially done. There'd be no motel rendezvous or late-night escapade in Alison Carver's three-story town-house. Durfee packed his camera into his 1982 Ford station wagon and drove off with the damaging photos. He'd have them processed in the morning. By afternoon, they'd be in Sarah Lewis's office.

Durfee left too soon, for Bret's evening was just beginning. Under the right front seat of his Lincoln, parked on the street, was a package wrapped in a plain brown wrapper. It was an explosive device, one of the three that Avery Masters had delivered to him that morning. Bret had gotten it out of the Pentagon easily, since the security people would never check him. In his attaché case was a small remote-control box whose signal was effective for up to 2,000 feet. Another phase of his plan was now beginning.

As a student of terrorism, the reporting of terrorism, and the psychology surrounding terrorism, Bret Lewis knew that nothing intrigued investigators and reporters more than a pattern. One incident was serious enough. Two or three were major news, and they directed the attention, and the thinking, of reporters and government officials. A pattern of incidents also meant more invitations for experts to appear on talk shows, which only increased the overall excitement.

Lewis started the car and headed out toward Falls Church, Virginia, a town adjoining Arlington. It was about five miles from the Pentagon, and was one of the bedrooms for the defense community.

The night was almost chilly, reflecting the erratic weather that had come in over Washington, and a light fog had settled in the low areas of the Mall. It was a feeling that was more London than Washington, yet it almost inspired Bret Lewis. This was a wonderful night for a crime.

Even with the fog, Bret got the same thrill he'd always gotten driving through the city and passing the White House. This time he saw it from the rear, gazing out over the great lawn, where foreign visitors were received, where, if his wildest dreams were realized, he himself would some day greet the powerful of the Earth. Everything was lit up, although the top of the Washington Monument was cut off by the fog. It was 11:34 P.M. and Bret found virtually no traffic on the roads to Virginia. Washington went to bed early and rose early, and the night life rarely boomed.

*   *   *

"Mrs. Lewis?"

"Yes."

"Al Durfee. I didn't wake you, did I?"

"Well ... yes, but it's perfectly all right, Al." Sarah had put the leftover Chinese food in the oven, on "low-warm," and had gone to bed. But now she sat up sharply, and snapped on a lamp. She knew that Al wasn't calling to discuss his fee, or his philosophy of life.

In fact, Durfee realized he had an obligation to alert Sarah immediately to what he'd seen, not even to wait for the photos to be developed. He couldn't know whether Bret would go home this very night and spring a divorce announcement on Sarah. He wanted her to have the latest, just in case he did. He called from a phone booth at the Washington Hilton hotel, whose lobby was filled with colleagues attending a tribute to a retiring federal judge. "Sorry to disturb you, ma'am," Durfee said, "but I think we've got the whole ball of wax right now."

"What do you mean?"

"I caught them having a very intimate conference—*very* intimate, right in the Rayburn Building. They didn't bother to lower the blinds."

"I see," Sarah said. Now her voice was chilly. "And this wasn't a good-bye kiss, I take it."

"This was hello, good-bye and let's go to Paris. And, as they say, I'll have film at eleven."

Sarah felt no shock, just a general letdown. This was confirmation, and it had shut her last window of hope. In a way, she was almost glad to know that Bret definitely was having two separate affairs. "I'm grateful that you called, Al," she said. "At least now we're sure."

"Very."

"And now I'll tell *you* something. This congresswoman isn't his only little pal."

"Oh, yeah?" Durfee replied. He loved the dirt. It was part of the attraction of the job.

"That's right. He's also involved with a close friend of ours. Her husband taped a conversation and played it for me today."

"Entertaining?" Durfee asked, then bit his tongue.

"In a way ... yes."

"Mrs. Lewis," Durfee replied, "how did you ever wind up with this guy? Don't tell me. He never showed that side. It's true. Happens all the time. They all say it. I hear it four times a week, sometimes five. I mean, Pat Nixon, she married Richard Nixon. Debbie Reynolds—I love her—she got stuck with Eddie Fisher. It happens to the nicest ladies I know. Really."

Sarah laughed sardonically. "That's very reassuring."

"But one thing, Mrs. Lewis. If this is true about the other, other woman—and we know it's true about this first other woman—then you need a sleazeball with vest."

"A what?"

"A lawyer. I really wouldn't wait so much as a single day. Even confronting the guy might be a waste of time. You might as well get the legal jump on him."

"You know, I was thinking about that. Maybe after the ceremony . . ."

"What ceremony?"

"You're not going to believe it. He wants us to get remarried. Next week."

"He wants to . . . what? If you'll excuse the expression, this is like overhauling a car just before you trade it in—not that I'm comparing you to my Ford."

"I understand. In a way, you're right. And it'll be a double wedding, a repeat of the one we had with our closest friends twenty years ago. The other bride is, as you say, the other, other woman."

Durfee took meticulous notes on a little pad that kids used for school assignments. *This* would go into his autobiography. *This* was a first. "Mrs. Lewis," he finally admitted, "I can't give you any more advice. This is the strangest man I've ever spied on. He's ahead of us. He's ahead of us both."

And he was.

Remaining ahead meant planning every detail, anticipating the next move of everyone else in the equation. Bret Lewis drove slowly through the Arlington area, on the way to Falls Church. Yet, despite his easy pace, despite the cool air blowing into the car, he could feel his hands sweating. He couldn't quite figure out why this was happening, though. He felt no particular nervousness. And he certainly felt no guilt over the person he'd become. A calculating man accepted certain moral ambiguities, a fairly generous description of his current situation. And in his profession, moral ambiguities were the norm anyway. Like a policeman, an antiterrorism operative can easily take on the characteristics of his opponent.

He wondered if there were something happening deep in his psyche that he hadn't anticipated. No, he didn't have any feeling that he should reverse course. And he surely knew how attracted he was to a new and glamorous life that could lead to the highest levels of power. And he also knew that he would not have dropped Sarah unless he felt he absolutely had to. But it was when he thought about Sarah that he felt his palms tighten. If this wasn't guilt, then what was it? Was some internal mechanism warning him that something was wrong, that there was danger where he didn't see it? Was it just a normal reaction to the violence he was about to begin? Or, possibly, was it the old touch of paranoia returning? Was someone on to him? Tracking him?

None of the above, he thought.

He realized, finally, that he still had feelings for Sarah, and that this was producing the odd reaction. And, yet, why should this be surprising? He and Sarah *had* gone through a wonderful twenty years, with the exception of the trauma over their child. Under any other circumstances, he would have given her that additional fifty. But he understood enough about himself to realize that he had this unique capacity to put feelings aside when they interfered with his destiny, as he saw it.

As he cruised along, he knew that something inside was pulling him back to Sarah, and probably would, long after she was removed from the scene. Thank God, he thought. Thank God I'm strong enough to resist.

He approached Falls Church and headed for an area that was under development. A company was building new houses and a small shopping mall on the outskirts of the town. Bret knew that there'd be little or no traffic at this time of night in the area of the development site, making it ideal for his purpose. He drove there and found, silhouetted against the cold steel sky, the spooky desolation of a construction area at night—the wood frames of houses, the silent bulldozers, the stores of lumber and brick, the inevitable piles of earth, arranged like miniature mountains around the site. There was a work shed, but it had been abandoned by the crew hours earlier.

Bret made sure to drive only on the paved road that went by the area. Driving on plain earth left tire tracks, and tire tracks could be traced. He stopped the car. He reached into his briefcase and took out a small cookie can, only six inches across and decorated with the flags of a number of European nations. Then he opened the car door and placed the can at the side of the road, about eight feet from the stilled bulldozer. He closed the car door and drove off.

His eyes searched everywhere. There were no cars coming, no one wandering near the sides of the road. He used the mileage gauge on his car to clock off a quarter of a mile. Still moving, he went into his briefcase again and removed one of the palm-sized remote-control devices that Masters had supplied. He grasped it in his hand.

He pressed the button.

Even at a quarter of a mile he felt the blast. And he distinctly heard the bulldozer either turn over on its side or be moved sideways along the ground. There was a secondary "pop" that he took to be one of the bulldozer's tires exploding. And he was sure he heard the sound of glass shattering in one of the uncompleted homes. The glass bothered him. It was one of the major unpredictables in any explosion.

It had worked.

Masters's supplies had functioned perfectly, and Bret Lewis was just not the kind of person to accept equipment unless he tested it first. He felt a visceral thrill at what he had done. He would have to press the button only one more time.

Bret drove away at a moderate speed. Never once did he hear a police siren. The radio news, which he listened to while going over Memorial Bridge on his way back to Washington, made no mention of a strong, mysterious blast near Falls Church. Utterly amazing, he thought. People could hear an explosion in the middle of the night and not report it. People just didn't care. They'd assume someone else would put in the call.

But they'd know in the morning. There'd be an investigation. And that's precisely what he wanted.

chapter
seventeen

"The Falls Church police are handling it, sir."

Bret raised his eyebrows. "That's odd. It has the earmarks of a terrorist bomb. Didn't the lab say they used C-4?"

"Yes, sir. But C-4 is so common, they don't want people to panic."

Lawrence W. "Simple" Simon sat in an oversized leather visitor's chair in Bret's office. He was a thirty-six-year-old Marine major who'd been temporarily assigned to Bret's antiterrorist operation. Specifically, he gathered intelligence and information on terrorist groups around the world. Slight and small-boned, Simon looked like anything but a mud Marine. He even spoke softly and played chess in his off-hours. He'd gotten the nickname "Simple" because he'd graduated first in his class at the Naval Academy.

"They're always afraid people will panic," Bret complained. "Maybe if they did a little more panicking, the world would do a lot more resisting. All right, so C-4 is common. But according to the morning report, whoever did this used a rather sophisticated remote control."

"We don't know how sophisticated yet, sir," Simon replied, checking his blue four-by-six note cards. But they're still considering this a criminal act."

"Any particular reason?"

"Well, the construction company ..."

Bret raised his hand. "Construction. Organized crime?"

"There are allegations, sir."

"And this was someone's warning about something or other?"

"The local police have that theory. No real damage was done, except to a bulldozer. But they think a message was being delivered."

"Well, maybe. But I'm not seeing it that way. I think it was a test."

"Oh?"

"Testing a device to make sure it worked. Maybe to see if it worked against heavy machinery."

"I see, sir. But . . ."

"I know. It's just a theory. But keep me informed, will you, Larry? I've got to go on to something else now."

Simon got up to leave, unaware that he, like Masters, had been made one more pawn in Bret's plans. Bret didn't really care whether the Falls Church explosion was seen as terrorism or some kind of organized crime love letter. He cared that mass spectrometry by the FBI lab had identified the explosive as C-4, a mixture commonly used by terrorists and manufactured in Czechoslovakia. He cared that remote control had been quickly determined to be the means of detonation. He cared that he was on record, in his talk with Simon, as suggesting that terrorists might have had a motive for setting off the explosion. When his murder bomb went off in seven days, the same physical pattern would be found. That was what he had in mind.

He turned to his private phone and dialed a number. Within moments a man across town answered on *his* private line. "Shel Jordan," came the jovial voice at the other end.

"Bret," Lewis answered.

"Right on time."

"Are you free for lunch?" Bret asked.

"Sure. I had something, but for you I can rearrange it."

"I want to plan the new wedding with you."

"Let's make it for one."

"One it is," Bret said, making sure to write down the time, and the person, on a calendar that would be kept permanently by his secretary. "I've got some stuff you'd like. I think we can use it."

"With you?"

"Right in a small box."

"Bring it."

Their conversation ended. Now Bret had to take every step with the utmost precision. No one knew the full extent of what he planned. Absolutely no one.

Bret left for lunch at twelve, although it took only half an hour to reach Shel's office in a sterile, modern building on K Street. He had another stop to make first. Wearing sunglasses, he drove to an electronics supply shop in Arlington. It was one of those places where skinny adolescents with concave chests, thick glasses and dreams of engineering glory come to buy obscure electronic parts dumped into cardboard bins, bin after bin, row after row. Behind the counter of Morry's was Morry, owner and sole employee for thirty years. Gruff, about sixty, Morry sat stone-faced with three huge catalogues before him and greeted customers with a warmth that was legendary.

"You're a jerk," Morry was saying to one customer, turned quickly into a victim. "This transformer wasn't made by no RCA. She was stuck in there by some English company in 1967. Now don't come in here and waste my time like this. I gotta sit on my butt and take care of people like youse all day. Next!" The customer was a regular. But Morry didn't remember regulars, or anyone else. His voice boomed. He knew everything. No one else knew anything. He could have built the atomic bomb with his own hands. People asked him. He guaranteed it.

"You're askin' for somethin' that don't exist!" he berated the next customer, a woman. "I can't do miracles. God I'm not. Send someone who knows. Next!"

The combative atmosphere was fine for Bret, who really didn't want to be noticed and who had no intention of lining up at the front desk to be executed. To him it seemed that some of those people on the front lines of Morry's rather liked being tongue-lashed by the master, as if it were some kind of rite of passage into the community of electronics nuts.

Casually, Bret passed down the aisles of cardboard bins, pretending to be interested in the endless connectors, potentiometers, circuit boards and resistors in this Edisonian heaven. He stopped at one aisle, where he was, for the moment, the only customer.

Smoothly, he reached into his right jacket pocket and removed a small brown envelope. He then inserted his thumb and forefinger into the envelope and withdrew a plastic card wrapped once in tissue. He looked around, pretending for a moment to show some interest in what was happening in the battle area around the front desk. Convinced that he was unobserved, he let the plastic card slip from the tissue and drop to the floor between two bins. Then, he placed the brown envelope and tissue back in his pocket.

He picked up a switch, examined it like any other customer, then placed it back in the bin. And then, as if he couldn't find what he was looking for, he turned to leave.

"Dropped something."

The voice was high and nagging. Bret's heart sank. He turned around, his sunglasses impeding any facial identification. "You talking to me?"

A customer with buck teeth and a goony smile nodded in the affirmative. "You should learn to use your fingers precisely," he instructed. "Then you wouldn't drop things." He slowly jutted out his finger, pointing to the floor.

But he didn't point to the card.

Bret looked down. On the floor, in front of a bin, was a narrow strip of white paper. "That's not mine," he said.

"Oh yes it is," the nag said. "I saw it drop."

Not wanting to make a memorable scene, Bret bent down and retrieved the paper.

It was his.

It was the fortune he'd gotten the night before at Jimmy Lee's. Somehow, it had stuck onto the brown envelope. He glanced at it for a moment: "What you don't know will always hurt you." He hadn't liked that fortune the night before, and he didn't like it any more now.

"Thank you," he said to the nag, who had a self-satisfied smile on a face that had no redeeming social value.

"Any time."

Bret left Morry's, hoping never to return. He walked three blocks to his car—he hadn't parked it in front of the store because he didn't want it seen there—and drove off. Mission accomplished.

"I feel for both of you. It's not that unusual a situation. I've had many patients in a similar predicament. I know the turmoil you must feel."

"Thank you," Sarah said.

"From me, too," Shel added.

The words were spoken softly, and Sarah was sure they were sincere. Dr. Lorenzo Rosenthal sat in an ordinary rocking chair as he spoke with Sarah and Shel. His office was more like a small library or study, with warm, dark wood paneling and rows of books, some of them rare and encased in glass. An eleven-year-old cocker spaniel appropriately named Sigmund slept in a corner, oblivious to the human trauma unfolding before him. The office was in a small brick house in College Park, Maryland, not far from the University of Maryland campus. Rosenthal was on the psychology faculty and also maintained a private practice, specializing in marital problems and parent–adolescent relations. He was a tiny man, no more than five foot three, fifty-five years old with a shiny bald head and a graying Vandyke beard. His ears were larger than necessary, as if supplied by the God of psychology to take in everything he heard. A patient once told him that he looked like the first therapist for leprechauns.

"So you've come to talk this out with me," he told Sarah and Shel. "I believe, Mr. Jordan, that you made the appointment."

"Yeah, I did, Doctor."

"Please call me Lorenzo. Even my plumber does."

"All right, Lorenzo. I checked around with people saying I was inquiring for a friend . . ."

"The traditional evasion," Rosenthal said. "It began with bladder conditions."

"Yeah. And your name kept popping up. When the best I know recommend someone, that someone is good."

"I'm flattered. Now, you know I'm a psychologist, not a psychiatrist. I don't deal with medical illness. If this is indicated, I refer you. I'm sure you noticed my name and my slight accent, so let me answer the question you'll ask each other when you leave, namely, 'Can he be a Spaniard with a name like Rosenthal?' I am from Cuba and came in the early 1960s after the great revolutionary and cigar smoker took over. As for Rosenthal, there are minorities in Cuba as here."

"That's interesting," Shel said.

"Especially to me," Rosenthal answered. "Also, you'll notice no wedding ring. After what I've heard in my years of practice, I'd never risk it."

Both Sarah and Shel laughed. Rosenthal had a storyteller's way of putting people at ease. "Also," he went on, "I want you to meet my associate and principal advisor, Sigmund, who lies in the corner. Don't be afraid to talk in front of him. He follows the ethics of the profession."

Sarah glanced over at Sigmund, who was still quite asleep.

"Now, Sarah," Rosenthal continued, moving his little body around in the rocking chair, which was too big for him, "I was fascinated by the fact that you and your husband grew up together. Tell me about this."

"We grew up in a New York suburb, although we didn't meet until high school. We were similar in some ways."

"Tell me."

"High achievers. Bret was president of the student council, I was vice president of the Greeters. We were the kids picked to introduce new students to the school."

"Very fine. So there was mutual respect."

"Always. I think there still is. In all the years since we decided to go together in high school, there was really no one else . . . until now."

"No one you're aware of."

"Well, yes, that's right."

"You went to college together?"

"We were physically separated. Bret went to Columbia. I was in upstate New York. But we were emotionally together. We ran up huge phone bills."

"So you think that absence did make the heart grow fonder."

"Oh yes," Sarah replied.

"I'm always happy to see a cliché come true," Rosenthal said. "Makes for an easier world, don't you think?"

"Yeah," Shel replied.

"Now, Sarah, you learned about—or suspected—your husband's

activity some months ago when he stayed out late and his excuses
didn't come together."

"Yes."

"Amazing."

"Why amazing?"

"Here is a man who deals with the scheming of international
politics, who is a student of military tactics. And yet, he couldn't fool
his own wife."

"Is that a compliment?" Sarah asked.

"Partially, yes. You know what they say, 'The wife is the first to
know and the last to believe.'"

"A lawyer once told me that," Sarah said.

Rosenthal shrugged. "I thought it was my line. But, people copy
me. To go on. You became suspicious, you hired a private inquisitor,
you discovered this affair. Now, you discover another affair—with
the closest of friends. And your husband suggests a renewal of vows.
You don't confront your husband because you want to save your
marriage by getting advice from me and others."

"Yes."

"You are wise. I will probe further, but my initial impression is
that there is much hope. I base that on the dual affairs."

"How so?" Sarah asked.

"The obvious," Rosenthal answered. "He can't marry both of
them."

Shel turned to Sarah, his usually bloodshot eyes growing bright.
"You know, that *is* obvious, and we never thought of it."

"In emotional situations, the obvious often eludes us. That's what
keeps gas in my Honda," Rosenthal said. "Now, you wrote on your
information form in the outer office that you two never argue."

"Correct."

"Never?"

"Well, we have disagreements, but not the kind you associate with
serious problems. I mean, no pounding on tables or screaming."

"There's been no change in this pattern recently?"

"No," Sarah replied. "Look, Bret can get tense at times. He's in a
tense business. And he's had bouts of paranoia and depression in
the past. But our relationship has been good. Never a threat. Never
regrets. He even suggested a second honeymoon."

"He's forty-one," Rosenthal noted. "Look, there is this midlife crisis thing. It's real. While it's true that some men leave their wives without warning—some even go away and are never heard from again—I don't think, from your description, that your husband fits that pattern. He's a proud man."

"Very."

"There are no guarantees here," Rosenthal said. "But I think your instinct may be right. These may be flings. The two affairs rather than one true flame, the new double wedding, the second honeymoon, the unchanging personal profile—all this gives me hope that he will outgrow this period. Of course, I proceed from very little information and can only guide you step by step. But I will make a suggestion . . ."

"Please," Sarah said.

"Both you and Sheldon here have had bad luck in the children department. You, Sarah, say you don't want to adopt because adoption sometimes brings bad results. Do I summarize right?"

"I was adopted," Sarah said. "Do you know what it's like to be a possession, not to have the same blood as your parents?"

"I have an adopted son," Rosenthal said, without missing a beat. "I am a single father. I don't own him. I do not examine his blood and he doesn't examine mine. He is fourteen now and we have a wonderful relationship."

The remark caught Sarah short. All her adult life she'd had "understanding" from others when she expressed her fear of adoption. Friends had sent her newspaper stories to bolster her prejudices. Bret, at least on the surface, had acquiesced in her feelings. Even her adoptive parents hadn't disputed her. Everyone seemed to know of some adoption that hadn't worked out. Rosenthal was the first to challenge her.

"I hadn't realized you had a son," Sarah said quietly.

"Adopted son," Lorenzo corrected. "I think you should explore this with your husband. Sometimes people suppress their wanting of children, especially after a tragedy like yours. But as they enter middle age, and their own mortality starts weighing on their minds, the parental instinct can surface. Explore your feelings on adoption again. As I say, probe with your husband. It could be that this . . ."

". . . is what's driving us apart?"

"Worth investigating."

Sarah remained silent. She understood, of course, that Rosenthal, in this first session, was presenting the obvious. The child thing, as she sometimes called it, was always a shadow on her mind. But Rosenthal was known for aggressive work and throwing out a multitude of suggestions—some of them based more on his observation of life than on psychology—and Sarah felt that this one was helpful, even exciting. Maybe the child thing *was* at the root of it all. Maybe Bret just didn't want to bring it up, knowing how she'd react to adoption. Maybe, she now thought, just maybe, she'd been wrong. "I'll think about that," she promised. "I should have done it earlier. Maybe if Bret had brought it up himself . . . but that's just an excuse."

"Life is a string of excuses," Rosenthal said. "It is the one area where man has reached perfection."

(At the moment that Sarah was pledging to open her mind to the possibility of adopting a child, Bret was placing a remote-control device in his jacket pocket, testing its feel, making sure it didn't bulge. And a child was in fact on his mind—the son he hoped to have with Alison Carver.)

"I will ask you one final question for this session," Rosenthal said, looking Sarah squarely in the eye. "If this should not work out—if your husband should leave you permanently—where do you see yourself in two years?"

Now Sarah turned uneasily in her chair. "I've thought about that," she said.

"They always do," Rosenthal added.

"I'd survive. I want to emphasize that. I'm not going to play tough lady of Feminist Row. It would hurt, and hurt badly. But I'd get over it, I'd keep my career, and maybe remarry if the right person came along."

"You have my admiration," Rosenthal told her. "That is a perfect attitude."

"Thank you," Sarah whispered. But down deep, she didn't know if she could really live up to what she'd just promised.

"Now Sheldon," Rosenthal continued, "this is a joint session, which I usually don't do. However, you both testified to the deep friendship between you, and you seem to have no secrets . . ."

"I wouldn't keep anything from Sarah," Shel insisted. "I would have said up to two days ago that Bret was my closest friend. It's pretty obvious that's not true any more ...."

"A bit harsh," Rosenthal said. "Emotions distort behavior."

"Well, I'm not that tolerant, Doc. I'm losing my wife. I told you on my form about that tape."

"Yes. You were saying about Sarah ..."

"I was saying that I thought Bret was my friend. But I *know* Sarah is. We're like one now. We're in this together."

"Yes, *very* together. You suspected nothing?"

"Before that tape, absolutely nothing. Oh, I mean, my Ramy had nice things to say about Bret ..."

"Like what?"

"Oh, the usual."

"Sheldon, what is usual to you may not be usual to me. Please be more precise."

"I'm sorry, Doc. Well, she'd say that she'd heard he was doing a good job over at DOD."

"DOD?"

"Department of Defense. And she'd say he looked nice one night or was intelligent. The usual things friends say. Hell, I didn't take notes on *that*."

"No, of course not. Have you been having problems in your marriage?"

Shel turned to Sarah, as if embarrassed, as if indicating there were things he *might* want to hold back. At first he said nothing.

"If you wish to discuss that privately, it can be arranged," Rosenthal said.

"No, I'll lay it all out," Shel replied. "We've had some shakes."

"Shel, I didn't know," Sarah said.

"Well, Ramy wasn't the kind to talk about it, even to you," Shel replied. "In fact, when we'd go at each other, I'd always ask her to keep it between us and she promised to. It wasn't that we didn't trust you. But I was sensitive about it."

"Many people feel that way," Rosenthal explained. "And you mentioned nothing to Bret?"

"No. Secrets are my business."

"Your shakes, as you call them. Tell me."

"Well, I really care a lot about Ramy. I mean, let's face it. Take a gander at me. I'm not exactly a movie star. To have a wife like that. Very attractive. Great at parties. Everyone's friend. I mean, it made me proud. But Ramy, well, I think she wasn't too proud of *me*. I'm not classy."

"Shel, I told you not to knock yourself," Sarah said.

"It's okay," Rosenthal interrupted. "We must show our true feelings." You believe, Sheldon, that Bret sensed this disaffection in Ramy?"

"No. Bret doesn't think that way. Ramy went after *him*."

"What?" Sarah exclaimed.

"She did it once before with someone else."

"This is new," Rosenthal said.

"In fact, she did it *twice* before."

"Ah, we get a picture," Rosenthal went on. "And she initiated each one?"

"We had it out. She admitted it. But they blew over. Bret wouldn't start with a friend. The guy's got a sense of propriety."

"That's true," Sarah said.

"I see the value in having you both here," Rosenthal observed. "You help each other."

"We always will," Sarah said.

"So," Rosenthal went on, "there is a history of indiscretion by your wife. And you, Sheldon?"

"Not once."

"Commendable. Unexciting, but commendable. A little joke."

They both tried to laugh, but Rosenthal had not brought the house down.

"I will assume," Rosenthal said, "even though further proof is needed, that Ramy initiated this. Being an attractive woman, she was able to make an impression on Bret. Since Bret is also apparently dallying with still another woman, we can surmise that she got him at a vulnerable time. These are theories. In further sessions we shall test them. Now, I only want to ask one more question. My first session is always short. I understand the stresses on patients. Sheldon . . ."

"Yes?"

"I ask what I asked Sarah. If this should not work out, if Ramy should leave you, where do you see yourself in two years?"

Shel looked at Rosenthal, then at Sarah, then back at Rosenthal.
He said nothing.

"Sheldon, are you uncomfortable with the question?"

"Well ... yeah," Shel replied.

"Perhaps you'd like to think about it, or answer it in confidence."

"I'll answer it now," Shel said. "Y'know, we guys all try to look
brave. I tried to look brave when I went to Sarah with that tape."

"Understandable," Rosenthal said.

"But I'm not so brave. If Ramy left me, where would I be in two
years?"

"Yes. That was the question."

"It wouldn't take two years," Shel said. "It would take more like
six months."

"And where would you be?" Rosenthal asked again.

"Dead."

"Excuse me?"

Slowly, Shel raised his right arm, formed his hand in the shape
of a gun and pointed it to his temple. "Bang," he said.

chapter
eighteen

Everything glistened at Sleson's except the reputations of the customers.

It was a new jewelry store, about six blocks from the White House, and within corrupting distance of many of Washington's major law firms, lobbying houses and influence brokers. It was a wonderful location for a place that celebrated greed and glitz—the twin commandments of the nation's capital. The "gem consultants" at Sleson's—none dared call them salesmen—had a pool to bet on which customer would be indicted within the month, which would never pay her bills and which would fake a robbery to collect the insurance on her jewels. Large sums were won on these wagers. The gem consultants knew their customers.

"I'd like the inscription to read, 'To my closest friend, Sarah, forever and ever.'"

"Very lovely, madam," Mr. Hans told Ramy as he carefully wrote the inscription on an order form. Lying next to the form, its case glistening in one of the special lights that beamed down from the ceiling to highlight the overpriced merchandise, was a gold bracelet billed at $2,450, giving Sleson's a sixty percent profit. Ramy had bought it for Sarah—because Bret had asked her to. It was all part of the plan, all part of the meticulous detail that would reach fruition in six days. The cost was insignificant. After all, Ramy reasoned, Shel would never live to see the American Express bill.

"Do you think there are too many words for the size of the piece?" she asked Mr. Hans.

Mr. Hans didn't look at the bracelet. He looked over Ramy's left shoulder at another customer entering the shop. Sleson's "gem consultants" were trained to show mild indifference to customers, never to make eye contact, always to act as if someone else in the shop were richer, or higher up the social scale, or more powerful. Pierre Sleson had taught, "Ignore them. They love it. It makes them want us more." He also knew his customers.

"No, madam, I think the inscription should fit in a most tasteful manner," Mr. Hans said. His name wasn't Mr. Hans. It was Irving, and he was from Brooklyn. But Pierre Sleson knew the customers liked salesmen with European names. It was worth another fifteen percent. Pierre had gotten his start as a Mercedes-Benz salesman.

"It's so special," Ramy told Mr. Hans, again at Bret's instruction. "I was married with this woman at a double wedding twenty years ago. We're renewing our vows."

"How very moving, madam," Mr. Hans said, now looking over her other shoulder. "Would you like this delivered personally?"

"No, I'd better pick it up. Tomorrow please."

"Of course."

"I don't care for this box."

"Madam will be given a selection of wraps when the item is ready."

"Oh, good. Sarah likes red."

"A red wrap it will be," Mr. Hans said, recalling that he had an extra red box in his desk drawer in the rear. It was from a birthday gift someone had given him.

Ramy left the shop, feeling the thrill of participation in a great enterprise. She still didn't know exactly why Bret had insisted that she have an expensive gift for Sarah, but he promised to go over the entire plan with her before the magic day. The logic, though, really didn't interest her that much. Hers was not to reason why. Hers was but to do and kill. She drove away from her parking space, her heart beginning to pound. In less than thirty minutes she would meet Bret—her first time with him since the dull anniversary dinner. Now they would be alone, if only to talk and to dream and to plan. Soon their path to freedom would begin. How could she know that her husband had just told a psychologist he'd put a bullet through his brain if she ever left him?

The point was moot at any rate. According to the plan, Ramy knew, *he* would be leaving her. And the bang would be bigger.

"Four ounces of this will throw a car several feet into the air and make it unrecognizable," Bret said. "I'm using only three. It's more than adequate and makes a smaller package. Very neat and clean."

He and Ramy were sitting in his car—the very car they planned to make unrecognizable—on the circular road surrounding the Jefferson Memorial. Bret always liked to pick tourist spots for his liaisons with Ramy, reasoning they'd never run into friends there. Washingtonians don't generally visit the Jefferson Memorial.

"It's so tiny," Ramy commented, gazing down at a black metal Mag-Lite flashlight, into which Bret had stuffed the makings of a remote-controlled bomb.

"That's the beauty," he said. "And with remote control, you don't have to hook anything up."

"*I* don't have to what?"

"You don't have to hook it up."

The western sun glared in Bret's driver-side window, making it hard for Ramy to look at him directly. But now she tried, taken aback by what he had said. "Me?"

"I thought we'd gone over this," Bret said.

"You said I would participate. I'd have a role. Look, I'm not a professional killer."

"Ramy, all I'll ask you to do is plant the device," Bret said. "That's it. You won't even see it go off."

She thought for a moment. Maybe she'd just blanked that out. Yes, that's pretty much what he'd told her before, but it was still hard to accept when he said it so starkly. "I understand," she finally said.

"At a set time after the ceremony, you'll inform Shel that you're going out to my car. You'll tell him you're going to put the bracelet for Sarah on the front seat, just the way you put her surprise gift on the front seat of our car every year. He'd never question that. Then you'll go out to the car. In your purse will be the bracelet and this little flashlight. You will actually put the bracelet on the seat. The flashlight will be wrapped in ordinary tissue paper so it can't be traced through fingerprints or fibers. You'll place the flashlight in the console between the two front seats.

"You'll return. You'll mention to Shell that you want to lure Sarah back to her car that night—even though we're staying over at the motel. You'll say you want her to find her gift. Suggest he get together with her and go out for some late junk snacks. God, we've done that before. I'm sure she'll agree. I'll urge her to. She may even suspect there's a gift waiting. They'll go out together. They'll get into the car. I'll be watching from a window. A small flip of a switch ...."

"I hope the window doesn't blow back and scratch you," Ramy said, with obvious concern.

"I've considered that." "I know where to stand."

"And you're sure it will do the job?" Ramy asked.

"The device will be between them in the console. It will strike both of them with the same force. It's an equal opportunity bomb."

"Bret," Ramy said, almost with passion, "you are always so thorough."

"It'll take more thoroughness than this," Bret said, virtually ignoring the compliment. "Our role isn't over when the device explodes. You're going to have to do some great acting. Your husband's been killed. You'll have to become hysterical, completely irrational. Don't try to make logical statements or speak in full sentences. Anyone acting rational in a situation like that invites suspicion."

"Shall I run to the car?"

"Yes. But understand ..."

"Understand what?"

"You may not want to get too close. It won't only be my Lincoln that'll be unrecognizable."

Ramy gulped. She'd understood this before, but, again, hearing the words brought home the reality. "I'll drop to my knees," she said. "Maybe pound the ground."

"That's good. And remember recollection."

"Recollection?"

"When people are hit by sudden grief they start recalling things out loud—like what they just did, how they were making a cake for the deceased, things like that. When you pound the ground remember to moan about how you just renewed your vows. Maybe even say something about Shel's plans for the future."

"Right," Ramy said, impressed, as always, by Bret's precision.

"Then go into a rage about who did this. Remember, you want to kill him, or them. And then . . ."

"I'd better write this down," Ramy said.

"Write nothing down. Memorize, even if we have to go over it ten times. Then, you'll realize Sarah is also dead. Rage about that. You can faint if you like."

"It'll probably happen anyway."

"Of course I'll do some shouting too, but most of my act will be stunned silence. I'll rush to your side. We'll comfort each other."

"I don't want to talk to reporters," Ramy said, "especially with tears running down my face. I'll look awful."

"You won't have to talk to anyone. I'll see to that. It won't be long before they'll start tossing out all kinds of theories about terrorism. The focus will switch to me. They'll never find out the truth."

"I have some thoughts about the funerals," Ramy said. "There are things Shel feels strongly about, and I want to honor them. It'll look right."

"We'll talk about that later," Bret replied. "Whatever you do, don't act as if you'd been thinking about funeral arrangements. Act confused. That's the way innocent people act—even days after."

"All right. But Shel wants music coming from his grave. One of those electric machines. I'm sure we can get it fast."

"Off the shelf," Bret assured her.

Ramy sighed deeply. "I'm beginning to feel it's actually real. I'm beginning to feel it all come together."

"It'll all be over in less than a week," Bret said. "Everything we've dreamed of, everything we've planned will come true."

"I just have one question," Ramy told him, now shielding her eyes so the sun didn't strain them.

"What's that?"

"It's been bothering me. I mean, I want to do everything for you—for us—that we talked about. But you want me to plant the bomb in *your* car."

"Yes."

"But why can't it be planted there already? Why do I have to carry it around?"

"In other words," Bret replied, with complete calm, "you think I should plant it myself."

"I'm not trying to get out of anything, Bret. But isn't that more logical?"

"No," Bret said. "There are several things wrong with that. First of all, the car could be stolen from the motel lot. Or someone could discover the bomb and possibly use it on innocent people. Even worse, they could blackmail me. And, more important, *Sarah* could discover it. I want there to be minimal opportunity for that."

Ramy leaned over and kissed him. "I should have known not to challenge your judgment."

"I think you'll be challenging it periodically in the coming years," Bret said, smiling at Ramy like the groom-to-be that she saw beside her. "I never mind when it's coming from you."

Their planning session ended, Bret explained that he was taking the device back for safekeeping, but would pass it to Ramy the night of the double wedding. She was to leave room in her purse. It would all be easy. Quick and easy. Just the way Bret planned it.

Bret began to pull out, stopping his car to let a group of Japanese tourists pass. When the way was clear, Bret accelerated, driving Ramy back to her Mercedes, parked nearby.

In a way, even he had trouble accepting all that had happened, all that was planned. It was difficult even for him to accept that two marriages, so solidly made at the double wedding twenty years before, had fallen into such complete disrepair. He wanted out because he'd outgrown Sarah, even outgrown the feeling for her. Ramy wanted out because Shel was Shel.

Bret had always considered himself somewhat unlucky—cursed by enemies and doubters who hadn't promoted him and sponsored him quickly enough. It was a touch of paranoia, a sliver of the disease that had plagued his personality. Now, though, he felt his luck changing. Ramy's interest in him was pure gold. Having Tim Curran behind him on Capitol Hill was platinum. And having Alison Carver was gold mixed with platinum, surrounded by diamonds from Sleson's. Everything *was* falling into place. Luck changed.

It was the year of Bret Lewis.

PART TWO

PART TWO

chapter
nineteen

The day of the wedding was sunny and balmy—perfect for the occasion, Sarah thought. She was sitting close to Bret in the Lincoln and fighting off any bad feelings about him, forcing herself into a high mood. Everything was in order—the green dress fresh from the cleaners, corsages packed in ice, the apartment alarm switched on. Bret hadn't let her pack his jacket and an extra shirt, but she understood. He was always particular, and maybe a bit edgy today. As they passed the landmark Shell station on the way to the Cheshire, he gave her hand a quick squeeze. A good sign, she thought. Maybe a very good sign.

Giving Sarah's hand that squeeze, Bret hoped his damp palm wouldn't give him away. The sweat signaled that his subconscious understood the chance of failure, but he didn't rate it very high. The plan was superb. The remote control was secure in the right pocket of his jacket. What he wanted now was Sarah's absolute trust, and absolutely no questions. For the last two weeks or so he had tried to be the model, loving husband. Now he wanted to prevent even a hint of nervousness that might give her a clue. This was a matter of pride. Professional pride. The father who had driven him from music and toward the more secure anchors of life would have been proud.

It was 7:33 P.M. as they approached the Cheshire. In ninety minutes, Bret knew, it would all be over. He would be going home in someone else's car.

But just as he was changing lanes to enter the motel's parking lot, a blue Toyota cut him off. For a moment Bret almost lost it, cursing at the other driver. When the brief incident was over he was angrier at himself than at the other guy, realizing he'd behaved like anyone with a new car who didn't want the paint scratched. He calmed himself, with an assist from Sarah's gentle pat on his right arm. He pulled into the lot, then turned to her, forcing a smile. Poor Sarah, he thought. It really was a shame.

But he admitted to himself that he regretted only one thing: Damn, he sure would miss the Lincoln.

Just then he caught sight of Shel in his rearview mirror, speeding into the lot, the SJ1 license plate, in gold frame, glistening at the front of the dark blue BMW 750i. How Shel loved it when heads turned to watch that car swing by, Bret thought. Even now he could see Shel beaming as a few motel guests stared at the BMW, as if royalty were coming in. And Ramy? She may have hated Shel's obvious pride, but she didn't mind the car a bit, or the heads it turned, or the whispers of envy it provoked.

"Wonderful idea of yours," Sarah was saying. "Just wonderful." She tried to make some chatter, but her mind started drifting out of its high and back to reality. Bret had been so different recently, and she didn't think she was imagining it. What, though, was he thinking of now, as he maneuvered the Lincoln toward a parking space? Was it Alison? Or Ramy? Or both? And once again she started thinking of her own options. *Should* she confront him on this special night? Should she even hint at what she knew? She realized she wasn't going to do that. She was going to wait, to play it out, to see what happened. But now she fought to keep her mind from drifting into despair. She figuratively shook herself, reaching for that high again, and pulled a lipstick from her purse.

The fact was, and it might not have surprised Sarah, that Bret was thinking of all three women in his life—thinking, while Sarah accidentally jolted the mirror while retouching her lips, that she measured up to neither of the others. She had none of Ramy's flair, none of Alison's outgoing brilliance. But he too fought to banish these extraneous thoughts. This was a night for action, not assessment. He readjusted the mirror and watched as Shel piloted the BMW into a slot far away. Trust Ramy, he thought. *She* picked that space so the blast in the Lincoln wouldn't even scratch the BMW. She knew what the car was worth, and she'd get her price.

The Cheshire had only twenty-three rooms, all in two long, white-shingled buildings with flat roofs, set at a ninety-degree angle, with the meeting and party building at the center. A small office unit was separate, and there was, as the moving sign said in flashing red, "ample parking for parties, weddings, lectures . . ." Only twelve rooms were occupied, but lights were kept on in most of the others to give the appearance of a prosperity that had long vanished. Some of the registered guests were doing business with the Pentagon. Others were visiting relatives in Arlington. Two more were spies, watched from still another room by FBI agents. And there were the usual one-night stands, which often made the difference between profit and loss.

Ramy darted out of her car, heading toward the Lewises. "This is eerie," she almost purred, hugging Sarah. "Just like twenty years ago." Sarah fought to stay in the mood, to stay in character, giving Ramy an extra squeeze. Suddenly both couples were talking and laughing at once, as if this were all real, as if stomachs weren't convulsing with tension. "The same green roof," Shel said. "Yeah, and still peeling paint," Bret added. "Didn't you try to climb it in the rain?"

"Me?" Shel asked. "I probably hired someone to climb."

"Do we have the same room?" Sarah asked.

"Surprise, surprise," Bret replied. He smoothly pulled a large key from his pants pocket and dangled it in front of Sarah. The tag with the punched "8" swung back and forth with a metallic clinking. "Care to join me?" he asked.

"I'll consider it," Sarah laughed. "Naturally, you thought of every-thing."

Ramy prayed that it was true. Had Bret left anything out? Had he screwed up anywhere? Was he as superb a planner as he advertised? Ramy knew that her whole future depended on the answers. And her role? That, she knew, depended on how well Bret had briefed her, and how well her tranquilizers worked.

"Why don't we go inside," Bret suggested. So they went to their rooms, just as they had that night twenty years before when feelings were so different, when all the world was theirs and they'd pledged themselves to a lifetime together. Now Bret Lewis carried in his suitcase a small, powerful bomb. And, as he unlocked the door to the first room he and Sarah ever slept in together, his heart pounded—not with passion, but with the anticipation of the horror that would soon engulf them all.

"It has the same smell," Sarah said.

"All motels smell the same," Bret answered. "That's what you're remembering."

They both looked around, smiling now. It was all so familiar, as if the years had been crushed into seconds. The small room, the double bed, one easy chair, the suitcase rack and faded wallpaper with Virginia scenes.

"It looks like they haven't changed a thing," Sarah said.

"It's probably replacement stuff," Bret replied, "but they kept the same colors." He moved to put his arm around her. "Remember, we couldn't get the TV to work?"

"Yeah. I was glad," Sarah recalled. She giggled. And Sarah *never* giggled.

"And it rained. It poured that night. We all went out late to try to get some snacks. All we got was drenched."

"Just a second," Sarah said. She walked into the bathroom. "In here," she called.

Bret dropped the two suitcases on the bed and joined her. "What did you discover?"

"Take a look." She pointed to a crack in the right bottom corner of the mirror over the sink.

"It's still there," Bret said. "They've really got a sharp crew. Want me to complain?"

"Oh come on."

"No, I'll say I complained twenty years ago and I'd like it fixed by, say, the year 2000."

"This time leave a tip," Sarah needled.

Bret glanced at a clock on one night table. A little more than an hour. He could already hear the screaming sirens, the panic, the weeping.

They started to unpack for their single-night stay. As he opened his black cloth bag, Bret pulled out a small vinyl business case that he often carried on trips. "Uh, this reminds me," he said. "I've got a list of things for the party. I'll just go over and check to see that everything's here."

"I'll go with you," Sarah said.

"No, why don't you stay. Just relax. I may have to argue with the florist or someone."

Considerate, Sarah thought. He knew how she hated confrontations. God, if he *only* knew.

It was the story of their marriage, Ramy was thinking. Shel didn't think to book their original room. No, he had to have the largest and most expensive suite in the motel—a corner unit with a separate den and a small kitchen. The color TV was a giant twenty-five-incher. There was even a little bar, which Shel had ordered fully stocked. Now, as Ramy poured two gin and tonics, watching him unpack, she steeled herself. Stay cool. In an hour it would all be over. Then, freedom. She squeezed the lime just as he liked it, and mixed the drink, offering it to him. But his head was deep in one of the Louis Vuitton bags and just muffled sounds emerged. Ramy set the drink on the bar. "You know," she said, "while you're doing that I'll check the party room."

"Why?"

"Well, you never know—things sometimes aren't right."

"Bret arranged it."

"Bret doesn't have the woman's touch. I'll be right back."

Shel's head was still in the $500 bag. He didn't challenge her.

Edging quickly out the door, Ramy hurried across the parking lot. The disappearing sun was casting a deep orange glow over everything. Cars were leaving as people went to dinner in Washington and the Virginia suburbs. Ramy could easily tell the one-night-standers. They were the smiling ones.

She entered the party building, a low, eight-sided structure with a brick interior. Right inside the door, waiting, was Bret. "Well timed," he told her. He looked around, making sure no one was watching them. Then, he reached into his business case and took out a small, black flashlight. Inside was the explosive and a detonator. Glued to the bottom of the flashlight, in a spiral, was a tiny wire antenna. Without a hint of emotion, Ramy took it and slipped it into the bottom of her bag.

"Done," she said.

"Remember," Bret said, "in the center console. Now, here's an extra key to my car."

"Why? Didn't you leave it unlocked?"

"Yes. But just in case Sarah goes back for something and locks it, you want to be ready."

"Thorough again," Ramy said.

"All right," Bret told her. "Let's go. Planning the renewal of our holy vows." He smiled. "Act one."

They both went into the main party room, whose inside reflected the eight-sided exterior. It was only twenty-seven feet across at any point, and the workmen hadn't yet removed the lectern from an afternoon slide show on how to profit from the coming East Coast earthquake. A chart on postquake real-estate bargains still hung. But the florist was already arranging the sparse bunches of carnations along the aisle, and not showing too much flair for the low-profit job. A workman was setting up folding chairs, many of them with rusting legs.

Taking a deep breath, Ramy approached him. "Could you pull these closer together and more toward the front?" she asked, with exquisite politeness. "There won't be all that many guests." It wasn't that she cared. She was just doing her part for authenticity.

Across the room, a man from the local delicatessen was setting out the cold cuts and beer—the same bare-bones menu the two couples had served to close friends on their actual wedding night two decades earlier. Bret was bargaining with the man for just one-half a roast beef sandwich—just a half—since he was one of the grooms.

Grabbing his half sandwich, he moved to the parking lot window. Ramy called one last instruction to the florist and joined him. They stood for a moment, silent. Bret stared at his car. Pity. He'd taken such good care of it. He placed his hand in his right pocket. Ramy caught the gesture. It was from this spot that he would detonate the explosive, changing their lives forever.

A chill came over Ramy, and she shuddered.

"What's wrong?" Bret whispered.

"I don't know. I have this rotten feeling that we won't be able to get those two in your car at the same time."

"Trust me," Bret assured her. "I told you how I planned it. It'll work. And look, at a party, with a few stiff drinks, people don't question. They really don't. Getting them into that car'll be easy."

"I trust you," Ramy replied. "Of course I do. But I'm getting the creeps."

"I know."

"It's starting to hit me. They'll be *dead*!"

"Very."

"Don't joke."

"Me? I'm not joking. This is necessary."

"I guess."

"It's no guess. It's God's truth." Bret loved that line. He thought it masterful to mix God with murder. Selected religious groups had been doing it for centuries.

"Excuse me. Mr. and Mrs. Lewis?"

Ramy jumped with a start.

"I'm Mr. Havalon, the manager. Is everything satisfactory?"

"Oh, uh, yes. Yes it is," Bret replied.

"I wanted to tell you," Havalon went on, "that the minister has arrived." He gestured toward a white-haired man across the room, hunched over in a folding chair, concentrating on a small black book.

"Oh, thank you," Bret said, and Havalon walked away.

"Just calm down. Cool it," Bret whispered to Ramy as he grasped her arm, guiding her across the room. "Mr. and Mrs. Lewis didn't sound that bad." They approached the minister, Bret noting the man's quivering hands.

"Uh, Dr. Clifton?"

Clifton turned around. "Yes?"

"I'm Bret Lewis."

"Who?"

"Lewis. Bret Lewis. And this is Ramy Jordan. You married us twenty years ago, sir. You're going to do it again tonight."

"Oh? Oh, yes. Brian Lewis."

"That's good enough, sir."

"And this is your bride."

Again the chill shot up Ramy's spine. Another endorsement by the Lord. Bret suppressed a laugh. "No, this is Shel's bride. We're just looking over the place."

"Oh, right. Yes, I remember you both. You were a lovely couple."

"Well, thank you, Doctor," Bret said. "We appreciate your coming."

"Oh, I appreciate *your* coming," the minister said. "It's very nice of you to remember God."

"Yes, sir. We'll, uh, let you read now."

"Sure. Don't be late."

Bret and Ramy awkwardly made their good-byes and walked away. "Jesus," Ramy said, "can he do it?"

"He's ninety-one," Bret replied. "Actually, he was pretty coherent when I called him. And he did get here. Yeah, I think once he gets revved up it'll be okay. These preachers go on automatic."

"I don't want him doing the funeral," Ramy muttered.

Sarah had just moved to the window, checking her dress in the fading sunlight, when she spotted them. Bret and Ramy—rather close as they edged out the main exit. Maybe it was just coincidence. On the other hand, maybe not. Now they were crossing the motel lot, and Sarah thought she saw Bret glance in her direction. Then, nonchalantly, as if it didn't matter at all, he raised a hand in casual good-bye to Ramy and made his way back to Sarah. Would he guess that she'd seen him, Sarah wondered? What would he say?

The door swung open. "Funny, Ramy had the same idea I did," Bret said as he walked in. "Just wanted to see how things were coming along."

"Shel's paying the tab," Sarah replied, brushing some lint off her dress. "You'd think *he'd* go out and inspect."

"Ramy said he was getting dressed. He'll take a look later. You know Shel. He just *expects* things'll be done right, once he writes the check. Oh, by the way, the party room's the same as before. Major tacky. But we'll love it."

Sarah slipped the green dress quickly over her head. Bret moved closer to her and zipped up the back, smiling at her in the mirror. In that same mirror he saw the alarm clock the motel had provided. Even with the numbers reversed he knew it was about forty-five minutes. Then, victory.

Walking over to the bed, Bret peeled off his jacket and tossed it down, then started to unbutton his shirt and undo the French cuffs. As he did, Sarah went over to his jacket and reached into its left pocket.

"What are you looking for?" Bret asked, fighting a sudden panic. The remote control was in the right pocket.

"I wanted to go out for some air. I need the room key."

Bret realized that, instinctively, he'd placed that too in the right pocket. "I'll get it for you."

"Bret, please, I'm not . . ."

"I'm in the service mode tonight," he said, praying that his gift for quick lies would not fail him. He reached into the pocket, felt the remote and the key. Stupid to put that key there, he thought. First blunder. Disciplinary action required. He took the key and flipped it to Sarah. "Don't elope with someone else," he grinned.

Forty minutes. Forty minutes to the moment when Bret would press a button and send his car several feet into the air. Ramy watched the time just as she watched Shel pull on a red silk jacket. It symbolized his taste in everything, she thought, turning away.

Ramy had more subdued plans. The press would see her after the blast. There'd be news cameras. She'd be "grief-stricken." So, she wore as little makeup as possible. Light on the mascara so nothing would run. She had chosen a modest blue dress with a white carnation—the press loved to focus in on flowers after a tragedy. Her long hair was pulled back and fastened in a graceful chignon at the nape of her neck. She never could stand how women looked after a shock—with mussed hair frizzing over their heads and strands dropping into their eyes. If she had to put on a show, she'd do it with some style, something worthy of the future Mrs. Bret Lewis. She readjusted her carnation and now, smiling at Shel, pinned another in his lapel.

Shel hadn't realized it, but she'd set her VCR. If she was going to be on the news that night, she'd want a tape.

They were all in the parking lot again, exchanging brief hugs. Ramy had her arm tight around Sarah as they made their way toward the reception building. Then, they all fell strangely silent. There were no jokes, no nostalgic stories, no bland comments about the wedding ceremony coming off without a hitch. These were now four people with precise missions, lost in very strange thoughts.

They entered the party building. As might be expected, Shel was the first to break the silence. "Look at this joint," he exclaimed, waving his head from side to side as if he had just bought the place, his eyes taking in the flowers, the rows of battered chairs, the table with the cold cuts, now covered in green and orange cellophane, and a make-shift pulpit draped in velvet. "Does it bring back memories or does it bring back memories?"

"It brings back memories," Ramy replied. God, be civil to the man, she told herself. His heart didn't have that many corrupt beats left.

Bret saw Dr. Clifton dozing in a chair, his large-print Bible beside him. He decided not to wake him until just before the ceremony.

Shel and Sarah drifted off to one corner together, now greeting some of the invited guests, who were just arriving.

Bret stayed with Ramy. "Do you have them both?" he whispered to her.

"Yes," she whispered back. "The thing is in the bottom of my bag. Sarah's gift—the bracelet—is just above it." Then she gazed over at Sarah. Her eyes became watery.

"Stop that," Bret said.

"I can't help it. She's my friend. She never hurt *me*."

"She's done enough," Bret replied. "Stay strong."

Bret noticed that Sarah kept constantly turning to look at Ramy.

Tim Curran, invited by both Bret and Shel, drove up in his maroon Cadillac Fleetwood, an illegal gift from a car dealer. Shel wanted him at the ceremony—"one of my dearest friends in Congress"—because Curran held the key to a bill that would benefit one of Shel's major clients, a waste disposal company whose competitors seemed regularly to wind up in barrels in the company dumps. Bret also wanted Curran—as a witness to the events about to unfold. Curran would always be able to testify to Bret's upstanding, loving behavior after the tragedy. Maybe he'd put something into the Congressional Record about the character and courage of the assistant secretary of the Navy.

Curran paid an attendant to park his car, which was placed two slots away from Bret's. Too bad, Bret thought, as he watched the attendant spin the Fleetwood into the space. Curran would at least be in for new windows, maybe a paint job, even some blown tires. But Bret knew that the congressman from Ohio wouldn't be angry. He'd simply announce that he, too, had been a victim of terrorism and had escaped death by a matter of inches. It would play beautifully in Columbus.

"Congressman," Bret exclaimed, as the king of the mentors strolled in. Curran, as usual, was alone. He never took his wife anywhere, which was probably a blessing for the lady. Tim Curran would almost surely humiliate her by assessing every other woman present and pursuing those he fancied. Curran walked briskly over to Bret, his hand extended, a ready smile now automatically generated by political instinct alone. He wore a boring but correct blue suit, and an equally boring white shirt and red tie. In his part of Ohio, anything more adventurous would get the gossips going, and Curran had constituents visiting him all day. He'd once advised a young protégé that the Lord and polyester, taken in equal measure, were the twin rocks upon which a career in his district was built.

"Bret," Curran said warmly. "What an evenin'. What an idea. It reminds me of my own weddin' to my wonderful wife of thirty-six years, bless her."

"Congressman, I appreciate your coming," Bret replied. Curran had not yet granted him the honor of first-name address.

"Wouldn't miss it. Canceled a dinner with the Egyptian ambassador to be here." Lie.

Sarah, spotting Curran, now walked over to join them.

"Unfortunately, the missus sends regrets," Curran went on. "She wanted mightily to be here, but she's a bit under the weather."

"I'm sorry," Bret replied, knowing the missus had probably never been told of the party. "Please send my regards. Oh, you know my wife, Sarah."

Now Curran gazed at the woman he'd trashed some months before, the woman who, he'd warned Bret, had become a political liability for her lack of social graces. "Do I know Sarah? I've had a distant crush on this lady since the first moment I laid eyes on her."

Sarah was startled. She knew all about Curran's cheating, and could even estimate the number of notches he had on his pistol, but had to admit she enjoyed the compliment of a man who, after all, knew women. "Why, thank you, Mr. Curran," she said.

"You are a perfect team. Now Sandy—Sarah—I'll tell you now what I've told hubby here, and what a night to say it. You two are goin' far. People talk about you. They admire you. You must tell me sometime all about your work at the museum. I love fliers."

"I don't actually fly," Sarah replied, violating Washington's first commandment: Never correct the powerful.

"Oh, I see," Curran said. He shot a glance at Bret, who winced on cue. "Well," Curran continued, not missing a beat, "I'm sure it's a fascinatin' place. I send my constituents there. The kids love it. They see John Glenn's capsule, and I know Glenn personally. He's from my state, don't you know. Not an excitin' man personally, but he represents the right values. I think that's awfully important for the kids."

"Absolutely," Sarah agreed.

"Ever have a party for him over at the museum, with his capsule and some kids from Ohio?"

"No, I don't think so."

"Plannin' one?"

"I don't think it's on the agenda, Congressman," Sarah replied.

"Well, it could be interestin'." Another glance at Bret. Double wedding or no double wedding, Timothy Curran always got his point across. Any sharp Washington woman would have known he was issuing a direct order. Any woman with ambition would have immediately promised to get that party on, to fight for it, to go to the wall for a John Glenn celebration in which Curran would be prominently featured, introducing Glenn to a middle-aged, adoring group who remembered his orbital flight in 1962. But Sarah simply hadn't caught on.

Curious, Curran thought, as he started looking around the room to see if anyone else was worth talking to—why this renewal of vows?

It had crossed his mind before, of course. Maybe it was just a ritual, something Sarah had thought up. Maybe Bret had felt he had to go along to avoid a premature rift with his wife. Curran hadn't asked Bret about it. That might be perceived as too much probing, too personal even for the mentor to ask. But he just couldn't put it together—what Bret Lewis was doing with this woman, why he hung in with her.

"I think we're about to begin, Congressman," Sarah said, glancing up at the cracked clockface on the wall.

"I'm sure it will be very moving," Curran replied. The whole thing was bizarre, he thought. Maybe Bret really loved her. Maybe he was one of those who couldn't break away because of some romantic notion about love. Grave error, he thought. Love was a political inconvenience.

But Curran had been had. Even the most cunning, skeptical mind on the Hill had not figured it was all part of a plan. Tim Curran had been used before, but he'd always known when, and for what purpose, and what to expect in return. Now, even *he* was being led around. Bret, eyeing him, sensed how he'd outdone even the great Curran, and allowed himself a small smile. A modest smile, yes, but a hint of triumphs to come.

chapter
twenty

It was eight-thirty.

The fourteen guests were in their places, Tim Curran right up front. "Always be up front," he'd taught Bret. "The row you're in equals your importance, even in a cemetery."

It didn't feel like a real wedding, which it wasn't. The guests, all of them in plain business suits or dresses, joked with each other just before the ceremony was to begin. A few exchanged business cards. All of them saw this as a sentimental social occasion, not anything particularly solemn. A few thought the whole thing was hokey, probably imposed on the Lewises by the less elegant Jordans. The cold cuts were still wrapped in cellophane, as they had been at the authentic wedding two decades earlier, but already the smell of corned beef filled the room, overpowering the carnations and even the one bottle of Air Wick that the management condescended to provide. There was an old upright Chickering piano at the rear, manned by someone Shel had hired. The pianist waited, shifting uncomfortably on the bench and checking his watch.

He'd been told not to play the wedding march. *That* would have been tacky in the extreme, Bret had thought. Although the event was simply a cover for his murder plot, why should his reputation for good taste suffer?

In the rear of the room, just outside the door, the two principal couples waited. Ramy carefully adjusted Shel's carnation, and Sarah pulled out a handkerchief, just in case. In Bret's right jacket pocket rested the detonator, placed with the button up, the correct position for the thumb. And in Ramy's bag—a bit large for the occasion, Sarah thought—was the explosive device and Sarah's anniversary bracelet. Ramy avoided Sarah's glance. She steeled herself, suppressing her earlier qualms and sentiments. Nothing would interfere with the plan.

"Any second now," Shel was saying.

"Yeah," Bret replied. "Anyone want out?"

There was some nervous laughter. Sarah glanced at Shel. She could see the tension in his puffy face, now lightly coated with perspiration. Poor Shel. With all his cash, what did he have?

"How's the Rev?" Shel asked.

Bret peeked through the door. Standing behind the makeshift pulpit was Dr. Clifton, and he looked remarkable. The man who had appeared almost terminal moments before was now standing erect, Bible before him, smiling at the guests, tapping one toe. "They changed his batteries," Bret said. "I think he's good for thirty hours unless you play him too loud."

He was trying to make jokes, Sarah mused. Men who had something to hide always made jokes.

The pianist started an uncertain rendition of a Vivaldi that Shel had suggested. "It's from that movie, *Kramer vs. Kramer*," Shel had said, demonstrating his mastery of the classics. The two couples started down the center aisle. They didn't march. They simply walked, the Lewises first, the Jordans second. Now, they all forced smiles onto their faces. Shel winked at a few guests, Bret even stopped to shake hands with a late arriver.

It wouldn't be long, Bret thought. He glanced around at the guests. He'd see them again at the funeral.

The Lewises and the Jordans reached the front, standing right before Dr. Clifton, who beamed like a proud father at the delivery of quadruplets. "Welcome, children," he said, his voice now firm, and utterly baritone.

And then . . . Bret couldn't believe it.

He watched, almost paralyzed, as he saw the strap on Ramy's large handbag begin to slip from her shoulder. He hesitated to move. Helping her might look suspicious.

The strap slipped farther and snapped down Ramy's arm. The bag fell to the floor. The whole room could hear the thud.

Someone in the back giggled. "What does she have in there, a bowling ball?"

"Sorry," Ramy whispered, addressing her apology to Dr. Clifton, avoiding Bret's eyes. Bret knew there was no danger of the bomb going off, but there *was* the chance that the thing had been damaged. Rotten break, he thought. She couldn't even hold the bag.

It wasn't a sure thing anymore.

He might press the button in his pocket . . . and nothing might happen.

This was the one hitch he hadn't anticipated. He would have to wait. He would have to sweat. It might go off. It might not.

Shel picked up the bag and handed it to Ramy, smiling. Ramy felt one speck of relief—Shel apparently hadn't noticed how heavy the bag was. She shot a quick glance in Bret's direction, a touch of guilt in her eyes. He avoided her.

"I think we can begin, children," Dr. Clifton said. But the minds of all four children were millions of miles away. They tuned in to Clifton only so they could follow his instructions.

"Ah," Clifton began, "love that is eternal. Love that is true. Love, in this turbulent time, that outlasts the years."

"Amen," Tim Curran said quietly.

"How often do we see love expressed this firmly?" Clifton asked. "Who cares?" Bret thought to himself. He kept eyeing Ramy's bag. Was there damage? If so, was there a way around it?

"For twenty years, Ramy and Sheldon, Sarah and Bret, have kept faith with their union . . ."

He could inspect the bomb before Ramy planted it, Bret thought. But where? How? There was too much chance of being seen.

"They come together again," Clifton went on, "to reaffirm with words what they have sealed with deeds."

He would just have to try it, Bret thought. If it didn't work, he'd have to improvise a second chance. But the murder *had* to happen.

"I have no doubt," Clifton said, "that here are people who would lay down their lives for each other."

"We would," Ramy whispered.

"A renewal of vows can take many forms," Clifton said. "Sometimes the loving couples write their own. Sometimes they repeat the words they spoke at their original joining. Sometimes they ask a member of the family, or a close friend, to write something for them. Sometimes . . ."

The guy is a long-distance runner, Bret thought. He hadn't remembered him that way, but Clifton seemed determined to hold the stage for the full three acts.

"Sometimes, we clergy simply do what we think is appropriate."

Bret could do nothing now but hope. He'd built the bomb strongly. The flashlight he'd used as a case was made of aircraft-strength aluminum. The manufacturer had advertised that you could drive a car over it. The brochure never said a word about usefulness in homicide plots.

". . . and so this is a rejoining," Clifton went on, his voice melting into a drone. He was well retired, but relished coming out for these last few opportunities in the sun, these moments where he stood before a captive audience, pretending to be the source of all wisdom and the appointed interpreter of God's word.

But suddenly Clifton stopped. He cleared his throat and stared directly at Bret, who, distracted, had begun to shift around, taking attention away from the minister. A man of the old school, Clifton believed he had a Divine right to stardom. Bret immediately fell still once more.

And the service continued. A few guests started glancing at their gold watches, sparkling below the overhead flush spots that lit the room. Finally, Clifton reached the key moment. "And so do you, Sheldon, once more take Ramy to be your lawfully wedded wife, to honor and to cherish . . ."

"Oh, I sure do," Shel replied, looking over at Ramy and beaming as broadly as the circumstances allowed. She smiled back, but her eyes maneuvered to avoid his. She couldn't bear to look directly at a man she would help murder within minutes.

"And do you, Ramy, once more take Sheldon to be your lawfully wedded husband, to honor and to cherish, in sickness and in health . . ."

Hell of a phrase, Ramy thought. Of course . . . he really wouldn't be sick. She tried to smile as Clifton went on with his question. ". . . and do you pledge this as long as you both shall live?"

Heavy, Ramy thought. She forgot to answer.

"Do you?" Clifton asked, a slight annoyance audible in his otherwise pristine voice.

"Oh, yes, definitely yes." Now she glanced over to Shel and forced a full smile, again avoiding his soon-to-be fixed and dilated pupils. But, then, quickly, she looked over to Bret, who stood without expression, annoyed to see her seeking out his approval, like some schoolchild.

Clifton now turned to the Lewises, and he could not resist the temptation to elongate his performance with a personal note. "I served as a military chaplain in World War II," he recalled. "I was aboard combat ships in the Pacific from Guadalcanal through Okinawa. So I feel a special connection with anyone who serves our Navy. Now Bret, my sailor friend, do you once again take Sarah ..."

Bret, who'd never quite learned how to swim, forced a respectful expression. "I do," he answered, when the time came, and beamed at Sarah, turning toward her so all in the room could see. No one watching that performance could possibly doubt his sincerity, his utter devotion to his wife.

Now Sarah gazed intently into Bret's eyes. This was the look she had seen, or imagined she had seen, for most of their twenty years. It was the look of total commitment that this whole renewal of vows was all about. That look in his eyes was saying *something*, and Sarah hoped it was saying that the extra-curriculars were over, that Ramy would be just a friend again, that Alison Carver would meet Bret Lewis only under oath.

Sarah's eyes drifted to Ramy. She still couldn't hate her. If there had been an affair, it surely had been Bret's doing. Despite what Shel had revealed about his wife's infidelity, Sarah couldn't believe Ramy would initiate anything but a redecorating job.

"Ah, and you, Sarah," Clifton went on. "Do you once again take Bret ..."

Sarah heard just the beginning of the question, then swayed on her feet, lightheaded. Could all this be real?

"Do you promise to cherish him in sickness and in health ..."

Sarah felt like asking Clifton if that included mental sickness, emotional health.

"... as long as you both shall live?"

"I do," Sarah said firmly, turning toward Bret and smiling.

Clifton beamed broadly, every wrinkle in his ancient face issuing forth in triplicate. "Well," he said, "I can't really pronounce you men and wives because that, as I believe the insurance men say, is a pre-existing condition. You know, we ministers had a difficult time deciding just what to say at this point in the ceremony. So I'll go with my own choice. I now pronounce your marriage resanctified, not only by the will of God, but by your own action and inner truth. You didn't need this ceremony to prove your devotion to each other . . ."

"C'mon," Bret thought to himself. "Hurry up."

". . . Anyone just watching all four of you would know that here, before us, are two perfect marriages. And yet, I'm glad you came before me today, for you serve as an example of what 'holy matrimony' really means."

"Maybe he *would* be good for the funeral," Ramy thought.

". . . And I stress the word 'example.' Everyone in this assemblage, everyone who knows you and knows of you, will be inspired by what you have done. To see two couples whose thoughts are so pure, whose intentions are so honorable, who are free of the evil and conniving and Godlessness we observe around us—that is a religious privilege in these painful times. Bless you, children. The service is concluded. Refreshments in the rear."

Now, with a great flourish, the pianist began the recessional. The Lewises and the Jordans congratulated each other, all gushing with sincerity, and thanked Dr. Clifton. Bret helped the minister down from the platform and back to a seat. "Thank you, bless you," Clifton said, in a voice suddenly weaker and unsteady, as if someone had pulled the Divine plug. "I enjoyed that, Jeff," he said, and Bret did not correct him. "Do you have my address?" Clifton asked.

"Yes, sir, I wrote it down."

"Send the check there."

"It'll be in the mail."

"Certified."

Bret hardly heard the instruction. His mind focused on what was ahead on this, the most decisive night of his life. Now he rejoined Sarah and the Jordans as they turned from the pulpit and walked halfway up the aisle, stopping to shake hands once more with their friends. Tim Curran rose to pat Bret on the back. "Real movin'," he said. "How about those vows." He barely acknowledged Sarah. In the kingdom of his personal God there weren't many blessings for women who couldn't throw a great party.

Now the guests pressed around the four born-again marrieds, and the small party began. Bret had rehearsed this part, too. He had stood in front of his bathroom mirror before every shower and practiced the greetings, the small talk. Now his mind was racing with thoughts of the next step. He tried for a moment to suppress the new frightening reality that the bomb might not go off because of Ramy's negligence. That was in the hands of the same God that had presumably just sanctified his remarriage. And so he began easing toward the row of windows that faced out on the parking lot. He could see his car clearly. He'd been concerned that someone would park so close that Ramy wouldn't be able to get the driver's door open, but he now saw that his fear was groundless. He'd also been concerned that some guests might hang out in the lot, but that too proved a false worry.

Not much time left, he thought.

Soon he would know if freedom would ultimately be his, if his life would indeed change.

"Hello, Sid," he said to Sidney Nelson, an assistant secretary of Interior, whom he'd known since college. "Thanks for being here."

"I love it," Nelson said. "Almost makes me wish I were married. But right now I'm going for the ham."

Bret eyed Ramy. By prearrangement, they weren't to talk with one another, except in a large group. Bret didn't want any guests recalling a conversation that could be pictured as conspiratorial.

"Meryl," Bret exclaimed, coming face to face with one of Sarah's friends from Air and Space, a rather striking woman in her thirties. "How've you been? Sarah always talks about the lunches you two have, but I never see you."

"You're seeing me," Meryl replied, "in living color and 3-D. You know, I almost cried at this ceremony. Of course, divorced women cry at a lot of things."

"Any prospects?" Bret asked. "Maybe I shouldn't have asked that."

"Perfectly okay. No, Superman hasn't flown into the museum just yet. I'm not sure he ever will."

"I just have an inkling things are going to improve for you," Bret told her, watching with some annoyance as one of Shel's guests pulled a chair to precisely the spot where he'd planned to stand when detonating the bomb. "Open to applicants?"

"Who isn't?"

"Sid Nelson's here, from Interior. Is an introduction in order?"

"Sure. I'll even supply a videotape and college board scores. But let me meet him a little later. I don't want to seem like I'm working the room, which I am."

Bret laughed, utterly uninterested. There'd be no introduction later. Later would be terror.

Bret watched as Ramy eased over to Shel, who was telling Tim Curran and a Washington lawyer about his new deal, representing a missile maker. Bret moved closer, pretending to get himself a sandwich, but trying to overhear precisely what was being said.

"Hello, all," Ramy was saying.

"Love, you know Tim Curran, distinguished congressman from the Buckeye State," Shel gushed. "And Wendell Morton of Ethridge and Morton."

"Of course I know these gentlemen," Ramy replied, directing a dazzling smile at Curran. God, Bret thought, the woman could turn it on, unlike Sarah, who had nothing to turn on.

"I've had a crush on this lady for longer than I care to remember," Curran said to Ramy. Now that was a slip for him, Bret realized. There was a time when he'd never use the same line twice at a party.

"Congressman, you've made a friend for life," Ramy replied. Bret focused on her handbag, which she now held tightly by the strap, making sure it didn't have a chance to slip off her shoulder. "Shel," she said, "I'm going out to Sarah's car."

"Sarah's? Why?"

"Guess."

"I can't."

"Sheldon, what do I do every year?"

Shel seemed to ponder for a moment, then started to laugh, as if embarrassed by his own slowness. "You know what she does?" he rhetorically asked the other two men. "She buys an anniversary gift for Sarah Lewis and leaves it on the front seat of her car."

"Real touchin'," Curran said, and the lawyer nodded, wondering when the business talk would begin.

"Of course," Shel quickly explained, "our gift for *both* the Lewises will be delivered. Can't leave a large-screen TV on the seat."

"Wonderful gift," Curran said. "I'd love a gift like that."

"I'll be right back," Ramy said.

"Make sure to lock their car doors," Shel reminded her.

"I will."

Bret felt his heart start to pound.

"And you know," Ramy said to Shel, as she started to leave, "after this shindig I've got a little job for you."

"Oh? You want to meet an ambassador, Ramy?" Shel winked at Curran and Morton.

"No, something a lot simpler. Remember the night of our real wedding, how you and Sarah went out and got snacks from some twenty-four-hour place? I think it was ice cream and pizza and some chips."

"Sure, I remember."

"Do it again," Ramy said, making it an order.

"Tonight?"

"Sure. We'd love it."

"Well," Shel replied, a bit embarrassed, "you sure you wouldn't want something a little more . . . elegant?"

"No, Sheldon. That wouldn't be half as romantic."

"Have you checked with Sarah?"

"No, but she'd think it's smashing."

Shel shrugged, raising his pudgy little hands as if the matter had been settled for him. "You've got it," he said. "Anything Ramy wants, Shel gives."

"See ya," Ramy said, now repeating Shel's wink at Curran and Morton, having let them know who the real power was. She started toward the door.

Bret watched Ramy, although he fought to look nonchalant. He saw her pause, look back at Shel, then at Sarah. By going out to that car, she knew, she was signing a death sentence for both of them.

Casually, Bret eased near the window he had previously selected. Shel's friend was still sitting there, shoveling most of a corned beef sandwich into his oversized mouth. Bret simply stood next to him.

He saw Ramy leave the building and walk out into the parking lot. She gripped the bag more tightly than ever.

Ramy didn't glance back. Bret had given her specific instructions not to. But she rehearsed in her mind how she would slip into the car from the driver's side, place Sarah's gift on the right front seat, lodged against the seat back, then place the bomb inside the console between the seats. The flashlight lens would be pointed up, exactly the way Bret normally kept it.

She walked further. Now she paused for a moment as a car rode by.

It was *happening*, Bret knew.

"Great beef," Shel's friend said.

"Yeah," Bret replied.

"You really had guts goin' through with this," the man continued, running an open handkerchief across his mouth.

"Thanks," Bret said.

"True love. What a crock. Y'know what I dish out in alimony each month?"

Ramy was almost there.

"No, I really don't."

"Take a stab."

"Thousand."

"Three. Three grand, and I only was married to her six months. What a crock."

"Yeah," Bret replied.

Ramy was at the car. She opened the driver door. She slipped inside.

"I like being single. But the three grand a month hurts. That's a baby Mercedes every year."

"Really a shame," Bret replied.

The car's interior light was on. Bret saw Ramy remove the gift from her bag and place it on the seat. Then, she returned to the bag. She took out the device, its lens glistening for a moment in the dim light. She opened the console.

"Nice party, though," the man said.

"I'm glad," Bret answered.

Ramy placed the bomb in the console.

Bret placed his hand in his right pocket.

He found the detonator.

"Dumb fool," he muttered to himself. "She bought the whole thing."

"Real blast," Shel's friend said.

Bret pressed the button.

chapter
twenty-one

The flash lit up the entire lot.

Then, in an instant came the deafening thud.

The sounds of shattering glass and shredding metal.

"Oh my God!" Bret shouted, spinning from the window to shield himself. But in that fraction of a second he saw the driver's door blow off his Lincoln. He saw the car's insides turn to fire. He saw the side and rear windows fly out in slivers.

He did not see Ramy. He didn't have to.

He heard the screams and gasps in the room.

His first thought: It worked. Well made. Well constructed.

And his second: His fears about glass coming back and cutting him had been exaggerated. The car contained most of the blast. The motel windows rattled, one cracked. None shattered.

Then, the room fell silent.

The lights suddenly went out—an overhead line snapped by the explosion.

"Jesus," someone muttered. "What happened?"

"Sounded like a plane crash," another said.

"No, something blew up!"

Pushing, shouting, some shoved their way to the window.

The Lincoln was blazing.

"Our car!" It was Sarah. "Bret, it's our car!"

Now a voice. "Ramy!" It was Shel. Again, with an impassioned shriek. "Ramy! Oh God, Ramy!" He started charging toward the door.

Bret rushed to him, stopped him. "Shel, calm down. Let's find out ..."

"Let me go! Let me go! She went to your car! A present! She left a present for Sarah!" Everyone could hear him. Sarah's face froze in shock. No. No, it wasn't possible that Ramy had been inside that car.

A low murmur began. In the near darkness, the room lit only by the shuddering orange of the blazing car, people stared at Shel, his face twisted and knotted with anguish. "Ramy!"

"Maybe she's in your room!" Bret shouted, as Sarah rushed over and threw her arms around Shel, now lurching closer to the door. Bret made a dash outside. "I'll find her! I'll get her! It'll be okay!" He ran out.

"Don't get too close!" someone screamed. "The tank could go!"

Sirens. Someone in the main office had called the police right after the blast. In the distance, flashing lights.

Others rushed outside to help Bret. Shel stumbled out, slowed by his weight, pounding one hand against another. Sarah rushed out with him.

"Got to get to her," Shel gasped. "Got to." Sarah held him back, pulling him away from the inferno that lay before them.

Despite warnings, Bret leaped onto a car parked close to his Lincoln. He looked through his car's front window, his face exploding in anguish. Then he looked back at Shel. But he said nothing. All he did was hold his hands out. There seemed to be tears in his eyes.

"No," Shel said. "Oh no, no, no."

Bret jumped from the car and rushed to Shel, grasping him by the shoulders. "Don't look," he said. "There's no chance. Just don't look."

Sarah overheard. By now she was weeping. "Why?" she pleaded. "What happened? Did the car just explode?"

"A bomb," Bret replied. "The car was rigged." And then, following the script he had rehearsed so many times, he backed up, leaning against the nearest car. "*I* was the target!" he shouted. "They wanted to kill *me*! Poor Ramy. Why her?" He slammed a fist against the trunk of the car. Guests tried to restrain him, but he raged on. Oscars have been won with less.

By now Shel was just sitting on the pavement, his hands covering his face. He was saying something, and repeating his wife's name over and over, but no one really heard. Everyone was still stunned, shocked. Nothing had sunk in. Time was frozen.

There was no way to approach the car. No way to pull anything out. The motel owner had rushed outside with a large, red fire extinguisher, but just stood helpless, watching the Lincoln as its black paint began to peel back, revealing the bare metal underneath. The gas tank had not exploded, nor would it. Anticipating the possibility, Bret had come to the motel with the gauge near empty.

Fire engines chugged into the parking lot, followed by a chief's car. Shel charged up to one of the firemen. "My wife is in there!" he cried. "She's in there, but she's dead, she's *dead!*" It didn't take long for the fireman to confirm that for himself. Sarah moved to Shel, her hand pressing his arm, edging him off alone.

Bret still leaned against that car, but now he watched as the firemen started working. Before they could even get their equipment out, though, a figure rushed up from behind him and slapped his hand on his shoulder. Bret, his eyes reddened from dabbing them with a mild detergent he'd packed in his handkerchief, turned. It was Tim Curran.

"Congressman, what a horrible . . ."

"I know, I know, Bret," Curran said. "It's awful. The woman was just remarried. The people who do these things—sick, criminals. But Bret, take my advice. The press'll be here. The TV. That bomb was meant for you."

"This is no way to be a hero," Bret muttered.

"You miss the point. They're vultures. No reporter ever got famous by coverin' an important story. They get famous by coverin' a spectacular one."

"What are you saying?"

"Dead woman. A government official who's alive and she's dead."

"You're not thinking they'll pin it on me . . ."

"No, but they'll want to know what you were up to. What did you do to draw a bomb?"

"I'm an antiterrorist officer," Bret said.

"You know it. I know it. But some of those boys'll make you the next Ollie North, and it won't be a compliment. Count on it. Be ready,

Bret. There'll be questions. Tell 'em you've simply been doin' routine work. Not directed at anyone. This shows how reckless these animals can be. An innocent woman dies because these bums have got some cause. Mention Iran and Syria. They eat it up. And try to focus on Ramy. Be human. Give her a eulogy."

Damned good advice, Bret thought.

chapter
twenty-two

It was Bret and Sarah's apartment. The time was twelve fifty-seven the next morning. Bret had insisted that Shel spend the night there, with his closest friends, in his seemingly insurmountable grief. Bret had disconnected three of the four phones, leaving only the one in the kitchen—explaining that he didn't want the shrill ring to disturb Shel. The District of Columbia police had posted a guard at the apartment door and one in the lobby, fearing that whoever had gone after Bret Lewis might try again. The FBI had already quizzed Bret because of the possible terrorist connection, and American embassies in countries with hostile governments had been alerted to the possibility of an international plot. Four funeral parlors had already called, one offering prerecorded eulogies to "our dear friend" by forgotten stars of stage and screen.

The apartment was hot. They had arrived only fifteen minutes earlier, after spending hours with the police, and after Shel had identified his wife's watch and necklace at the morgue—the only dignified way he'd had of identifying what had been Ramy. The air conditioning was just taking effect, supplying background hum that seemed much louder to anyone in shock or grief.

"I want to watch," Bret was saying. "I want to make sure they're treating Ramy right."

Bret, Shel and Sarah were in the living room, Sarah with her arm around Shel, still trying to console him. All of them had grime and cooled cinders on their faces and clothes, and their hair was disheveled and filled with dust from the explosion's aftermath. What Bret wanted to watch was a 1:00 A.M. local newscast, and what he really wanted to see was how *he* was portrayed. Ramy's reputation was entirely irrelevant. In fact, she was hardly in his thoughts at all, and would be banished from his memory by morning, except when he needed to say the appropriate things to the necessary people in a moving and convincing way.

"Yeah. Maybe you'd better watch," Shel said.

Bret excused himself and walked slowly into the bedroom, his body tired and stooped. He snapped the black remote control to switch on his Mitsubishi television. Then he sat on the edge of his bed and waited while Ed McMahon explained some of the benefits of life insurance for the elderly.

In the living room, Shel was muttering as he sat next to Sarah, seemingly unable to come to grips with what had happened. But now, with Bret out of the room, his tense and strained words took on a new meaning. "I forgive her," he said to Sarah, words, Sarah knew, he could never speak in front of Bret. "I forgive whatever she was doing. I hope she hears me."

"She does," Sarah said.

"She was a decent person, a good wife. Maybe I was the problem, but what does it matter now." He laughed, bittersweet. "We'll never have to see Lorenzo Rosenthal again."

"No, I guess we won't."

"You know, I always told her how to act if I died suddenly. I said, 'Ramy, don't go to pieces. Just handle things and go on with your life.' I never thought I would have to do this. I mean, you just don't think of women dying suddenly. I can't figure that out, but it's true. It's always some fat guy keeling over from his heart."

"Maybe you should just rest, Shel," Sarah said.

"No, I like to talk it out. It's better for me, Sarah. If you don't mind."

"Of course not."

Then he paused and took a deep breath, letting it out with a wheeze. "So this is what it's like. A bomb. It could have been a car crash. Or a house fire. Or some other kind of accident. I guess you sit with friends, just like this. I mean, sudden death. Maybe I expected drums to roll or everyone to collapse. I guess it's like this."

"Yeah, it's like this," Sarah said.

"I want to know who did this."

"We all do. We all want to know."

But there was something else on Sarah's mind. Yes, Ramy's violent passing utterly stunned her, but her shock was blunted by a strange, indescribable numbness. After all, Ramy had been one of the other women. What would her death do to Bret? What effect would it have on their marriage? Sarah was strangled by a clutching guilt as it all raced through her mind. Something would now change, but she could not conceive of what it could be. Bret seemed completely grief-stricken by Ramy's murder, but beyond his grief he was impossible to read. It seemed sinful, Sarah thought as she tried to comfort Shel, that the death of her best friend had to he stained and violated by thoughts of Ramy's infidelity.

In a way, Sarah realized, her life was no less complicated than it had been ten hours earlier.

The faces on Bret's TV screen were all smiles as the news began. One male anchor, one female, with assorted specialists sitting off to the sides and in the rear. Bret hoped he would be the lead story, a distinction he'd never had in all his years in Washington.

He was.

"It came with a sudden flash and a deafening roar," the blow-dried male anchor began, his voice resonating through the bedroom. "An innocent woman, a possible terrorist plot." Ramy's picture flashed on the screen. "Washington hostess Ramy Jordan was killed instantly tonight by a car bomb in Arlington, Virginia." Then, on screen—the burning Lincoln, and firemen trying to put out the blaze. "Ironically, the wife of prominent lobbyist Sheldon Jordan had just repeated her wedding vows, some twenty years after . . ."

Bret tuned it out, allowing himself to hear every few sentences, as if fast forwarding and pausing on his VCR. He wanted only to know how he came off.

"The FBI was called in when terrorism was suspected, and an agent said the bomb was probably set off by remote control. The car belonged to Bret Lewis . . ."

Bret's ears perked.

". . . an assistant Navy secretary who has been identified with antiterrorist policy. Police speculate that the bomb was meant for him, possibly put there by someone retaliating against the United States."

Then, Bret on screen. Haggard, deep in sadness, his arm around Sarah, who stood by him. "I still can't believe it," he was saying. "This was one of our closest friends, a gentle, gracious lady. We were here for a ceremony that was holy to all of us. Whoever did this . . . we will track them to the ends of the earth."

"Do you feel it was meant for you?" a reporter asked.

"Well, no one would want to kill Ramy Jordan. Yes, it was meant for me."

A woman print reporter stepped forward, in full view of the TV cameras. "Mr. Secretary, are you involved in any secret missions that would provoke this?"

It was the Ollie North question. Tim Curran had called it. On the screen, Bret could see himself staring into the face of the reporter. He knew her as someone who believed all evil rested in Washington. "No," he replied. "There are no ongoing missions, just a constant watch on terrorist activities. As far as who did this . . . there've been stories in the press about Iranian students right here in Washington. There was that blast in Falls Church. I think they found Semtex traces, which is the kind of explosive used by these terrorist groups. And of course we know about the Syrians. And there's always Colonel Kaddafi."

"Do you have proof that any of them is involved?" the reporter asked.

"I'd rather not comment on that."

Good, Bret said to himself, as he watched the screen. He left them with a little mystery. Maybe he knew something. Maybe he didn't. He came off like the man at the center of the action, the gutsy guy who'd narrowly escaped death, and he was diverting attention away from Ramy. Fine performance, he thought—a real Curran performance—especially the part coming up: "Look, I've got to end now," he was telling reporters. "This woman had a wonderful husband and our place is with him." Patriot. Public servant. Family man. Good friend. It *would* be the year of Bret Lewis.

Bret was about to go back to Sarah and Shel when he saw another image flicker onto the screen. It was plainclothes investigators poring over his car after the fire was out. He watched the TV intently. He hoped they were good. He hoped they were thorough and professional, and driven. For those were the kind of investigators the remainder of his plan required. And if they didn't do the job, he'd make sure the authorities assigned people who would. They would find what they were supposed to find, what they had to find to make Bret Lewis's plan complete.

Bret returned to the living room. "So?" Shel asked. "What did they say?"

"It was handled very well."

"They didn't bring up my business?" Shel asked.

"There was nothing like that, Shel. There were nice things about Ramy."

"That's good. I want people to say nice things about my wife."

"We'll all miss her," Bret said.

Neither Shel nor Sarah answered that. Sarah wondered precisely what Bret had meant by the comment. What had been their last words together? And why had they gone through with that double wedding? Shaking the thought, she forced her attentions to Shel.

"I want to help," he was saying.

"Help?" Bret asked.

"With the investigation."

"Look, there are professionals ..."

"I want to help. I intend to."

"Shel, I'm not sure there's anything you can do. I was the target. It looks like a terror bomb. I mean, we can't be absolutely sure, but what else could it be? You just try to recover, try to get over the shock, maybe go away somewhere."

"No, I'll be here. I want to talk to the police. You know, maybe it was meant for Ramy."

"What?" Sarah asked.

"To get at me. I'm not loved. Sarah, I'm involved with some pretty tough people. You just wouldn't believe some of the ..."

"Shel," Bret asked, "how would they know Ramy was going to go to my car?"

Shel hesitated, then he shrugged. "Maybe they got our cars mixed up," he said.

"Not very convincing," Bret replied.

"Then let's figure out something that is. I'm on a manhunt, Bret. I'm on a goddamned absolute manhunt."

Sarah was sure she saw a smile in Bret's eye as Shel said that. She couldn't figure it. Was Bret ridiculing Shel? Was he thinking of his affair with Ramy? Was he uneasy with Shel's zeal?

Sarah stared at Bret, studied him. A sense of foreboding came over her. Suddenly, it seemed that the tragedy was not only the end of Ramy, but the start of something else, something even more sinister. She did not like that look in Bret's eye. He was a man of secrets, the eternal calculating man. What secrets, she wondered now, lay behind that strange little twinkle?

chapter
twenty-three

"I can truly say that I loved her. It's not an exaggeration. It's not something I say simply because she's gone. It was true. People who knew Ramy long enough all loved her. Everyone here knows of her warmth, her generosity, her devotion to charity. Most important, everyone here knows her devotion to Shel, who is left only with beautiful memories."

Bret Lewis was standing at the pulpit of the modern chapel, a gray, raining sky intruding through the arched skylight, the chapel's red brick walls almost covered with flowers and wreaths. The 200-seat auditorium was filled to capacity, with a small group standing at the rear. An organist played softly in the background, and a choir, hired for the occasion by Shel, stood behind Bret in purple robes, holding psalm books. Ramy's coffin was in front of Bret and below him. It was solid oak, and on top lay a single rose, snipped from one of the gardens she carefully tended around her house.

As Bret spoke movingly of Ramy's devotion to Shel, he looked out and saw the nods. He knew, of course, that most of the people at the funeral hardly knew Ramy and therefore could not possibly know whether she was devoted or not. But they had to nod. At a funeral you nodded in the designated places. You could be burying a war criminal, but nodding was required by the rites of all religions.

Even Sarah nodded, although the muscles in her neck tightened when Bret spoke of Ramy's devotion to Shel. All she could think about was that tape Shel had brought her on that afternoon at the museum. How could Bret lie so blatantly at Ramy's funeral? But a funeral was the time for lies. Like nodding, lies were part of the ritual.

The place was packed with lawyers, congressmen, Defense Department purchasing agents, judges and assorted influence peddlers whom Shel had graced throughout his career. They came for Shel, not for Ramy, and, Bret knew, maybe five percent really cared. The rest kept eyeing the large roman-numeraled clock behind Bret, thoughtfully placed to tell unmournful mourners when the last good cry was about to begin. It was as close as Bret had seen to a funeral for a middle-management executive in organized crime. There were even policemen at the doors, although all clad in respectfully dark plainclothes.

"I recall when I first met Ramy more than twenty years ago," Bret went on. "I thought to myself that this was a first-class young woman, someone who could light up the world. Little did I know that her voice would be stilled at such a young age, and under such violent circumstances."

More nods. The heads were really going now, as the eyes watched that clock.

Bret glanced over to one of the TV newsmen who was taping the service for the evening news. He cleared his throat. "For Ramy," he continued, "especially for Ramy ... and for Shel ... we promise today to hunt down whoever did this to our friend, and to seek final justice. We promise that we will hunt them to the ends of time."

At this there was even a smattering of applause—a little out of place even at a Washington funeral, but useful both to Bret and the unmournful mourners nonetheless.

Bret spoke for a few more minutes, and then some more eulogies were read. Finally, at eleven-thirty, allowing guests time to get to their horse-trading lunches at Washington hotels, the service ended. Shel stood at the rear of the chapel and greeted each guest who came through. He knew maybe half. But all had a little remembrance of Ramy, a little anecdote they wanted to tell Shel, even if it were made up. Bret and Sarah stood by Shel, also greeting some of the possibly bereaved. There was a visitors' book—the most important ornament at a power funeral—so each guest could leave a written reminder that he cared enough to come and was available for business meetings once the deep sense of loss began to give way to more important things. "In memory of Ramy Jourdan," one guest wrote, not quite recalling the spelling of Ramy's last name. It was, of course, the thought that mattered, whatever that thought happened to be.

As the last guests were heading for the valet parking, Bret spotted a man leaning against a door, looking directly at him. He was about thirty-five, tall and muscular, with an utterly bald head and a well-trimmed, short beard. He looked like something off a Russian wrestling team, but, with that body-tight shirt and tapered trousers, he had an aura of the rugged, lonely American—a cross between Hulk Hogan and G. Gordon Liddy. Bret had never seen him before, and he didn't particularly care for the stern, beady look the visitor was throwing at him. Yet, the guy didn't budge.

Finally, Bret walked over, uncomfortable with the stare and wanting to put an end to it. "Did you want to see me?" he asked.

"Yes," the visitor replied.

"Well?"

"You are Mr. Lewis."

"Yes, you know that. My name is in the printed program. You saw me up there."

The guest finally smiled. "Just a routine question. No offense meant." Then, nonchalantly, he whipped out a badge, thrust it into Bret's face and slipped it back in his breast pocket. "My name's Kyle King. I'm assigned to this case."

"No one has a name like that," Bret said, thinking the guy was a little weird.

"You're right. Born Francis Lafayette Undermeyer, but I started in show business. Tap dancer. My agent gave me the name."

"I see. A tap dancer turned detective."

"Yes, sir. We all evolve."

Bret did not appear to be amused. "I thought all this was being handled by the FBI."

"They're helping. I'm homicide. There has to be a homicide investigation while the Bureau works on the terrorism angle. I know it's a bad time. But there's never really a good time, is there? You must be pretty broken up over this."

"The lady was a close personal friend."

"They say that in show business a lot."

"Excuse me?"

"Forget it, it's inside. Look, I don't like to butt in, but there are questions, and I know you'd like to catch the people who did this as much as we'd like to catch them for you."

"Look, uh, Mr . . ."

"Detective would be fine."

"Look, Detective, I'll be happy to give you all the time in the world, but we're on our way to the cemetery."

"I'll get them to hold the hearse," King replied, again with a smile. "Not to worry. We do these things without upsetting the loved ones. But I've got to talk to you now."

"Has something new developed?" Bret asked.

"No, but we'd like it to."

"Step outside," Bret said. He looked back and saw Shel and Sarah saying a few words to the choirmaster and the minister who had presided. He thought King's intrusion was rude and uncalled for, and he didn't much care for this tap dancer turned detective with the Hollywood name. King looked like a guy stuck in police work while waiting for a part in a revival of *Wonderful Town*. He was nothing like the modern, scientific cop Bret wanted assigned to the case. They stepped into the corridor, not far from where departing guests were exchanging business cards and signing the visitors' book.

"All right, what's this about?" Bret asked.

"We want to try to reconstruct this whole case, starting with the friendship between all of you."

"Why? Look, this is terrorism. I mean, a remote-controlled bomb. The FBI called me late last night and said the chemical composition was identical to that device in Falls Church. Why do you need our life story?"

"Mr. Lewis, I've got bosses."

"All right. I understand. I'm in a bureaucracy myself. We've all known each other more than twenty years."

"All?"

"The Lewises and the Jordans."

"You were in close contact during the entire period?"

"Yes, extremely close. If we were separated by distance, we spoke by phone. These were real friendships."

"Any incidents like this during that time—attempted violence, death threats?"

"No, although my wife worries about me."

"Because of your antiterrorism work?"

"Yes. After this she's going to worry a lot more."

"Any attempts on the Jordans?"

"No, of course not."

"Either of them ever mention any threats? I mean, this man Jordan must deal with some pretty tough people."

"Well, yes. He deals with people who want a lot. There may be some tough elements among them. But he never mentioned any threats, and his home security system is pretty thin. I mean, he doesn't even have a watchdog. So he never thought he was in any particular danger. Look, that's not even a factor. The bomb was directed at me. It was *my* car."

"That's our assumption."

"Assumption?"

"Well, you never know. The perpetrator could've mixed up your car with Mr. Jordan's."

"Not probable. The man drives a BMW."

"Or he could've placed devices in both cars, not knowing which one the deceased would ride in next."

"That's stretching it," Bret insisted.

"But it's possible. Something else is possible."

"What's that?"

"It's possible this wasn't a terrorist attack."

Bret just looked at King, a look that held more ridicule than Bret had ever heaped on anyone. "Come on. Two and two always equal four."

"This isn't arithmetic, Mr. Lewis. This is murder. In murder we score the test differently."

"What do you mean by that?"

"I've been working on a theory," King said. "Consider this. I mean, think about it: Why would a terrorist plant a bomb in a console between the two front seats of your Lincoln?"

"Why *wouldn't* he?" Bret demanded. He pretended to be annoyed, but actually was quite pleased with King's approach. Playing right into my hands, he thought. He's doing everything he was supposed to do. King suddenly appeared very useful.

"Because the device could've been detected so easily," King replied. "You could have seen it. Or your wife. And why would he hang around to detonate it by remote control? He could've gotten into the engine compartment and wired the ..."

"I've got a hood lock with a siren alarm. You should've checked that, Detective."

"Yes, you're right, Mr. Lewis. I flubbed my lines on that one, didn't I? But it doesn't change my theory. He could've jammed the bomb under the dash and connected it to the ignition. Then he could've walked away. I mean, this perpetrator had to be within fifty yards of the car when it went off. He *knew* someone could've seen him. He could've been caught."

"If someone was watching, and apparently no one was. And it was night."

"Still risky. I say it might not have been a terror attack. I mean, you're not that visible a figure. Not to insult you, sir, but your death would not have brought the flags to half staff."

"True." That drove Bret crazy.

"Maybe this Mrs. Jordan was the target. Or your wife. Whoever set off that bomb knew a female was entering the car because he had to be watching it. That's got to be right. Right?"

"You don't leave me too much choice," Bret said. But then he paused, as if pondering the detective's point. "On second thought, you do. Look, I myself wondered why the bomb was set off when a woman entered the car, rather than me. But there are two explanations. First, the bomber may not have seen *anyone* enter the car. We don't know what his vantage point was. There were other cars in the lot that could've blocked his vision. Maybe he only saw the door open. Or maybe he only saw the light go on inside."

"Possible," King said. "Very possible." His smile, awkward for the solemn occasion, grew wider, but Bret got the feeling that it was the smile of a vulture about to strike.

"Second explanation," Bret said, "and you don't know how much I hate to say this ..."

"But your wife may have been the target," King interrupted.

"Yes. Get Sarah to get at me. No, I'm not a high official, but I do work in antiterrorism and there are people who have my name on lists. And they attack families."

"Everything you say is possible," King conceded. "But for a terrorist attack, certain things are missing here. No one has taken responsibility. No one has sent a threatening message."

"They don't always," Bret pointed out. "It depends on their strategy."

"True. But put together my main objections," King said. "One, the method of bombing was crude. Two, although you or your wife might have been the target, I really don't buy that the bomber didn't visually identify the party entering the car. It's not human. People don't plan anything this risky and then guess at who's getting into a car."

"Yes, that's a point," Bret agreed. "But you're assuming the world is rational. Terrorists act strangely. A lot of them are jerks. But, let's say it wasn't a terrorist attack, though I certainly think that it was. Why would it be directed at Ramy Jordan?"

"Could be almost anything," King replied. "A personal grudge. Frustrated lover. That's my pet theory. Here it was, the night of her renewal of vows. Note the timing, Mr. Lewis."

"Noted," Bret replied. "I'm far from convinced, but you've raised some points. Still you'll have a pretty tough time explaining why someone out to get Ramy Jordan planted a bomb in *my* car, or why he'd use a bomb at all. It doesn't sound right."

"Just a theory," King assured him. "A lot of things here aren't right."

"What do you do next?" Bret asked.

"We're still getting lab results. You'll be available, I hope."

"I'm always available."

"I'm sure we'll be talking. I'll also be talking to your wife and Mr. Jordan. Thank you, Mr. Lewis. My condolences."

Without a word, King turned and walked off toward his car outside, and Bret could almost see THE END superimposed on the screen. King traveled with a kind of graceful swagger that instantly reminded Bret of every hero who walked into the sunset. Yes, they would certainly be talking again. Bret's initial dislike had turned to a resounding like. With no coaching from the studio audience, Kyle King, né Undermeyer, had taken the investigation in the very direction that Bret had wished. It was only a matter of time before the break would occur, Bret was sure, only a matter of time before the next phase of the plan began to work.

chapter
twenty-four

Flanked tightly by Sarah and Bret, Shel shuddered at the first thunderclap. They all huddled closer as the rainstorm began and quickly increased in intensity. The mourners who had come to the cemetery were under canvas, but the coffin was not, and the rain splattered and leaked off its brown wood sides as the clergyman, who insisted on standing in the downpour in nothing but a clerical robe, spoke. His words—forgettably standard—were regularly interrupted by the thunder and streaks of lightning.

"God is crying," the minister said, the stock line for gravesite rainstorms. "He is crying because he has had to separate Ramy from Shel."

Sarah could not help but think that God was the ultimate divorce lawyer.

"And well he might cry," the minister droned on. "For this was a marriage truly made in Heaven."

And wrecked on Earth, Sarah thought.

"In a way, it will never end, for Shel and Ramy will some day be reunited in that glorious place we mortals can only dream about."

Shel was crying, too. The tears didn't come easily, but his body shook and the flab under his chin quivered as he listened to the final moments of the service. Besides Bret and Sarah, the guests were members of Ramy's and Shel's families and a few friends. Each was lost in his own thoughts. There were occasional sobs, some genuine, some required by graveside etiquette. Sarah, though, was still caught in her strange ambivalence—genuine grief for the friend she'd lost and horror at the manner of her death, yet an embarrassing relief that a competitor was no longer in competition. The tumult in the sky was the right symbol, she mused. A terrible fracture had broken these two marriages—the affair between Ramy and Bret. Maybe Ramy's death was an act of Providence to restore, at least to the Lewis marriage, what had existed before.

In these two weeks, Sarah had come far from the rational, methodical engineer to a woman now grasping for something, anything, to explain all that had happened. No one had ever told her why, and no one ever could. She tried to push out of her mind the idea that her own husband was still in danger from whoever planted the bomb that had killed Ramy.

Now she looked in his direction. Strange, she thought, that he didn't say anything or even gesture to her. Was that important? Was she imagining? Was his mind elsewhere, on the woman of Capitol Hill? She and Bret had spent remarkably little time alone since the bombing. It had been more important to devote themselves to being with Shel. Sarah realized that she would have to get to know Bret once more, to see if there would be a new Bret with Ramy gone.

And she thought it strange, too, that Shel hadn't mentioned a thing to her about the events that had preceded his wife's murder. It was as if he were trying to sanctify her. Not a word about her affair with Bret or the devastating tape that he'd brought to the museum. Sarah had feared he might explode at Bret, confront him with his resentment over the affair. But Shel had said nothing. That affair, it seemed, was history.

Every now and then Bret reached over to pat Shel on the back, the only acceptable male gesture of comfort he could think of. At one point, though, he glanced out to the left, into the distance, to the road that passed this hilly section of the cemetery. There, in the mist, was an old Plymouth. And standing next to it, under an ordinary black umbrella, was Kyle King. King just watched, sizing up his characters, assessing those he would engage in verbal combat in the days ahead. Bret was pleased, but made sure to frown as he looked in King's direction.

The service soon ended. Each guest braved the wind and rain to approach the grave and place a rose atop the soaked coffin. The wet roses adhered to the wood and stayed in place despite the weather. Then Ramy was buried on the hillside of her choice, facing east, toward the morning sun. And Shel said good-bye to most of the guests, who hurried back to their cars, parked along the same road where King stood watching.

In the end, after all the others had gone, only Shel, Bret and Sarah remained. Despite the continuing downpour, they approached the edge of Ramy's grave and paused for a few moments in silence.

"I want to thank you both," Shel finally said as they prepared to leave the site. His voice was hoarse, the strain on his heart evident. "If you hadn't been here during this, they'd be putting me in the ground, too."

Sarah embraced him. Bret put an arm on his shoulder. "I just want to have good memories," Shel went on. "Anything that might have happened, well, who knows why?"

Maybe that was it, Sarah thought, Shel's one hint that he'd known about the affair. She looked over at Bret, but he didn't acknowledge, not visibly at least, that he'd picked up on it.

"Life continues," Bret said, to no one in particular. "But I'll always know that Ramy died in my place."

Now, as Sarah watched Shel grab a faltering Bret by the arm, it occurred to her. Of course. Bret had to be affected by Ramy's death in another, special way. Guilt. The guilt of the survivor. It should have occurred to her earlier, she realized.

What did not occur to her, even now, was that it was all an act.

Kyle King, his pants legs drenched from the rain, returned to his cheap metal desk at police headquarters in Arlington. He tossed his umbrella into a corner, spraying a good part of the wall. Then he slumped into a chair, exhausted by the morning's work on the Ramy Jordan case and by the rotten weather. As usual, a copy of the *Hollywood Reporter* was on the desk, and he glanced through it, absorbing the latest news on the business that he really loved best. Secretly, King had made several applications to become a technical adviser on TV police shows and feature films, but he had always been turned down. No one wanted a cop from a small Virginia department, where nothing ever happened. Hollywood wanted someone from New York or L.A., or somewhere picturesque like New Orleans. It made King more than a little bitter. They'd take a guy from Washington, right across the river, but they wouldn't take one from Virginia. Maybe some good, flashy work on the Ramy Jordan case would convince them. It was major, it had made the headlines, it had all the earmarks of a big-time operation. But, luck being what it was, he thought, it would probably wind up as a bit player terrorist attack with the perpetrator already back in his own country, getting a stamp issued in his honor.

Still, King was troubled.

He'd meant everything he'd said to Bret at the chapel. He was not yet prepared to accept the conventional wisdom that the murder of Ramy Jordan had been an act of international terrorism. There was something an older homicide detective had said to him over and over: "Everyone has a reason to be murdered." Even a saint could have enemies, King knew, and often did. And Ramy Jordan, considering who she was, her wealth, her status, her husband, certainly had enemies, even if they smiled to her face and complimented her hair.

King's skepticism was reinforced by a preliminary report of his own department. It referred to a number of investigations of Shel Jordan's business practices. "Subject," the report said of Shel, "has been photographed by law enforcement agencies in the regular company of known members of organized crime associations." Now, King knew that this could have been exaggerated, and he knew that being photographed with a criminal didn't make a man one. But what if Shel's link with these people were serious? King knew all about reward and retribution in the world of major crime. The murder of family members was part of the system. If Ramy didn't personally have enemies, her husband certainly did.

And there was something else in the report that troubled Detective King: "Neighbors report frequent quarreling during the last three months within the Jordan household, sometimes followed by Mrs. Jordan exiting the house and driving away."

King decided to speak with Bret Lewis at least one more time, then go on to Sarah and to Shel Jordan. He didn't bother making an appointment with Bret. Appointments put people on their guard, tempted them to memorize statements or develop acute laryngitis. King simply walked back into the rain, got into his car, tuned his radio to a station that was playing nothing but Sinatra for a week and drove over to the Pentagon.

It was Bret's first time back at his office since the bombing. There were some condolence notes on his desk from staff members who knew how close he was to the Jordans, and there was the expected list of those who had called in his absence, including the Secretary of Defense and Tim Curran. He was greeted in muted tones by friends in the halls, just as a man would be if he'd had a brush with death in combat or a peacetime accident. He got some stares—everyone knew he was the official who'd been targeted by some group unknown for some purpose unknown. The whispers followed.

His initial appointment was with Captain Avery Masters, the very officer who had in effect supplied the murder weapon. Bret was fully confident that Masters would never make the connection between those supplies and the explosion at the Cheshire Motel. Even if he did wonder, Masters's career was heavily dependent on Bret, and Masters was not the kind to let anything stand in the way of ambition, certainly not anything as minor as a little package of fireworks.

"It was a remarkable experience," Bret was telling Masters, leaning back in his chair and fingering a baton that had once belonged to Leopold Stokowski. "I guess you uniformed guys have all been shot at from time to time, but I've never been a target."

"Concentrates the mind," Masters was saying.

"They've got a guard temporarily watching my rented car," Bret said. "I think I may begin to feel like a prisoner. I guess it's necessary, but I'm a pretty free spirit and I kind of resent it."

"You can't be too careful," Masters replied. "I was a terrorist target when I was assigned to Greece once. Someone put a poison snake in my car. Fortunately, I saw it before it saw me."

"A snake!" Bret exclaimed. "I'll have to watch the insides of my car from now on, whatever new car I happen to pick up this week. You know," he continued, "the explosive was the same kind you supplied to me for my . . . . operation. You don't think someone could have gotten it from our stores, do you?"

"Sir, it's always possible," Masters said. "Unlikely, though. As you know, everything has to be signed out, and nothing has been reported missing. But records are strange things. Magical things happen to them. I've known a lot of magicians in this business."

"I'm going to requisition some more of that," Bret said. "I wish I could let you in on some of the things we're doing."

"I understand, sir."

Bret was looking Masters up and down. The captain showed not one sign of suspicion. Bret was requesting more materials to give the impression of continuing operations. He didn't want Masters focusing only on the last order.

"So I'll get a list together after some meetings," Bret said, "and pass it on to you. Oh, by the way," he added, "before I forget—as far as the little matter of your personnel difficulties, the Kearns report and all that, I think things'll be just fine for you. I've started sending out feelers, and there's no real desire to nail you to the wall."

"Thank you, sir," Masters said, visibly relieved.

"In fact, I rather like working with you, Captain," Bret went on. "I'll make sure the right people in the bureaucracy know of your effectiveness. Just be careful about any violations. I wouldn't want a great career ruined by some foolish action."

"Caution is my middle name," Masters said.

Good, Bret thought as he ushered Masters out. The captain was in his vest pocket and would likely stay there until old age and a retirement parade in front of the Pentagon building.

Bret started leafing through the Washington and New York papers. Remarkable, he thought, but there was very little printed about Ramy's death. The Washington papers did run stories with headlines like FBI PROBES TERROR LINK IN MOTEL KILLING and NAVY MUM ON LEWIS ROLE IN IRAN. But the stories were deep in the inside sections. It was three days after the blast, and there was not much more to say, pending the naming of a suspect. Also, no one had come up with definite proof of anything, and Ramy Jordan was not the high government official whose murder would have stayed on page one.

Tim Curran's prediction that the press would hound Bret about his involvement in possibly illegal operations had not materialized, at least not yet. Bret had already been tipped that some reporters were working on that angle, and the headline NAVY MUM ON LEWIS ROLE

IN IRAN showed that the issue was alive in the newsrooms. But no reporters were camping out at his door. Bret had already prepared answers in case he had to use them, and the Pentagon press office had volunteered to help him.

As he started through the *Washington Times*, his intercom buzzed. "A Detective King to see you, sir," his secretary said. "About the incident."

Bret was surprised, but smiled to himself. This King was showing signs of doggedness, signs Bret enjoyed and admired in a useful pawn. "I'll make a call, then show him in," he replied. Bret called only the weather bureau, a stalling tactic to avoid appearing too eager to see King. The eager witness is always suspicious. He piled some reports on his desk, uncapped his Mont Blanc diplomat fountain pen and pretended to be fully engaged in the business of the United States Navy when King was escorted in, displaying his usual rubbery swagger.

"Detective," Bret said, rising and extending his hand. He noticed that the bottoms of King's trousers were still damp. "I'm sorry we gave you such a miserable day."

"I'm used to it," King said. "Look, I apologize for coming here so soon. I know we talked this morning, but I've got some further questions."

"I'm surprised you didn't use the phone," Bret said.

"Hate the thing. I like the visual. Live theatre. Film. You get a better sense of mood and feeling."

"Mood and feeling," Bret echoed.

"Yes, sir."

"Sure. Sit down, Detective. What can I do for you?"

King sat, but as he did he gazed around the remarkable office, focusing on the collection of sleek batons and the old model airplanes. He said nothing about them, though, his mind riveted on Ramy's murder. "Uh, I'd like to pursue some questions about Mrs. Jordan," he said.

"Why? Is there anything new?"

"Oh no. Just getting additional details."

"Still don't fully accept that it was terrorism?" Bret asked.

"Pursuing all leads," King replied.

"All right, go ahead."

"Mr. Lewis," King began, "I'd like you to forget that possibility of terrorism for a moment. Can you think of anyone in this world who'd want to kill Ramy Jordan?"

"You do get right to the point," Bret responded. "But I'll try to help." He pretended to ponder the question. "You realize, of course, that I don't know everyone who knew her."

"I understand."

"No, I can't come up with anyone who'd want her dead."

"I see. Did she ever joke about enemies?"

"Joke?"

"Sometimes," King explained, "people make light remarks about problems they're having, but they're really quite serious. Someone once said that comedy is tragedy plus time ..."

"I've heard that definition," Bret said. "But Ramy wasn't very funny. In fact I don't remember her ever telling a real joke. And if something *was* bothering her, she'd come out with it."

"Like what? What was bothering her?"

"Well ... look, I didn't say anything was."

"But was there?"

"Now, Detective, remember that everyone ..."

"I think you're holding back, sir. What was bothering her? Could it have been her husband?"

"Did someone tell you that?"

"Yes."

"Then you know Ramy had some strains in her marriage. Look," Bret said, picking up the Stokowski baton, rolling it rapidly between his fingers, "this happens with married people. You married?"

"Divorced twice."

"Then you know."

"No, I was married to two dancers," King replied. "They're not like people."

"I see. Well, being a friend, she'd confide in me. After all, I was a friend of Shel's as well. I think she wanted to salvage things, and thought I could help."

"How serious were the strains?"

"I had the feeling they were serious. But they both agreed to our renewal of vows, and I'll admit that I came up with the idea in part to try to rekindle things for them."

"Why did you feel that would work?"

"I didn't. I was just hoping. There was no rational reason for the problems between them. It was emotional, and that's the hardest thing to deal with."

"Did Mr. Jordan know anything about explosives?"

"Not that I know of. Hey, come on."

"Did Mrs. Jordan?"

Bret paused at this point and stared directly under King's shining bald head and into his large brown eyes. "Look, what are you getting at?"

"Just asking."

Bret's gaze turned hard. "You're asking whether Mrs. Jordan could have blown herself up accidentally while trying to plant a bomb to kill her husband. Isn't *that* what you're asking?"

"Mr. Lewis," King replied, "we have to consider all possibilities in our line of work."

"Number one," Bret replied—and now his voice had a sharp, hostile edge—"she wouldn't have planted it in my car. Number two, Ramy couldn't plug in an iron. Now let's cut it out." Then he slammed his fist into his desk, making a penholder bounce and pop over the side.

"No need to get passionate," King said, not showing much feeling himself.

But Bret held an icy stare, trying hard now to lay it on. "Detective King," he said, "Ramy Jordan was a friend of mine. She didn't have a malicious bone in her body. She died in an explosion meant for *me*. Do you know what it's like to realize that, to realize that someone you practically loved died in your place?"

King didn't answer. He was not yet convinced that Ramy Jordan died in *anyone's* place.

"It'll be with me the rest of my life," Bret added.

"You have my genuine sympathy," King told him. "And this may not be the best time to go further with this. I think I have what I need." He snapped shut his rain-splattered, dog-eared notebook. "Please understand that I only collect facts."

Bret tried a weak smile. "I understand. I do. It's just that ... it begins to hit you."

Later, alone with his door closed, Bret jotted a few notes on his conversation with King. It would be important to remember exactly what he'd revealed and *hadn't* revealed. Then, with a feeling of sublime contentment, he moved across the room to his stereo system and snapped it on. He placed a disk of Handel's *Messiah* on his turntable, gently advancing the Fidelity Research arm to the seventh groove. He eased on his Stax earphones, and heard the first strains of the "Hallelujah Chorus." Appropriate, he thought. Very appropriate. Kyle King was moving in exactly the direction he'd planned, so music of celebration was fitting.

It would be only a matter of time before Detective King, or one of his cronies, would make the ultimate discovery.

chapter
twenty-five

When Kyle King first looked up at the *Spirit of St. Louis* hanging in the National Air and Space Museum, his only thought was that Jimmy Stewart had played Charles Lindbergh in the film. In King's world of values, if they didn't make a film of it, it didn't happen. He glanced over to the space capsules on display and recalled some of the actors who'd played the original astronauts in *The Right Stuff*. Ed Harris, he remembered, played John Glenn. That reminded him that Scott Glenn played Alan Shepard. He had an image in his head of the grinning wise-guy type who played Gordon Cooper—Dennis Quaid. King thought he himself would have been very good as one of the astronauts, although none of them was known for a bald head or short beard.

King had never been in the museum. Now he had come, not to contemplate the history of flight or to immerse himself in space fantasies, but to interview Sarah Lewis. He had to change jurisdictions to conduct the interview, coming from the State of Virginia into the District of Columbia, but he had made the necessary arrangements with the District police.

A guard told him where Sarah's office was. He walked to it and knocked on her closed door.

"Come in."

King opened. "Ma'am, are you Sarah Lewis?"

"I am," Sarah replied, looking quite haggard. "Are you Professor Levy from M.I.T.?"

"Uh, no, ma'am, I'm Detective King of the Arlington police, about the Jordan murder."

"Oh, I see."

"I spoke to your husband about this, ma'am, and I'd like to speak with you."

No response at first. Just a vague, uneasy questioning across her face. King waited.

"Do you have any identification, Detective?"

"Of course." King took out his black leather wallet, which he kept highly polished. He opened to his badge and laminated I.D., offering them to her.

Examining the I.D., Sarah wondered why Bret hadn't mentioned King. Ramy's murder was the central event of their lives, a detective had visited him, and Bret never mentioned it. So strange. Glancing up from the I.D., Sarah thought King's appearance pretty strange as well. He looked more like a hip bartender than a detective. But she nodded her approval of his credentials and motioned for him to sit.

"I know this is difficult for you, ma'am," King began. "I understand Mrs. Jordan was a very close friend."

"The closest," Sarah replied. Again, that ambivalence. Closest, yes. But rival, also yes.

King sensed a certain coolness in Sarah's reply, something not expected from the deceased's closest female friend. Maybe she was trying to be dignified. Maybe it was nothing. "Ma'am," he continued, "I'm just developing some information on Mrs. Jordan. You know, we have to explore every aspect of the case, as I told your husband. The more we know about the deceased, the more it helps."

"But if it's terrorism," Sarah replied, "and was directed at my husband . . ."

"It might not have been, ma'am."

"Oh?"

"Your husband didn't mention this to you?"

"No, he didn't."

"I'm surprised."

"Maybe he was protecting me." She was defending Bret, Sarah thought. She was actually defending him. Why was she doing that?

"Well, why don't we just chat," King went on. "I'm here specifically to ask about some stories I've heard. They involve Mrs. Jordan's marriage."

Sarah seemed to freeze in place, although every muscle in her body fought not to make it obvious. Did King know? How much did he know? And how much would eventually get into the papers? She picked up a small desk model of Amelia Earhart's Lockheed Electra and started turning one of the propellers nervously. "What about her marriage?" she asked.

"Strains."

Sarah paused for a moment. That word—strains—it might mean that King had discovered what she'd hoped no one would ever discover. "I see," she replied. "Tell me, Detective King—did you discuss this with my husband?"

"Yes I did, ma'am. Apparently, Mr. and Mrs. Jordan were having some problems. Were you aware of them?"

"Everyone has problems."

"What about *their* problems?"

Again Sarah hesitated, continuing to spin the propeller.

"Ma'am, do you have any information?" King asked, showing some impatience.

"Detective," Sarah replied, "you're putting me in a very awkward position. This woman is dead. I was brought up to . . ."

". . . speak no ill of the dead."

"Correct."

"I'm not looking for gossip, Mrs. Lewis."

"In a way, you are."

"I'm looking for information. Strains in a marriage can induce a person to do some pretty weird things. And if there was another man . . ."

Sarah stifled a gasp. "Excuse me?"

"You seem upset by that."

"Look," Sarah replied, "I really didn't expect to be questioned. I just assumed that everything they said was true—that this *was* an act of terrorism. Now you're asking me to discuss someone's marital problems. I wish Bret had alerted me to this." She stopped abruptly, collecting herself. "Please tell me," she went on, "what my husband said about the subject."

"About Mrs. Jordan?"

"Yes."

"Just that he knew about some problems she'd been having. He said she'd sometimes discuss them with him. I'd imagine you two had conversations about the same thing."

"Well, no, actually we didn't. I can't explain why. Ramy knew Bret very well, and she obviously chose to confide in him. It's understandable."

"In what way, ma'am?"

"Sometimes men give better advice on handling men."

"That's true," King replied. "But this strikes me as odd. Your closest friends, and you and your husband didn't discuss their marriage. Doesn't that strike *you* as odd?"

Now Sarah tried to smile, if only to give herself a few seconds to frame an answer, to backtrack. "Look, Detective, the truth is that we occasionally did mention things to each other. We just didn't have long conversations, that's all. I never thought the situation was that bad between Ramy and Shel. And I really don't like talking about it. I feel as if I'm prying."

King was unmoved. "Did Ramy, Mrs. Jordan, discuss her problems with *you?*" he asked.

"As I said, I don't like . . ."

"Please, Mrs. Lewis, I'm trying to solve a murder. Would you cooperate?" King's voice, the product of some acting lessons, was firm and unyielding. "I'll ask again. Did she discuss her marriage problems with you?"

"No, not really. Detective, sometimes even close friends hide things from each other. There's pride involved. Ramy would mention when they'd had a little fight, but that isn't the end of the world."

"It sure was the end of *her* world, Mrs. Lewis."

"You're not suggesting that Shel . . ."

"Oh no, no, no. It was just a figure of speech," King said. Then he stopped, obviously frustrated. He reached his right hand up to his shiny head and simulated brushing back hair, something he unconsciously did whenever he felt he wasn't getting what he wanted. "Ma'am," he said, "why do I get the feeling you're holding out on me?"

Sarah paused as well. "I don't know why you get that feeling," she finally replied. "But you know, Detective, I'm getting that same feeling as well."

"Are you, ma'am?"

"Is there something you're not telling *me*?" Sarah asked. "Something you know about Ramy, about her marriage?"

"No," King replied.

She looked straight at him. Maybe he was telling the truth. Maybe he only knew there'd been problems between Shel and Ramy. It didn't mean he necessarily knew about Ramy and Bret. And certainly Bret wouldn't have told him. Why would he reveal a secret that Ramy had taken to her grave?

"Okay, Detective," Sarah finally said. "But the fact is, I really don't know much."

"I see."

Now more in control, Sarah held her stare firm. Sure, she was holding back information, and technically that was wrong. It was also pride—a gut desire to avoid laying bare her apparent failure to keep her husband. Besides, Bret and Ramy's affair couldn't possibly have had anything to do with the murder. Don't reveal more, she told herself. Just get through this.

"All right, Mrs. Lewis," King continued, now trying an entirely new tack, "did Mrs. Jordan seem depressed to you?"

"Not really. She was very up for our renewal of vows. Look, when they fought she wasn't a barrel of laughs. But I never saw her very depressed."

"Did she ever say anything like 'I wish I were dead'?"

"We all say that."

"And most of us don't mean it."

"If you're suggesting that Ramy was suicidal, I'd have to say she wasn't."

"You're sure of that?"

"No. It's my impression."

"Was she afraid?"

"Of what?"

"Of anyone?"

"Like her husband?"

"We'll begin with him."

"No, Ramy wasn't afraid of Shel. He isn't that kind of man. As far as anyone else, she never expressed any fears. Sure, she sometimes had some doubts about Shel's business associates."

"Doubts?"

"There were some pretty seedy characters. It's in the nature of influence peddling. But there was never any talk of violence, or threats."

"I see. She died in your car."

"Yes," Sarah acknowledged. "That's why they think it was terrorism."

"Of course," King replied. "And that's what we'll have to nail down."

King stopped and reviewed his notes, flipping the pages of his notepad with an uncommon grace. Sarah could hear his shoes tapping on her tile floor. She guessed he might have an artistic background, yet couldn't quite square that with his job as an investigator of knifings, shootings, unexpected exits through windows, and death by dynamite. She neither liked nor disliked him. Like so much that had happened in her life in the last weeks, she felt his presence was just one more intrusion, one more thing she didn't need.

"I don't think there's anything more I can ask," King said, finally smiling, a smile that struck Sarah as mildly sinister, or at least conniving.

"I wish I could have been more helpful," Sarah replied.

"So do I, but thanks anyway . . . and I might be back. Each witness suggests a new line of questioning. I appreciate your time." King shoved his notebook back in his inside jacket pocket and started to get up.

"Detective King," Sarah interrupted.

He sat down again. Maybe she'd gotten religion. "Yes?"

"I don't mean to appear petty, but please tell me: Did Ramy have another man?"

King shrugged. "I don't know," he replied.

"Based on what you know, do you *think* she had another man?"

"Why do you ask? You seemed sensitive about that before."

"I was just wondering," Sarah replied, icy calm.

"I still don't know," King replied. "If she did, I'll want to talk to him." Then, he gazed directly into Sarah's eyes, like some military sergeant staring down a scared recruit. "You don't have a name, do you?"

"Of course not."

Kyle King left, frustrated. Instinct told him that the Ramy Jordan murder wasn't the clean act of terrorism touted by the FBI and the Washington commentators. But so far he'd come up with no good motive for the killing. He guessed—and guesswork, he knew, was the first fifty percent of a murder investigation—that Shel Jordan held the key. It had to be Shel—a man of influence and power, but a man who inevitably had kicked some shins in his lifetime.

Now, King thought, it might be time for Shel to have *his* shins kicked.

chapter
twenty-six

In the days following Ramy's murder, it struck Sarah that something new was going on. Bret was around a great deal. No more reports of late-night meetings or trumped-up crises. He was home by seven almost each evening. And, despite Ramy's murder, he seemed more at peace, more serene than she'd seen him in a long time. Maybe, in the strangest of ways, Ramy's murder had jolted him into it.

There was not a hint of Alison Carver. Sarah had thought of hiring Al Durfee again to do a follow-up, but, with no late-night excuses, there seemed no particular reason to do so. She read an article in the *Washington Post* reporting that Carver was about to go on a two-week inspection tour of American military bases in Europe. Good. If things had been hot and heavy with Bret, Alison Carver could easily have gotten out of that junket.

The Lewis apartment had taken on the character of mourning. The piano top, decorated with anniversary cards just days before, now was filled with condolence messages, the anniversary cards relegated to a desk drawer. Although the Lewises and the Jordans weren't related, everyone knew—or thought they knew—how close the couples had been, so condolence cards to Bret and Sarah were considered proper. Besides, the circumstances of the bombing—with the press saying Bret had been the probable target—had encouraged many friends to try to comfort the Lewises. A few had sent flowers, and one had even begun a Ramy Jordan scholarship fund.

The funereal atmosphere at home made it easier for Bret to hide his elation over all that had happened. He gave thanks each day for Ramy's cooperation, for the quality of the materials Masters had provided, for the gullibility of official Washington in thinking a terrorist attack had occurred, making him an instant celebrity, and for Kyle King, whose investigation was proving outstanding, relentless— everything Bret could want. Bret sometimes felt that he was being guided by some great spiritual force, so complete was his gratitude for the fruits that good fortune had provided.

But he began to wonder if he'd been wrong in not telling Sarah of his conversations with King. He'd originally felt that the less discussion he had with her over Ramy's death, the better. Discussion, after all, led to questions, and Sarah's questions were not in any script, first draft or otherwise, that Bret had written on the dark side of his mind. Yet he knew he should have anticipated that she'd bring up King once the detective visited the museum, and that his silence might then arouse her suspicions. But this was a minor hitch in an otherwise perfect plan, whose climax was soon to be played out.

"I felt so awkward," Sarah was saying over a diet dinner of steamed vegetables the day King visited her. "I just didn't like his probing."

Bret sat opposite at their kitchen table, his jacket and tie off, his shirt unbuttoned. The heat, which had broken for a few days, had returned, and their air conditioner provided its usual accompaniment. "I was a little annoyed, too," he said. "But he's just doing his job."

"Why don't they leave it to the Bureau?"

"They've got to do their own investigation. Besides, I think they're starting to shy away from the terrorism thing."

"How come?"

"Didn't he explain it to you? A lot of inconsistencies, a feeling that Shel had enemies."

Their conversation then ceased for more than thirty seconds, each one of them maneuvering.

"He kept on emphasizing their marriage," Sarah finally said.

"Why not? When we do a security check on someone, we have to probe into their personal lives. This is no different."

"I'm very surprised you didn't tell me what he'd asked *you*," Sarah said. She wanted to do a little probing of her own.

"Why rehash it?" Bret replied, not missing a beat, while showing no great interest in the steamed vegetables on the table before him. "It's the kind of thing I want to put behind us. Maybe I should have told you that he'd quizzed me, but I didn't see the point of the aggravation."

"Ramy was my friend, too."

"Yes, Sarah, I know."

"He seemed to think you knew more about their troubles than I did."

"Really?"

"Yes, Bret. Really."

Now Bret stopped eating altogether. He looked up at Sarah, the stubble of the all-day beard on his sweat-moistened face giving him a tougher aura than usual. "Well, okay," he replied, "I guess I'm going to have to come clean with you."

Abruptly, Bret got up. He thrust his hands into his pockets and started pacing the kitchen, knocking over a salt shaker that had rested on a counter. His sudden movement sent Sarah's heart into an arrhythmia. This she hadn't expected. She had expected the usual evasion, maybe an apology, but "come clean" was out of the blue. How much "coming clean" was he prepared for? Was this the mea culpa over an affair with Ramy, the final admission after the corpse was duly put away? Or was Alison Carver the subject of this sudden confessional? Sarah said nothing.

"I meant to talk to you about this, I really did," Bret said. "Well, maybe I didn't. Look, it's a very sensitive thing."

"Sensitive?" Sarah prepared for the worst.

"They were really having problems, and Ramy came to me. I mean, she asked me to meet her several times."

"What did she want?"

"Advice. She and Shel seemed to be drifting apart. She began to dislike the guy. Look, let's face it, I can understand that. We're not talking Prince Charming. But she did want to save the marriage. She wanted to know if I knew professional counselors or psychiatrists who specialized in this."

"What did you tell her?"

"Frankly, not much. We didn't get the chance. We'd just begun having these talks when ... we did the double wedding."

"She didn't mention much to me," Sarah said, almost matter-of-factly.

"She told me she wouldn't. I don't know, she just felt sensitive about it. Maybe she felt she'd failed at her marriage, and you'd succeeded at yours."

Lying through his well-bonded teeth, she thought. There wasn't an honest thing he'd said, but he was saying it with such utter conviction. "Go on," she continued, restraining herself.

"That's about it," Bret said. "There was serious static between them. I thought the double wedding might help. You know—emotion, nostalgia. Ramy thought so too. Frankly, we discussed it in advance."

"Uh huh."

"And I was about to get some names for her, some very good doctors, when this thing happened."

"That was the only reason you saw Ramy privately?" Sarah asked, coming closer than ever to going over the line.

"Yes. What other reason could there be?"

No, don't blow it, Sarah thought. Don't blow it when the sailor seemed to be coming home. She shrugged. "Just asking," she said.

But now Bret threw a stare at her that was somewhere between hostile and hurt. It surprised Sarah. She'd expected him just to go on to something else, but the stare signaled that he wanted to anchor on that last point. And then he started shaking his head negatively from side to side, as if stunned, baffled. "You weren't just asking," he said, and his tone was intimidating.

"What?"

"You *know* what I mean."

"No, I don't."

"You really think there was something going on, don't you?"

Jesus, Sarah, thought, *he* was bringing it up. She was completely unprepared. Instinctively, she shook her head no.

"Oh yes you do," Bret said. "That's why you asked. I saw that suspicious look in your eye. Sarah, I just can't believe this. A few days after Ramy's murder and you suspect there was something going on between us. After twenty wonderful years, after our renewal of vows, after this tragedy, I can't believe it. I . . . I just can't believe it."

"No, Bret, you've got it wrong," Sarah found herself saying. What did he think he was gaining?

"I'm hurt," he said. "I'm shocked."

"It was a foolish question," Sarah said. Somehow she couldn't bring herself entirely to soothe his anger—she had enough anger of her own to make that impossible. But this was the man she was trying to keep, and to confront him now could easily destroy all she'd hoped for. "Just forget it," she said. "Ramy's gone."

"But you suspected. Admit it, Sarah."

He'd never spoken to her that way. It seemed reckless, the opposite of any man's wish for secrecy about his affairs. "No," she said.

"Do you love me?"

He was becoming more bizarre by the minute. "Bret, how can you ask that?"

"I asked it. It was a simple question."

"I answered it at the double wedding."

"Please answer it again."

"Bret, of course I love you."

"And I love you, too. And I'd never cheat on you. With anyone. I want you to understand that. In all these years I have never cheated on you. I will stay with you for the rest of my life. I said it at the ceremony; I'll say it again."

"I do appreciate that," Sarah said, still shaken, still stunned by Bret's sneak attack, almost whispering her words.

"And I don't think you've ever cheated on me," Bret added.

"No."

"Do you promise me that, Sarah?"

"Of course I promise it," Sarah replied.

She was assuring *him*, she realized. It was crazy. Here she was assuring the man whose voice had been on that sizzling tape, the man who'd been in every one of Al Durfee's prize centerfold snaps, the man who'd lied about his extra-hours forays. Maybe it was still the shock of Ramy's death, but Sarah found herself completely disoriented.

"Your faithfulness means a great deal to me," Bret said. "There is nothing else."

"Bret, I think you're exhausted," Sarah responded. "Why don't you lie down? The strain is showing."

"You always take care of me," Bret smiled. "You don't mind if I don't finish dinner?"

"No, of course not."

"You're right. I'll try to sleep. I'm glad we had this little thing out."

Bret went over and kissed his wife on the forehead. Without another word, he walked slowly into the bedroom. As he did, far from Sarah's sight, away from the anxiety of her glare, his slight smile broke into a wide, gawking grin. He fought to control himself, to suppress the laughter that was building inside him, to restrain the absolute exultation that he felt. "Why do I have this power?" he asked himself, actually moving his lips as he did. "Why can I manipulate people so superbly?" He glanced at himself in a bedroom mirror, delighted at the person before him, content with another day's work.

It was all perfection.

And it would all be over soon.

chapter
twenty-seven

He was a pathetic figure, sitting in his lavish den in a satin bathrobe, with a black mourning band pinned to the left arm. It was not the Shel Jordan his friends and cronies knew. It was not the Shel Jordan who could walk into the Capitol and be greeted by name by three-fourths of the Senate and at least half the House. It was not the Shel Jordan who'd been a VIP at six Cape Canaveral launches. It was not the Shel Jordan who could pick up the phone in his office and dial the private numbers of royalty in half a dozen countries. The man on the couch, ample stomach bulging, chins folded down against his thick neck, eyes bloodshot and sagging, was a vast contrast to the man in the pictures that neatly lined the wall—smiling with presidents and ministers, gladhanding with the virtuous and the corrupt.

This Shel Jordan in extreme mourning was the man Kyle King encountered as he continued his probe into Ramy's sudden, violent death. For an instant, at the start of the interview, King wondered whether Shel could even handle the questions. But a private nurse, hired for the mourning period, nodded that it was okay, that talking about Ramy was good therapy.

Shel didn't look at King, who sat in a copy of the rocking chair that President Kennedy used. He remained almost motionless on the couch, except for the curious habit of rolling a ballpoint pen in his hands, then, reaching over to a table to replace that pen with another, rolling the next one for a time as well. The pens were part of his most prized collection—pens used to sign bills into law and Shel Jordan contracts into the millions.

"I know this is difficult for you," King said, his voice subdued and more dignified than a detective's had a right to be.

"Yes," Shel whispered, slowly twirling a black Parker pen.

"My mother was killed in a hit-and-run," King went on. "I was thirteen years old, and I saw what happened to my father. So I understand."

"Thanks," Shel said.

"Would you like to talk about her?" King asked.

Now Shel raised his head slightly, while still rolling the Parker in his stubby hands. "What's there to say?" he asked, his voice so weak that King had to turn one ear toward him. "Did you see her afterward? Did you see what they did to her?"

"No, sir," King replied. "But it's not good to dwell on that. Think of the good times."

"The good times," Shel said with a heavy sigh that seemed to undulate through his entire body. "I try to think of them. There were so many. Even the sad things could be good when I was with Ramy. We have a son, you know."

"Yes, sir."

"We don't talk much about him. There I go using the 'we' again, but it'll take me a long time to get over it. Our son, he has problems, mental problems. You saw that he wasn't even at the funeral. But he always knew he had a mother and father. There were good times with him. But, you know, it's funny. Most of the good times were with the Lewises. Always so close to them, closer than family. Strange how Ramy died in Bret's place."

"If she did, sir."

"You doubt it? I read something in the paper that you people were onto something new. I don't know."

"It may not have been terrorism, Mr. Jordan."

"Then what?"

"That's what we're investigating."

"Well, keep on investigating," Shel said, making a fist now. "Investigate the hell out of this, no matter where it leads you."

"Sir?"

"Did I say something?" Shel asked.

"Uh, that last phrase, 'no matter where it leads you.' "

"What about it?"

"What did you mean by it?"

"Nothing in particular. Should it mean something?"

"Well, sir, I was just wondering. And again, I know how this is going to feel. But you're a man of some influence in this town, and to gain influence you sometimes have to . . ."

"Make enemies," Shel said.

"Yes, sir. I know that sounds offensive. I didn't mean to suggest . . ."

"It's not offensive," Shel said. "It's true. Oh God, it's true." He returned the pen to the table next to the couch and took another one, a red Waterman, and started rolling it between his palms. "Do you know how many times since this tragedy I've thought about that, Detective King?"

"I can imagine," King said.

"Every waking minute. Do you know what it's like to wonder if anything you did led to the death of your wife?"

"No, sir."

"It's hell. You go over names in your mind. You begin to make lists. Here, right here—in the pocket of my robe . . ." Shel reached into his right pocket and pulled out a piece of paper with names scrawled all over it in no particular pattern. "I made a list. People who might have had a grudge. Oh, I mean, most of this is stupid. These people wouldn't . . ."

"Could I have that list?" King asked.

Shel hesitated. "Well, I . . . I guess so. But look, I'm in no shape to be reasonable. These names, they're just names . . ."

"We're used to that, sir." King had made his point, but didn't make any effort—at the moment—to reach over for the list. He knew Shel might be sensitive about anything involving friends or business associates. There was a guilt factor, a powerful guilt factor. "Besides the names on the paper," King went on, "is there anyone, a particular person, who had a *real* grudge, a serious grudge?"

"Against me or Ramy?" Shel asked.

"Either."

"Against Ramy, no one. People loved her. You were at the funeral."

"Yes I was, sir."

"You see that crowd? That's the size crowd that comes out for a senator, or a CEO. They came for Ramy, my wife of twenty years. Even an old lawyer came. She'd been his legal secretary before we were married. An excellent legal secretary."

"I'm sure she was, sir."

"No, no one hated Ramy. As for me, you're asking a lot. You step on toes, people scream. Sometimes they don't scream, they just hold in the pain. They're the ones you worry about."

"Have you had threats?"

"Not recently."

"But you've had them."

"Couple of years ago I greased some wheels for a firm that wanted a contract to repair runways. You know, for the Air Force?"

"Sure."

"Their competition didn't care for my efforts. There were some phone calls about my head."

"Your head?"

"How it could get detached from my body."

"I see," King said. "And yet, I understand you've never had much of a security system."

"I won't live like that," Shel said. "I've got some machinery in the house—the usual alarms. But I'm not going to live in a bunker."

"You don't have a dog."

"Oh, I'd like a watchdog. That would be great. But my allergies . . ."

"I see," King said, duly writing that down in his pad, which now had only six blank pages left. "Uh, sir, I've got to bring something up," he said.

"Oh? You found out about someone?" Shel asked. "About someone after us?"

"Well, not exactly," King replied. "I haven't come up with anyone after you. But there's a subject area I've got to discuss."

"If it's that tanker deal, I'm an innocent man, Detective. And that's a federal matter, not even in your jurisdiction. The IRS won't leave me alone. Their tactics are like a secret police. They came here one night. Ramy was in her nightgown. They wanted to . . ."

"It's about your marriage, sir."

Shel fell silent. Now the pen he'd been rolling in his hands dropped into his lap.

"I'm sorry, sir," King said. "But we have information to the effect that . . ."

"Is that why you came?" Shel asked. He really wasn't angry. He seemed too drained, too weak in the blood for any real anger to mushroom. But a look of hurt was etched all over his beaten face. "My wife's body, *parts* of her body, are still warm in the ground and you come with rumors about us."

"Sir, again I apologize. I don't mean to cause you any pain."

"Empty words, Detective."

"But every angle has to be tracked down. You yourself said to investigate the hell out of this. Now, sir, there were reports that you and Mrs. Jordan had some . . . well, some difficulties."

"It's true. There's no shame in that, and it didn't change my feeling for Ramy. Yes, there were rough spots."

"Would you care to go into them?"

"Tell me what you know."

"Only that, Mr. Jordan. Arguments. Mrs. Jordan sometimes driving away after a scene."

"That's true, too," Shel conceded. Now his chest appeared to cave in, adding to the aura of weakness, the picture of a beaten and broken man. "I wasn't always Mr. Right."

"Was there another Mr. Right?" King winced at his own question. He'd hit it so hard, so fast. He hadn't built up to it, and for an instant he was ashamed.

And yet, strangely, Shel smiled. It was a weak smile, but one that had the effect of unburdening him, of freeing him from some terrible secret. "Interesting question," he answered cryptically.

"Was there, sir?"

"Detective, I've been quizzed by the authorities many times. I know every technique, every style. You guys never ask a question unless you already know the answer. So, I guess you've got this answer too. You tell me. Tell me all about my wife's affair with Bret Lewis."

King didn't budge. An old police mentor had taught him never to show shock—it makes the detective look unprofessional. But he caught Shel's admission in the gut like a fighter in his prime. He groped for the next words, even the next idea. He began writing precisely what Shel had just said, but his pencil was shaking. The bombshell had come out of nowhere. "My information wasn't that specific," he said, almost nonchalantly.

"Yeah, right," Shel answered, not really believing it. "I guess you've got a real scoop."

"How long did it go on, sir?"

"I don't know. I taped a phone conversation between them. It was pretty strong stuff, but I forgive her. I forgive her because it was probably my own fault. I should have done more for her."

A tape. There was evidence. King couldn't even guess at its significance, but it opened up a can of worms that had to be examined closely. So Bret had lied, or at least held back information. And that called into suspicion everything else Bret had said. "Did Mr. Lewis ever give you any hint whatever that he was involved with your wife?" King asked.

"Never. Look, I don't want to talk about this. It's over. Bret is still my friend. Maybe he loved my wife. Maybe she needed him. But I can overlook that now. I can overlook a lot now that Ramy is gone."

"Sure, I understand, sir. And in a way I guess it's good that Mrs. Lewis never knew."

"Are you kidding?"

"Sir?"

"I told her. I played the tape for her."

"She *knew*?" Now King almost lost it.

"Yes. I was sure she was the one who told you."

chapter
twenty-eight

"What did you want me to say?"

"I wanted you to tell me the truth."

"Look, all right, I held it back. I'm sorry. I didn't think it had anything to do with this case. I was embarrassed . . . and I didn't want to hurt Ramy's memory."

"Your apology is accepted."

King was back in Sarah's office, the door tightly shut. Sarah's eyes were bloodshot now, but she had fought back the tears, steeling herself. "So Shel told you . . ."

"It came out in conversation," King replied. "He had only great things to say about you. He wanted this to be kept private and it will be, to the best of my legal and professional ability."

"You just left the barn door open," Sarah said.

"I know. I'll try to keep it from getting out, but I'm not God." A new heat wave had started, and King was dressed in a painfully creased light gray suit whose left shoulder was lower than its right. Beads of sweat decorated his bald head, and even his neatly trimmed beard seemed matted and shriveled.

"Well, you know the story," Sarah said "Shel brought me the tape."

"And you'd had no hint of this before?'

Again, Sarah balked.

"You'd had no hint of this before?" King repeated.

"I didn't know about this one," Sarah replied. "About Ramy. But I knew there was another."

"A second other woman?"

"Yes, I'm afraid Bret worked in duplicate. The only reason I'm telling you this is because I don't want to be accused of holding anything back again."

"A wise lady."

"I'll be the judge of that," Sarah replied. "I want your word that none of this gets back to my husband. I'm trying to save my marriage, Detective. Please try to understand that."

"Mrs. Lewis," King answered, "I'll try to help you do that. The only things that interest me are facts that might help solve this murder. I don't know what those facts are. Most things we collect in a case like this are useless, but right now I can't separate the useless from the critical. So I ask a lot of questions."

"You sure do."

"And I hope to come up with something. I will not inform your husband of anything you're saying, unless called upon to do so in a court of law. And if it comes to that, the whole mess will be all over the kitchen table, so to speak."

"So to speak," Sarah murmured.

"Now, the second other woman."

"Congresswoman Alison Carver of California." Oh how good it felt finally to get that out. Sarah almost laughed when she said it, but thought better and kept her satisfaction to herself.

"I see," King replied, writing down in his brand new notepad, which he'd bought especially for this interview. "A congresswoman." He was rocketing to gumshoe heaven. This was the big time, page one, film at eleven and a "technical advisor" credit at the end of a Hollywood film. The thought "book contract" floated through his mind, and already he saw himself sitting in a bookshop autographing copies with his picture on the back cover, and dishing with Larry King on the decline of Washington morality.

"Yes, a congresswoman," Sarah replied.

"You had proof?"

"Pictures."

"Is this ongoing?"

"I don't know. I'm hoping that it was just a fling. Bret has been keeping regular hours since Ramy's death, and I don't see any hint that he's wandering again. Maybe it was just an interlude."

"Let's hope so, Mrs. Lewis," King said. "You never brought this up to your husband—either woman?"

"No, not really."

"Not *really*?"

"I hinted at it a few nights ago. It almost slipped out. I don't know if Bret caught on to how much I know, but I doubt that he did. He just got very emotional and denied he'd ever cheated on me."

"And you didn't believe him, did you?"

"The camera doesn't lie. The microphone doesn't lie. When I've got a regular audiovisual presentation on my husband, belief goes into the shredder."

"Sure," King said. "I'd feel the same way."

"But there's tomorrow, Detective, isn't there? Didn't Scarlett say something like that?"

"Yes, ma'am, she did. Right at the end of the movie."

"Unless it's legally necessary," King was saying to Bret at the Pentagon a little later. "Nothing you say to me will be reported to your wife."

"I love my wife," Bret replied, visibly shaken by what he'd heard so far.

"I'm sure you do," King said, utterly without expression, not giving Bret's words an undue amount of weight.

"And this thing about me and Ramy—it just isn't true."

"You telling me that on the level?" King asked.

"Absolutely on the level. I know Sarah suspected something. We had it out about that. She'd just gotten a wrong idea."

"There's a tape," King said.

"Excuse me?"

"A tape. You know, a cassette thing that goes round and round."

"What kind of tape?"

"A tape with you and Mrs. Jordan on it."

"How do you know?"

"Police officers have ways of finding out."

"Oh. You were bugging Shel's phones."

King just shrugged, keeping his pledge not to reveal his source. "You have anything to say about the tape?" he asked Bret.

"I haven't heard it, Detective," Bret said, now pacing the office, gazing into his prized display cases each time he passed them. "I don't know if you have. But I'm sure it's just a misunderstanding. Ramy and I were certainly close—very close, but not in the way you think. I cared a great deal about her and tried to help her. That's all."

"I understand the tape doesn't confirm that line of thinking at all," King replied, glancing down into his notebook. He avoided eye contact with Bret, trying to make Bret feel uneasy, disliked, disbelieved.

"But you haven't heard it?"

"No. It's been described. I'll hear it at the proper time."

On Bret's desk was a diplomatic message reporting that Swiss intermediaries in Lebanon were negotiating for the release of American hostages, but were facing escalating demands from the kidnappers. They'd wanted a million dollars a day before. Now it was two, and counting. For a moment Bret broke off his talk with King, sauntered casually over to the desk and studied the message, using the few moments to gather his thoughts. He knew the rules of engagement: Voices don't rise, brows don't sweat, hands don't shake, eyes don't shift, mouths don't twitch. He followed them all like a Boy Scout shooting for a merit badge in lying.

Not that King's visit was bad. No way. It was wonderful, perfect. It was just that Bret wanted to be sure to play *his* part perfectly, for he knew how critical this meeting was. Kyle King was on the right track, and Bret had to keep him there.

"Detective King," Bret finally said, "you've had close friends, haven't you?"

"Sure."

"I mean, close female friends. Not romantic gigs, but just close."

King shrugged and actually had to think back to some actresses he liked to describe as "my very close friends," but who never were. "No, actually I haven't had any close female friends."

"Then you can't possibly understand. Sometimes, words are used, expressions, that you wouldn't use with a close male friend."

"Uh huh," King replied.

"If you heard the tape, you'd see what I mean," Bret said. "I'd even volunteer to listen to it with you. I think everything would be straightened out."

"We might be able to work that," King said. Now he was starting to hedge his disbelief, but, professional skeptic that he had to be, he hardly abandoned it. After all, the information he'd heard about Bret revolved around more than Ramy Jordan. His own wife had volunteered that her husband had, at least for a time, cheated. "Uh, another thing, sir," King continued.

"Yes?"

"Alison Carver."

Bret hardly reacted. "Alison Carver?"

"The congresswoman."

"Yes, I know who she is. What about her?"

"Do you know her?"

"Of course. She's very important in areas that I deal with."

"Your relationship with her . . ."

Now Bret flashed some anger, swinging around and approaching King, towering over the detective, who was spread out in a visitor's chair. "Why are you asking these questions?"

"Because I have to," King replied, used to being challenged. "This case didn't turn out to be elementary, my dear Lewis."

"What does a congresswoman have to do with it?"

"Not *a* congresswoman, Mr. Secretary. *That* congresswoman. And she has everything to do with it. I've seen some strange marriages here—I mean yours and the Jordans'—and strange marriages produce strange ideas, and strange ideas produce strange motives. And, do I have to tell you, strange motives produce fees for morticians and stage time for priests."

"You're bonkers."

Now King flashed a rare smile, a smile so deep that the creases extended down below his beard to his neck. "Amazing how regularly my sanity is questioned," he said. "Usually by a man with something to hide."

Bret hardly reacted. "I have nothing to hide. The congresswoman and I are close friends."

"You have a lot of close female friends," King observed. "Or had."

"There's nothing wrong with that. I have a lot of business with Alison Carver."

"At what hours?"

"Many hours."

"Like midnight?"

"Where'd you get that?" Bret asked.

"You denying it?"

"Where'd you get it?"

"Philanderer's hotline," King replied. "Just answer the question."

"I sometimes see her after hours. I like her. You can have friends. There's no law."

"I know there's no law. But there's decency. What do you tell your wife?"

"What the hell do you care, King?" A good snap to that, Bret thought.

"I care, I like gossip," King snapped back. "Besides, I have a professional interest in you."

"Am I a suspect?"

"Yes."

"That's obscene."

"You want to call the Supreme Court?"

"If I'm a suspect, I won't answer any other questions without an attorney."

"Oh, you watch crime shows. Okay, Perry Mason's in the yellow pages."

"I've got someone better."

"Then I suggest you call him."

"Of course, you have no evidence against me. I don't need an attorney to tell me that," Bret said.

"But I've got hunches," King replied, now getting up and piercing Bret with the laser stare reserved for those he'd begun to loathe. "Hunches are big with me. They lead to facts."

"Detective King," Bret countered, "may I gaze into my professional crystal ball and offer a prediction?"

"Without a lawyer?"

"Without a lawyer."

"Certainly."

"I predict, Detective King, that you're about to make a complete ass of yourself."

"I'll take it under advisement," King said.

Now both played at ignoring the other. Bret turned to his desk and sat down, busying himself, not even bothering to say good-bye. King carefully shut his notebook and slipped it into his inside jacket pocket. Then, without another word, he got up and left, smiling at Bret's secretary as he stepped into the vestibule.

As he walked the Pentagon corridors, brushing past officers with stars on their shoulders, King sensed that a break in the case was coming.

So did Bret.

Each knew the dangers, the risks.

A bombshell was ready to explode.

PART THREE

PART THREE

chapter
twenty-nine

But the bombshell didn't explode immediately. It took three months. Still, when it happened, it rocked Washington and swept across the TV networks. Washington was used to political scandal. It had grown accustomed to murder in darkened streets. But it couldn't recall anything like this. It was too juicy to be missed, and better than any hearing Congress could create for competition.

No courtroom in Arlington was big enough. It wasn't going to be merely a trial. It was going to be a circus, and the local authorities accommodated the ticketholders. A new auditorium being built at a school was quickly modified so the media would have plenty of access and the crowds could get their peek at the fallen defendant and, equally important, the celebrities from the news programs. The streets outside the school were filled with vans with microwave antennas on top, ready to beam pictures and sound to the public watching at home. Neighborhood lawns were trampled. Hawkers were selling soft drinks, maps, and pulp biographies of the main personalities in the case. Even the international press was there. The Lords of Fleet Street loved a good trial, and the paparazzi were determined to make European celebrities of all the combatants.

There had been rumors for weeks before the indictment was announced and the trial date set. The word "terrorism" had dropped from all mention of the story. Kyle King, ever mindful of Hollywood hype, had tickled the ears of gossip columnists and a local magazine writer who specialized in sleaze. And some reporters had developed some theories of their own, based on their private probings. The name "Bret Lewis" had crossed a number of journalistic lips. Ambitious. Conniving. A fixer. A man on the make. A water boy for Tim Curran. The term "physical evidence" cropped up in press speculation—physical evidence that clinched the case, that tied all the human threads together, that was there from the beginning but had to be reexamined once King had opened the secrets of the Lewis and Jordan marriages.

It was fall. The weather was reasonable. The auditorium was ultramodern, with tall windows on each side allowing beams of light to stream in, cathedral style. The stage had not yet been installed, so a temporary floor was put in to create the trial area at the front of the mammoth "courtroom." It wasn't only justice, it was show business, and both the media and the local populace loved it.

The first rap of the gavel brought no great cooperation from the eager audience, any more than the first downbeat of the orchestra at a Wednesday matinee. Right in the second row sat Al Durfee, having decided to sacrifice a day's work tailing a salesman suspected of stealing from his firm. Next to him were Phil and Francesca Black, who couldn't have been more pleased by developments. The pictures Durfee had sold them on the cheap were now worth the tabloid equivalent of Rembrandts, and the price would surely climb after conviction.

"You have 'em locked up?" Durfee remembered to ask.

"Sure," Phil replied, forgoing even an attempt at the Australian accent.

"Where?"

"Al, I can't tell you that."

"I don't mean exactly where, but what city?"

"Here."

"Mistake, Phil. Get 'em somewhere else. The kinda people who don't like that stuff published—they drill through walls. And have copies made."

"That I've done," Phil replied, a bit testily. "We're professionals, Al. Please don't insult us."

"Just being thorough," Durfee remarked.

Another rap of the gavel. And then another. This time the crowd began to quiet down. On the bench, Judge Thomas "Bo" Meeker looked stern and unruffled by the commotion around him. Meeker had been a practicing lawyer for most of his career, but had been made a criminal court judge four years before this trial. He was fifty-one, heavy, round-faced and small-eyed, with a shock of flowing gray hair.

"Court will come to order," Meeker said with a Southern accent that went well beyond the modest dialect of northern Virginia, where the trial was being held. Actually, Meeker had worked on his accent over the years, honing its courtly, patrician tones—the better to play for press and public. He had graduated from Harvard Law School, but never emphasized it, and in fact deleted it from all press releases. Now he played the good ol' Southern boy, someone locals could trust. But he wanted it both ways—good ol', yes, but also a legal Solomon, a mountain of respect.

"Come to order, please," Meeker repeated, now clearing his throat. "I apologize for the crowded conditions, but we've done everything we could to accommodate the public interest in this case. As long as everyone is orderly and there's no buzzing and no outbursts, we'll get along fine. If there's any behavior problem, I will take action. Everyone who's ever sat in my courtroom knows that."

Meeker wore half spectacles, and now peered sternly over them to gaze around the auditorium, satisfied he had taken control of the proceedings. The place was silent. Anticipation radiated from every row. It tingled down to the hands of each reporter with a pencil and pad.

"This case has drawn more interest than any in a long time," Meeker went on. "I can understand that. But my job is to make sure justice is done, and that doesn't depend on the size of the headlines. This will be an honest trial conducted the same as any other."

At the word "honest," Meeker looked down sternly at the prosecution table. There, staring right back with barely concealed contempt and twelve gold fillings, was L. Howard Gresh, who would prosecute the case. And it was evident from Meeker's stare that he was in contempt of Gresh even if Gresh wasn't in contempt of court. If Meeker was patrician, Gresh was anything but. He was, in fact, Meeker's opposite in every conceivable way.

Only a mother could love Howie Gresh, and even his mother

found it an unspeakable burden. Howie Gresh, only thirty-two, transplanted from Philadelphia, was a squirt. He was a weasel. He was the ninety-pound weakling. He was the kid every kid loved to hate long before they knew what hate was and how good it felt. He was no taller than five-four, telephone-pole thin, with a narrow face that opponents envisioned at the end of a fishing line. He also wore glasses, thick glasses whose frames were too big for him and extended beyond the edges of his temples. And he had that voice. Call it soprano, and that might put it down a couple of octaves. It wasn't for nothing that Howie was called the piccolo of lawyers. In law school he had had to get special dispensation to graduate without a required class because the professor refused to admit him, on general principles alone.

But the public loved him. Howie Gresh was every shlump who made it, every kid who couldn't get a date for the senior prom, every wimp who threw up on the school bus. The fact was, the guy was a terrific little prosecutor who got back at the world by sending people away, sometimes for sentences that seemed a bit much for their relatively minor offense. To Howie, everyone was guilty of something. The innocent? "An innocent man is someone about to make his first mistake," he often chuckled, a chuckle that sounded like a mouse choking to death. But the public loved that, too.

The judge shifted his eyes from the revolting Gresh to the defense table. It was Woody Evans for the defense, the best dressed man in the courtroom, his black silk vest adding an elegant touch to his perfectly tailored suit. Evans was twice Gresh's age, and, unlike Gresh, he exuded a kindliness that was half put on and half accidental. He'd watched too many Spencer Tracy movies and fancied himself *that* kind of advocate, the kind you'd come to for advice on any manner of subject, from taxes to the right person to marry. He was famous for the line, "The wife is the first to know and the last to believe." He was also famous for divorce cases that stemmed from that eternal truth and for fees that themselves could mean eternal payments. But Judge Meeker liked him. They were soul brothers in the oozing of lawyerly charm, and Howie Gresh was vermin in the court, a disease that had not yet been cured.

"This is a heinous crime," Meeker intoned, now grim-faced and somber. "A woman has been murdered. Brutally taken from her family and friends. In my years as a lawyer and a judge I have rarely seen any felony so heartless and cold. It is a case that cries out for justice and punishment, but punishment only of the right person. We are here to try one individual for the crime, and it will be up to the jury, and only the jury, to decide whether that individual is innocent or guilty."

All eyes were on Meeker. He had an imposing presence. Within minutes he had taken utter command of the huge hall to the point where only a few scattered coughs marred the absolute silence. Once again, he looked at the defense table. "Will the defendant please rise?" he said.

Now all eyes shifted to the defense. Only two people sat at the table, Woody Evans and the defendant. Evans gestured to his client to rise. It was the moment the entire hall had waited for, the moment the press corps had awaited for months.

The defendant rose.

"You are charged with the willful murder of one Ramy Jordan," Meeker announced. "How do you plead?"

"Not guilty," Sarah Lewis whispered.

Bedlam. Bedlam in the court—even though the plea had been expected. It was the reality of the moment that counted. It was hearing Sarah actually say the words. Judge Meeker rapped his gavel three times, and the bedlam quieted, but only to a din of murmurs.

Barely aware of the excitement around her, Sarah swayed on her feet. From the corner of her eye she spotted Bret in the first row. His jaw was forward, strong and defiant. As she uttered "not guilty" he threw her a solid thumbs-up. It was a small sign, he knew, but all that was needed. Many eyes in the court were on him, and he could count on at least three reporters in row two to see his gesture. One reporter right behind him was known in the trade as Purple— for thirty-three years she'd covered every major trial in northern Virginia, always appearing in a purple outfit. "A low-key but angry badge of support" she wrote of Bret's thumbs-up to Sarah. "A gesture that told the world he would stand by his wife no matter what."

Purple knew a trial needed heroes, and she adopted Bret for the role. "Eyes bloodshot, face drawn" she wrote with quick, though slightly wrinkled hands. "The indictment and the screaming head-lines, and now this tumult in the court was taking its toll on both of them."

On the other side of the room, behind the prosecutor, an impassive Shel Jordan registered almost no reaction to the "not guilty." Slumped, looking ten pounds beyond his normal roundness and saddened beyond description, he sat unflinching through it all, occasionally staring at Sarah with a curious, incredulous expression.

"Order, order in this court," Judge Meeker demanded, holding the proceedings until there was silence. And then, jury selection began.

The serious action would not start for as much as a week, old hands knew, so they looked to what the cynical called "the real trial" to provide the enlightenment during that period. The real trial occurred in the streets, during recesses and after sessions, played out for the press and, especially, the television cameras. The real trial took place in the court of public opinion, in some respects the highest court of all, for Sarah's fate could ultimately rest with an elected appeals judge or an elected governor, or even some appointed prison official watching which way the political winds were blowing.

And so, after Meeker rapped his gavel signaling the first recess, the reporters made for the doors, setting themselves up like snipers, ready to ambush the principals in the trial. The auditorium, the temporary courtroom, was attached to the school, and students released for lunch were pushed, knocked over, shoved and shouted away by the scholars of the press as they jockeyed for position and camera angles.

First out, as he always was when he prosecuted a case that he thought was in the bag, was the diminutive and despicable Howie Gresh, beaming with pride after a first morning that he felt went extremely well. As assistant district attorney, Gresh had his eyes on higher things. He knew precisely how to play for the cameras and microphones, even though his personality fought him every step of the way.

"Mr. Gresh, how do you think it went?" was the standard first question.

"Very well," Gresh replied, pushing his way to the front of the crowd. His screeching voice preceded him. "I'm glad people got a good look at her. I'm glad they heard her whisper. You see, when they're guilty they whisper because they're ashamed."

"And jury selection?"

"We selected two. I'm very happy. These are solid citizens who'll never let some overeducated intellectual get away with murdering a family woman."

"Are you sure you'll ask for the death penalty?"

"Of course. What else is there? If you were Ramy Jordan's mother, wouldn't you want the death penalty?"

"The defense is saying that you really haven't got any evidence."

"They always say that. And I always win. How do I win without evidence?" He chuckled. It could ring in your ears.

"And you're satisfied you have enough of a motive?"

Gresh scowled. The questioner seemed skeptical. "This is the best possible motive," he answered crisply. "She killed someone she thought was trying to steal her husband."

"Was she?"

"Was she what?"

"Was Ramy Jordan trying to steal Bret Lewis?"

"Why don't we wait and see," Gresh replied, and then slipped past the cameras to head for a mobile van nearby, where he was scheduled to give an exclusive interview to a network anchorman.

One reporter saw Sarah slip out a side door, heading for a car that would whisk her away for lunch. With her, holding her by the arm, was Woody Evans. He may have been in his sixties, but Evans had been a sprinter in his youth and still took some turns around the track. When he saw reporters he prompted Sarah, and they both dashed for the car. "No comment!" he shouted at the press. "Mrs. Lewis will not be interviewed at this time!" It was part of his strategy. He knew Sarah was still too traumatized to face reporters. "You'll be fine," he told her, as he took her away. "It's just too soon." A little more experience in court, he was thinking, and then he could present her to reporters—a falsely charged woman, the victim of an ambitious prosecutor.

Besides, Woody Evans knew there was good fodder for the hungry press inside the courthouse. Bret Lewis, waiting in there by prearrangement with Evans, had no qualms about speaking with media. In fact, he had volunteered. "I'll be your public point man," he'd told Evans, who thought it a fine idea. Bret, loyal husband, would fight in public for Sarah's innocence. And Sarah had no real objections. No matter what she knew about him, or thought she knew, or thought he'd done, she needed his help.

But Bret didn't confront the press uncoached. Tim Curran had not only given him advice by phone, he'd sent him a handwritten note with the political wisdom of the ages:

> Bret—
> No matter what the woman has done, you must defend her, and passionately. Remember, no one ever forgives a man who abandons his wife. So, as far as you're concerned, she's innocent. Even if they've got a picture with the bomb in her hands, she's innocent. She could be lighting the fuse. She's innocent.
> Those people out there—they cheat on their wives and husbands all the time. But it makes them feel good to stand up for loyalty. It's part of the great lie. It's what our profession is all about.

Bret agreed. Had the letter not been so private, he would have framed it.

"Mr. Lewis," a reporter shouted as Bret emerged from the courthouse, "how did you feel about the first morning?"

"Rotten," Bret replied. "The whole thing is a farce. The police couldn't find the real killer, or chose *not* to find him, so they blame my wife."

"Will you stand by her?" a woman asked.

"To the end." The reporters wrote down his answer, though a few thought it a bit odd that he would already be talking about the "end."

"How can you be sure your wife is innocent?"

"Because I've known her for more than twenty years. Ramy Jordan was her closest friend."

"But they say you and Mrs. Jordan ..."

"A lie. It'll all come out. If Sarah ever thought it were true, she would have asked me. She's the gentlest person alive."

"What did you mean when you said the police might have chosen not to find the real killer?"

"Look," Bret replied, "I'm angry. I'm angry because a good woman is being put through all this. Maybe I was out of line. But *I* was the target, and, frankly, there may be some people who don't want to *embarrass* certain parties."

The reporters pounced. "What parties?"

"Certain foreign countries."

"Would you be more specific?" a TV newsman shouted, over the giggles of schoolkids who were passing by and pointing out the TV reporters they often saw on the screen.

"I'd prefer not to. But terrorism is touchy. Sometimes we have interests in countries that support it."

"Are you accusing anyone?"

"I'm just stating a theory. Look, the most important thing is, Sarah is innocent. I will fight for my wife and I will never leave her. Now if I can go . . ."

He brushed past the reporters, having given them a sound byte that could easily fit into the six o'clock news. Fighting words, yet loving words. He was proud of how he'd handled himself. He was also proud of the way he'd manipulated the justice system.

He fought the temptation to smile. As he had before the bombing, he'd practiced a grim, fighting expression in front of his mirror and in his new Oldsmobile. But it felt good, he thought, as he maneuvered away from the press. When things went right, it always felt good.

Shel Jordan was the last person out of the courthouse during the lunch recess. As might be expected, he had a public relations man with him. Earl Willingham had been an editor with a number of trade publications before starting his own firm in Washington. He was forty-five, well-read, and often bordered on the pompous. He had the aura of a man above-it-all, better than the media rabble, merely assisting a client who wanted nothing more than to be left alone to do charity work, feed the hungry and clothe the poor.

Shel was silent. "Mr. Jordan is understandably upset," Willingham said, in a cultured, baritone voice. "I'll answer any questions."

"Can't he speak for himself?" a reporter asked.

"He'd prefer not to. This gentleman's wife has been murdered. He's asked me to assist him."

"What does he feel about Sarah Lewis now?"

"Distress," Willingham answered. "Obviously. However, Mr. Jordan is a fair-minded man. He wants to await the presentation of evidence. But, from what he has heard, he's anguished over what a friend may have done."

"Are you anguished?" asked a reporter, still pushing to get an answer from Shel.

"As I said," Willingham firmly replied, "Mr. Jordan . . ."

But Shel interrupted. "I'll say something," he began, his voice shaking and drained. "I'll say something for the one member of our double wedding who isn't here. Ramy would want justice. Nothing more. Nothing less. I wasn't the greatest husband, but she was the greatest wife. I'm here to see that she gets that justice, no matter where it leads."

chapter
thirty

The jury was selected. Seven men, five women. Nine white. Three black. Of the seven men, three were retail clerks, one was a retired airline pilot, one was a carpenter and two were middle-management executives. Of the five women, two were homemakers, one was a computer programmer, one a school administrator and one a biologist. Both sides were reasonably pleased.

"Call Shel Jordan."

Howie Gresh's off-key soprano scratched through the packed auditorium, and a hush fell over the place. Gresh had kept his tactics secret. No one had expected his first witness to be the husband of the victim, although it was evident from his past trials that Gresh loved to charge in with an opening surprise.

"Do you swear to tell the truth, the whole truth and nothing but the truth?" Shel was asked, his hand on an old Bible with a cracked, burgundy cover.

"I do," he replied, in a remarkably strong voice.

Gresh wasted no time with preliminaries or niceties. He didn't even bother with the usual condolences over Shel Jordan's loss. His style was shock trial. "Mr. Jordan," he began, "did you tell Sarah Lewis that your wife was having an affair with her husband?"

"I did."

"Did she believe it?"

"Yes."

"How do you know?"

"Well, I played her a tape that I had made. I sometimes tape phone conversations at home. Y'know, for business and things like that. It was Mr. Lewis and my wife. They were ... affectionate."

"And what was Sarah's reaction?"

"Well, she obviously wasn't pleased."

"Did she say she intended to do anything?"

"Oh, yes. She wanted to save her marriage."

"I see. She, uh, loved her husband."

"Oh, yes."

"Did the affair between your wife and Mr. Lewis come as a shock to her?"

"Well, in some ways, yes; in some ways, no."

"Explain that."

"She felt he'd been ... well, she told me that she thought he was seeing someone else."

"And who was that someone?"

"A congresswoman. Alison Carver."

There was a loud gasp in the court, answered by Meeker's gavel. "This isn't a soap opera," he warned. "You will remain silent throughout. Go on, Mr. Gresh."

"So now Mrs. Lewis believed her husband was possibly involved with two women ..."

"Yes." Shel looked over at Sarah as he answered. She sat stoically, concentrating on Woody Evans's instructions: Show no emotion, stay in control. "Above all," Evans had told her, "be *likable*. Between facts and likable, juries choose likable."

"Did she have a plan of action?" Gresh continued.

"Sure. As I said, she wanted to save her marriage. And I wanted to save mine. So we decided to see marriage counselors. You know, psychologists and the like."

"And you did?"

"We got to one. Lorenzo Rosenthal. Then the double wedding and ..."

"I see. Tell me, did Mrs. Lewis at any point express vengeance toward your wife?"

"No, she didn't."

"Are you sure?"

Now Shel leaned back and thought. He was almost elegant in a dark blue suit and maroon tie, the picture of refined respectability, except for the bulging weight. And, of course, he carried a reputation for wheeling and dealing that no tailor could fix. "Well, she was angry."

"Describe her anger."

"After I played her the tape she referred to the people on it as conniving. She said, 'That conniving little . . . *those* conniving little . . .'"

"That's all she said?"

"Well, she said other things. She said it wasn't the Ramy she knew."

"But no threats."

"No."

"Didn't that strike you as odd?"

"What do you mean?"

"Well," Gresh said, staging every moment of it, "didn't it strike you as odd that someone who'd just learned that her beloved husband was having an affair with her best friend *wouldn't* make threats— like 'I'm gonna get her.' Something like that?"

"Well, yes, I guess it did. I mean—God forgive me—I actually described my wife as a bitch to Sarah, after I played her the tape. But Sarah, yeah, her reaction was pretty mild."

"How mild?"

"Well, after hearing her reaction I said, 'You're an optimist, Sarah Lewis.'"

"And until the end of Ramy's life, is it your testimony that Sarah never said anything harsh to Ramy, never confronted her, never indicated to her in any way what she knew?"

"Sure. That's my testimony."

"Doesn't that sound like a woman who's figuring to do something and covering it up?"

"Objection!" shouted Woody Evans, now on his feet.

"Sustained!" Judge Meeker barked. "Mr. Gresh, you knew perfectly well, suh, that such a question would never be allowed. It's pure speculation."

"I apologize, Your Honor," Gresh said, with the gooney smile that belied his razor-sharp mind. No matter. He'd made his point to the jury, even if the question would never appear in the record. Purple, jotting it down from her perspective in the second row, saw this as the first attack on Sarah. Knowing Gresh from past trials, she predicted he'd carry it all the way. Point by point, he'd paint a picture of Sarah as actress—playing the long-suffering wife, pretending to save her marriage while plotting Ramy's murder. Purple had it right. Shel Jordan was the ammo in Gresh's opening gun.

"Now, finally, Mr. Jordan," Gresh went on, "I must ask you a difficult question. It may be painful, but it's important that the court know."

"Yes. Go ahead."

"Was this the first time your wife was . . . involved with someone else?"

Again, murmurs in the court. Meeker cast a stern glance at spectators and press, and the murmurs subsided.

"Well, no," Shel answered. "There were other times."

"Was Sarah Lewis aware of this?"

"Objection!" Evans shouted again. "Irrelevant."

"Your Honor, it's very relevant," Gresh insisted, propelling his meager frame up to the bench. "If Mrs. Lewis was aware of Ramy Jordan's . . . dalliances, it could affect her opinion of her, her mindset."

"I'll allow it," Meeker ruled, "but don't pursue it too far, Mr. Gresh."

"Of *course* not, Your Honor."

"Mrs. Lewis was aware of it," Shel replied, a little catch in his voice. "I mentioned it in Dr. Rosenthal's office." He shifted in his seat, stifling a gasp. Then, as an already riveted courtroom looked on, Shel Jordan apparently cracked. Shoulders heaving, his head buried in chunky, sweaty hands, his whole body shook uncontrollably, his muffled voice barely audible. ". . . Ramy's best friend. Her best friend . . ." The moment was right. Howie Gresh loved it. He loved Shel. He was in ecstasy.

"Thank you," Gresh said. "I assure you, we all share your loss. I have nothing further, Your Honor."

Meeker looked down at Shel. "Can you continue to testify?" he asked.

"Yes," Shel whispered.

Meeker then turned to Evans. "Questions, counselor?"

"No questions now," Evans replied.

Evans was playing it right, the reporter in purple jotted on her pad. Shel Jordan, the husband of the deceased, was an inherently sympathetic witness. Now he was even more so. Attacking him made no sense. It would just antagonize the jury.

"You may step down, Mr. Jordan," Meeker instructed Shel.

Shel Jordan got up with some difficulty and stepped down from the witness chair. He walked toward a side door to leave the court, but, as he did, he hesitated for a moment. He shot a glance at Sarah. Her eyes were lowered. She couldn't look at him. Although she was innocent, she was embarrassed that he might have *thought* her guilty.

As for Shel—his face showed hurt, pain. But, beneath the pain, the spectators in the first few rows saw a seething anger. They were sure he'd already made up his mind. He and Willingham, though, still insisted on "no comment" as they rushed by reporters outside.

It is hallowed tradition in the American press to assess the condition of the prosecution and defense after each witness. And so, during a ten-minute recess, reporters buzzed over the impact of Shel Jordan's testimony. Purple was in the thick of it, her silver hair a contrast to a smart, purple suit. She wrote: "Shel Jordan has been damaging to Sarah Lewis, but not fatal." Pursuing her usual practice, she jotted down lines that would find their way into her full story, lines that confirmed her earlier prediction of the prosecution strategy: "An aggressive Howard Gresh is painting a stark motive for the defendant—jealousy of the deceased." And later: "He showed that when Sarah Lewis heard that tape she reacted strangely, was just too cool, too saintly." Purple summed up: "Gresh is carefully building the image of Sarah Lewis as a suspicious, jealous wife." She added one more note. "But was she?"

It was during the same recess that Alison Carver issued a statement from her office absolutely denying any romance with Bret Lewis. She expressed outrage at the suggestion that she'd break up a marriage, and made it clear that she thought Sarah had a vivid imagination.

Hinting that she believed Sarah was guilty of Ramy's murder, Carver told a reporter that afternoon, "Frankly, I'm glad *I'm* alive." It was stark, but Carver believed the statement would stick.

Carver's denial danced in the heads of Phil and Francesca Black, who were sitting on Al Durfee's photographic gold mine. Print the photos? Wait? Sell them for a mint? They decided to wait, hoping for some explosive revelation that would make the pictures even more valuable. They also knew—as did Sarah in her innermost thoughts —that the pictures, while tantalizing, were not conclusive. Bret and Alison weren't really *doing* much. And either of them could claim that the pictures were doctored. The power of the pictures was in suggestion, in sowing the seeds of scandal.

"Call Morry Sherman."

Gresh smiled as he said the name, as if he knew his next witness would begin tying the noose firmly around Sarah's neck. Morry Sherman, looking his sixty years, hunched over slightly and wearing a suit that didn't fit in any significant dimension, marched up to the witness stand and snapped his right arm into the air. He was duly sworn and sat down with a thump.

"Your name?" Gresh asked.

"Morris Sherman. They call me Morry."

"All right, Morry. What do you do, Morry?"

"I run and own Morry's. That's an electronics shop in Arlington." The voice sounded like a lawnmower in distress. "We are a professional store. Our customers know what the hell they're doing."

"I'm sure, Morry."

"Ask me anything about electronics. I'll answer."

"All right. Now Morry, I'm going to show you some wire." Gresh walked back to the prosecution table and picked up a clear plastic envelope with small bits of electric wire inside. He returned to the witness chair and showed the envelope to Morry, who grabbed it. "Recognize that, Morry?"

"Sure. I sell it."

"Is it a common product?"

"No, it's specialized wire. Very few places handle it. I'm the only one in this area. Y'see, most of these stores ..."

"All right, Morry. Now you're *sure* you recognize it."

"Sure I'm sure. I'm Morry. I can go back to my store and show you the whole roll."

"Commendable, Morry," Gresh said. He loved Morry. The guy was almost as obnoxious as Gresh, but the jury knew he was the real thing, and that's what Gresh wanted. Morry couldn't be bought or swayed. It was written all over him. "Your Honor," Gresh said, "I enter this as the People's Exhibit A. Testimony will identify this wire as coming from what remained of the bomb that killed Ramy Jordan."

"Misuse of equipment," Morry mumbled.

"Now Morry, I want you to think back," Gresh continued. It was an act. Morry had been well prepared for this and rehearsed over and over. "You found a credit card in your store recently, didn't you?"

"Sure did. Hate that."

"All right, you held it, didn't you?"

"Right. Well, y'know, most times when they drop a card they come back and look. I mean, you give it back to these card companies, they cut it up. The people get angry, they ..."

"May I ask the name on that card?"

"Sure. It was Sarah Lewis."

"No!" Sarah snapped, now slipping from the absolute control that Evans had prescribed. "Our lock was broken. The card must have been taken from the apartment."

Murmur in the court. Experienced reporters got the connection immediately. Sarah had been in the only store in the area that sold the wire used in the bomb. Why? Why was she even in Morry's, if not to buy that wire? This hurt. Again, it wasn't fatal, but it wasn't something that would make a defendant run out and order new furniture.

"Do you recall Mrs. Lewis coming to your store?"

"No, but y'see, we got these aisles. Tall boxes."

"So it's possible for a customer to come in and out without your seeing him ... or *her*."

"Sure. I trust my people."

"Was wire of the kind we examined sold on the day you found Mrs. Lewis's card?"

"Oh sure."

"To whom?"

"Well, I don't remember. Look, you ever been in my place? I mean, we get mob scenes."

"I'm sure it's a wonderful store," Gresh replied. "Oh, by the way, Mrs. Lewis didn't call for her card, did she?"

"No, she didn't."

"Didn't that strike you as odd? A woman goes into a store, obviously opens her handbag. She'd remember being in that store. You'd think she'd call to ask if you found her card."

"Objection! Speculation again," Evans shouted.

"Watch it, Mr. Gresh," Judge Meeker intoned. "Ah'll allow this, but watch it."

"Morry," Gresh continued, undaunted by the opposition, "isn't it really true that Mrs. Lewis might not have called because she didn't want to bring attention to herself?"

"Objection!"

"Mr. Gresh," the judge insisted, "that was foul."

"Your Honor," Gresh replied, "I profoundly apologize for my professional indiscretion."

Again, the jury got the message.

"Nothing more," Gresh said.

The judge turned toward the defense table. "Mr. Evans?"

Now Woody Evans rose. He made his way slowly toward the witness chair, grasping the lapels of his suit, his polished demeanor lending an air of sobriety to the proceedings. He spoke in the measured, modulated tones of the wise old barrister, the man who'd seen it all.

"Now Morry," Evans began, "you consider yourself a decent man, don't you?"

"Honest and decent."

"Of course. And we applaud that. Now, Morry, you wouldn't want to see an innocent woman's life destroyed, would you?"

"No."

"All right. Now I want you to look over at my client, sitting right over there." He gestured toward Sarah, now in control, her eyes lowered once more, demure and dignified in a gray suit. "Morry," Evans continued, "I want you to tell the court whether you have *ever* seen this woman in your shop."

"No, I've never seen her before. But those tall boxes . . ."

"But if she bought anything," Evans reminded Morry, "she'd have come out from behind those boxes and up to the front. And then you'd have seen her, right, Morry?"

"Yeah," Morry replied. "That is on the beam."

"But you didn't see her."

"Well ..."

"You didn't, did you?"

"Well, I can't recall. I mean, we got all these customers. A lot of regulars."

"So many regulars that you'd spot a stranger?"

"Sometimes yes, sometimes no."

"You wouldn't want Mrs. Lewis *convicted* on the basis of your testimony, would you?"

"No," Morry answered. "Look, just because she dropped a card ..."

"If it *were* she who dropped it."

"Yeah."

"But a card bearing her name wasn't *necessarily* in her possession, correct?"

"Objection!" Gresh shouted. "Speculation, speculation, speculation." He made Pee Wee Herman sound like Macho Man.

"I guess it is," said Judge Meeker.

"I withdraw the question," Woody Evans conceded. Like Gresh before him, he had made his point to the jury. "And I have no further questions for Mr. Sherman."

Morry Sherman stepped down. He didn't look particularly happy. He was an electronics man. He dealt in precision and numbers. But somehow, as he made his way out the side door, he felt vaguely uneasy about his testimony. He felt it had become enshrouded in a fog.

He was right. The word in the hall was that Gresh had scored a good point about Sarah's credit card having been left in an electronics store, but that there was still no smoking gun. What if the card had been lost? What if she'd gone in to make a phone call? What if the card itself had been a forgery? The testimony hadn't helped Sarah, but it was far from conclusive. Purple wrote it this way: "With this witness the prosecution proved only that something belonging to Sarah had been found in the only store in the area that sold some wire used in the bomb. But there are still too many ifs, like what if the wire had actually been bought in some other part of the country."

"They haven't got a thing," Bret told reporters during a recess. "What've they got? That credit card was missing for days. We had a break-in at the apartment. I, uh, told my wife the lock had broken. I didn't want to alarm her."

"Did you report the break-in?" a newsman asked.

"Sure. But who cares about a little burglary, with all that's going on?" He, of course, had faked the break-in, but hoped the jury would surmise that *she* had faked it to cover the card's loss. And so he was quite pleased by Morry's testimony. He knew the credit card wasn't conclusive evidence, but it was one more piece of suspicion, one more mental nudge that the jury would need when deciding its verdict.

"If the prosecution can't come up with more, I'll ask my wife's attorney to move for dismissal," Bret went on.

"How are your relations with your wife?" a reporter asked.

"Excellent. When the truth comes out, you'll see how excellent they are. There've been some real sleazy charges here. They're just not true."

"... a proud and dedicated husband," Purple wrote.

She knew what sold.

So did Bret.

chapter
thirty-one

What reporters found remarkable about Sarah Lewis during the early stages of the trial was her control. Only once had she spoken out, protesting the credit-card evidence, and even then her interruption hardly qualified as an outburst. Inside, though, she was seething, the shock of her indictment wearing off and the fight within her building. She would defeat this, she kept telling a very supportive Bret in their constant conversations. They even had a few laughs together, for the first time in a long time. Through Sarah's eyes the marriage seemed to be healing under the onslaught of this miscarriage of justice. That was good. She was sure the healing would last and that, once exonerated, she would be with Bret for the rest of her life.

Still, a discordant thought sometimes struck her. Had Bret not had that fling with Ramy, there'd have been no murder motive for her, Sarah. And without a motive, there'd have been no indictment and no trial. But Sarah couldn't cope with that thought for long, and tried to focus on the battle at hand.

This wasn't someone's mistake, she was sure. It was intentional, a frame-up at a high level. They had to have a killer in a high-profile case, so they found one with a clear reason to kill. All the evidence was rigged. Sarah was sure of it, and Bret's support fed her certainty. She was also sure that she'd be able to prove it.

Sarah told that to Woody Evans every day, and he always agreed with her. He had to. He'd heard it hundreds of times before. All defendants, innocent or guilty, thought pretty much alike.

*   *   *

"Call Kenneth Warren," Gresh intoned.

Kenneth Warren, about twenty-eight, with the ramrod straight bearing of a general, strode toward the stand and sat down. He looked around the court—at Sarah, at Bret behind her and looking intensely at him, and at a worn, beaten Shel Jordan. Warren caught the quizzical look on Sarah's face. Although she knew he was going to testify, she didn't remember him. Of course. How could she? They'd been together for such a short time.

"State your name," Gresh said.

"Kenneth Lawrence Warren," Warren replied.

"Your occupation, sir."

"I'm a waiter for a catering service."

"I see. And were you assigned to the Lewis/Jordan reception the night of their renewal of vows?"

"I was."

"And were you in close enough proximity to overhear conversations between the members of the Lewis and Jordan families?"

"Yes."

"Mr. Warren, it's been established that Mrs. Jordan went out to the Lewis car to deposit an object. Would you happen to know what that object was?"

"Yes. It was an anniversary gift for Mrs. Lewis."

"A gift. How did you find that out?"

"Well, I overheard Mr. and Mrs. Jordan talking about it. Then I heard Mr. Jordan mentioning it to Mr. Curran and another man."

Ordinarily, there would have been an immediate objection from the defense table, for this, like some of Shel Jordan's, was hearsay evidence. Warren was being asked to repeat what *others* had said. But Evans had decided not to object. He knew from his own investigation that everything Warren would say could be confirmed by someone else. Get it out of the way fast, he reasoned. Avoid confirming witnesses who'd just reinforce the story.

"Mr. Jordan say anything else?" Gresh asked.

"Yes. He said Mrs. Jordan left the anniversary gift on the front seat of Mrs. Lewis's car every year."

"So Sarah Lewis knew in advance that Mrs. Jordan was going out to the car and that the gift would be on the front seat."

"Oh sure. I heard every word. Every year the same. Every year the same."

There was a buzz in the courtroom, too low for Meeker to rap his gavel, but present nonetheless. The buzz was saying that this hurt, that this testimony answered one of the great questions about the crime. Sarah could only be guilty if she'd known in advance that Ramy would go out to the Lewis car. Then Sarah could plant the bomb there. But how *would* she know? Now the answer came. She'd know because Ramy did the same thing every year to celebrate their anniversary.

"Mr. Warren," Gresh continued, "did you hear Mrs. *Lewis* say anything about this tradition?"

"Well, not that I heard. But she did see Mrs. Jordan go out to the car."

"Oh? How did she see that?"

"She waved to her from across the room. Then she definitely saw—we all could see—Mrs. Jordan through a window."

"Thank you. I have nothing else."

"Defense has nothing," Woody Evans announced. Purple wrote that Evans looked disturbed by the testimony, even though he'd seen it coming. Warren was more articulate than Evans had assumed he'd be. And Sarah also looked upset. Warren, after all, had provided a crucial piece to the murder puzzle, and Sarah knew it could be used powerfully against her.

Bret Lewis held a grim, hostile expression as he watched Warren stride from the courtroom. Despite the look, he was privately wishing he could give Warren a generous tip. Of all the conversations he'd staged that night, at least one waiter had overheard and remembered. And he'd remembered so well and come forward with such damaging testimony. It was not looking good for Sarah Lewis. Purple, originally hoping that Sarah would come out a heroine, wrote nothing more about the testimony on her pad.

The next witness took only thirty seconds. She was a heavy-set maid from the Cheshire Motel, about fifty-five, with prematurely gray hair. Gresh himself seemed to give her short shrift, hoping to throw Woody Evans off, make him think this was a minor witness. But she was major. She was very major.

"Did you see Mrs. Lewis get out of her car when she arrived?" Gresh asked.

"Sure did," the maid replied.

"Was she wearing her wedding dress?"

"Nope."

"Was she wearing it when she emerged from her room?"

"Yup."

"Did she go directly to the party or did she stop at her car?"

"Went direct to the shindig."

"Thank you. I'm finished."

Judge Meeker turned to Woody Evans. "Do you have any questions, counselor?"

At first, Evans didn't answer. He simply sat in his chair and stared at the maid, trying to figure out exactly why she was there. He hadn't been thrown by Howie Gresh. He'd seen this tactic too many times before—the quick kill questions, going by so fast that their significance isn't immediately apparent. But Evans was working on a theory, and, within moments, he was sure he'd determined exactly why this woman was on the stand. So, he got up and slowly walked toward her.

"Uh, ma'am," Evans began. "Do you wear glasses?"

"Yes, sir."

"Do you need them for normal seeing?"

"Beyond about five feet," the maid answered.

"You have them on that night?"

"Oh yes, sir."

"Okay. Can you explain to the court why you were able to observe Mrs. Lewis so closely when you were supposed to have been working?"

"I knew that would come up," the maid replied. "And I don't wanna lose my job. But, well, y'see, we don't get that many weddings at the Cheshire, and it's pretty excitin' for us workin' people. So I kinda hung around outside the rooms."

"Just hung around."

"Yes, sir. I get a kick out of that stuff. I sure do. I never had no wedding."

That line did it for Evans. He realized that this witness, like Shel, was too sympathetic to attack. Forget the theory about why Gresh called her. The best thing was to get her off gracefully. "Thank you," he said. "You've been most helpful."

A series of technical witnesses followed, presented to fill in little mechanical details and get basic facts about the crime on the record. But there was a sense in the courtroom that something big was coming—that Howie Gresh was just coasting with the witnesses presented thus far. It was about six days into the trial when the sense of the court proved correct. Gresh made his major move at ten in the morning, early enough for TV reporters to shoot and edit their stories for the five o'clock news shows. Purple knew this would be the day because Gresh appeared in court with freshly cut hair—done by one of Washington's hairstylists to the corrupt—and with a light blue shirt that wouldn't glare in the cameras.

"Call Detective Kyle King," Gresh announced.

From the back of the hall, swaggering as if all cameras were rolling, Kyle King started his march into judicial history. He wore a suit borrowed from a lawyer—a $1,200 job complete with vest—and shoes borrowed from his brother, Alan McAfee, hand-sewn. He'd rubbed some wax on his bald head for a soft sheen, and a little hair cream in the beard to give it perfect body. This was a chance, King knew. The TV people were in the courtroom. The guys from the networks—the ones who bought the two-hour movies of the week—were probably monitoring the trial. This could be a great two-parter, King thought to himself as he approached the witness chair. Monday and Tuesday nights. Four hours. He could play himself. Maybe coproduce. Bottom line—technical consultant.

King was sworn.

"Good morning, Detective King," Gresh began. "You are a detective with the Arlington Police?"

"That is correct," King replied. He'd practiced a firm, yet mellow tone into a dictation machine for about a week.

"And you were assigned to investigate the murder of Ramy Jordan?"

"Correct again."

"When you were first assigned to the case, was there any police mind-set that you confronted?"

"Yes, sir, there was. Pretty much everyone thought this was terrorism. You know, Mr. Lewis is an official with the Navy. That's his specialty. We knew there were some foreign groups operating in the vicinity. And there'd been this blast in Falls Church just a little while earlier."

"A similar explosion?"

"The lab tests showed the materials were identical."

"How did you feel about the terrorism theory, Detective?"

"Oh, I don't think I felt passionately about it. I like to cover all bases. That's the kind of cop I am."

"Commendable," Gresh said. "And you interviewed the principals, is that correct?"

"Yes."

"Were they cooperative?"

"At first I thought they were. Mr. Jordan was cooperative. He told me everything I had to know, and he didn't hold back. The Lewises . . ."

"Go on."

"Well, there were some funny things happening with their marriage, and they weren't straight with me."

"Explain that."

"Mr. Lewis didn't tell me about his extracurriculars, and Mrs. Lewis didn't tell me that she knew—at least not until I confronted her with the fact that I'd found it out."

"In other words, Mrs. Lewis was . . . evasive?"

"Objection!" Evans shouted. "This is all hearsay."

"Your Honor," Gresh replied, "this testimony is critical to my case. What I'm pursuing is not the specifics of the comments Mr. or Mrs. Lewis may have made to Detective King, but Detective King's state of mind in response to those interviews."

Meeker brooded a few moments. "Well, ah'll allow it if you restrict yourself to that, Mr. Gresh."

"I will, Your Honor. To repeat, Detective, was Mrs. Lewis evasive?"

"Yes, I'd say she was evasive."

"Did this whet your detective's appetite?" Gresh asked.

"Sure. How could it not?" He looked out at the crowd in the courtroom and saw several television executives. "When you have the kind of experience I have, day in, day out, working the front lines of crime, you . . ."

"While you were conducting these interviews, was other investigative work under way?"

"Yes," King replied, now stroking the top of his shiny head, wondering how he could get his self-advertising into the testimony.

"You have the results of that work?"

"Yes. It all came through me."

"I'd like to review that now." This was one of Gresh's techniques. While other lawyers depended on technical experts to give technical testimony, Gresh felt that expertise was oversold in courtroom trials. Within a few moments, Gresh was convinced, the jurors forgot they were listening to an expert. They'd react the way they'd react to any person—to voice, demeanor, personality, style, attitude. So Gresh preferred to have a good performer on the stand, presenting evidence originally developed in laboratories. King was that good performer. Gresh depended on him the way a producer depended on a leading man to fill the seats on Saturday night.

And so the scene was set. The obnoxious little prosecutor would orchestrate the words of the articulate, showy cop on the stand.

"Now Detective King," Gresh continued, "would you describe the explosive that was set off in the Lewis car?"

"Yes. It was of the C-4 variety, called Semtex, and it was inserted in a flashlight. The explosive was set off by a blasting cap powered by a battery."

"And how was the device detonated?"

"By remote control."

"How much of the explosive was found?"

"Well, only fragments. But these things don't explode clean, if you follow me. The flashlight blew apart, but there were sections of its case still intact."

"Did these segments exhibit anything . . . unusual?"

"Yes, they did."

"Explain."

"One of them had several strands of human hair attached."

"Was an examination done to determine whose hair it was?"

"Yes."

"Is that person sitting in this courtroom?"

"Yes, sir."

"Would you point out the person."

Dramatically, forcefully, Kyle King thrust his index finger toward Sarah Lewis.

Uproar.

"That's a lie!" Sarah gasped, ignoring Evans's advice and jumping up from her seat.

Bret also shot up. "They faked it! I've seen this stuff done!" he shouted. "They can fake anything they want!"

Meeker rapped his gavel. "Mr. Lewis, sit down!" he snapped. "Sit down or I'll throw you out. Mrs. Lewis, the same. D'you hear?"

Woody Evans reached up and pulled Sarah down. But Bret remained standing, red-faced, jabbing *his* finger at Kyle King. "They're covering up! This was terrorism! Someone's being protected!"

"Bailiff!" the judge demanded. A burly bailiff in full blue uniform charged up the aisle and grabbed Bret. The court was in chaos. Bret resisted. "Don't you try to mug me! That's my wife they've got! It's her life!"

"Remove him!" the judge ordered.

The bailiff yanked Bret into the side aisle and then out the door. "You're not gonna shut me up!" he shouted, before the door was slammed behind him.

It had been the most dramatic moment of the trial, and even Sarah was overwhelmed. How could she doubt Bret now?

The press recorded every detail. Interviews with Bret would be lined up with every major station, network and newspaper. Now, as the bailiff marched him down the hallway, he felt a moment of exhilaration that he hadn't felt since setting off the bomb. He'd practiced this outburst in his car for weeks, and it took a complete crushing of his inhibitions to pull it off. He could already read the public reaction. He'd be the man who stood by family and country, the man who was ready to fight for the old, decent values in the face of the unspeakable Howie Gresh.

How easy it had been, he recalled, to snip off a few strands of Sarah's hair as she slept, and plant them in the bomb.

The courtroom settled down. Kyle King was still on the stand. Terrific, he was thinking. Reports of the outburst would mention his name. He'd get more coverage than he'd ever gotten before.

"Now Detective King," Gresh went on, "I'll ask you to ignore the most recent theatrics. As we all know, people get emotional when confronted with the truth. Now I ask you whether any other human hairs were found in fragments of the bomb."

"They were not."

"All right. Then I ask you whether the contents of Mrs. Lewis's motel room were examined."

"Yes. We got a warrant."

"Was anything of significance found?"

"I would say so. Gloves."

"Gloves?" Gresh repeated, following the script. "Why would that be significant?"

"Well, first of all, we kinda wondered why anyone would pack gloves in June."

There was a commotion at the defense table. Evans should have been informed of the gloves in pretrial discovery, but wasn't. He now whispered to Sarah: "Did you have gloves?"

"No," Sarah whispered back. "I don't ... think so."

"You don't *think* so?" Evans asked.

"I brought some little cases of accessories. A pair of gloves could've been ... I don't know. But I never *wore* any."

"Detective King," Gresh went on, ignoring the side conversation, "did the gloves reveal anything?"

"Yes. They had traces of the explosive."

Another uproar.

"No!" Sarah shouted. She snapped her head around, searching for Bret. But Bret was gone. Her eyes met Shel's. And *his* were burning. Suddenly, he shot up. "You bitch! You did it!"

Meeker slammed his gavel. "Bailiff!" This time the bailiff rushed over without further instruction.

"You killed her! You lied to me! You never wanted to save your marriage! You used me!"

"Shel, it's not true!" Sarah gasped, now breaking down in sobs.

"Request a recess!" Woody Evans demanded, and Judge Meeker had little choice but to grant it, prompting a dash for phones by every reporter in the hall.

Veering away from the phone booths, one reporter tracked down Bret. His reaction to King's bombshell could be too good to pass up.

Bret appeared furious when the reporter told him what King had said. "Planted evidence!" he exploded. "She never wore gloves!" He was even angrier than he'd been in court, and might have gone on if the bailiff hadn't pulled him away. Of course, Bret had known about the gloves all along. He'd packed them himself, stuffing them in the bottom of the case after lacing them with particles of explosive.

As for Kyle King, he ducked out of sight of all reporters. Publicity glutton though he was, he knew that this was not the time to speak to the press. He was testifying. He was still under oath. Maintain style, he instructed himself. Impress them with complete professionalism.

But Shel Jordan made himself available. He waved his public relations man away as reporters surrounded him. "I never wanted to believe it!" he said bitterly. "I never wanted to think that Sarah was capable of something like that. But I've heard enough. There's no doubt in my mind."

"But could she *build* that bomb?" a reporter asked.

"You kiddin'?" Shel shot back. "She's an engineer. She works with pilots and military people. Her husband probably talked about explosives all the time. There's no problem. One of the cops told me it was a simple bomb anyhow. The parts were nothin'."

"Are you going back in the courtroom, Mr. Jordan?"

"If they let me. I gotta be there. I gotta be there for my late wife."

Another reporter spotted Woody Evans rushing to speak with a new lawyer who'd been brought in to advise the defense team. Evans waved the reporter away when the newsman approached. Evans wasn't smiling. He wasn't calm. A button on his vest was open, and Woody Evans never left a button opened. To the reporter, the signs were clear. Evans knew his client was in trouble. While he pretty much knew the entire prosecution case, he'd never expected Gresh's witnesses to have such emotional impact. Gresh's questioning was masterful, his choice of dramatic moments perfect. And now Evans knew what every defense lawyer knew—that despite the heroics of television's criminal lawyers, there came a point when events, and feelings, began to overwhelm the most skillful legal strategy.

The worry on Woody Evans's face showed how close that point was. Observing the beleaguered lawyer, Purple now recalled a popular Woody Evans quote, one usually reserved for lectures at law schools. "The lawyer should be the first to know . . . and the very first to believe."

chapter
thirty-two

When proceedings resumed, Kyle King was back on the stand. He'd had a chance to freshen up, change his shirt and apply a dab of makeup to lighten the shadows under his eyes, making him look friendlier and younger. He sensed from the murmurs that greeted him that he was now the star attraction, and he knew—because he'd rehearsed his testimony with Howie Gresh—that he was very likely to remain so.

It was a full and buzzing courtroom, with every available seat and inch of standing room taken. Judge Meeker had given permission for both Bret Lewis and Shel Jordan to re-enter and sit among the spectators. But each had been warned that he'd be barred permanently if he caused another serious disruption.

The Blacks were in the courtroom again, planted in the fourth row with Al Durfee. Durfee had attended enough trials to be able to read faces, and the face he was reading now was Sarah's. No doubt, Durfee thought to himself. Evans had talked to her heart-to-heart during the recess, and what he told her was less than optimistic. King's testimony had not helped her cause, and his credibility and style had obviously impressed the jury. Sarah looked older and tired. The assertiveness that had marked her spirit in the early moments of the trial now seemed to have been chiseled away. Her face read trouble, with a hint of desperation.

"Detective King," Gresh began, "I'd like to turn to the matter of Mrs. Lewis's dress. Was this an object of investigation?"

"Yes, it was."

"And could you tell us why?"

"Of course. Any garment sheds fibers. It leaves a trail. We know where it's been. In this case, it might tell us something about the movements of the accused."

"Was this a new garment?"

"Yes. It was picked up two days before this new double wedding."

"From what you gathered, had Mrs. Lewis ever worn it before that night?"

"No. When we interrogated her just before her arraignment, she told me she tried it on at the shop, then once at home for her husband, then put it away for the ceremony."

"And how was the dress brought to the Cheshire Motel?"

"In a zippered garment bag. No one disputes that."

"I see. Uh, Detective King, did your lab examine the upholstery of the car in which the bomb went off?"

"Yes. Of course, most of it was burned out, but there were enough remnants to examine."

"Did you examine the driver's seat?"

"Oh, yes. That came first."

"What did that seat tell you?"

"Well, there were fibers. Most of the ones we found were from Mr. Lewis's clothing—usually his business suits. Then we found fibers that we traced to the Jordans. They sometimes rode in the car, and fibers can spread around. And we also found fibers from Mrs. Lewis's wedding dress."

"Oh? But Mrs. Lewis didn't wear the dress before the ceremony."

"Yes, that's right," King said. "So she must've entered the car *after* the ceremony."

"That's a lie!" Sarah shouted, as the courtroom again erupted in bedlam. Now she turned to Evans. "It's a lie! He's lying!" Durfee watched her from his seat in the fourth row. When a defendant thinks she's got to convince her own lawyer, he knew, she's in big trouble.

Meeker as usual rapped his gavel, but his demeanor toward Sarah was considerably milder than before, as if he sensed he was dealing with an already condemned woman. "Now Mrs. Lewis, please don't do that again," he admonished.

Bret had his head in his hands. The press would report that he was "increasingly anguished." Shel Jordan simply stared at Sarah, his mouth hanging open. As if in shock, he quietly repeated King's charge: "After the ceremony, after the ceremony." Of course. She'd entered the car after the ceremony to place the bomb.

But Gresh wasn't entirely satisfied. It all had to be hammered home. "Detective King," he said, "perhaps we're a bit confused. Isn't it possible that *Mister* Lewis touched Mrs. Lewis's dress, maybe helped her zip it up, then went back to his car, depositing some fibers on the front seat in the process?"

Suddenly the courtroom fell into a hush. Howie Gresh couldn't be helping the defense. No one seriously believed that. The question had to have an ulterior motive.

"We considered that," King replied. "But the dress itself answered the question."

"Oh? In what way?"

"We found traces of grease near the hem. We traced the grease to the door mechanism of Mr. Lewis's Lincoln."

That did it. The murmur in the courtroom had that "she's dead" sound to it. Sarah turned to Evans, who avoided her anguished gaze. Evans stared straight ahead. Maybe his great aunt was right. Maybe he should have been a surgeon.

Everyone admired the thorough job that Howie Gresh was doing. But it wasn't Gresh who was thorough. It was Bret Lewis. He'd arranged everything, down to the spot of grease on Sarah's dress.

And through that ominous murmur that continued in the courtroom, only one voice was discordant. "Frame-up," Bret Lewis muttered, just loud enough for reporters sitting nearby to hear. The defense table heard it too. Sarah turned around to look at Bret, her expression almost numb. *Obviously* it was a frame-up, Sarah thought. It was not, after all, the first time the word had been used during this trial. "Frame-up," Bret charged again.

And yet, the word had remarkably little impact on those who heard it. Why should there be a frame-up? Who would want to frame Sarah Lewis? She certainly had a *motive*, a powerful one, a classic one. She had the means. As an engineer, she could assemble the bomb, and materials were easily obtained by those with scientific or military connections. And she had the opportunity. Planting the bomb in her own car was simple. The remote-control detonator could have been hidden in her clothing or handbag.

Motive, means, opportunity—the foundations of a criminal case. Sarah seemed to score in the superior zone in each category. But, of course, in the mind of every spectator and reporter was a single question: Did Woody Evans have some trick up his sleeve? Was there some surprise witness, some mystery personality, who would come forward in court to give Sarah the golden alibi she needed?

"Detective King," Howie Gresh said, "I have no further questions. Your testimony has been most enlightening."

"Mr. Evans?" asked the judge. Inwardly, Meeker was rooting for Woody Evans, a colleague in spirit. He despised Gresh, the conniving upstart, and Gresh enjoyed every bit of the loathing.

Woody Evans slowly rose from his chair and approached the witness. Up to this point, King had appeared relaxed, thoroughly confident. Now he would face the opposition, an opposition that had been backed into a very small corner by his testimony.

"Good morning, Detective," Evans began.

"Good morning," King replied coldly.

"You've heard the word 'frame-up' in the court, haven't you?"

"I've heard some . . ."

"Pretty important word, it seems to me," Evans interrupted. "You, uh, have some heavy evidence in your file, Detective, but something is troubling me."

"Oh?"

"Yes. No witnesses. Isn't that true?"

"I beg your . . ."

"No witnesses," Evans repeated. "Just some hair. You talk about strands of hair found in the remains of that bomb. But no one *saw* Mrs. Lewis with the bomb. You didn't find anyone who saw her, did you?"

"No."

"And the gloves. You have any witnesses who'll say they saw Mrs. Lewis with them on?"

"No."

"Fibers from Mrs. Lewis's dress in the car. Anyone see her getting into that car?"

"No."

"Anyone see her get grease on that dress?"

"No, but . . ."

"But what, Detective? The fact is, no one saw much of anything. Oh sure, you've got all this lab stuff, but what does it prove? Do you have a witness who can place Mrs. Lewis with that explosive, or who saw her set it off?"

"No, I don't. That's why we *have* those lab tests."

"I repeat again," Evans said, now allowing his voice to rise, "you haven't got any witnesses. Access to Mrs. Lewis's belongings is easy. Her hair? There are strands on hairbrushes, left out at night. The wedding dress? Anyone could get strands from that and leave them on a seat . . . or get some grease on that dress. Did you investigate the possibility that someone was doing that, Detective?"

"Uh, not directly, sir."

"Oh, I see. Not directly. Well maybe you'd better get started."

Evans was reaching and he knew it. Who was the someone he was talking about? Terrorists? They usually took responsibility for what they did, if only through an anonymous phone call. Shel? Evans had thought about that. Shel had a motive for killing Ramy—she was cheating on him. But he was no technical expert, had no motive for framing an ally like Sarah, and probably would have been happy to humiliate Ramy in a divorce, if he wanted to rid himself of her. Besides, Shel would never have had the opportunity to plant the evidence.

There was always Bret, Evans thought, even as he stood before Kyle King. Bret had means and opportunity. In fact, he was the only one who had proven access to Sarah's possessions . . . and her hair. But where was the motive? If he were having an affair with Ramy, why kill her? If he *had* to kill her—if Ramy had something on him —why frame Sarah? A man like Bret, with his connections, could have had Ramy disposed of cleanly. And if he *weren't* having an affair with her, why murder her? If he were involved at all, why shout "frame-up" in a crowded courtroom? It didn't figure.

Everything pointed to Sarah—the motive, the forensic evidence, the choice of a device that a scientifically trained person would be likely to build. Even Sarah's alleged attempt to save her marriage— visiting Lorenzo Rosenthal with Shel—could easily be seen as a convenient cover-up. Evans could not escape the conclusion that he had a guilty client.

"No further questions," he announced to Kyle King. "But the defense requests a short recess."

"Without objection, so ordered," Judge Meeker ruled, rapping his gavel twice.

The rumors started almost immediately. A deal was in the works. Sarah would either plead guilty to a lesser charge, or would change her plea to "not guilty by reason of insanity." A psychiatrist would be found who would issue the proper certification. To most courtroom hands, it seemed the only way. Absent a miracle, Woody Evans could offer no credible defense other than some temporary lapse of his client's mind.

But courtroom hands also knew that Sarah would have to go along with this defense. Sarah was a proud woman. She'd gone for a "not guilty" since the start of the trial. Her demeanor at the defense table—disciplined most of the time, with brief interruptions of anger—gave no hint that she was ready to cave in.

Nonetheless, a mid-afternoon TV newsbreak in Washington began with, "At the Sarah Lewis trial, reports are circulating of a deal. Defense lawyer Woody Evans and prosecutor Howard Gresh were locked behind closed doors ..."

The Associated Press reported that Sarah and Evans had met for a full hour in a small room near the judge's temporary chambers. No journalists were allowed in, but one who got close reported hearing considerable commotion.

Speculation went beyond a deal. Virtually everyone in the press thought Sarah would escape prison, that at most she'd serve time at a mental facility. And what would Shel's reaction be to the arrangement? No one knew.

But would Howie Gresh accept a deal? He seemed to have an airtight case, so why not go for conviction on the maximum charge? Because, the old-timers felt, he realized that Sarah was essentially a sympathetic figure who thought she'd been wronged, and that Ramy had been a wealthy socialite.

Finally ... the word.

Woody Evans called a press conference. Everyone knew what was coming. Sarah was beside him. She looked grim, yet unshaken.

"There will be no deal," Evans announced. "Mrs. Lewis wants full vindication."

chapter
thirty-three

Woody Evans was fond of quoting the old lament of the bar that a lawyer who represents himself has a fool for a client. He was also fond of modifying it: "A lawyer who takes a client who makes her own decisions," he often told young attorneys, "has a fool for himself." He thought about that now. He thought about it over and over as the clerk of the court polled the jury after it returned its verdict. He felt like turning to Sarah and quietly saying, "You should've taken my advice. You should've made a deal." But he didn't. That would have been too cruel. And so he sat silently, listening to twelve men and women, good and true, confirming to the judge what they'd decided.

"Philip Gruson," the clerk called out, with studied attention to each syllable. "In the matter of the people versus Sarah Lewis. How find you?"

"Guilty."

"Liza Farrell. In the matter of the people versus Sarah Lewis. How find you?"

"Guilty."

"Robert Jefferson." He was the first black juror polled.

"Guilty."

"Brock Lawrence." Retired airline pilot.

"Guilty." Firm, clear voice.

"Mary Bellows." Homemaker.

"Guilty."

"George Baker." Clerk in a Seven-Eleven.

"Guilty."

Yes, she should've listened to me, Evans kept saying to himself, over and over. He knew he was starting to think more about his practice, his reputation, than his client. But it was understandable, for this was a catastrophe. An utter rout. His entire defense came down to the fact that no one actually *saw* Sarah plant the bomb, but the jury wouldn't buy. All the other evidence was solid and unshakable. And there was that overwhelming motive—a motive that anyone could understand. Sarah had wanted to testify in her own defense, but Evans wouldn't let her. He'd been afraid she'd come off as the curator from an elite museum, the kind some simple jurors might not care for. The court never had a chance to hear her, the press never got the opportunity to assess her, even to know her.

"Roy Queensbury."

"Guilty."

"Alexandra Burke."

"Guilty."

Maybe I was wrong, Evans now was thinking. Maybe she should've taken the stand and met the evidence head-on. They'd be debating it in the law journals, he knew, and now he wondered how he'd come out.

"Suzanne Hodges."

"Guilty."

"Andrew White."

"Guilty."

"She has a perfect record as a citizen," Evans knew he would say, when standing before Judge Meeker for sentencing. "She has led an exemplary life—the life of a scientist and public servant. She is respected throughout her community."

"John Muller."

"Guilty."

"Beatrice Oliver."

"Guilty."

"The woman who *may* have planted that bomb is entirely different from the woman standing before this court today. She is a woman who grieves over the loss of a close, dear friend. She understands . . ."

Evans stopped thinking about his sentencing appeal as the clerk ended his poll of the jury. The buzzing in the makeshift chamber rose to an excited roar.

Guilty. Premeditated murder.

Eyes turned to Sarah, who sat staring vaguely at the jury box, not ready to accept the fate that twelve jurors had handed her. And as the reality began to hit, she fought the temptation to scream, to heave contempt at the jurors, at Howie Gresh, at Meeker, even at her own lawyer. "They won't have that satisfaction," she insisted to herself. "They won't go out of here saying I'm a nut." She knew she would win on appeal. The prosecution's case would ultimately be exposed as a fraud, a hoax, a perversion of justice. Bret would help her. He was a brilliant man. Bret would see it through.

Eyes then moved to Shel. His head was down, as if in deep prayer. Reporters nearby clearly saw him reach unsteadily into his inside jacket pocket, pull out a picture of Ramy, gaze at it for a few moments, then kiss it. For Purple, that was a feature in itself. Vindication. Justice. The grieving widower remaining loyal in death, bringing his marriage, finally, to a shattering close as he watches his wife's murderer convicted. "For Shel Jordan," Purple wrote, "the agony will never end. But perhaps this moment of justified revenge will help ease the indescribable pain."

It was tabloid heaven.

Bret was first out of the courtroom. "I'd like to read a brief statement," he said, as reporters from as far away as India crushed around him, almost knocking him over. "Would you stand back a bit?" he asked. "Just a bit. Would you give me some air?" The press complied, except for the radio and TV people, who jammed microphones into Bret's face, each one bearing the call letters of a local station.

Bret's statement was handwritten, something he'd scrawled on a piece of notepaper while he listened to the verdict. Reporters had seen him scrawl it. What they hadn't seen was how he'd perfected it on his word processor over a matter of weeks, then memorized it. "This is a time of great sadness," he began, his face looking drawn and tired. He'd kept himself up all night to create the look. "But it is a time when I must stand by my wife. It is a time for loyalty, for love, and for trust. If you ask me if I'm angry, the answer is yes. Absolutely yes."

"Look this way and say that," a television reporter demanded.

Bret obliged, looking right into the camera. "Yes, I'm angry. Justice wasn't done in there today. You had a slick prosecutor with a lot of circumstantial evidence. I won't rest until this verdict is overturned. My wife is innocent. I'll fight to my last breath to prove that, and I'll give up my life if that's what it takes."

A few spectators behind the reporters applauded.

"Have you spoken with her?" a reporter from the *Washington Post* asked.

"Just briefly. As you know, they won't release her, even with a bond. Too dangerous, the judge said. Might even take her life. Can you believe that? I did get a chance to speak with her after the verdict, while they were taking her away. I don't know if any of you can imagine what it's like seeing your wife in handcuffs, knowing that she's going to jail. Just the way Sarah looked back at me . . . ."

"What did she say?"

"She was more concerned about me than herself. I think she now knows there was no affair between Ramy Jordan and me. Just a close and caring friendship. Sarah worried that I'd go to pieces over this. I told her that I wouldn't. That the fight inside wouldn't let me. Then she had to go."

At that moment Shel Jordan emerged from the courthouse. Some reporters turned to rush toward him, leaving an opening in the crowd around Bret. Shel made a move forward, but then stopped, spotting Bret. He looked straight at Bret, a look that said everything that had to be said. It was bitterness, it was hurt, it was betrayal, it was, as Purple wrote, "a seething, dark fury that Shel Jordan contained with superhuman dignity."

Bret turned away. His face, too, registered pain. "We were such good friends," he confided in the reporter standing closest to him. "We'll never exchange a word again. What an awful thing."

"Will you be . . . ?"

"No more questions," Bret replied, quickly turning and pushing his way through the media mob. "Please, no more questions."

*   *   *

"Your Honor," Howie Gresh began on the day of sentencing, "in
all my years of practice I have rarely heard such anger expressed at
a convicted murderer. This woman, Sarah Lewis, had everything. She
had a fine home, a prestigious position, a husband who, despite her
hallucinations, *cared* for her. And yet, when she thought her best
friend was endangering her marriage, what did she do? She murdered
her. She murdered her in utter, cold blood. She never even confronted her, never sought her out, never so much as wondered
whether she could possibly be wrong. She simply planted a bomb
in a car to make it look like an act of terrorism, and pressed the
button on a remote-control device ..."

Sarah watched Gresh intently, too numb to hate him, too overcome to take open offense at his words. But each sentence seemed
half an eternity. "How much time does he get?" she whispered to
Woody Evans.

"As much as he wants," Evans whispered back. "But he's usually
brief. And blunt."

"Blunt," Sarah repeated.

"Ramy Jordan had everything to live for," Gresh went on, his
voice getting higher and higher. "She was young, vivacious, a con-
tributor to charity, always willing to give of herself ..."

Bret, in the second row, looked stern and angry, but had to fight
to contain his amusement. Ramy? Give? This was funnier than the
funeral.

"I received a letter from an orphanage that she personally visited,"
Gresh continued. "Those children loved her, and they will miss her.
They say so, one and all." He kept watching the judge, but Meeker
made it a point to sit stone-faced at these sentencing hearings.

"We ask," Gresh said, "what is the proper sentence for someone
who has taken a life as good as this? Nothing can bring her back.
Nothing can give Sheldon Jordan the wife he had cared for during
a blissful twenty years. But we can achieve justice, and we can send
a message to all the smart little Sarah Lewises out there, those people
who think *they* make the rules in this society, the intellectual snobs,
the elite, the partygoers ..."

Sarah was now visibly agitated. "Despicable little runt," she whispered to Evans. "What does he think he's doing?"

"Running for governor," Evans replied.

"The court can strike a blow for the families, the survivors, of innocent victims all through this state." Gresh glanced in the direction of the spectators and press. They were silent, and he sensed he was having the impact he wished. "Your Honor," he continued, "I have thought long and hard about this and have asked for Divine guidance in speaking the words I am about to speak. After the most serious contemplation, I must ask that you impose on Sarah Lewis the only fitting sentence for her crime ... the sentence of death."

There was an audible gasp throughout the court. Meeker showed no emotion, but even hardened reporters, even the unflappable Woody Evans, were stunned by the request. It was all show, of course. This was sentencing day and Meeker had presumably already decided on a sentence. But the idea of executing a young woman with no criminal history sent quivers up the spines of even veteran trial watchers.

Bret stared at Howie Gresh, rage in his eyes.

Even Shel seemed a bit surprised, but, after a few moments, nodded his head "yes," ever so gently.

Howie Gresh loved the reaction. This would get 'em in southern Virginia. This would make the news. This would make him a mini J. Edgar Hoover among the fry 'em set. Some women might object to his plea, but they weren't the kind to vote for a tough prosecutor for governor anyway.

Meeker rapped his gavel to quiet the buzz that floated through the crowd. "Court will come to complete order," he insisted. "This is not a circus. Mah court is a serious place." He turned to the defense table and nodded. Now would come the expected plea for mercy.

Sarah slowly rose. Again the murmurs started. She would make her own plea. For the first time at this trial, she would speak in her own defense. The murmurs quickly faded. The room fell utterly silent. The moment was electric, made for the media. Kyle King watched intently from the third row. Definitely, he thought. Definitely he'd have to advise on this film.

Bret followed Sarah with his eyes as she made her way forward. He looked proud, even moved. Shel followed her too, but his expression registered only revulsion.

There was the constant sound of rustling paper as reporters flipped pages, making hurried notes on Sarah. "She wore a simple blue dress," Purple wrote, "with not a single accessory or piece of jewelry. She even abandoned the watch she'd glanced at continually during the trial. It was as if she wanted to appear as humble as possible. She did wear lipstick, but any other makeup was barely visible. Her blonde hair was shorter than shoulder length—not worn to be shown off."

"Your Honor," Sarah began, and her voice now was surprisingly strong, as if she had garnered all her strength for this last appeal. "Your Honor, I know that within a few minutes you will impose sentence. And again I must plead my innocence. I did not commit this crime. I *would* not commit this crime. I have never committed any criminal act. The evidence is tainted. The jury didn't believe my attorney when he said that, but I believe we will eventually prove it. These things were planted. I don't know why. I don't know by whom. I was never in that electronics store. I never got grease on my dress. There's no legitimate way that strands of my hair could've been attached to that ugly explosive.

"Mr. Jordan, when he was called back, testified that Ramy never received an anniversary card from me this year, although I'd always sent her one. Mr. Gresh suggested that there was no card because I knew that . . . Ramy wouldn't be alive to receive it. No, Your Honor. If I had testified I would have told you that I didn't send the card because I was hurt, because I believed Ramy was trying to take my husband from me. All right, maybe I'd exaggerated. Maybe both Mr. Jordan and I misinterpreted that telephone tape. But that was the explanation."

She stopped, and seemed to grope for the next words. Her breathing suddenly became forced. Some in the first few rows leaned forward. Was she going to faint? It looked as if she were. Woody Evans moved to rise, pushing his chair back with a scrape. But Sarah turned and vigorously motioned him away. Then she went on. "Your Honor, I can't ask for mercy because I have done nothing wrong. I only ask that you recall the number of defendants who've gone to prison in this country and were later found innocent. Please recall the cases, Your Honor. Please recall the names and the names of their loved ones, whose lives were shattered, who were forced to

live in darkness and shame. There have been many mistakes in our
judicial system. Some of those mistakes were put to death.

"So I ask not mercy, but cautious wisdom. I cannot read your
mind, Your Honor, so I don't know how you assess the evidence
presented against me. But my conscience is clear, and history will
prove that I am speaking the truth.

"It is now in your hands."

Sarah finished. Meeker, as usual, appeared unmoved. Neither
Sarah nor Evans took this to mean anything. They knew it was the
man's style.

Rather than turn around, Sarah backed up slowly to her chair,
never moving her eyes from Meeker's. The only sound in the court
was the clicking of her shoes against the hardwood floor. Then, she
sat down, strangely disappointed. Somehow, she'd expected a sign
of support from the crowd. There was only silence.

Meeker had a reputation for handing down tough sentences. But
he could also be compassionate when the occasion demanded it.
The odds during the recess that followed Sarah's plea were lopsided.
Most reporters thought Sarah would serve no more than eight years,
and the trial junkies thought pretty much the same thing. First offense,
passion killing, otherwise solid citizen, not involved in the drug trade.
There were mitigating circumstances and it seemed a foregone conclusion that Meeker would use them.

But there were those who knew Meeker more intimately . . . and
they weren't so sure. He had, on several occasions, and only in private
conversations at his exclusive club, expressed a particular loathing
for the female murderer.

And so they waited. Some chose to go outside the court during
the recess, their hands in coat pockets to protect against the chill.
The trees were thinning, the Washington area had lost the aura of
southern charm that hung over it during the warm months. The brisk,
damp breeze seemed appropriate for the sorry events inside the
temporary courthouse. And so did the shivering crowds that waited
outside—the trial junkies, the fans of live soap opera who saw the
Sarah Lewis trial as something of a perverted love story. Some jour-

nalists spent their recess interviewing spectators. Some TV reporters spent theirs signing autographs for gawking members of the public.

In fact, a market for autographs sprang up. Anyone who could get Sarah's could easily pull in a fast hundred bucks. Shel's drew fifty and Bret's about the same. The lawyers' didn't command much and the judge's nothing. Other markets sprang up as well. Street vendors appeared selling hot dogs and slices of pizza. Already the "free Sarah" buttons were on sale, one vendor explaining that "there's always a crowd that believes in the guilty. My father sold John Dillinger buttons."

"Court resuming," someone said near the main door. The rush began to get back inside. Now, the final chapter was about to unfold.

"Ah don't think ah've ever anguished so much over a sentence," Meeker began, holding in his hand the written words that would determine Sarah's fate. Sarah stood before him, Woody Evans at her side. She used every muscle within her to remain erect and dignified. "The crime was utterly brutal. And the defendant is without remorse, still clinging to a claim of innocence that only she apparently believes. Even the manner of execution—and this *was* an execution—was particularly heinous. Not only was the victim killed, but scores of others might have been as well had they been passing by, or had the car's gas tank exploded. The sheer selfishness of the deed has given me nights of unrest."

Some reporters thought they saw Evans edge away from Sarah as Meeker finished that section.

"On the other hand," Meeker continued, "ah have seen these romantic situations before. Ah know what they can do to someone's mind. Ah know the pain that they can bring, and with that pain all reason can disappear. The defendant before me, after all, has no criminal record. She has been a credit to the community, a model citizen . . ."

And then, an outburst from the second row. "Until she murdered my wife!"

The court was in an uproar. Meeker slammed his gavel. "Order!"

A bailiff rushed to Shel, but Shel quickly sat down. Meeker, with a wave of the hand, signaled the bailiff to ease off. He didn't want Shel dragged from the court at this crucial moment. He had a right to hear the sentence.

Quiet returned, and Meeker continued. "This defendant can probably be rehabilitated. She can perform useful work, work that can benefit society."

Evans inched closer to Sarah, and Sarah herself breathed a bit easier.

"Ah have weighed these things carefully," Meeker assured the court. "The crime. The defendant's flawless past. The anguish of a grieving husband. The defendant's potential for good.

"And ah have made my decision."

Every head in the room leaned forward. Sarah fought to show no emotion, her teeth clenched so tight she cracked a filling. Shel Jordan's eyes were riveted on the judge, eyes that would soon show either approval or contempt.

"Ah have concluded," Meeker announced, "that the horrible nature of this crime outweighs all else. I therefore pronounce upon you, Sarah Lewis, the sentence of death, to be carried out . . ."

No one heard anything else.

PART FOUR

PART FOUR

chapter
thirty-four

"The sentence was just, and it fit the crime. God save her soul."

That was Shel Jordan's only comment, released through his office.

"This is obscene."

That was Bret's, shouted defiantly to a TV camera outside the courthouse.

"I will fight to my dying breath," Sarah told Bret, who relayed her words to the press.

No one, presumably, wanted to say more.

And yet reporters demanded more. They descended on Shel's office and his house, only to be handed a statement by uniformed guards: "Mr. Jordan has gone into seclusion at a spot known only to him and a few close associates. He wishes, at this emotionally stressful time, to be alone with his memories of his wife."

Bret, too, slipped away. But a Pentagon release said he would take only the remainder of the day for himself, and would be back at his desk in the morning. He would be available to the press later in the week.

And so it ended. There would be the usual appeals, of course, but a woman sat on death row in Virginia. Stations interrupted their programs for special bulletins on the death sentence, newspapers broke out the kind of headline type usually reserved for major calamities. Washington braced for still one more debate on capital punishment. The trial, and its outcome, was essentially the only topic of conversation in bars and restaurants throughout the area. Barbara Walters was reported ready to fly to Virginia for an exclusive interview with Sarah, if Sarah would accept. But Mike Wallace was also applying the heat for *Sixty Minutes.*

That evening, Shel Jordan sat in a small cottage about eight miles outside Charlottesville, Virginia, watching the news. The cottage was borrowed from a sympathetic friend, who offered it as a secret refuge from the constant crush of the press. Charlottesville was a good ninety-minute drive from Washington, and the cottage itself, white-clapboarded with dark green shutters, was on a piece of private property in the woods, completely isolated from civilization. The only access was by way of a dirt road usually full of mud puddles.

It was just after midnight. The weather was cool, with a slight drizzle beginning to fall, pattering on the leaves of the large trees around the cabin. Except for two inside lights, and the flickering images on the television screen, the area was pitch dark.

Then a pair of headlights appeared at the bottom of the dirt road. When the driver was sure he'd found the road, he shut off his lights so as not to be seen by anyone passing by. He turned on an ordinary Eveready flashlight, beaming it ahead to negotiate his way along the bumpy, muddy road. He held the light in his left hand, driving slowly with his right. It took him about four minutes to maneuver the length of the road, finally pulling up to the cottage. He snapped off his flashlight and picked up a package that lay next to him on the seat. Taking care to make as little noise as possible, he opened the door, eased out of the car and gently closed the door again. He walked up to the green front entrance of the cottage, and rang the bell.

It took some time, but finally he heard the TV set being turned off. Then, footsteps toward the door.

The door swung open.

Shel Jordan stood there, staring at his visitor.

Bret Lewis stared right back.

Not a word was exchanged. The eyes of each remained riveted on the eyes of the other.

Finally, Shel backed up and Bret entered. Both men held their silence.

And then, slowly, Bret raised his right hand. Shel raised his as the two moved toward each other. Their hands came together in a clasp—a firm, resolute clasp.

A slight, mysterious smile took shape at the edges of Bret's lips. Then Shel started to smile, too.

The smiles grew, and swelled, and then erupted in a fit of uncontrolled laughter. Bret and Shel slapped each other's backs. They jabbed ribs like two college boys after a hot date. They hugged. And the laughter, a macho self-congratulatory laughter, went on.

"We did it!" Shel exclaimed, only the choking laughter preventing him from screaming.

"A complete, unconditional victory," Bret replied.

"I never dreamed it would be this perfect," Shel went on. "Bret, you planned it, old chum. You get the credit."

"We *both* planned it," Bret insisted. "Just two guys trying to get rid of their wives by murdering one and framing the other for the murder."

Still laughing, still rejoicing, they dropped into easy chairs, exhausted. "No divorces," Shel boasted. "No sharing with those bitches. No mess, no bother."

"Pretty much the way I explained it to Ramy at Arlington Cemetery," Bret said. "Except I left out a couple of details."

"Yeah, like who the victim was going to be," Shel chuckled.

More laughter. Now Bret reached to the coffee table for the package he'd brought.

"I look back," Shel reflected, "on how much detail went into this. My father taught me that the difference between the successful man and the failure was detail. The way you lured Ramy into that affair . . ."

Bret shrugged. "You were the key man there, Sheldon. You made her ready for it." He moved the package toward him, ripping open the paper. "She knew you weren't interested any longer, and she was just as easily manipulated as we thought she'd be."

"The double wedding was brilliant," Shel threw back. "What a cover for a murder."

"You resisted at first," Bret teased.

"Sure. Made it realistic," Shel said, accepting a glass Bret offered him from the package. "And that terrorist killing story you dreamed up. Even setting off an explosion in Falls Church. Really, old sport,

I admired that. It gave the whole thing size, style. You really *should* be in public relations."

"Right now we're *both* in public relations," Bret said, pulling out a glass for himself. "What was the trickiest part?" he asked. "You know what I think?"

"What?"

"That tape. That goddamned tape."

"Stupid Ramy," Shel nodded. "It took us about ten taped phone calls before we had one where she didn't gush all over you. I loved the way you told everyone that the tape really showed nothing, even though Sarah thought it showed everything."

"Well, the tape did its job," Bret said. "It gave you the reason to go to Sarah. It gave Sarah the motive. That was the lynchpin, my friend. The rest was easy—planting all that evidence. Even getting Ramy to go out to my car. Look, she was ready to love me, to go to the end for me."

"She did." Shel burst out in more laughter.

"You know, I must admit, we're damned good actors," Bret said. "I saw Sarah before I came here. She's really convinced I'm fighting for her. She's also convinced they'll reverse her sentence."

"No way," Shel said, "especially after I fixed it so Meeker got the case. The guy has always had this hatred of women who kill. Lot of people don't know that. They won't reverse anything. It's airtight."

"Let's drink to that," Bret said, pulling a bottle from the package.

"You went out special to get champagne for us?" Shel asked.

"No, that would have been too risky," Bret replied. "I asked Sarah to buy it—for a little celebration after the double wedding."

"You snake you," Shel said. His face was more alive than Bret could ever recall. It was sheer enjoyment for Shel Jordan, life's greatest triumph.

"We've deserved this for a long time," Bret said, holding up the champagne and looking at the label. "Dom Perignon. Nineteen eighty-two. Excellent."

"I wish Marlene were here," Shel lamented.

"You speak with her today?"

"From a pay phone, like always. When this whole thing cools down, I'll fly her in from Dallas. I hate this discretion business."

"It'll all be over soon," Bret replied, now removing the foil from the bottle. "Then you can show Marlene off wherever you go."

"And Alison Carver?"

Bret paused. "Ah, Alison," he said. "The one thing that almost went wrong. You know, I never thought Sarah would discover that affair. She really was very ingenious about it. And hiring a private eye! It's the strangest thing, though. In a way that worked for us. It made her look even more paranoid than I'd planned."

"You think you can marry Alison?" Shel asked.

"A delicate question. I want to. She'd be so useful to me. But she came up at the trial. It may take a long, long time before it's respectable. But I'll marry her. Sure. If I could work all this, I'll work that."

Shel grinned. "Think we can have a double wedding?"

"I'll pretend I didn't hear that," Bret said. He popped the cork. "Frankly, I've had enough ceremony for a lifetime—although Sarah's funeral should amuse."

Shel moved the glasses forward for Bret to pour. "From this moment on," he said, "we drink as free men, and pillars of the community."

They raised their filled glasses and faced each other. A symbolic, moving moment. "To us," Bret said, "and our new loved ones." They touched glasses.

"And to the justice system," Shel responded. "It served us so well."

They lifted their glasses. Shel downed his quickly, joyously. But then he noticed—Bret had barely touched his glass to his lips. "Hey Bret, aren't you . . . ?"

"Just a sip," Bret answered. "I'm driving."

"Oh, sure, I under . . ." Shel stopped. A quizzical expression crossed his chubby face. "You know, I don't feel . . ."

Bret said nothing. He simply stood there and stared, just as he had stared at Shel when he first came in.

The look on Shel's face shifted to anguish. "Bret, you son of a . . ."

Those were the last words Shel Jordan spoke. He slumped to the floor, the force of the fall causing vases in the room to rattle. He looked up at Bret, the anguish turning to anger, then questioning, then blankness, in a smooth progression.

And he was still.

Bret stood over him. "You know, Shel," he said, as if feeling some compulsion to explain to the corpse, "I always liked you. You were fun to be with. Always had a joke or a good story to tell. Always threw a class-A party. Trouble was, Shel, I never really respected you. You always had a big mouth, and too much of a taste for alcohol. You were the only other person who knew what we'd done. I couldn't trust you, Shel. In my business, you learn pretty fast what loose lips can do. I just couldn't trust you." Then he glanced at Shel's empty glass, lying beside the body on the thick beige rug. "I tried to make it painless, Shel. Believe me. I always had your comfort in mind."

Bret then sat down, let out a deep breath, and allowed himself some time. Two of the four principals in his original plot, Shel and Ramy Jordan, were now dead. And Sarah was on death row with little chance of a reprieve. The complete victory he'd boasted about to Shel was close to becoming reality. But it was no time for self-congratulation, Bret knew, no matter how deserved. There were some critical things still to be done. He had to dispose of Shel. He had to stage a "battle" for Sarah's life, making sure nothing he did was too effective. Finally, he had to finesse his relationship with Alison Carver. His political future required that the marriage meet public approval.

Bret got up and started a thorough sweep of the two-bedroom cottage to eliminate any trace of his presence. First, he put on rubber gloves that he'd stuffed in his pocket. Using one of Shel's own towels, he wiped every surface for fingerprints. Still wearing the gloves, he took the two champagne glasses, the bottle, and the cork and placed them in the bag he'd brought, planning to take them and bury them. Next, he checked Shel's meticulous personal papers, particularly the leather-covered calendar in his briefcase, to be sure there were no references to his visit. There weren't. Shel, the note keeper, knew what notes not to make. Bret even checked the tape in Shel's dictation machine. It was blank.

And then came the body.

Bret went out to his car and got two steel-reinforced lawn bags, which he brought into the cottage. He pushed one bag into the other for strength. Then he loaded Shel's body into the double bag and hoisted it over his shoulder. He almost buckled under the weight, and began to fear a backstrain that could alter his walk and look suspicious in the days ahead. So, slowly and carefully, trying to balance Shel as best he could, he lugged the body down the three front steps of the cottage and to the car, easing it into the trunk. Next to the body lay a shovel and a pickax.

Finally, Bret brought a small vacuum cleaner from the car into the cottage. For the next half hour he vacuumed the place, hoping to suck up any hairs or threads he might have left behind. With that finished, he felt satisfied. He'd done the job the way a calculating man would do a job. It was time to leave, time to end this visit with his old friend.

He even shut off the front light. He always did admire Shel's frugality.

The drive to the predetermined spot took about an hour. It was just off a little-traveled road between Charlottesville and Washington. Bret had dug the grave in dense brush several nights before, covering it over with branches and leaves. Now, working quickly, he transferred Shel to the grave and filled it in. One car did pass while he was working in the brush, but the driver never even slowed down. After all, there was nothing unusual about a car parked at the side of the road.

"Well, good-bye old buddy," Bret whispered as he smoothed the top of the grave. "I hope you like the accommodations. I'll have the mail forwarded."

chapter
thirty-five

It took four days.

That's pretty much what Bret had expected.

Shel's secretary tried to call him for the first three, and got only the answering machine. When she didn't hear from him, she assumed he wanted to be alone or had gone on a private side trip. His lawyer tried reaching him, and came to the same sympathetic conclusion. People understood. For three full days no one was *that* concerned, although Shel's friends did worry about his ability to bear up.

But when he was out of touch for four days, his secretary decided to call the Virginia state police. A state trooper drove out to the little cottage where Shel had been staying and spotted his car parked outside. He realized it hadn't been driven for a time, because rain had fallen the previous few nights and there were no tracks behind the tires. The trooper walked up to each window of the cottage and peeked inside. He saw only a neat, clean dwelling, with no sign of life. Then he went up to the front door and was surprised to find it unlocked. His inspection of the cottage confirmed his earlier hunch. No one was there. There weren't even footprints on the carpeting. He was sure no one *had* been there, possibly for days.

The police sent out an all points bulletin with Shel's description. The press picked up the story: SHEL JORDAN MISSING.

It made all the news programs, including a few on the national networks. Reporters sought permission to interview Sarah about

Shel's disappearance, but were turned away. Sarah simply issued a statement saying she knew nothing about it.

The press gossips had a feeding frenzy. Had Shel *decided* to disappear? Had his grief been too much? Had he done away with himself? Had some crazed person kidnapped him, holding him for a ransom to be demanded later? Had Shel been murdered, perhaps by some ally of Sarah? Had he been murdered in a robbery attempt by someone who tracked him after the trial?

No one even thought of suspecting Bret Lewis. After all, in the minds of press and public it was Shel who had the grudge against Bret—Bret had "stolen" his wife. But what possible motive could Bret have had for killing Shel?

In fact, when Shel's disappearance was announced, Bret immediately called Kyle King and volunteered his help.

But Shel wasn't really hot copy. He wasn't on trial. He wasn't charged with anything. The story of his disappearance was page one for five days, then it started to fade. Again, it was precisely what Bret had anticipated.

In the meantime, Bret maintained a constant drumbeat on Sarah's behalf. Eight days after Shel vanished, he formed a committee called MERCY FOR SARAH. He rejected the more insistent JUSTICE FOR SARAH to avoid any implication that she'd not had a fair trial. MERCY simply sought to have Sarah's sentence commuted while legal experts looked into her case. Bret was sure it would go nowhere. Working diligently, he collected character references from everyone who knew Sarah— including the few politicians who allowed their names to be used. The letters were meaningless, but they kept his name in the papers and smoothed his image.

"You're developin'," Tim Curran told him. "You're doin' just fine. When the time comes, I want to talk to you, man to man, about how a husband acts after an execution. There's points to be put on the board."

Bret looked forward to that. There weren't too many handbooks on the etiquette of executions.

"I feel we're making progress," he told Purple in an exclusive interview in his Pentagon office. "People in the Navy have been very supportive. The museum has raised funds. You know, people really love Sarah, and they believe in her. Eventually we'll win this thing."

A poll taken by Purple's newspaper showed that sixty-three percent of Washingtonians thought Bret Lewis was the kind of man they'd want their daughter to marry.

The jail cell where Sarah was kept was ten by twelve. Her bed had a lumpy mattress that had been Army surplus in World War II. There was no window. There was no chair. But there was one "amenity"—a constant din from the other women in the block, many of them convicted murderers, child abusers and prostitutes. Every second word was obscene, every second shout a racial epithet directed at whatever race the orator happened not to be. Some choice remarks were occasionally aimed at Sarah, not because she'd been convicted of killing Ramy Jordan, but because she'd gotten so much publicity.

The National Air and Space Museum this was not. There were no guided tours for Girl Scouts.

Bret visited Sarah every day. She was taken from her cell, and they spoke through the usual wire-mesh barrier. They always spoke in whispers, for there were rumors that guards recorded these conversations for later sale to the quality press.

"I want to bring in new lawyers," Bret told Sarah at one meeting. "I don't think Evans is doing his job."

"I'm beginning to feel the same way," Sarah replied. "Who were you thinking of?"

"Lionel Merton. A top criminal man from Richmond. I've made inquiries. He's the best appeals lawyer in the state."

"But the cost . . ."

"Money? You're thinking of money? Look, Sarah, we're getting you the hell out of here. You're innocent. We'll rebuild everything, even if we have to do it from scratch. I've told you before, I'll tell you again. There were some misunderstandings. It was terrible for all of us. But that's past. You and I are inseparable."

She believed him. What choice did she have?

"I think we should go with Merton," Bret went on. "He'll review every page of that trial. The whole thing was a circus. Maybe he can get it thrown out."

"All I want is the verdict thrown out," Sarah said.

"You'll have it. Look, I'm on TV and radio all the time. People are with you. I've been approached by at least three New York publishers. I think the women's groups may take it up."

Sarah felt complete confidence in Bret. Her suspicions about him, already dulled by the trauma of the trial, were fading into the recesses of memory. Sometimes she even felt that the entire nightmare was ordained—a mystical means of putting their marriage back together. But in more realistic moments she was terrified.

"How about the investigation?" she asked.

"Into your trial?"

"No, into Ramy's murder."

"Sarah, I tried to explain before. There really isn't any investigation. Oh, sure, there are reporters who are following up. Some of them don't buy the verdict. But as far as the police—their role is over for now. When we have the new lawyer we can talk about a private investigator to look into things correctly. The lawyer takes care of that."

Sarah tried a vague smile. "Maybe I'll be a TV show," she said.

"Only if it's about the triumph of justice," Bret replied. He almost winced as he said it.

"God," Sarah went on, "I'd give anything to know who really did this. There are times when I just feel like . . ."

"I understand," Bret interrupted. "Someday we'll know. And we'll know why the police wanted to frame you. They got orders. Believe me, they got orders."

"From whom?"

Bret just shrugged. "I go over that evidence in my mind every day," he said, "and I see how masterful they were in putting it together. I know about corruption. I see it all the time."

Now he reached a hand toward her and they tried to touch through the wire mesh. A heavily set female guard wearing tinted glasses watched them warily, concerned that Bret might transfer a weapon to Sarah. A few minutes later the guard moved in, indicating that the time for the meeting was up. Bret, as always, forced tears into his eyes and made his mouth quiver with emotion.

"I hate it when you have to go," Sarah said.

"So do I," he sighed. "But I'll go back now and make some more calls. It's only a matter of time." He paused. "This is the kind of thing that only happens to other people, isn't it?"

"I say that to myself every day," Sarah replied.

They threw each other a kiss through the wire.

During the drive back to his Washington apartment, Bret assessed his session with Sarah. He found these jailhouse meetings more difficult than anything he had done in carrying out the plot—even more difficult than killing both Ramy and Shel. He hadn't realized how hard it would be to sound convincing when facing a wife sentenced to death. He was a good actor, a good liar, but he was becoming increasingly uncomfortable seated across that wire mesh. Was it guilt nudging the back of his mind? Was it fear that he wasn't coming across? He didn't know what it was, but he hoped Sarah's execution wouldn't be long delayed, and that he would be spared these awkward, unseemly ordeals.

He snapped on the radio, barely listening as the announcer went through the latest report of economic indicators. That was followed by a story about a toxic waste dump near Bethesda. Then, buzzwords: "Shel Jordan." Bret's grip on the wheel tightened. He turned up the volume:

> Virginia police sources revealed that they may have scored a
> major breakthrough in the Shel Jordan inquiry. These sources tell
> CBS that they may be much closer to cracking the case than they
> had been just this morning, but they refuse to reveal the details.
> Meanwhile ...

Bret was baffled. How could they be closer? They certainly hadn't found the body—it was buried in the middle of nowhere. *No one* could find that body. And there wasn't a clue left in the cottage. If there were, it would have been found days before. Unless ... did some lab report reveal something? Was there a witness who'd come forward? What witness? The cottage was isolated. No, maybe the radio report was a fake. Maybe some cop was playing games. But maybe not.

There was nothing he could do. *That* was the most frustrating feeling of all. He couldn't ask questions. He couldn't try to find out what the police had, if anything. It would look too suspicious. He could only wonder. Had there been a mistake? Was this perfect crime less than perfect? What *had* been left in the cottage?

Bret arrived home and flipped on the TV, hoping for something further. There was nothing. Maybe, he thought, it would fade away. Maybe the breakthrough would turn to dust by the next news broadcast.

But, for the first time since he hatched his plot, Bret tossed in bed that night, sleepless. Delayed reaction, he rationalized. Pent up nervousness. Understandable. Explainable. It would pass, just as Sarah would pass.

It didn't pass.

When the barrage began, it was announced by a quiet phone call.

Bret was at home. He'd come from visiting Sarah and was just finishing a salad that he'd thrown together for dinner. When the phone rang, he was sure it was his office with an update on the capture of a major terrorist. But the voice was not Navy.

"Mr. Lewis?"

"Yes?"

"This is Detective King. Remember?"

"Oh . . . yes, of course."

"Uh, Mr. Lewis, I wonder if I can drop over. It's very urgent."

"Urgent?"

"Yes, sir. Something's come up. I've got to speak with you."

Bret knew not to probe on the phone, not to appear nervous or apprehensive. "Of course. Come right over."

"Thank you, sir. I'm on my way."

Bret hung up, and waited. He was thoroughly in the dark. But King had sounded friendly, not hostile. He'd called for *permission* to come over, he didn't simply appear at the door. He didn't mention that he was bringing other cops. This really didn't sound dangerous at all. Maybe King had come up with something insignificant about Shel that he *assumed* was important. Bret guessed that King had discovered some criminal activity of Shel's, and would try to link it to his disappearance. Fine. Perfect. That would create no problems.

So Bret relaxed as he waited for King, figuring by King's demeanor on the phone that this meeting might actually be pleasant.

King appeared less than twenty minutes later. When Bret opened the door to greet him, the Virginia detective flashed a broad smile, his best "I want to be in pictures" smile. It was more reassurance for Bret. He thought he might have King in his hip pocket.

"Hello, Mr. Lewis," King said. "A pleasure to see you again."

"Come in," Bret replied.

King strode in, carrying his beaten briefcase. "To what do I owe this honor?" Bret asked.

"To fate," King replied. He savored the line.

"Fate?"

"Exactly, Mr. Lewis. I think I have some very good news for you."

Bret shrugged at that, not wanting to appear overanxious. "Always glad to hear good news," he answered. "Let's go into the living room."

As they sat down, Bret watched King's eyes sweep the room. There was mail piled up on every tabletop and even on some chairs. "Excuse the mess," Bret explained. "There's a lot of mail here for my wife. You know, letters of support. Even prayers."

"I understand," King said. "Many people believe in her."

"They *love* her," Bret replied. "Absolutely love her. Now, what's this good news?"

He saw that King was still smiling. And the smile grew. "Mr. Lewis," King said, "we've made an important discovery."

"You found Shel!"

"No."

"Then . . . ?"

"Even more important. We've been conducting this investigation into Mr. Jordan's disappearance. We were getting nowhere, absolutely nowhere. We'd searched his houses, his cars, his office. Nothing turned up. Then *I* decided to search again. Y'know, sometimes you've just got to trust your own instincts."

"Sure."

"So I went to Mr. Jordan's main house. I had everything removed.
I had carpeting ripped up—all with a search warrant, of course. And
then I found something, under one of the carpets."

"Oh?"

"It was a safe, sunk into a floor. Really, a very well designed thing.
We blowtorched it open. Inside . . . it was just remarkable."

"What was it?" Bret asked, still in the dark, yet starting to sense
that this might not be as wonderful as he'd hoped.

"Well, sir, apparently Mr. Jordan liked to keep notes."

"Yes, he was very thorough about business. He kept good records."

"And these notes told quite a story," King went on. "*Quite* a story."

"What do you mean?"

"Mr. Lewis, hang onto your seat. It apparently was Mr. Jordan who
killed his wife."

Control it, Bret told himself. Stay cool. Let the reaction come out
slowly. He stared at King, then allowed a quizzical, skeptical expression to cross his face. "What?" he asked quietly. "Repeat that."

"Jordan killed his wife."

"Are you kidding?"

"Do I look like I'm kidding?"

"And you have proof . . . ?"

"We found notes on the crime in Jordan's safe. They were things
only the murderer could know—about the bomb, the remote control,
and . . ."

"That's . . . incredible. I'm utterly stunned."

But Bret's heart was sinking. King was a manipulator. He knew
how to peel back information for maximum impact. What would he
say next? "What else was in that safe?" he asked.

"Well, there was some stuff about *you*."

"What stuff?" That was it. It was a trap.

"Memos to call you. Nothing of importance."

Nothing of importance? No, it wasn't a trap. But . . . if the police
now thought Shel was the killer, then Sarah . . .

"This Mr. Jordan," King went on, "he was over at your apartment
all the time, right?"

"Sure."

"We think he took things your wife owned. He might even have done that break-in. A strand of her hair—could've gotten it from a brush in your bathroom."

"Yes," Bret replied, trying to appear dazed by it all. "Yes, he could have. This is ... it's unbelievable."

"*Very* believable, Mr. Lewis. A little awkward for us, of course, for obvious reasons. Faces are very red."

"I'm sure."

Actually, King relished the moment. He was delivering a happy ending. Red faces or not, this was great copy. "We now think Mr. Jordan killed his wife because he thought she was having an affair with you," he went on. "He tried to frame your wife because she *also* had a motive, so framing her could work. And we now doubt that he just disappeared. We think he ran because he got scared we'd figure it out. Wonderful guy."

"Yeah," Bret agreed. "Real wonderful guy." But Sarah. He had to mention Sarah. He was groping for time, for some strategy. Now a sense of utter horror erupted inside him. "But this means my Sarah ..."

"We already contacted the Arlington courts. The ball is rolling. If this new evidence checks out, Mrs. Lewis could go free. It's great news, Mr. Lewis." King smiled. Bret hated him. He'd been so happy just an hour before. Everything had been going so well. Now, because of some notes that stupid fool left in his safe, he saw his new world starting to crumble.

Notes. The jerk kept notes!

And Sarah.

Sarah.

My God, Bret said to himself, I'm going to have her back!

chapter
thirty-six

"I've reached a decision," Meeker said, adjusting his reading glasses and picking up a legal-sized piece of paper from his large mahogany desk.

He'd decided to hold this hearing in his chambers—a warm, comfortable office lined with shelves of books, most on law, but many on the history of the South. Howie Gresh had been in here many times, and each time had been sure to express admiration for the history collection, especially the autographed edition of Douglas Southall Freeman's four-volume biography of Robert E. Lee. Woody Evans had been in here too, but Evans was far too much the gentleman to curry favor with the judge.

Only Meeker was sitting. Howie Gresh stood before the imposing desk, as did Evans. Next to Evans was Sarah Lewis, wearing an ill-fitting, gray prison outfit that still bore stains and cigarette burns from a previous prisoner. Meeker had expected to see her happier, considering the circumstances of the hearing. She had, after all, been delivered from a death sentence. And yet, she barely smiled. Maybe the whole ordeal had been too much, Meeker thought. Maybe the impact of the latest bombshell had not yet hit her. Maybe it was unrealistic to expect an instant recovery.

Behind Sarah, by special permission of the judge, stood Bret. He had no legal role in these proceedings, but asked to be there to lend his support to his wife. He affected a look of vindication and gratitude.

If Sarah did not yet have a glow, Bret did. He stood almost touching her, his eyes on her constantly. Judge Meeker thought him a fine young man.

Inside, of course, Bret Lewis still boiled. He loathed Shel for taking notes. He loathed King for finding them. He loathed the judge for his devotion to justice. He loathed Sarah for being alive, and his wife.

"This case cries out for an additional dose of justice," Meeker said. "The district attorney informs me that his office has not yet reached a decision on whether to re-try Mrs. Lewis. They are, they inform me, still examining the new evidence that's come out. However, I am convinced that no legitimate purpose would be served by the continued imprisonment of the convict. I therefore am prepared to release you, Mrs. Lewis, on your own recognizance. Obviously, you'll have to make yourself available should there be further proceedings."

"Of course," Sarah replied softly.

"But now . . . you may go."

Bret stepped forward and kissed Sarah. "Thank God," he said to her. "Thank God it's over."

Sarah returned his kiss, but without passion. Judge Meeker looked on, and understood. It would take time, he knew, and possibly some professional help. But she would heal, with the help of that fine young man.

"Congratulations," Howie Gresh said, stepping up to shake Sarah's hand. Privately he was crushed that the conviction of Sarah Lewis was falling apart, but he could sense the direction of the political winds. He slipped through an easy transition from Gresh the knife to Gresh the man of compassion. There were consolations. After all, he was already talking to Kyle King about a possible movie.

Meeker had a trial to run, so, after wishing Sarah and Bret well, he left for court. Sarah slipped into a side room to change. But when she emerged a few minutes later, she was noticeably nervous.

"What's wrong?" Bret asked.

"Freedom nerves," Woody Evans replied. He'd seen it all before. He was pleased that Sarah was free, although he wished it had been *his* doing. Still, he was far from sanguine about her future. He gave the marriage about a month. These things never worked out.

*   *   *

Bret drove Sarah back home. The security of Meeker's hearing had been maintained, and the press wasn't even aware that she was free. It should have been a time of celebration, but there were actually few words spoken between them. Each was lost in his own thoughts, very different thoughts.

"I'd love to take you out," Bret finally said. "But it's impossible. You'd be recognized."

"I don't want to go out," Sarah replied. "I just want to be at home, with you."

"Do you want to see a doctor?"

"Yes, eventually. But I can put that off. I want to see my apartment. My plants. My refrigerator. You don't know what these little things mean."

"I think I do."

"I don't believe I'll ever understand exactly what happened. It's too bizarre."

"Just put it behind you," Bret said. "It shouldn't be part of your future."

"Oh, it won't be. Not at all."

Bret pulled into the apartment garage. He handed Sarah a pair of dark glasses and a kerchief that he'd brought, so she wouldn't be easily recognized as they made their way upstairs.

Minutes later, Bret opened the door to their apartment. He'd decorated it with welcome home signs and balloons—personal security in case the story leaked out and reporters descended on the place. He was still calculating. He was still maneuvering. There had to be some way out of this.

"Welcome home," Bret said. "Forever." He almost choked on the words.

She was *back*. Alive.

The only presence he'd planned for her was an oil portrait, done after her execution, to make him look even more devoted. But this picture moved. It talked.

Now he'd have to live with her, to pretend to love her, to show every attention to the woman whose death he'd engineered. His immediate objective was to make sure no question ever fell on him. The police were being helpful. They were all too eager to blame Shel exclusively for Ramy's death, and to take full credit for the solution.

Bret and Sarah embraced. "It'll be like old times," he told her. "You tell me anything I can do."

"You can just be here," Sarah answered. "And *I* can just be here. I want to walk around. I want to study this place again. There are no bars here, are there?"

"Only in the neighborhood."

"I'll get used to it ... awfully fast."

She was walking around the apartment, opening almost every drawer, picking through the mail, even wiping some dust off the top of the toaster oven in the kitchen. Bret watched her closely, still not believing it. Maybe it was a mirage. A bad dream.

But it wasn't.

It was her.

Back.

And then, unexpectedly, the unwanted returnee approached him. Her expression was serious, even grim, as if a burden still weighed on her mind. "Bret," she said, "I'd like to discuss something with you."

"Oh?"

He knew by that expression that this wasn't show and tell.

"It's about ... what we've just been through."

"Of course," Bret replied. "We'll talk about whatever you wish."

Sarah walked over to the small tan overnight case she'd brought from prison and zipped it open. "Isn't it incredible, that something they found in Shel's safe led to my freedom?" she said, while looking for an item inside the bag.

"It certainly is," Bret answered, wondering what she was driving at, what she was going to take out of that case.

"They found other things," Sarah said.

"Really." He didn't like the sound of those "other things."

Then Sarah pulled a sealed, business-size envelope from the bag. "They found this."

"What have you got there?"

"It's a letter addressed to 'Sarah Lewis—personal.' It's from Shel.

On the bottom of the envelope he wrote, 'To be delivered in the event of my unexplained death or disappearance.' "

At first Bret said nothing. He was baffled, but becoming very uneasy. "Why would Shel do that?" he finally asked. "Have you read what's inside?"

"Yes, I have. And now I think *you* ought to read it."

"Me? Why ...?"

Sarah handed him the envelope. "Out loud, if you would," she said. "For both of us."

Bret removed the letter from the envelope. He unfolded it.

"Out loud," Sarah reminded him.

Bret didn't like it. The feeling was not good. But, without missing a beat, he began:

> Dear Sarah—
>   I hope you never read this because, if you do, it means something has happened to me. What I say is really going to floor you. It may even make you sick. Maybe you better sit down.

Bret stopped for a moment and gazed at Sarah. She was staring at him intently. He continued:

> I want you to know that ...

He froze.

"Go on," Sarah ordered, and there was jagged ice in her voice.

"This is ridiculous, it's ..."

"Just read it!"

> I want you to know that Bret and I murdered Ramy and set you up to take the blame ...

Again Bret stopped. "Look, Sarah, the man was always jealous of me. You know that. You said it. This is just ..."

"Go on!" Sarah snapped. She was stonefaced.

And Bret did go on. He'd even manage this with some style.

We were two guys bored with marriage who thought we could get rid of our wives easily. Kill one, frame the other. Hey, you avoid a lot of paperwork that way.

We planned it all, from the tape you heard in the museum to our own faked emotions after the blast and at the funeral. I've got to hand it to Bret. He played his part brilliantly.

I know you're wondering why I'm admitting this. Look, I've known Bret a hell of a long time. I like him. Always have. But, I'll put it bluntly: I don't completely trust him. It's just this gut feeling I've got. He always seems ready to do almost anything to get what he wants—like putting his own wife through a murder trial and seeing her executed. You, Sarah—who he's been married to for twenty years.

And I figured this: If he'd do that to you, what would he do to me? I mean, face it. I'm the only other guy who knows the whole story. And Bret is a calculating man.

So, if something happens to me, this letter will go to you. That'll be my revenge against Bret. You'll know everything. He'll never get away.

Look, this is something I've got to do. I just can't live with the idea that someone could screw me in a deal . . .

Bret stopped, letting his hand, still holding the letter, drop to his side. Dead men tell no tales, he'd thought when he'd killed Shel.

But a dead man had returned.

And he was telling tales.

"Shel had a way of ruining things," Bret said, to no one in particular.

Sarah said nothing.

She just stared at Bret.

Then, suddenly, without warning, he bolted for the foyer table where he kept his pistol. He flung open the drawer.

"I have it," Sarah said sharply.

And she did. "I took it when I went through the apartment before. Sorry you didn't notice."

Now she pulled it from a deep pocket on the side of her dress.

"You put us through such hell," she said, with a firmness she'd never shown before. "You put us all through such rotten hell!"

"It was a lot of work," Bret said.

"You know," Sarah continued, "I think finally, after all these years, Bret, I've begun to understand you, to know what you really are. When I first read Shel's letter I wondered why you didn't just kill me. But oh no, no. That wouldn't be *like* you. You'd calculate that if I died suddenly, and you married Alison Carver, there'd always be lingering suspicions about you."

"Quite right."

"And divorce? No, you wouldn't just divorce me either, Bret. You'd think, 'That Woody Evans. He's a shrewd lawyer. He'd inject things into her head that she'd say at the divorce hearing—things that could hurt later on.'"

"Yes, that's right, too."

"And besides," Sarah pressed on relentlessly, "who would care about the divorce of an assistant secretary? But this way, with all you've done ... Bret Lewis, you became a star."

"And right again," Bret replied. "You know, Sarah, you may have had more potential than I thought."

Upon hearing those words, calmly, and with no emotion whatever, Sarah squeezed the trigger, and pumped five bullets into Bret Lewis.

His face tightened.

But he managed to stand up, as if it were the honorable thing to do.

He stood, motionless, for a few horrifying moments.

Then he collapsed.

As he slumped to the floor he gazed up at Sarah one last time. "Plead temporary insanity," he whispered.

Always, always, a calculating man.

epilogue

Sarah Lewis, represented again by Woody Evans, was exonerated on a claim of self-defense. The district attorney for Washington, D.C., choosing not to prosecute, accepted her contention that Bret's lunge for the gun proved his intent to kill her. Purple wrote that public opinion was so completely on Sarah's side that the D.A. could come to no other decision and still expect to keep his job.

Sarah was free. She went back to work but resigned from the National Air and Space Museum less than six weeks later. Her presence attracted too much attention. She moved to Pittsburgh, settled in, and taught aeronautical engineering at a local college. She never remarried.

Bret was buried in a small family plot just outside New York City. He'd always wanted to be buried at Arlington, and a surviving relative did file a request with the Department of the Army. It was rejected. A meticulous career planner, Bret hadn't planned this one well enough: He didn't meet the service requirements for Arlington.

The Blacks printed their pictures of Bret with Alison Carver, but they were complete duds. Readers weren't interested in the romantic entanglements of dead men. Alison Carver charged that the pictures were fakes, and was reelected. The Blacks sued Al Durfee to get their money back, but were fined by the court for filing a frivolous lawsuit.

Shel Jordan. Ah, what can be said about the man who distrusted Bret Lewis, yet drank his champagne? Shel Jordan did make another appearance ... in a way. Bret hadn't known it, but the land where he deposited his oldest friend had been sold to developers. Shel's remains were unearthed during excavation. They were, however, immediately reburied, without being identified. It is a commonplace of builders not to report the finding of bodies. Police departments don't want to know. The evidence trail has usually run cold; investigations are costly and time-consuming. And, as one detective put it to a builder in a similar case, "If a guy is buried there, he probably deserved it."